THE BATH FUGUES

THE BATH FUGUES

Brian Castro

WUNDOR

Editions

First published in 2009 in Australia by the
Giramondo Publishing Company

This edition published in Great Britain in 2018 by Wundor Editions

Wundor Editions Ltd, 35B Fitzjohn's Avenue, London NW3 5JY

wundoreditions.com

Book Design – Matthew Smith

ISBN 978-1-9998996-2-2

Printed and bound in Great Britain by TJ International Ltd

The Goldberg Variations ... are a set of 30 variations for harpsichord by Johann Sebastian Bach. First published in 1741 ... the work is considered to be one of the most important examples of variation form. It is named after Johann Gottlieb Goldberg, who may have been the first performer.

– Wikipedia

It is, in short, music which observes neither end nor beginning, music with neither real climax nor real resolution, music which like Baudelaire's lovers rests lightly on the wings of the unchecked wind.

– Glenn Gould

I

BECKETT'S BICYCLE

... panting up the hills in bottom gear, refusing to give in, like my father.

– Samuel Beckett

1

My friends, there is no friend, Michel de Montaigne had written. He had in fact said there was no *perfect* friend. When my only friend Walter Gottlieb asked me what I was writing, he received an outburst from me bordering on abuse, as I was on the inner path of my trance. What is it about? Gottlieb insisted. I turned his questions upon themselves. What would I be writing? How could I complete it now? Is not your interrogation ruinous? Here, take my work. Critique it thoroughly. Destroy my vision before it has had a chance to bloom. Explanation, I said, was shortening my breath, the plague of description poisoning my thoughts.

I was in Paris at the time, having given up art fraud. I still had a passport and Paris was occasionally home. Walter Gottlieb was passing through. He said he had just *made a pilgrimage* to Portugal. I didn't ask him any questions. He was on sabbatical from Sydney University and I knew he was working on something secretive from those little signs he made: a nervous flicking of his fingers. We went back a long way. In 1972 I had read High Modernism and politics in a Roman jail … two years in the company of Joyce and Gramsci, after being sentenced for supplying money to the Red Brigades. I gave up my art practice when the French mounted an exhibition of famous forgeries at the Palais Soubise. They catalogued my work in detail and I was released soon after, having achieved both fame and notoriety at the age of thirty-five. Walter Gottlieb found me a job. He may even have petitioned to have me released (rumours said Sartre also signed), though I didn't presume Gottlieb was ever my benefactor. An artist, he said, offering me a cigar, had to do it tough.

Twenty years later I was back in Paris living on a writing grant and Gottlieb turned up again. Anyway, to satisfy him, I said I was writing my memoirs, a choppy musical dedicated to counterpoint, without the axes of time and place, collapsing in upon itself because the notes will inevitably run out, returning, elaborating, criss-crossing, double-handedly creating variations upon a theme. But wouldn't readers be hindered? Gottlieb argued. No good turns came out of such curiosity. I was through with explanation. Montaigne was right. Scribbling was selfish and secretive; genius was in learning how to be a thief. Now, nearing the age of fifty-five, I, Jason Redvers, specialised in cataloguing the lives of others.

Walter Gottlieb died within three months of our exchange. You can imagine how suffused with guilt I was. How right was he to warn of literary ambition! I was still idling in my studio, trying to write, when I received the news. I immediately began an apostrophe to my dear friend. His wife Marie rang from Double Bay in Sydney, requesting me to collect my things. Marie was an heiress. I could hear her rings clacking across continents. She recited an address – *Colo Heights* – where I might find alternative lodgings – it sounded colonic, gut-wrenchingly vertiginous. Might it not have been *Apollo Heights*? I had been occupying a room in the East Wing of the Gottlieb mansion where I'd kept a stretcher, a bicycle, some books and a jar of my kidney stones.

Marie said that Gottlieb had suffered an infarct in his bathroom. She was proud of her medical terminology, but the possessive adjective meant they hadn't slept together since the tragedy which changed their lives. Retirement had not been easy for him. The cause of death was that having taken Viagra with his Prozac, Gottlieb had sought relief between Eros and Morpheus. This tug of war in the bath had proven too much. He must have swelled and choked next to the toilet bowl, his face turning red, then purple, then blue, a Francis Bacon triptych I once forged. I believe he owned an original. Poor Gottlieb. I had given him much in the past. Because I'm not a systematic thinker, I saw little use for writing stories about my life, so I spoke them to him in order to fill his priestly days ... hours so solitary ... like his journal, grey with drizzle ... whence he gleaned nothing but beads of sweat and prayer from his great desire for fame.

For years Walter Gottlieb had shuffled up and down the university corridor. I attended his lectures in the late 'sixties. (He was only five years older than me, but he looked ancient. I, on the other hand, possessed the youthful insouciance of a perpetual student.) There was one week when all he discussed was Jean-Paul Sartre. Then it was Simone Weil. I was only interested in whether the philosopher banged the nun. The contemporary novelist ... Gottlieb began his discourse at the college high table one evening during dinner (it was warm, the wine was terrible) ... was a bum – at best, a product of confession, he said. A novelist was nothing but a grafter, a hack, a grubber with prurient leanings and huge repressions. Novelists were at the end of the line in these, the closing days of the Western Canon. Wood-tongued theorists were taking over; tin-eared reproductionists; counterfeit drummers. To publish a novel, he said, was to make yourself suspicious. Unmediated personal expression in the face of disinterest. Nothing new there. Every kid was doing it, trying to become memorable in the age of forgetting. They were all robots. Etc. Etc. And so the night wore on.

In his daylight hours, Walter Gottlieb lectured on *Montaigne and Disdain*. In twenty years, the last two as an associate professor, Gottlieb had not published anything. He taught love during Lent term, friendship during Trinity, death in Michaelmas. Epicurus, Montaigne, Socrates; it was a hard road to take in order to arrive at contemporary literature. When he said *Mann*, we thought him hip. So modern, so chic. *Literature ended in 1939*, he would declare provocatively, a smirk creasing his face as if he'd suffered a stroke. Speech proclaimed his genius; rumour brought him fame; rhetoric fought off adversaries. He *was* Socrates. He always argued with a remote elegance bordering on self-pity. A malicious gossip ran in the corridors that he was pathic. I don't know if there was a student hanging on his every word. Maybe they meant he was pathetic. But in truth, I didn't care for any kind of public manifestation at the time, even of intellectual hatred. I was deeply into art forgery and was learning how to be a revolutionary. I didn't think a state of serenity could ever be achieved by *saying* anything out loud ... I was in flight from presence. For someone who was plotting a break-away Department of Comparative Literature, Gottlieb read neither French nor German, spoke a slightly accented English, wore loafers and loved to boast he ate only wafers for dinner, holding up each sliver like a Communion Host before our bloated faces. (At high table there were only two or three disciples left.) I didn't see him again until he turned up in Paris shortly after my release. Had he ever been a Jewish refugee, he had certainly eaten a lot of wafers since. He was catholic with a small *c*, he said. He was beginning to waddle. His centre of gravity was very low. He had not managed to get promotion and had sunk into a terrible gloom. Perhaps he suspected he was going to die. There are a few portraits of him in Paris still in existence. Not all of them by me.

Five years after my release I returned to Australia with a woman who was to become his wife. Marie was an art dealer with Christie's. Gottlieb found a new lease on life. He wore polo shirts and a baseball cap, squirted soda into his scotch and considered flying lessons. He insisted I should rent the East Wing of their Double Bay double-storeyed villa on Sydney Harbour. The fee would be very modest; Marie was making a fortune. I was wary at first and only went there on weekends - floated by the marina in a rubber dinghy listening to seagulls and the Gottliebs' incessant squabbling, watching the harbour water, which was never completely calm.

While there, I bought an old bicycle from a garage sale, a Swift Safety, circa 1928, with rusting rims and torn leather saddle. It was said to have belonged to Samuel Beckett. Somebody had brought it out from Ireland, dead clover still stuck in the sprockets. I repaired it as best I could and rode it like a hippo treading water, slowly. Cross-winds were the worst. Soon I was reaching the mountains from the sea then squeaked home in time to take my tea beneath the jangling spars of unused schooners. Out-of-town millionaires appreciated my watchdog insomnia. I disturbed their children deflowering one another in the stoop. I frightened prowlers with fireworks and warned off sightseers with a water-pistol. I wore cricket whites; a cap, gold-embroidered with the word *Security*. Since the rich were only threatened by the thought of poverty, they trusted me to some extent, and when I warned them the sea was tatterdemalion or the wind boreal, they noted my Brahmin weather eye. In any case, I supplied vocab for their boardroom bullying, once told them a story they thought taxing, about a great white whale. Still, *Moby Dick* became a much used phrase on the floor of the stock exchange … along with red herrings, white elephants and flying pigs.

But nothing could excuse my meanness to Gottlieb, who died without literary success, a clutch of mysteries still in hand. Marie had not mentioned the beautiful woman from whom he'd regularly bought dried flowers, nor could anyone explain that large hourglass he lugged home like a signal lantern, clogged with grey, wet sand. Looking back, I can now see his infatuation with Fabiana. She must have been the muse who lit his hidden self.

I returned from Paris but I didn't make it to Gottlieb's funeral. So the week before I was to vacate the East Wing, I resolved to ride from the War Memorial to Colo Heights. My state of mind was cenographic, as I planned a humble tribute to my friend. Gottlieb's death revealed to me my own. Any future project seemed inane. I began at dawn, on a marathon during which I expected I would die. I wove unsteadily out towards Windsor, then along Bell's Line Of Road, a haunting rosary of dead explorers who'd navigated the rise and fall between light and shade, through a miasma of blue eucalypts and rank rainforest. I felt fit. My legs were good. I crossed the Colo River where children had been lately drowning. Soon I was mending a puncture by the side of the Putty Road. The sunlight was now agony. I heard wings; explosions; bombs. I might have been in

Guernica. Despair broke in at noon with the Angelus of migraine.

I was at the entrance to a public road, the kind of unsealed by-way I seldom explored, hollowed with ruts, the median peaked with gravel, bends raked with corrugations. Such tracks were always disappointments, ending in tips or quarries. Where you expected soft glades and groves you often came upon police and their sniffer dogs searching for bodies in sunken shafts. Spindrifts of dust rose up from the cleared hills. I read anxiety everywhere. I tested my tyres for a mile or so and thought how deliberately Gottlieb had pressed on with his poetry; how he fiddled on board his sloop on weekends, hunched in the bleached transom penning lines reminiscent of more famous harbour poets. In the East Wing of his house I used to watch the red glow go down behind him and hear the tiny bell in the tower of the Stella Maris convent pealing five times from a distant hill. I would sip a martini and look up at the regularly departing jets etching contrails into a deeper blue. The moment was significant; the gathering clouds threw up a tableau: a scene at Gethsemane; a soaring crucifix: for Gottlieb's tiny, stooping figure spoke to me of passion, failure and futility, and of the tragic deafness of the world. It was a very Australian moment ... with olives.

I did not realise how rapidly I was descending. Freddy Mercury's lyrics buzzed in my ear: *I want to ride my bicycle, I want to ride it where I like.* Mercury: my father injected it, I don't know why. No wings sprouted from *his* ankles. He once owned a bicycle shop in Macau. I, though, flew; from the past. The vegetation was suddenly looming up above, and the road was speckled with light and shade and the Swift was bouncing over treacherous tree roots. I tried to correct my discomfort by gliding from one rut to another – a fatal error, for I should have held my line – and came down heavily on my side, rolling into a creek full of pickled stone. For some time, although I had no idea of time, the bittersweet world of the half-coma manifested itself in gentle constriction and gay abandon not dissimilar to that experienced in love. I peeped into a golden corona of light, blindingly soft. Then upon regaining full consciousness and experiencing the first stabs of pain, my first thought was of

Gottlieb's little daughter, I don't know why. The water was cold. I may have been drifting towards the darkling riverbend; all around, the contrapuntal chittering of grebes. But it was of Blimunde I first thought, when consciousness brought back the anxious world without. Blimunde, one of Gottlieb's twin daughters.

I attended university at the age of thirty. I was a slow learner obsessed with badminton, having spent several years swatting shuttlecocks on the international court. *Gap years*, the young would now say, justifying my laziness. Gottlieb was already a rising star, a senior lecturer defending New Criticism, an old school in brief renaissance before French theory poisoned the ivy league. He wore sky-blue cardigans and read closely for tone, not for feeling. But when language was totally severed from meaning, when The Word finally separated from The Thing (a nut pounded since the 1920s), something harder cracked; a synapse failed to fire among the believers and those who spoke in toneless paradiddles began to sound more brilliant.

A slow learner always plumped for loyalty. I think there were five of us who still refused to believe a poem was all sociology and subtext, let alone symbols and syntagms. We did not see any social function for any of it. We liked it for itself. Held in the oral stage, we sucked language like a lozenge. Besides, a poem was less to carry, could be dissected endlessly for sweetness and light. It didn't have to mean anything, but it contained secrets, perhaps even exuded its inheritance. Such dubious legacies may have been dangerous in greater minds, but none of us was ready for Gottlieb's mental challenges, though we pleased him, at least, by nodding at the right places. He oiled his bat. Took to the crease against the French. A short man with an enormous mane of greying hair (you could have sworn a Persian cat was curled up on the lectern), wearing braces and spectacles, he delivered his lectures in a powerful bass voice. A talking bow tie, Beethoven-like, he used his deafness to record deep structures in the resonances of ideas. He handled himself well:

Regard the Intentional Fallacy – the text means only what it says. The author's intention is irrelevant. Meaning can only be textual, without personal reaction. Now that was put forward by Wimsatt and Beardsley in 1954. What then, was this French nonsense about the author being dead? A copy, no doubt.

Gottlieb would adjust his collar and push up his chin. The glint in his eye said he was having fun.

Maybe meaning is merely a copy of itself ... its self-importance. The author knows all that. Knows it's all smoke and mirrors. Knows that you know that meaning is always a manipulation, that there are only copies, echoes of previous profundities, so powerful that you want to be deceived because you are literary; you assent more than you dissent because you have been chosen. Go with it. The Greeks gave us mimesis. Have you never cried at the movies, at the copy of reality, knowing the light outside would make you foolish? You see, we are all in the know.

Gottlieb touched a flaring nostril. We didn't understand. We'd never wept. We thought the sunlight outside was cartharsis, or even peripeteia. It was all French to us. Layer upon layer. We longed for a smoke. That would surely mist up our eyes. When Gottlieb said theory was just a form of doubling, or as he sometimes said, dubbing, he looked to us like he was winning. During high summer, in low dudgeon, we ran past his college garden on half-marathons and saw him in his shirtsleeves watering weeds in the hot wind, his dribbling hose annointing the hordes, believing he was warding off the threat to civilization.

In those days I used to run all day, sometimes in tweeds, always conscious of my weight. At lunch I ran around the campus with several others, clockwise, anti-clockwise wound by a repetition-compulsion to circle the university until time stood still. One day we passed the student regiment with bayonets fixed, marching over protestors who were lying on the road. We ran faster than ever from the goad, threading through cries of rage and outrage, to catch Gottlieb's lecture on W.B. Yeats: *Sex, Uprising and the Spirit of the Age*. We were his chosen ones – he was peeved if we were late – and while he spoke directly to us about *tone* and the deception of *finer feelings*, we sat in a weightless pool of cool, stared up at ceilings and floated upon his buoyancy. Later, we asked sententious questions while row upon row of jealous eyes burned holes in our bobbing heads.

It was Gottlieb who encouraged me to travel. Where do you want to end? he questioned through a fumy cigar. My thoughts began to unravel. I did not want to end, simply to be in motion. I remembered my schooldays, that same inquisition from the vocation counsellor, his radio voice crackling from afar. My answer then was that I wanted to be a piano-player in a New York bar.

One afternoon, Gottlieb invited the Disciples to a regular tea where he ordered in cucumber sandwiches. He lived on campus at the time, master of a male college which grieved him with its lax dress code. The Vice-Chancellor had overruled him on the wearing of gowns. His rooms overflowed with manuscripts, some secured in stacks with red bow ties. His tools of trade were few: some pencils; a black Olympia typewriter; blue rustling carbon paper. His leather Chesterfields were worn and mined with dirty whiskey glasses. Almost every book on Post-Structuralism was marked with slips of paper, so one guessed at whether those pages were important or whether Gottlieb had simply given up. The fight against theory had taken its toll. He had an air of weariness. So sure, he kept repeating. Theory is always so sure. Perhaps he was mumbling *Saussure, Saussure*. He certainly *looked* like he had given up. The rings around his eyes were permanent. He handed out easy passes and urged us all to travel. Go and look at how the French did things. It was too late for him, he said. I went home that night resolved to spend some time abroad. I stayed away for ten years.

I don't know what it was that made Gottlieb suggest I should rent the East Wing of his mansion upon my return. The East Wing was approachable down twenty narrow stone steps past the neighbour's bougainvillea. It was self-contained and private, with partial views of the harbour. Perhaps he thought that a jail term and years abroad had tempered me, had caused me to repent, to renounce revolution, to embrace civil society. After all, what would an ageing forger do when his cover was blown? Where could he hide all that secret admiration? I accepted almost immediately. More than twenty-five years out of university, I still felt like I was his student, living off his magnanimity. Gottlieb and Marie must have wanted to lodge an intimate in their midst for ballast. Then again, I did appear a little down and out. I wore a dirty-cream linen suit, my shoes were scuffed and one lens of my spectacles was cracked. I took private students and taught bad Italian. Crooning maniacally at the piano, I may even have inspired them. They showered me with useless gifts. People always wanted to give me things I generally did not need. When my father died, Gottlieb was so depressed himself he bought me a brand new suit for the funeral. He did not hide his feelings, which I took to be deep. He wanted to know about my grandfather. I said my grandfather had been dead a long time. He asked me for a photograph, which he took to have framed. I accepted his gift and stored it in a suitcase. I didn't need to move. My lodgings in Newtown, mice-infested, had given me no bother. I called the rodents by name. They came, bolder and bolder, and suffocated in the blankets at the foot of my bed. My sticky linoleum floor squeaked with mournful song, rattled with black rice, and the television took me back to monochrome days of pure good and evil.

Looking back now, I believe Gottlieb wanted to keep a close eye on my working methods. He was my keeper. Had I returned to a counterfeit life or was I really trying to write? There was no difference. Nevertheless he was a sleepless spy. To think I entertained the idea of a *ménage à trois*. But in those days triangles were my speciality; I was looking for angles, the *hypotenusa* – what used to be called the *screw*, that *subtended* – the feminine side equal to the power of both the others, and I was sure I would find her hidden somewhere, for it was not Marie, but Gottlieb's secret lover, who intrigued me ... but what the hell, the harbour was languid and fresh and when the gusty wind whipped up spindrift, my heart galloped along excitedly.

It was the tragedy that brought things to a head.

At first I used to visit for weekend barbecues. I wasn't sure about staying, but there were free hot meals. In place of saying grace I had to put up with Marie speaking of her illness. She bore down on our company. She had never mastered the art of conversation and reverted to some complaint which replaced my self-pity with hers. When her face thickened and crumpled into pain Gottlieb made excuses for her to retire hurt. He and I then sat on silently with our whiskeys. It was still early and vesper bells sounded five times across the water. Then he looked at his watch and ordered the tiny twins to fetch bed-slippers for me and to recite from Beatrix Potter. At forty-nine he was quite old to be their father. There was no clapping. He did not like applause in case it spoiled them for life's disappointments, but he did conceive then, his now famous line, embedded with a double meaning, embossed on his linen business card: *Dr Walter appreciates your talent and will write you in the future.*

Another 'ski? It was the question he loved most to ask, which for me, had always been the pinnacle of any hospitality. He bought nothing but the best: fifty-year-old malts with unpronounceable names. We would stand atop the windy highlands at midnight quoting Burns and I would play *O Danny Boy* on the piano while we slurped Marie's chicken soup for chasers. We always hugged before I made my way under the ferns and creepers to the East Wing. Propping my bike up on its centre stand beside my bed, careful of the counterpane which in the past had fouled the chain, I set out on a stationary ride to formulate my thoughts before sleep ... reciting Attic poetry, for instance, listening for strophes and antistrophes ... and from one squinting eye observed the last ferryboat flit like a firefly across the oily water before chesty tugs churned out for early morning duty.

I didn't miss my Newtown digs and had quite forgotten my father's death but for the smell of old prawns which rose from the net someone had left beneath my window. Shrimp paste had been my father's favourite condiment. Akin to fertiliser on dying lawns, my father called it *balichão*. An odoriferous fish sauce, fermented to perfection, its name needed to be sung to compensate for loss of appetite. It cured minor ills – the wriggly tilde above its vowel is best articulated with a cold. The secret, Father said, was in shrimps, so transparent and fine you could hardly see them in daylight. Rare, found only in the Pearl River near Macau, they were dried, salted and bottled in rice wine. My father was their sole importer in Australia. He mixed in Portuguese brandy, tore up bay leaves, added peppercorns and chillies. He simmered everything until old Mrs Harris complained in falsetto from the far end of our apartment block. She was his oven clock. He pretended he was deaf. His jars were sealed for three months. When my father died, I used his *bali-chāo* to lure bait. Dragged it over the shore in a football sock. I never had long to wait for the fat lug worms to wiggle up, a tribute to the chef.

I used to tell Gottlieb about my father – that he was the sporting son of an obscure poet who smoked opium and begat children while my father boxed and raced bicycles. My legacy was contradiction. And your anxiety is illegitimacy, Gottlieb would say. Sometimes his smirk looked like Adolf Eichmann's. He would interrogate me on them, hardly letting up when I pleaded exhaustion.

I could never sleep in Gottlieb's East Wing, upon the rosewood Marie Antoinette bed, for more than two nights in a row and when the nights were balmy, I sometimes camped outside, naked, lying on fustian I'd found in the boatshed. Fig trees rustled in the August wind. I thought of Gottlieb's maid, a girl from Ashton's Circus who folded down the sheets so tightly my feet ached from their imprisonment (sometimes she left a rose upon my pillow). Marie became a fast friend of this procrustean, a grim girl with an undershot jaw who I didn't think would stay too long. But the latter knew her ropes and there was something of the guillotine in the profile of her nose. Charlene was obviously good for the twins. She dandled them upside down and swore she'd teach them how to trapeze and swim.

The house seemed outside Gottlieb's range. He was more at home in college, where before his marriage, he had busily posted exam marks on bulletin boards and then appeared bat-like in his chalk-smeared gown at casement windows, pushing out rippling panes through reddening ivy to announce the Medallists. In the summer months when all was quiet, he would patrol the lawns and hockey fields where years before we had discussed his leaving the Catholic church. I was about to leave for Rome. He had worn a furrow that night, weighing up the pros and cons. The Vatican exacted an examination of conscience and then there were the usual threats – a secular life of perpetual guilt. All kinds of dispensations and preliminaries would have to be negotiated with neither impatience nor rebellion. It had not been an easy decision and he told me that he had good reason, and that he would take his secret to the grave. At the time I presumed the secret to be some sort of perversity, but now that I know the truth, I blush at my naïvety. He had slept with a young student.

During barbecues at Double Bay we often sat on a terraced lawn, which at four squares of turf was itself worth a million dollars, while his daughters giggled and plashed in the spa adjoining the pool. I made no reference to dormitories, or to long walks, or to nights discussing Kierkegaard. Marie said I was such a godsend for her husband. *You'll see him waiting for you at the balcony*, she said to me. *He always watches for you there.* Whenever I rode down to the house at the end of Bay Street after a morning's tutoring, I would see him hunched over the railing, motionless, expectant, and strangely tense. These were drowsy afternoons without philosophy. That was the failing. Philosophy would have kept me alert. One day, while the twins were painting fairy rings on the garden rocks with Marie's supply of nail polish, my happy hosts seemed particularly keen to absent themselves. It was the first time I'd seen Gottlieb giggle. I don't know what brought on this frivolity – I suspect it was the season – when they went upstairs to check on a roasting lamb. I recall the twins happily engaged in their practical work. I remember Marie in a black swimsuit which did not flatter her shape. I still see Gottlieb appearing briefly at the bay window without his dressing gown, reminding me of the pale underside of a flounder. I dozed on and off astride the banana lounge and toyed with dialogue, glad I'd postponed lunching with a blocked writer who'd fallen foul of melancholia. I drank my gin and avoided nibbling on *schadenfreude*.

I was dreaming of Benares, of dipping into the Ganges where once on such a humid afternoon as this, treading water amongst some half-cremated bodies, I was suddenly coated with such disgust for humanity I'd not eaten any meat since. A recurring nightmare featured pyres where night vultures looped like bats, picked at roasted morsels and roosted on my windowsill. I felt their down-draught in my dream and in the morning found their droppings on my floor. I was halfway between India and Double Bay and was half-seeing the harbour wavelets lapping beyond the swimming pool disgorging blackened flotsam, when one of the girls ... it was Blixen ... began tugging at my arm. Through half-closed lids I saw sailboats skimming past. A loathsome southerly was about to blow. The halyards tinkled with alarum. And that was when I noticed Blimunde at the bottom of the deep end of the pool, motionless, face down, her useless water-wings circling near the filter. I dived in, but was too late. Her lifeless body was blue, icy cold and heavy. I tried resuscitation knowing it would do no good, and blamed myself for half-heartedness ... perhaps because the neighbours may have looked over the fence and thought I was a paedophile. I had missed the flight from Delhi, the southerly had come in, and the Ganges was afire. I looked up and called, weakly at first, for help, and saw the pale figures of the Gottliebs appear naked, briefly at their window, and knew things would never be the same again.

2

Summer always had its own particular trials. For decades, siroccos, föhns, khamsins, tormented me with dry lunacy. I was a cyclist, and winds were anathema, but now I just took interminable baths. In the south of France the *vent d'autan* blew for three, six or nine days at a time. It was odd, the effect of breathlessness it had on me; I panicked; ran from room to room. It blew with such ferocity I closed my shutters and wept in the howling dark. It was neither warm nor cold, a Devil's fart that sent Van Gogh crazy. It caused migraines, made cattle charge, provoked snakes to attack. Rabbits burrowed deeper, fish would not bite and philanderers returned home to plead with their wives for forgiveness. Wine turned into vinegar, wildfires erupted and lunatics in the Albi asylum formed a conga line, a dancing marathon which lasted for weeks. In Australia, the hot north-westerlies brought me chronic desperation and intensified my alcoholism as all thought dried, ink turned to rust, words to dust. Lust evaporated in the gibbering desert. Yes, of course I heard voices. Each birthday I attempted suicide while the sirens wailed. Saved from death by chance – a loose knot, failed short-circuit, pills untried, the sudden and unexpected return of an old lover dragging me from my overdose – I exercised, sexualised, till all thought ceased, for that was what was expected in Australia. Erudition implied mental effort, so in accordance with the culture, I took up sport. A sporting death was the ultimate credential, I was saying to Doctor Judith Sarraute, my GP, who was stretching gymnastically, reaching backwards for a syringe (Chagall would have painted her), fitting a needle, which until now I had disavowed, having preferred love's prick as a cure.

My father had prostate cancer, I said to Doctor Judith, angling for sympathy. He was from Macau and came to Australia for his own funeral. Australia, my father pointed out, had lots of room for the dead. He wanted to be buried by the sea, facing Antarctica. A *southern death*, he called it. It was quite sudden. He loved cold water. He had always been a swimmer, and each morning he performed a freestyle crawl, half-stooped, before his full-length mirror. He even turned his head to breathe, his eye cocked in alarm and his mouth in a rictus, gasping for air. His reddening face soon turned purple. So when a pain developed in his back I suggested he stop this channel-crossing. He went to a chiropractor who sold him a newfangled machine to heat up his spine. I tried it out. It reduced muscle mass and I was keen to be greyhound lean. It heated up my chest and shoulders and redirected whales, but did not bring me the famine victim's featherweight or a lighter cage for my heavy heart to flutter in. The pain in my father's back increased and he died within two weeks, I said to Dr Judith. The cancer went undiagnosed. His heart gave out in the Bondi surf. The coroner said it was a drowning; a sick man out of his depth, it was not uncommon. A sign of other drownings. I would flee to Paris again and again, the city of refuge, where I would spend endless hours sitting by the Seine.

Doctor Judith neither discouraged nor encouraged speech, though she never answered personal questions. She was young and balletic, but there was no point in flirting. She treated me professionally, calling me *Justin*, a misnomer I kept correcting. There were prints on her walls, fine drawings of jellyfish by Pehr Forsskål (b. Helsinki, 1732, d. Yemen, 1763). Not originals? I inquired, obsessed with authentication. Surely not? There was a cuttlebone on her desk which I accidentally knocked onto the parquet floor. Such an object spoke volumes: inky mollusks; the uncanny detritus of homelessness; bone-food. My inadvertence was surely a sign of evil. Dr Judith performed general practice twice a week, in order, she said, to *keep in with normal people*. I don't know where she operated on other days, but I suspected she was a specialist of some kind. She told me depression was always difficult, that most of her patients were migrants. I don't know why she made that connection. Was I one? Was she one? There was no home if you had ambition, I said, staring at the bone, thinking of hermit crabs. No friends either. I remarked that Nature was evil. I don't know how this idea arose, perhaps because someone was beating a child in the waiting room. She looked at me, pushed back her raven hair and flexed her waist. She did not bend at the knees. If you are reading the Marquis de Sade, Justin, the signs are good, she said swaying her hips while annotating my card.

One afternoon, when her patients were dwindling and the receptionist had slipped out for a moment with the pathology courier, she snapped on a surgical glove and inserted a finger into me. Just checking, she said. She had expert digits and reminded me of Arabian nights, the symmetrical arabesques of double-entries, before a poster on the wall halted me abruptly with the words: *Prostate cancer: all the early signs.* Accountants would know how to work it out. I was broke. I had no private cover. Jellyfish, I kept thinking, reproduced if cut. Not money though.

Back home, I no longer had my five o'clock seizure. Watching the trees sway in the pall of a dying afternoon from a porthole in my bathroom in Gottlieb's East Wing, I reflected on Nature and the body's imperfection. There was always an invitation to voyage: *luxe calme et volupté*. I suffered from reflux, bad karma, my soul walloped with wind. I read Baudelaire and was going blind. Diabetes, probably. On my wall, a triptych by Francis Bacon: a toilet bowl, two contorted figures, bloated faces. Bacon made few friends and terrible enemies. When a friendship revived ... as they often did ... he changed his mind and swabbed his canvases with turpentine.

In my tub I dreamt only of drifting, watching the passers-by, now appearing evil in their maniacal purpose. Heading somewhere seemed to me an inherent illness; linear, venal, well-plotted. My own form glowed palely beneath the water; limp and unrefined. I remembered Bacon giving me one of his pentimentos in London, the panels washed out with rusty paint he'd poured over them in rage and self-mortification. You can have the whole box and dice, he said to me. The triptych was too large to fit through the door. I wished it folded like an Oriental screen. I had to cut it up. I suspected his portraits were of me, naked. He paid me nevertheless for his failure. I spent several weeks unsuccessfully rubbing them back. My friend, my friends, I cut through everything. It would have been better to have been satisfied with the maestro's russet bath. When I finished, there was a peroration of brown and jade. I painted over them with super-human recollection and sold them to the Red Brigade.

The trees are bending. I lie unconscious in the tepid water while it swindles me with winter currents. Bath fugues: I return to Berlin, Paris, Vladivostok in a vertigo. A clawfoot tub is always good for spirals; to be carried away in the present tense by a griffin on curlicues of dreams; flights of fancy. I will now submerge. To practise a bath fugue is to ride a bicycle underwater. Walking while sitting, motion in place. Beneath the suds all is calm, quite circular, grey, with minor variations. Hello! It was Marie. I will have to hide. The dragon breathes at my keyhole which I've recently stoppered with chewing gum. The knob is swivelling back and forth. I wonder how long I can stay under. The past rushes forward. Drifting. Even Montaigne liked to drift, but only on holidays. I decided everybody was a contradiction, selling ideas at two prices. Fatal to follow any one. Hello, Jason; I know you're in there!

3

Michel de Montaigne. There was a deep emptiness at the centre of everything he wrote. His friendship with Etienne de la Boétie, or 'Booty', corrupted his marriage and ruined his kidneys. He no longer had sexual relations with his wife, preferring to quote Socrates: *He who takes a wife shall repent of it.* How true, how true, how true. I've had three, and the ternary, a psychoanalyst, nailed me to the mast. Gisela said I was lacking a notion of the real, like the phallus, which only existed in a dialectic of the eye, in terms of what it had missed. I had no idea what she was talking about as I was blinded by love, but every time I read the phrase *trompe-l'oeil* in art catalogues, I thought of the way she spoke to my penis, wagging it like a finger puppet, practising ventriloquy. I was measuring up one-eyed, Cyclopean, missing my strumpets and oils. That marriage was supposed to be third time lucky. We spent three years together. Gisela liked things in threes. The first orgasm got rid of the pain; the second, she said, was plain pleasure; the third however, was bliss. She had never reached the third. Never lost control. Hard work for me. The simple truth was that there was Man's love and then there was Woman's. The former ran on one rail; the latter derailed everywhere. One day I got on my bicycle and forgot to return for six weeks. I cycled into the worst storms in history. Met Napoleon at Waterloo. Hannibal in the Alps. Was alone on the Russian steppes.

In Hanoi I sat beneath rattan ceiling fans batting at tumid cigar smoke exhaled by droopy desperadoes – man's estate. When I returned, Gisela told her friends I was affected by a mild psychosis. It wasn't mild. The police were on my trail.

4

Montaigne was on his travels, approaching Rome. It was the summer of 1581. He was heading for San Sebastián, where natural springs produced miraculous cures. He was a connoisseur of water. He drank a quart an hour to rid himself of kidney stones. All that gaseous liquid gave him wind. He would spend nine days at San Sebastián. It was in an old Roman bath, where men and women sat together, naked in the fresh and lively stream for the sole purpose of conversation, when he felt the sudden stab of love. She was Spanish and shapely, her face dark and pretty, and she rubbed him down with quicklime for depilation, her Iberian novenas gurgling over his neck and back, readying his body for the burial pit. For Montaigne, it was a good reminder of the need for eros. In his essays thus far, he had only managed stale solitude, empty eternity, ineffable infinity. Time was running out. He needed a friend.

Montaigne had no friend. Booty had died on him prematurely. Brevity was, Montaigne surmised, perfection. Grief washed over him in little particles. The Spanish woman noticed his melancholy and waded around to edge upon his knee. Together, some tickling. Nothing like paid pleasure to guarantee happiness. I see them wedged together in a darkened corner. Their niche. He wore a short beard. She had a mole in the small of her back. Upon an unsuccessful orgasm, an internal return, Montaigne experienced the sharpest pain. It was pleasure, he wrote, inflamed with difficulty: *stinging tingling and smarting with arrowes*. Marriage had blunted all of that. For a moment he thought he had triumphed over

Socrates, for whose decrepit wisdom no maiden was ever going to trade her thighs. That night, Montaigne thought again of Booty's early death. Down the road at the church of San Giovanni Porta Latina, he heard fireworks, as priests performed gay marriages. He went to the toilet. There was no other person there on the long bench. He squatted over an asphixiating miasma ... the wooden wall against which he leant was impregnated with the odour of decaying cabbages. He tried to pass water. No success. Anyone who entered would have seen him grimacing with pain, a non-committal smile upon his face. It had plagued him all his life, this non-commital smile – his portraits confirmed it – hiding his anger and contempt for those who only *pretended* suffering. Poor Booty. At least his friend had written sonnets in all his youthfulness and had had no thought of failure. Booty, after all, had suffered the real thing: death before fame. A fate worthy of a true friend. Montaigne began something of a movement amongst philosophers in losing one's friends. In 1654, exactly eighty-three years after Montaigne retired to his tower to begin writing his essays, the philosopher Blaise Pascal suffered an intense spiritual crise. He became an ascetic and grew wary of affection, abandoning all his friends. Friends were crutches.

I was interested in Montaigne's determination to disavow intimacy, avoid melancholy and turn his life towards an inquiry into learning how to die. It was self-discovery at its best. At thirty-eight, he ensconced himself in a round tower with his books. At the completion of his *Essays*, towards the end of his life, he would come to the conclusion that nothing was perfect, least of all, friendship. His best friend, Étienne de la Boétie, had been dead for many years. His own essay on friendship was meant to be both an introduction and a monument to Booty's *Discourse on Voluntary Servitude*. Discovering that this had already been published, or that it was too republican and volatile, he decided on reproducing the sonnets. When he found that these too had been published, he excised them completely, making only a mention of them in the empty parentheses of his own introduction. Disappointed his own writing was ant-like and prudent rather than reckless and brilliant – a writing that nevertheless persistently undermined itself, since *it* desired to be art – Montaigne entombed the sonnets in silence. Was he honoring his friend or was he protecting himself? Perhaps he was embarrassed at revealing the fragile noise of Booty's youthfulness. Then again, perhaps he wanted his own essays to shine without the colouring of others. We will never know. It was posterity creeping up, something quite a few of us come to hear at the end of our lives: time's collapse before naked ambition. Montaigne noticed that his testicles drooped. He looked in the mirror and plucked the dead blossoms from Booty's grave. His essay would be the final word on friendship and there would be no poetry.

Impressed by Montaigne's austerity, this farewell to poetry, I tried to make my mind as sceptical, my body as ascetic, my curiosity as intrepid. I rode my bicycle endlessly, a pathetic martyrdom to failure, since staying upright was dependent upon perpetual motion and resting was an eternal falling. It was hell. But once at speed, on a reasonably flat surface, it became effortless, gravity-defying, other-dimensional ... plunging into new territory, where no friend existed, dead or alive, to hold you back. *Being,* wrote Montaigne, *consists in motion.* Pascal would reproduce that phrase: *Our nature consists in motion.* Copy-cat Blaise. Such surface meditation always brought me meaning. *Motion erases emotion,* I wrote vertiginously.

So much for philosophy.

5

Dr Judith was staring into my eyes. Hers were violet, without shrinking. Like love, the deep resulted in occlusion. I had already lived too long to dive into those cupidinous weeds. Whenever Judith examined me, I followed rivers of thought. For one who does not exist fully as himself, a woman doctor gave direction. With a mind that knew my body thoroughly, Dr Judith was both Mother and the Marquis de Sade, whom I paid for extra consultations outside of surgery time. Judith Sarraute, a cycling physician, could speak of the *Tour de France* and *Oulipo* in one breath, the *Nouveau Roman* and *Paris-Roubaix* in another. She challenged me to a hundred-kilometre *randonée* during which we had to randomly select our favourite books whose titles did not contain the letters *a, e, i* or *o*. We would then have to defend our choices. I was found wanting. *Tunc!*, she yelled as she rode off, leaving me far behind. *You have to read me backwards!* When I caught up I told her about Guy de Maupassant; about his gregariousness ... he was riparian as well ... how he rowed up the Seine every morning, fifty kilometers without fail, against the current ... until he got the pox. Then his face shrivelled up and his mouth drooped, leaving only enormous eyes fading with the light of fatality. One day he fainted on the towpath while riding his bicycle. He was wearing an all-in-one suit pioneered by Jules Léotard, the trapeze artist. When he recovered by the side of the canal, he started to howl like a dog. Passers-by didn't help. They didn't like the look of him. Imagine wearing something so immodest out on the promenade! He must have had evil intentions. *Mauvais passant.* Up to no good. *Pédé!* Gustave Flaubert said he couldn't understand how anyone could have spent so much time having so many love affairs. *You don't need that much experience to learn the monotony of passion*, he wrote to a woman friend.

In the winter of 1853, Flaubert, novelist and bourgeois, was reading Montaigne in bed. Like his eiderdown, he found Montaigne's absolute doubt about everything extremely warm and soothing. In the winter of 1573, Montaigne, essayist and ascetic, took a turn in the library of his cold stone tower, picked out a book on Diogenes of Synope and read it in a Bordeaux tavern by a roaring fire. In the summer of 323 BC, Diogenes, cosmopolitan and cynic, took up residence in a wooden tub outside the temple of Cybele to demonstrate his freedom from material desire. He drank water from his cupped hands and ate only onions. He emerged from his bath before noon and walked through the marketplace at midday with a lit lantern, looking for an honest man in the canicular heat.

All three understood the irony of authenticity.
Dog's breath. Dog years. Old dogs.

6

Where was I? In what era? I was fleeing, as I had always done. The flapping sign on the Putty Road had taken hold in my mind's eye: *Martins Boarding Kennels*. Unnecessary apostrophes appeared daily on roadside notices, but here I found their absence annoying. I remembered turning into that dusty road on my rusty Swift and I remembered seeing the swinging board. Made from pine or rosewood. I remember my father's funeral. I remember Charlie Walsh, an old school friend who was an undertaker. Pine or rosewood? was Charlie's only question. I got it on a discount. Now I was lying in the creek thinking of Gottlieb's little daughter. I was confused. I wondered if she were mine. Although a twin, Blimunde was dark and Blixen fair. Northerners were fair, southerners dark. All could be transmogrified, Doctor Judith said.

Upon my liberation from Rome I had found myself on the banks of the Rhône (or was it the Saône), when a slanting rain washed away the circumflexes in my diary. Without a roof, with no means, a *sans abri*, I was advised to call upon the nearest jail for soup and beans. But I was proud and clung to poetry, not to the coat-tails of the *gendarmerie*. My family had sprung from the Pearl River estuary in China; they were riparian to say the least – hark, one diverse branch of my name: *De Rivière*, whence one derived the name *Redvers*. I found the confluence of rivers congenial. Currents of East and West, Europe and Asia. People mistook me: in certain lights I could be an Eskimo, Latin American, Nepalese. The light in the south of

France was harsh, but at dusk it was mixed with lavender. Here, in the purple light on a large river, they saw me as Vietnamese, casting my net in my conical hat. The banks had been newly concreted and reinforced with a mosaic of pipes and tunnels. These were storm-water drains or flood relief viaducts. Egress and ingress. There I had my dwelling for several weeks hoping the river wouldn't rise beyond its runnels. Rats were more than company. Their chattering moni-tored water levels. Before long I had constructed a raft from debris and poled downstream each day to forage through restaurant bins. I ate well without illness, thanks to punctuality and discrimination, avoiding truffle tins and cognac glasses in which the well-to-do stubbed out their cigars. I collected what kitchen-hands trimmed in preparation when they were distracted, or on the phone. Those healthy shards freshly shaved in the early morning made me stout, sustained me well: discards, disjecta, scraps, excisions. Such margi-nalia invited memory to dine out. Years after my father's death, I started missing him, his scratchy hi-fi, the smell of *balichāo*, his eau de cologne.

I was poling my craft upriver, struggling with the afternoon current and a headwind, when I looked up and suffered a romantic *crise*. A woman was hailing me from a bridge. She was astride her *mobilette*, a baguette in her knapsack, her arm upraised. The pylons loomed up suddenly ... some frieze of popes carved in stone ... I was moving backwards battling to stay upright, feeling my way from dark to light ... the remedy was to head diagonally for the nearest shore. I could no longer see the rest of her, but she had flashing teeth and looked like an American Kennedy. As I passed under, she followed my regress, appearing on the other railing to toss the bread to me. I caught the manna miraculously, performed a salutation, but she was gone. A perfume lingered on the loaf. It was almost dark as I worked my way through the loam along the bank, oblivious to the fact that I was still some miles from home.

I did not see the woman again until an exhibition in a small gallery in Toulouse. By this time I had developed something of a reputation as a 'river artist', a painter of tramps under bridges, weeds and booze. Her name was Marie de Nerval, and she was a friend of the curator of the Bonnefoi Galleries. Marie had put on weight. She no longer rode her *mobilette*. She was the daughter of a marquis and she invited me out to her château for Sunday lunch *en famille*. We were interlaced in conversation during the meal and then we pored over a few sketches before her father, a deaf old man in plus fours, applied his seal to them and ushered us into different rooms. He then proceeded to ask me about the calendar of events for the summer season of opera. He was under the impression I was a musician, but when I assured him I was tone deaf, he smiled and hugged me as though he had found a long lost friend. When are you getting married? he asked. I answered in halting French: *Honi soit qui mal y pense. What ho, ill seen, ill said*, I continued, and then he complained of ancient laws and gleaners on his estates. He was powerless, he said, to rescind a sixteenth century decree permitting them to gather grapes that had escaped the harvester. *Well, worstward ho! For to end yet again amongst the grapes of wrath*, I sympathised, *that's how it is, with mice and men*. We patted each other's backs upon parting.

The year turned yellow. It felt like 1554 ... I don't know why that date came to mind. I was probably rapt with the penal code which permitted vagabonds a second harvest. The Marquis was smarting from a costly legal suit to have it overturned. Marie de Nerval and I were married in the spring. Provence was where she yearned to live and we moved into her thirteenth-century house in Rousillon d'Apt. I could not rid myself of habit and in the early mornings set out on my bicycle for orchards with my waxy carton to gather fallen fruit. Marie started a private press, the *Editions Nerval*, and published obscure writers in limited, signed editions, printed on Magnani Velata Avorio paper in Bembo twenty-four point. These were all lost in the great Avignon warehouse fire of 1978. The insurance payout was hefty and rumours spread, accusing the Marquis of arson, but the police could prove nothing. They suspected me instead. I had a record.

Marie and I spent many afternoons gazing over the Roman ramparts at the red soil and lavender hills of the Vaucluse. The colours still stay with me. Beneath the town were two stone wash-sheds; one for the healthy and one for the sick. They were built in a time of plague. In June 1585 it reached Bordeaux. The mayor, Michel de Montaigne, fled. For six months he wandered nomadically around the countryside. He suffered guilt over this dereliction of duty. He threaded his way through the civil war that followed, passing as both Protestant and Catholic. He shortened his name to Michel Eyquem. He was no hero. The only thing that kept him going was his reading. I too, read by the wash-sheds. Cholera came rattling through here after Napoleon; *vibrio comma*, a bacterium, sabre-curved, faster than a horse. When the rains came, I noticed a touch of madness in Marie's dark eyes, in the long dank hair with which she used to shield her face; in the unattractive smocks she began wearing, stained under the arms, moping around the courtyard wielding a scythe, trying to weed the unruly garden, applying only a few half-hearted strokes. The Roman waterspouts were broken and muddy water spewed over her. O Marie, I pleaded, don't try to be a peasant! Step out from that dungheap. O Marie, how distant were you when you lapsed into anomie, unconscious of my presence! How infected were you by that congenital disease, the *de Nerval syndrome*, whose classification and symptoms are still hidden in the National Archives at the Palais Soubise under five hundred years of legal silence! (Modern terminology would have you *slumming it*, or *addicted to bohemianism; dressing down*.) Nights you floated past the end of my bed with a bottle in your hand, the dark stone wall behind you weeping with centuries of damp. I did not understand how hard you were striving for the fever to break. All I heard was the generator switching over in the storm, your yearning for the noisy labour of child-bearing, your fears of the madness being passed on. I did not comprehend the obsession you had with your family portrait – your sisters, wearing large crucifixes around their necks, seemed destined for bordellos. I was not as self-involved. I sought other intimacies. There were degrees of lunacy that could coexist. Your smiling sibling Lisette screamed obscenities as I read Sade to her with my hand beneath her skirt. (This tableau is familiar. I must check who painted that first.) Of course I have always led a clandestine life. In a way, this secretiveness was my truth. Marie tried to pry it out of me at every opportunity and all I needed to do was to appease her, to say the appropriate thing about my clumsiness, my misdemeanour with her younger sister, but I did no such thing. More than a matter of pride, I saw it as a kind of creative intervention, justified by the fact that it was consistently rekindled *as a method of saving Marie*. With such healing power, a secret had to remain just that. One late morning, perhaps it was at the break of noon, I cannot remember, I heard a tremendous crash. She had thrown my typewriter out the window. My Olivetti Lexikon, one of the first electric golfball portables, solid, heavy as a set of weights. I saw the memoir I was writing roll end over end, down into the river.

It was then that I took to straying even further. Each morning I cycled to escape Marie and raced up and down the hills, but kept returning in the afternoons, sometimes to her father's château, since he paid the bills. The old Marquis and I conversed in tongues. He slid along a rolling ladder hooked before his books and threw down selections aristocratically. I stood on the lower rungs propelling him with one foot as on a scooter. He had a hooter strapped around his neck which he blew upon for me to stop and while we paused, I scavenged the splayed volumes for the old man's evening reading. He hardly spoke about his daughter except to mention Marie had always chosen lovers badly. She tossed a slice of bread to them and believed they would be eternally grateful, he said to me. Most of all she wanted them to suffer, at least share a portion of her pain. I thanked him for this advice.

Marie had always wanted to see Australia and since I was Australian, she hung onto me, though our relationship had all but ceased. I was not one to cling, since she was incurably insane. In her father's library I spent hours reading Montaigne for ballast. Happy to have a foot in each camp and a travelling companion who paid for everything, I carried her bags from airport to airport while my hands grew calluses.

It was not long before I introduced her to Walter Gottlieb. She liked older men, ex-priests, intellectuals. And that, they say, was that. A quick divorce. Glad to get her off my hands, though there was no recourse to any money. She was much taller than Gottlieb and they walked awkwardly together whenever it rained, the ribs of his umbrella poking her eye while she chattered about death. I imagined her stature impressed him. She dragged him around like a teddy bear. I saw neither of them for some years. That was my second liberation.

In Sydney I painted a little, taught part-time and published modestly – some tiny introductions and mini-biographies of well-known jailbirds like Genet. My publisher, George Brezinsky, was also a libel lawyer. He drew a line down the centre of a blank page. On one side he wrote *Nervous* and on the other, *Crazy*. He tapped his pad with his fountain pen. I think you're heading for ulcers, he said to me. Orgasmic black ink spurted onto paper. I saw swans on a lake and a castle emerged from a deep blue mist. Brezinsky excised five characters from my *Brief Lives (I)*. It stayed on the bestseller list for three weeks. Such brevity was important. I was driven by a contempt for writers – hating their hypocrisy and inauthenticity – the fact that they desired publication above all else and cared nothing for the preservation of friendships – the fact that they had never lived. Those still living would have sued. In the process of writing, I was filled with such immense self-loathing that only in censoring my own insights and revelations could I have been redeemed from their company. I had material for another two books.

Gottlieb read of my success. He wrote to Brezinsky for my

current address. He wanted me to be godfather to his children. He was almost fifty, with twin girls of three: Blixen and Blimunde. I could not refuse. I didn't know they were at that age. Brezinsky, who knew everything, said he and Marie had adopted them. I did some calculations. The pregnancy must have been proleptic. I felt somewhat sad, I think, for myself, almost the same age as Gottlieb, to be drifting thus, into and out of other people's lives, lampooning them without reason, with not even one illegitimate child who might have taken my name.

I visited them in Double Bay. It was then that Gottlieb invited me to rent their East Wing. Marie looked terrible. She'd grown much rounder, and for one so wealthy, wore third-hand frocks from a Paddington charity. She and Gottlieb seemed happy enough. She was a stranger to me now, and she seemed guilty in my presence. I didn't wish to remember our intimacies, but after a drink or two I discovered she might still have had a hankering, which surprised me.

7

That was my first thought, upon regaining consciousness in that cold creek bed somewhere off the Putty Road. I was shivering. I was bleeding a little, a slight gash at the temple. I was thinking of Gottlieb, finally in his bathrobe. His face not only reflected trauma, it signalled the end of his responsibility to me as friend. It released him from guilt. I thought I saw half a smile, obviously from fear. *I had caused his child's death. It was my fault now.* Why then, after the event, did he still allow me to rent half his house?

A thin stream of muddy water was dribbling over the rocks. My body stung. Along with the ache of my depression, which came abruptly with consciousness, I felt disoriented. My heart was beating irregularly. Coughing, wet, heavily wet, I sat down on one of the large smooth stones. A kingfisher fluttered and then hovered. The secret lives of birds. I don't know how long I'd been unconscious. A pleasurable calm had come upon me. I recalled one thing: I had already mentioned this; it was simply a matter of realigning my life, of measuring triangles and distances, of constructing a grid. But at that moment there was uncompassed existence, spread-eagled on the riverbed; I was swallowing up the treetops, the powder-blue sky, the flitting bird. There was a voluptuous sweetness and a soft slumbering. I recalled saying aloud that the present tense was all I had. *I'm asleep.* I debated this with Gottlieb once. The present tense, I said, is the tension of pleasure. *I'm dying.* We have no torment upon its real approach; that only comes with grammar, but to exclaim is the experience of release. Gottlieb said the present was only unawareness.

I had written to him from Paris, of the need for a spare bicycle. Not a new one, but an other; *in steed of,* as Montaigne had said of the Roman cavalry, whose riders always rode with their right hand holding the bridle of a spare horse, upon which they could jump when the present one grew fatigued. A spare bicycle too, should be within reach to provide continuity, for a bicycle deteriorates like the body and is prone to falling, since that is its natural state when not being ridden. An impossible machine except in motion, its every attempt is to keel over. I have fallen countless times. It is only in motion, when the mind and body are in equal harmony that one can do philosophy, for mere intelligence cannot save you from falling, but together, a mind mechanised and a machine anthropomorphised, can have the effect of producing understanding and insight. *Falls happen because of a lack of self-awareness,* Gottlieb used to say. But cocooned inside oneself on a bicycle, at speed, seeking the path of least resistance in the perpetual present, one could be aloof, obsessed, inaccessible *and* thoroughly aware.

There was a law in Montaigne's time when noblemen who owned horses were not allowed to travel on foot, so they conducted all their business and pleasure on horseback ... their women sat backwards, astride their laps for hasty assignations, this reverse cantering bringing laughter and orgasm; quite rightly ... there was no time like the present ... and one should never have to get off for the sake of hunger, or an itch, or post-coital practicalities ... though Montaigne wrote that in warfare men did dismount, not least because if the horse was frightened, its rider would be carried away.

The business of life is consciousness, but to persist like a machine, like a bicycle which marks time and yet moves swiftly, like water running over rocks ... that is the way my mind has taken me these last years, I was saying to Gottlieb after I had broken a hand in a fall, and I saw him rush over for a pen and paper, not having seen him move so fast since his stroke ... *since flight*, I said, *is my natural state. I am never here.* I used the tense of death. There is no greater freedom than to be journeying on a bicycle, or, as one who has adopted a mode of travelling which others would call *vagrancy*, is there any further fall. Gottlieb offered to buy me another bike if I felt the need for a spare. No! I objected, unless it be a Swift circa 1928. It had to be absolutely identical.

I didn't hear the car approach. I saw it quite suddenly, pulling over in a cloud of dust. A Range Rover. A woman getting out. Green scarf, sunglasses, straw hat, which she removed and tossed back through the open window. Fine, soft hair like winnowed hay. She stood on the edge of the road. Was I all right? Nothing broken which cannot be mended, I said as would an archaeologist. That reassured her. She came closer. Climbed awkwardly down the bank while hanging onto the branch of silky oak. With some sadness, I noticed a flash of beauty in her smile. She was about forty, with an olive complexion and a lurching gait. Broad-shouldered, full-breasted, swivel-hipped. Involuntary, her smile; cruel for me. It broke upon her face like a Melbourne spring which easily darkened into showers. I had done with the idea of finding myself attracted and was disappointed to rediscover it was not an idea. The heart is an ancient muscle. It learns very little voluntarily. I reassured myself that concern by others for me came not from the attractive or the well-heeled; it arrived broken and deformed. The ugly, it seemed to me, always had more compassion. Unjust but true.

Closer. Her sunglasses defended her. I avoided proximity, a long sufferer from emotional sclerosis. I feared more the passion and the pain which came in waves, the surf of her smile which touched me here and there. Her eyes, when she pushed up the shades, reflected a blue eternity which guaranteed the loss of everything; my freedom, my art; for I had already begun denuding myself, lowering barricades, fearing still the crack to come, the flood of agony called lust, and I knew that only he who was beyond it could ride a bicycle, for a bicycle guaranteed balance, equanimity and flight. For example, I returned to Gisela, my third wife, after six weeks of riding through the Auvergne. Six weeks, I figured, would jinx the hex of the ternary. I saw, through the light of the upper bedroom window, a looming male form, bouncing, trampolining. Six weeks was all it took. Gisela's flushed face rose at the other end of this gymnast's calves, ectoplasmically. I was surprised. I was aroused. By her enthusiasm; her contortion; my own release. I dreaded the return of lust; saw it approaching with unequal power, the roar of a hail-storm, the blackmail of it. I had freedom finally. I balanced, tip-toe, in the shrubbery and then rode off forever.

Would you like some coffee? The woman held out a hand. She was tall. Maybe it was an introduction. I bowed, more from vertigo, and said I was Jason Redvers, claiming descent from Richard, Seigneur de Reviers, First Earl of Devon. My fluorescent sash was missing. I was Portuguese-Chinese; from Macau. No! she said, she was holding out a hand to help me up. I was still concussed. Her hand was warm and moist. I tried to exert as little pressure as possible. I realised my hair was wet, long, I looked Columbian; pre-columbian. Her soft limb was useless as an aid, but my heart seemed to revive from slumber and I swung giddily onto the road. She had run over the back wheel of the Swift and it was twisted like a potato crisp. I'm sorry about your bike, she said. She helped me wrestle it onto the roof rack, adjusted her glasses over her hair. She seemed short-sighted and squinted at the warped wheel. She brought out a thermos. Her eyes smiled without giving up their secrets and they presumed much. Eyes recollected in tranquillity. You could say she had the face of a movie star, beauty diluted, a faded Dietrich underneath the lamplight. Inside the car I smelt *Thé Vert*, by *L'Occitane*, Marie's favourite perfume. And tobacco. There was a huge Alsatian dog in the caged rear compartment, suddenly thumping around like a bear. I hadn't noticed it until now. It was drumming its tail against the window. I closed the door. Odour of raw steak. The dog's panting made me frantic. That's Rajah, she said. He's just a cuddly bear. We drove along the dirt road tasting of dust. I swallowed some coffee. Either blood or sweat trickled down inside my arm. The dog was curious, nosing the back of my head through the grille. We passed a woman in jeans and a white tee shirt holding a longbow. I was starting to hallucinate. A colony of women. Amazons. The huntress was angrily driving a cow off the road, wielding a branch. That's Miranda, my rescuer said, pulling a face. She took out a packet of cigarettes. Smoke? No thanks. She tapped one out on the wheel. Wedged it between her lips and pushed in the lighter. I stole Miranda's husband, she said. Just for one night. She lit the cigarette and smiled crookedly when she exhaled. Miranda's never forgiven me. She lives in town. In fact, she hates me. A sniper. I think one day she's going to shoot me from afar ...

I was still in some kind of delirium. I doubted my existence; there had been a metamorphosis; I was a stag in this world of women. But because I was not myself, I said, in order to complete her sentence, I would stand before her like a shield. She looked over and smiled sweetly. My aches erupted. She was luscious.

The Rover agonised uphill. She shifted gears from first straight into fifth. I'm Fabiana. She held out a hand and the car, over-geared, lurched from rock to rock. She drove only with one hand, urging the Rover on like a team of horses; the other she waved about, explaining the vegetation, pointing out the boundaries. The car spewed smoke and dust. I told her my name, which I had some trouble remembering. I wished to sink into her expressive arms. Charmed, she said, and considered my hesitation. Hardly, I replied. No, I mean it, she said. (What was it she really said?) It's rare to meet a cosmopolitan. She tugged a little harder at the wheel on the bends, ash from her cigarette spilling onto her lacey bra. We arrived at a cream stone bungalow beneath a stand of pines. The plaque on the wall said *Barringila*. Dogs appeared out of nowhere. Packs of them. All sorts. There must have been twenty. Tails whipping. There was no barking, just some false yawning, a scratch or two. Dogs are sensitive; dissimulators; they can fall victim to madness. They leapt up, scratching at the door. Out of the way. She spoke firmly to them from her window. She eased the car over to the side of the house and did not apply the handbrake. I got out. The dogs could smell blood and they lunged at my arm, obsessively licking. Out! Fabiana cried. Stay! She seemed pleased by the sight of blood. I was apprehensive, looking out for people who might appear; men in overalls, barefoot children screaming, shotgun-toting youths. But the house was silent. We stepped onto a cool verandah. Cane rocker. Smells of paint, stone, pine. The dogs were disinterested now, hot and sleepy, slinking off towards shade, settling down melancholically under a tree, panting and watching, half-lidded. She opened the door, took off her shoes. I followed. My socks had holes. I pulled them off as well. It was dark inside and I squeaked to the window and could see a green tractor beyond and smelt dead flowers and saw corpses wheeled past in caskets, my memory of Gottlieb still fresh as they lowered him into the ground, the soil dark and wet beneath. He was my only friend. Walter Gottlieb. I was remembering names. Bookshelves. Taps. Funereal drumming of dripping water. Soft explosions of ignited gas. Fabiana's toenails painted blue; I was looking at a painting, swirls of blue, a figure, a woman seated. Fabiana putting on the kettle. As she walked past me in bare feet I noticed she was so much taller than me, and she walked with a kind of lurch and sway, seductively, vertiginously. The coffin of a baby grand in one corner. Sit down, she said and returned to the kitchen again, just checking on me. Good to be checked on. I'm a stranger, I have no means to get back to the city, I was about to say, but I heard the gas go off and she yelled, for she was a long way off ... on second thoughts, do you want some whisky instead? Returning with a bottle of Dimple and two glasses and she poured, then settled herself into a deep sofa, her feet rising as she sank so I was looking again, at the twins painting rocks with blue nail polish, her feet so fine, the skin alabaster, nails blue, Blimunde sliding beneath the surface, and Fabiana wearing a black silk top so she's obviously gone and changed and here I am. I asked about the paintings instead. European landscapes? She nodded. Whisky warming my belly. Things leaping about inside my head. I remarked lightly that she shouldn't give alcohol to accident victims since it could kill them. It's okay, she poured another for us immediately and I sensed the woman was capable of murder.

I used to take trains in Europe with my bicycle lodged in the last car and sometimes they would uncouple half the train and I'd have to make my way back miles to fetch the bike, I was saying to Fabiana, and she was listening in the same way Dr Judith did, though with the doctor I was aware of my past, since I had a record, having had several episodes as a *fugueur*, and had lived under different names in different places and had already been classified and diagnosed by a Parisian psychoanalyst, who told me I was living three lives, which surprised me because I thought he would have uncovered more. So I told the story of stopping at train stations because they looked good, had nice flowers, were clean or because there was mist settling at dusk, with snow-capped mountains behind, or I'd seen a family sit down to supper in the soft glow of a weak electric light and felt comforted, *at home*. This vicarious joy became more powerful as I felt the urge to paint. I didn't wait for reality to arrive, since I knew it always came, a kick in the belly at the end of my money at the end of a dark road where thugs inevitably lurked. It was called *being an artist*. I was protected by a shell, I said, born with a caul; Fabiana was leaning forward, looking rather clinical. I said I had always found money by going to the Australian embassy or the consul-general or wiring the arts council, and they seemed to agree there could be a kind of standing loan in small instalments providing I brought results. But of late, there had been too few results. Fortunately, I was found by Marie de Nerval, who convinced me that I should paint over the paintings of others, after swabbing them down with turpentine. That way, she said, the ghosts of the past were always present.

Fabiana took all this in, but all the time I felt she had done a million riskier things and she was weighing up where I came in on her scale: liar; drunk; vagabond; thug. A game you played with buttons. She had undone the top ones of hers. You're an artist? You appear so different each time I look at you, she said in a soft voice. I stared at her for an explanation. I just wanted to hear it again. The *non-sequitur*. Perhaps I missed something. The remark was not unpleasant. A most expressive face; beautiful eyes; my head was spinning. She removed an ice cube from her drink and held it to my temple. Outside, the wind arrived in violent gusts. All was dust; a khamsin, a desert visitation. A voice arose. It said: *In Egypt this wind blows for fifty days.*

8

I had given up poetry for painting after university, I said to Fabiana, claiming how lucky she was to have this peace in the countryside. Poets should die young. Painters can paint badly for a long time. She laughed and the dogs embarked on a chorus of whining. They give no peace, she said, but I love them. It's free-range boarding, she added. We don't believe in caging them. The plural signalled a partner. Gottlieb would have been compiling a list of questions by now. I hated his curiosity. What was the point in finding out? Should she have a husband? A lover? Was I beginning to be interested? She left off the apostrophe in Martins Kennels, I remarked. Oh, let me not begin, she said. Her father was Brazilian. Alfredo Martins. I'm no longer married, she said, wagging her ring finger. There was a sad silence. Apostrophes implied possession or absence. We seemed to be speaking at cross-purposes; in a void; to or about the dead. The sky outside was turning cobalt.

I needed to go. It was getting dark. Considering the fact she'd run over my wheel, I could not expect her to do much else than drive me to the crossroads where I could hitch a ride. Out of the question; she said I was in no state to travel. Come. We went to the verandah and put on our shoes and with the packs of dogs running behind, she drove us to another part of the property where two small silos reared against the sky like mini-lighthouses in a sea of spent wheat. Fabiana walked with her hands behind her back, stepping over the flattened stalks. A hare bounded away up the hill. I've had this one converted into a studio, she pointed. She was slightly out of breath. I paint, but it was my grandmother who was the famous artist. She and a friend went to France and they joined an artists' commune, sometime in the 1920s, I think. Fabiana opened the door. Took a lantern hanging from the back of it, raised the glass and lit the wick with her cigarette lighter. The butane-inspired flame roared like an oxy-welder. Smells of kerosene and turpentine. She found a switch on the wall and around the roof a pink circle of fluorescent tubes glimmered and ignited. It was a clean, well-lighted place. A rose pagoda with a brass bed. I imagined things: her soft voice between a child's and a seductress'; undressing between the sheets, a spilling of flesh; the long screech of a frogmouth owl outside; her leaning over me, the steady exertions. I longed for my stretcher like Peter the Great, who when offered the grand suite in the hôtel de Lesdiguières, unfurled his bedroll over the stone floor. You can stay here, Fabiana said, gently taking me by the elbow. I informed her that I seldom stayed overnight anywhere without considering whether I would be able to die there, divested of all the paraphernalia of gloom, amongst harlots and jesters. She smiled the sort of smile for which some men would have died. We walked to the centre of the wooden floor. Perhaps we could have danced. Smells of resin and oils. There were five small square windows cut into the circular wall. You can sleep quite well here, Fabiana said, and if you're bored there are plenty of books on the shelves, if you get to them before the mice. There's a washbasin and a tap. I'll move these frames and canvases out in the morning. When you're ready, come over for dinner. It's about a ten-minute walk … at a leisurely pace.

I'd forgotten the damned summer light. She turned, cutting a lonely figure through the stubble. Her Range Rover growled through dust. She neglected to change gears. A little later, headlights flicked on, and the car disappeared. We had withdrawn from intimacy for practicality's sake, I imagined. But the way she touched my arm ... the closeness of her body. A rising wind fanned my anxiety. I washed my face, studied the paintings. Cubist influences. A girl with donkeys. Angular landscapes: southern French villages bathed in limestone light. Powerful women with cone-shaped breasts and cyclists' thighs. Indigo panels. Then everything was transformed – the painter may have had an eyesight problem – I recognised the changes straight away – from strong colours to faded landscapes, a deliberate flouting of perspective, a renouncing of distance, for such space beyond the intimate world which one could no longer see turned one infinitely sad. A later period perhaps. The houses had been rendered amorphous, floating in ether; human figures standing on cliff-tops now had the measure of a mountain. It was all very Chinese. Stirred, impressed, I thought how strange it was for her grandmother to travel backwards from Cubism into the heart of ancient China. I stretched my eyelids. Nobody understood hybridity. I was forged myself, with impressions of authenticity.

I pulled out the crumpled letter Marie had written to me whilst I was in Paris. She had mentioned a house for rent off Martins Road at Colo Heights. I had gone way past that turn-off in my fugue. But why this coincidence? Why am I at the right place now? Why Fabiana? Well, there are stranger things in the countryside. I did some calculations. Fabiana had made ends meet by selling art works. The kennels kept the taxman from her door. Wheat had been grown in the two lower paddocks. There had been some logging of the hardwood forests and timber trucks have destroyed the track, leaving one side of the hill exposed to erosion. Gorse and blackberry were multiplying.

There was a man here once.

9

I have taken a *Montaigne* turn. I question and analyse, but cannot enter into feeling, yet love is a strange animal which persists, appearing out of the dark, bleating and alternately threatening. Indeed, Montaigne had written that no relationship failed sooner than that which was concluded for beauty's sake. I preferred to be left alone. A friend, though, was loved because he was my self. And so, I must have loved Gottlieb, for reasons which I still cannot fathom.

Gottlieb liked repeating the phrase that *life was not art*. That it wasn't, was obvious. But the corollary was more difficult: that art was not life needed explanation. Mathematical differentiation, he said. Just as a parabola approaches a straight line and only touches it at one point, so life only touches art at one perfect moment. You only peak once, you mean, I said to him. I think he liked me for this simple-mindedness. My admitted failure. Few will ever touch the line, Gottlieb shook his head as he spoke. I reflected on this in silence. I knew that art admonished life for the latter's failure to risk itself. I was sure Montaigne knew that art was brave. Unlike Booty, Montaigne didn't have a death warrant in his pocket. But did Walter Gottlieb?

Within three months of Blimunde's death, Gottlieb suffered a slight stroke. He had been drinking heavily for some time and that seemed the most likely cause. After the stroke, his speech became slurred; he stuttered; he drank little, but he always appeared drunk. One eye had almost closed. But his wits were still as sharp as ever and when he rang me in the East Wing of his house, he quoted from Mao and said *The East is rrr-Redvers'*. He was working then on a series of what he called 'wordless poems', though I inferred from this he meant he was doing nothing. It's a ch-ch-Chinese thing, he said.

He was almost inconsolable after Blimunde's drowning but he forced me to stay close. He said he could not trust himself. I feared he would take his life. Each morning we would work on our respective *oeuvres* and at one o'clock Gottlieb would ring me from his study to suggest lunch at the brasserie near the Marina. We walked slowly, and I noticed he was slurring his left leg, in time with his speech. He always wore one of his bow ties and lugged a black briefcase. We never discussed our work, but he was always asking me whether I had read one thing or another and in this way I suspected he was building up a file. He hardly slept at night. He said he was overloaded with ideas. In winter he started bonfires in the garden and sat in a wicker chair, clasping a sheaf of papers to his chest. I stopped paying attention to his ravings and his stuttering was neither worth repetition nor anticipation. No pearls gleamed in deep frustration. I spoke of my grandfather the Macanese poet. I said his *Water Clock Poems* were tears of time, filtering through each stanza to resonate with the ground-bass of *tristezza*. My grandfather was lost in contradiction, torn between cultures, between love and homesickness. Sometimes a poet should not have a heart. He should deal in blood. Ha! Gottlieb shook a finger at me. He was taking notes. For a while I clammed up. Writing isolates, he said, putting his arm around my shoulders, it tears us away from our mythic states, our communal tongue, our shared sense of terror. Your stories of Macau keep me alive. I would have liked them to be my own, but alas, your constant supply of them fills my life while Marie howls and laments and jets off to London. There is no question of their ownership, but anonymity is more virtuous. (I was pumping up my tyres. It matched his insufflation.) Writing is the ethics of high envy, I suggested. A higher mind knows what to borrow and what to steal and conceal. Anything less than genius turns art to suspicion. Marie, Gottlieb said, changing the subject, has taken to wearing large crucifixes around her neck. She brings home priests and has them visit me in my study. I detest this intrusion. I need to be exorcised from priests. I am not dying. Not yet.

I know, I said. I meant I knew about Marie and her crucifixes. She was killing him.

Gottlieb devoted himself to Blixen, lavishing all his attention to educating her for something other than literature. He bought her microscopes and telescopes and encouraged her to bottle ants.

Since Blimunde's drowning, he suspected all emotion. He seemed only to be playing at feeling, constantly on stage. Marie may have had him under surveillance. He declaimed his lamentations in the spotlight. Charlene, the maid with the guillotine nose, was never far away. Once when Marie went to London, Gottlieb took a flight to Melbourne for an assignation – a slim, dark girl in black lace and shiny stockings. She may have been a former student. They went to the art gallery on St Kilda Road to look at a Giacometti exhibition. Gottlieb seemed grotesque, portly amongst all those stick figures towering over him. A photographer snapped them, he and Jet Gems, for that was her name, she said, smiling a white smile, flicking back her raven hair. And you sir? The camera was thrust in his face. He would give his name as Redvers ... he secretly enjoyed these trysts, assuming names, tried to coach Jet to assume them too ... use any friend, he said ... but she already had one and was not about to ruin her professional career. Walter Gottlieb grew anxious. This was a *photo. Ceci n'était pas un texte.* He walked off quickly; fled without the least sign of a stroke. The photographer snapped Jet on automatic, arms akimbo, leaning against the wall. He knelt on the floor for more shots, lay down, chatted her up. Another journalist joined them. They were on assignment for Fashion Week. She dazzled them while Walter waited in the bookstore. He stood on tiptoe, peered up over the lower shelves. Was she through yet? Look at those sleazebags. The Giacomettis shimmered like burnt trees in the middle distance. His heart was pounding. What if the photo appeared in a national daily? He could see it. What would he say to Marie? He would be out on the street. He was already planning how to cancel the paper delivery, train next door's labrador not to retrieve what he threw over the fence; no, maybe he should write to the arts editor, explain he didn't want to be exposed; men alone understood these things. His heart started behaving strangely, the world swelling and subsiding, systole and diastole, life-giving, gift-retracted. Indian giver, they used to call him at school. It was true. He hated parting with things; pens, comics, cap pistols. He gave them away to make himself more likeable. He had bought Jet

Gems some very expensive French perfume, but now this whole trip was ruined. Never mind her friend, a big man in a loud tie was shooing the photographers away. He was touching her arm. Alberto. Was that his name? Was he inviting her to lunch? No, he was a friend of Giacometti's. Jet looked across and signalled. Gottlieb smiled. She was still his.

More shock in store. When Gottlieb arrived in Sydney, Charlene met him at the airport with Blixen in her arms. He thought she was abducting the child. He was confused, reached out to grab his daughter, but there was Marie a few paces behind, a darkness veiling her face. They were leaving. Leaving him? It was something not even Thomas Hardy could have plotted. Marie was at the domestic terminal because her plane from London had been diverted to Melbourne. Sydney was shrouded in fog that morning. They had been on the same plane. She had a migraine. Her face was puffy. *Les réactions ...* she said, *they give me a 'eadache ... pas confortable.* Her eyes had by now shrivelled to dark sultanas. Reactions? Gottlieb translated to himself, knew she was cryptic when flustered. *Yes, jets.*

I had known from the moment Gottlieb lectured on the split narrative at university, that his personality was itself a split narrative. An imaginative person always led two or more lives: that which he projected for others and those which he hid even from himself. So Gottlieb was *naturally* duplicitous and this naturalness did not warrant rationalisation or condemnation, but carried him through life; indeed, *it enabled him to live.*

10

Bats were gliding between the trees. While I was washing my cuts over the enamel basin, they emerged from the sky and sailed past the window in slow flurries of black snow. They made for the orchards, where a night of fruitful and silent savagery began. I remembered Fabiana had primed the gas lamps which lit the silo.

I was disappointed she lacked concern over my cuts and abrasions, but she had seemed preoccupied with something else. Perhaps there were other vampiric guests. Not all the dogs followed her. One was silhouetted on a windy ridge, remaining still for a moment, its ears against the early moon. I looked at some of the canvases turned against the curving wall. More oils of heavy women chiselled from stone, sketches of hilltop villages, and then indigo. Indigo everywhere.

Just before Etienne de La Boétie died at the age of 32 in 1563, he repeatedly called for Montaigne to be close to his bedside. *My brother, stay close to me, please.* The name *Brother* is indeed a glorious name, but as Montaigne wrote, the sharing of goods distempers all alliance. It was in the priesthood that Walter Gottlieb began his adult life and it was in the seminary he learned goods were there to be used only as needed for existence. He appropriated the intimacy of others. Without question, he said, I thought that to be called *Father* was so much better than *Brother*. Paterfamilias; bequeather; testator. He was to lead the chosen: disciples; epigones; ephebes. The rest could be spurned, or as Gottlieb had it, were common goods used to advance the intellect a little further for those who lacked other means. Knowledge is not held by any one of us for himself alone, he said to me one day as we played squash on the university courts – I was still far from graduating – Gottlieb had attached rubber bands to the heavy frame of his glasses and he looked like a wild Apache chief suddenly intent on arc-welding – knowledge, he said, supercedes personality. I teach, you acquire. There is no need for return save friendship and devotion. The Greeks knew all about that. Call me *Fra Gottlieb*. I am no padre, but a professor partial to Marx. As always, Gottlieb had his arm around my sweating shoulders in solidarity with my failure to win a point, yet I could not shake off the thought that for him, the word *Brother* had always been a legal fiction. I lost on purpose. Fathers, though, were there to be murdered.

I was thinking about this as I began the walk down to Fabiana's house in that speckled moonlight which drew the tide of instinct. I was thinking how Gottlieb had said all friendship was debt and labour. Sex, he said, was only the *expectation* of capital, for orgasm was not enlightenment, the phallus a one-eyed waiter in the dim refectory, bringing up food we had all seen before. It's best to pay for prostitutes, for honest labour which *delights by numbers and by difference.*

My problem with Walter Gottlieb, I was going to tell Fabiana when I arrived at her house, began when our long lunches at Double Bay stretched into evening dinners and then to late-night drinking sessions. Gottlieb had unlimited cash, which he unleashed upon obsequious waiters to keep them at bay. They were not to stack up chairs upon the stroke of midnight. Gottlieb suggested he write something on my grandfather ... nothing really intricate, he said, just a kind of introduction to his work and then some balanced critique. I winced at the word 'critique' but went along with it. Feed me information, Gottlieb said. I need to know not only the work, but the man. There is a nuance to all these things and I do them best, he said. He was the expert of tone and feeling. You and I, he said, find refuge among the great dead. Read Hermann Broch, he suggested, *The Death of Virgil.* You, however, are a synthesiser who has not realised himself ... you feel too keenly the imperfection of life and that defeats your will. You studied painting and forged a few. You were the filter of others and you brought out their imperfections. You are not a writer, but you can translate your grandfather's poems, can you not? Even imperfectly?

That was when I began telling him all. My grandfather's life, which left me with nothing. His spirit stolen. The great poet Camilo Conceição, whom nobody had been able to pin down. An insatiable succubus inhabited me by day, for I was manic with ideas of image and advertisement and I reached out for his posterity, but in the dead of night it bit back with guilt and distrust. My father never spoke about his father. He was a poet, my father said. You must never consider that as a legitimate title. Discourage all research. I told Gottlieb that. Friendship was poison. Was not Gottlieb inquiring into this for me, out of respect, friendship, honour? Why then, did I feel so empty? So insincere? The rosewood bed in the East Wing felt like an empty tomb, a stolen monument, a theft of my legacy.

I sought refuge in alcohol. While Gottlieb refilled my empty glasses, I supplied him with stories from my grandfather's past. How we were all connected by illegitimacy. Grandpa had three concubines, I said. I think after three or four *Nights at the Brasserie*, which is what I began calling these sessions, he knew that I knew that he knew I was more than myself. I was being sacrificed for his art. It must have been how Booty felt, with Montaigne sitting by his bedside. Booty in a dream-fever, saw things through imperfect understanding. He knew he was being etched into a minor history.

I make my way down the track to Fabiana's cottage. Moonlight glosses my path; it is a safe light and it shines on Jason Redvers. I am fighting for my originality, struggling against being swabbed out with turpentine. Of late I have ceased creating. My optic nerves enter the back of my eyes at right angles, so there is some retinal separation. There have been four operations, but my vision is now blurred and I have many blind-spots. It is perhaps the reason why I ride a bicycle. Though I cannot see what is to the side of me, my hearing is extremely keen. The night is busy with voices. Unused to walking, I imagine riding. I coast through the grizzle and hiss of marsupials. I hear whispers in the wind. Ghosts come down to water. A zone of sound. Music would surely kill me with its beauty. But there it was, a Beethoven sonata in C major, coming from her bedroom.

I was telling stories to Fabiana over our omelette and crisp white wine, which was thoughtful of her. She had side dishes of prosciutto and assorted cheeses, and she had baked her own bread. It was simple and tenderly served. She let me talk. I was primed by my nights at the brasserie and was professionally entertaining. I was a native son of Macau, born sixty years ago, resident of the Côte d'Azur for twenty years. But having lived in Australia for a much longer period, I was nevertheless unknown. It was as though I had always painted in another's name. It was as though the country didn't know how to recognise me. Fabiana didn't intrude and nodded in all the right places. After a while I felt I was the only one filling the silence. She brought more wine. I tried not to stare and avoided her eyes through which I would have fallen and not have found bottom. An old fool can only feel pride. Somewhere in primeval history, a stirring. She wore stockings and heels. Lilac slacks. A shapely woman in an indigo cashmere pullover, fluffy and tender. She listened to my nonsense with wide green eyes. I was father to the child. Though if you ask me now what she looked like, I cannot quite say. Creating an identikit mugshot is quite impossible, I told the detectives.

For almost a year, I told Fabiana, I worked at the Villa d'Este on Lake Como in Italy. It used to be a grand hotel, though I don't know what has happened to it since. It stood on the site of an old convent, with rolling hills and parklands which commanded views of the lake on three sides where in summer you could see the sailboats keel over in sudden squalls. I earned my living as a waiter and rose in rank to Maître D' as I was fluent in Italian and French and had references from the Negresco in Nice where I was the barman at La Rotonde Brasserie. It was easy work. From June to September I plied old dowagers with champagne, after which they snoozed in the cool parlour beside the frieze of Cupid and Psyche, their snores circling up to do battle with the ceiling fans. The town of Cernobbio was a short walk away and I had the afternoons off to browse at one of the three bookshops which sold rare books, in one of which I found a sixteenth century volume published by Cardinal Gallio. The Cardinal, a great stroller around the parks, often seen striding forth in his crimson robes, had met a French nobleman by the name of Michel de Montaigne. Montaigne was undertaking a voyage in search of mineral spas. That was in the year 1581. The Villa d'Este had been a meeting place and hospice for travelling poets, artists and men of science. Montaigne stayed in one of the rooms on the second floor of the old wing. There you can still make out an inscription on the blackened beam that runs beneath the ceiling. Montaigne was famous for leaving graffiti and this must have inspired Cardinal Gallio to have his carpenter chisel deeply into the wooden beam, the philosopher's remark that he, the Cardinal, was *an affable boulevardier of considerable charm*. For this had been written in the visitors' book. It was mostly in Latin, and *boulevardier*, being such a typically urbane French term, was rendered more respectfully as *ambulator*. The Cardinal was not aware Montaigne had published this very sentence in French in his travel diaries, with reference to the typical Bordeaux dog, a *boulevardier* which he described as *très gentil*, when it was not urinating.

Thank goodness there are no beams in my studio, Fabiana laughed a laugh sweet as wild honey. She ran a finger around the rim of her glass. The ghosts were close by. I took the opportunity to explain my mania. I find silence soothing, I said, when I'm with someone else. I hold silence dear, not only in complete solitude. My kidneys are aching. It probably accounts for the fact that I've never had a long-term relationship with anyone. I pass stones which grate like rosary beads. The noise of contrition is deafening. Fabiana is shifting in the lounge, placing her feet up so she is looking away from me, as if to be nearer to me at the same time. Confiding, I noted, was also a turning away. She knew me without need for any further explanation. The walk from the silo had been a test. Perhaps it gave her time to look me up on the internet, make a few phone calls.

I offer a story for a story, she began. I left my husband a year ago. He was a farmer and owned this property. There are rivers enough here … I'll show you the pool where you can swim … a spot with deep icy water all year round … you can hang and jump from springy willow branches. I left him; left all of this. She inscribed a semi-circle with her index finger. He was a good man. Dull, but good. A man of routine. You would hear the tractor come round the hill at precisely five o'clock in the winter. I cooked him steaks. The fire crackled and the wind howled outside. Do you like Brahms? I was crazy about Brahms, but Roger hated any kind of music. He said incessant music repulsed him. It was a kind of terror. I think he was jealous. Not of me, but of Brahms. He hardly lived indoors. He would have the milkers penned, the pails washed, the floors hosed and he would be up at four-thirty the next morning. It was not a life of feeling. I stuck with him, then I got pregnant. The twins were not his. Roger and I lived separate lives, but we did not move away permanently. I wanted to play the piano in Sydney. It was not unpremeditated. My friends Claire and Nikki used to come up on the weekends. We formed the Sibylla Trio. We were friends at the Conservatorium and had already given several concerts together. Though rusty, we practised hard. We started playing lunchtime concerts at the Art Gallery of New South Wales. I stayed in town more and more, and then six months later Roger disappeared. At first the police said he was crushed under his tractor. Then they said there was no body. At first they said it was an accident. Then they said it was no accident. He was hauling a trailer with a full water tank to douse some flames in the western paddock. Lightning had sparked a grassfire. The flames went through. He may have dragged himself down to the waterhole. There were no clues. I think he just gave up. Neighbours said he gave up. Stopped applying his routine. Things ran down. His heart wasn't in it. Should I feel guilt or blame? I was the one who was pregnant, who was all on her own, with very few resources. Neighbours here don't talk to me anymore, Redvers. Just the dogs.

You said there were twins.

I fell pregnant to another man. My daughter's extremely bright, though I don't say that as a mother.

You play Brahms, you paint. I hear your antiquated refrigerator rumbling in the kitchen and all around you things run down. I dream you in your past, long-married and suffering the wordlessness of Man, his flannel shirt stuck with burrs, the grease-stained overalls flapping on a cold line startling the pink galahs. I lie upon the procrustean bed in my tower-silo hearing the wind explore a cavity in my soul, staring at a false dawn waiting for the scabrous intimacy of too much significance, or not enough, as when you said to me as I left that night: *Tomorrow's Saturday and I work in a shop in Sydney, so I'll drive you in to get your things.* I fill a missing place for now, but it's in neither of our hearts to love again. And yes, you play Brahms in the night and you paint. I think of why I did not take her in my arms and kiss her two or three times. I think she would have stopped me, stoppered them, told me to get on my bike. It seemed that upon too much intimacy, she turned abruptly cold. Good. But return to me.

I'd like to think it was the story I told that inspired you to make the offer of letting me rent one of your silos, Fabiana. Maybe I was just in love with your name. Maybe your name inspired my stories. Fabulation. Your name in Cantonese starts with the word for flower. *Fa*; A note. A pressed flower. Preserved perfumes. You settled down on the lounge, put your feet up beneath you and I began.

At the north bank of the west end of Qutang Gorge on the Yangtze river there are caves in the cliffs. During the Ming Dynasty, Zhang Xiangzhong, an *insurgent*, so the label went, was driven with thirteen of his followers to take refuge there. The Emperor's soldiers blockaded the river just below the gorge, hoping to starve them out. But they didn't count on Zhang's ingenuity. He got his men to chisel holes in the rock below the cliffs during the night. Then they used what was left of their fighting sticks and staves and cut them into sections, which were then fitted to the holes. In this way they descended, one by one, removing one rung at a time to place it in the slot below. At the bottom, they were able to drink and catch fish. But unless they swam, they could not escape from the cliffs. The current was too fierce in the narrrow gorges and they would surely drown. Each night, they performed what they called their *water-stealing*, and each day they dried the fish they caught. Meanwhile, the Emperor's men were finding it difficult to maintain their siege, for they were recruited from the cities and did not know how to fish efficiently, needing to be supplied by road. They did not understand how the insurgents could have survived. Morale started to deteriorate. Zhang's rebels hung their fish out in full view. They toasted the soldiers below with their plentiful supply of water, holding out their ceramic bowls. Then they mocked their foes, punching holes in their bowls so when they held them up, water dribbled out. This was in mocking reference to the way the Emperor measured time with his dripping water-jars. The soldiers were frustrated. Rumours became rife about this being a hundred-year siege. Their archers could not reach the cave with their arrows. They soon withdrew. Zhang's band did not leave the cliff. They felt so secure there, so *untouchable*, they overstayed Nature's welcome. A monsoonal flood cut them off. There were no fish in the water. They died inside their caves. There were rumours of cannibalism.

Fabiana listened. When Redvers finished his story he had a strange look on his face. He often felt himself leaving his body when he told stories, as if he didn't belong to himself, the words working against presence. She led him to her study, where amidst the books and jars of paint and writing implements, she drew out from a cupboard carved with Chinese characters a small *doucai* cup decorated with blue and red flowers and butterflies. Redvers commented on its beauty. The blue flowers in the thin white glaze were translucent. It's not very old, she said. About 1927. This was made by my grandmother's friend. It was one of the very few things she made with clashing colours... that's what *doucai* means. Her name was Anna Ångström. She was obsessed with Chinese porcelain, but she was not at all brittle. It was at the moment when he returned the cup to her that she held his fingers, just for a few seconds.

I'd given up *amour*. It was a strangely ancient experience, like a sound of chariots. I recalled the last time a woman kissed me. Then there was the sound of wheels on a gravel drive. I was teaching English in a high school in Paris. It was after I had left Marie de Nerval and had cycled all the way to Paris from Provence. I had to record my voice on tape for the language laboratory and was sitting at my booth one afternoon when Céleste, the philosophy teacher, entered and quite suddenly kissed me on the back of the neck. I heard a car crunch up the gravel drive outside. I was wearing a collarless shirt and the mark of her crimson lipstick was quite visible, though I didn't realise it was imprinted there, and all day the students were smiling at me in a strange and knowing way and when the deputy headmaster offered me his half-bottle of wine at lunch, saying I needed inspiration and courage to fight with one arm tied behind my back, I became suspicious. When I met Céleste's husband, I saw he only had one arm. He was a charming host, a man of *esprit*. He asked me if I could give him a lift home in my little red car, my *bagnole*, my chariot, for he could not drive. I left the school soon after.

11

I think Fabiana made an offer to me because we traded stories. I don't mean the offer to drive me to Double Bay – Marie had already indicated I should be gone when she returned from Europe. I mean if only Fabiana could drive me to my single room in Newtown, my old abode, which would depress her no end if she saw my live-in garage and stretcher bed and the dog shit dotted outside, she would ask if I wanted to work in her studio for a modest rent, and I could board there, for at least until she sold the property. She did make the offer. It would be a few months yet, she said. My first thought, I don't know why, was of my heart in a state of siege. Timetables filled me with anxiety. *Deadline* was an apt term. It got the wind up me. A Simoom blew through the arid regions. I saw long depressive afternoons. I saw engorged bloodworms sliding down the cliff-face of the Qutang Gorge.

I ache all over, not from my fall, but from all the dehumanisation since the Enlightenment. In Fabiana's machinery shed I repair my wheel. There is no thought but that of rotary motion, balance, rolling resistance. To *true* a wheel is more than to make it round. Being *well-rounded* is perhaps the least scientific, least engineered of all mechanical principles. Where the eye senses perfection, the flaws are abundant. A spinning wheel reveals all the bumps and crookedness, all the rocking and rolling, the swivelling and swaying. And so inside a human being, the diffracting motion of X-rays can show up the crookedness of a spine, the fracture of the first metacarpel, the loss of movement in the primate's opposing thumb due to violent impact. Only in motion and against the wind do we find some kind of perfection. It is better that grief strikes us dead than we have words to frame it, for my sorrow, weighing upon suspicion of my friend Walter Gottlieb, pained me more than any injury. I collaborated with Gottlieb; helped him write, as he said, *this novel of huge import* to uncover an unknown poet. I did not speak my discontent and squashed any thoughts of propriety and jealousy. Montaigne had taught me well: *I am little subject to these violent passions. I have naturally a hard apprehension, which by discourse I daily harden more and more.*

12

Many years ago, I lived in Paris. Down-and-out. I scraped by, working as a barman and waiter. That was after I did time for forging famous paintings. Gottlieb came to Paris. He saw the state I was in and promptly arranged for me to take up a job as a gallery guard in an art museum. He was ecstatic. He liked being a wheeler-dealer. I complained at first. A gallery *gardien*! Gottlieb smiled. Humility, Redvers. Besides, you'll be near your favourite paintings all day long. You won't have to speak at all, not even to raise your voice at miscreant children. To be in uniform! What a position! You can almost smell the paint! You'll be the guardian of civilisation. Wouldn't you rather sit in a warm museum, muffled in a comfy chair between *Velasquez* and *Vermeer* than ply the streets in your condition, pockets charged with garlic and chives you'd stolen from the fuitshop near the Métro station?

Walter, I said, a museum's not alphabetical.

We were sitting outside a brasserie near the Picasso Museum. They had gas heaters on tall stands. An icy wind funnelled up the rue du Temple. Gottlieb was in shirtsleeves, wearing braces and a bow tie. You do smell bad, he chuckled, fiddling with the wings of his spectacles, staring at the other patrons. His mind was on some practical task. Droplets of perspiration appeared on his forehead. There'll of course be a queue for the *carte de travail*, he said, but it could all be done with some clever shuffling, quiet words upstairs and quick signatures on the sly. I said you were a famous painter ... in Australia. The French are always lucid when it comes to frontier places. They like naïfs. But don't mess up. You would, in no time at all, be a *fugitif*. French law has always been flighty, my dear Redvers. You could go back behind bars without seeing a lawyer.

Gottlieb pronounced French words badly and loudly. He was newly converted to deconstruction. His bow-tie was colourful and his suit impeccable, and the well-to-do customers nodded as though they recognised him. Perhaps he was Henry James. Parisians of course, dwelt in different time zones.

At the *musée*, there wasn't much to do. It wasn't as though I was watching the Mona Lisa watching me. Gottlieb took me to dinner several times in the ornate dining room, and when I changed out of my *gardien*'s uniform, nobody recognised me. Parisians triaged their lives in Cartesian form: mind, body, food. Gottlieb was rubbing his hands together. He was pleased I liked the job. He took special delight in drawing me out. I was obsessed with Vermeer. (It was after my Francis Bacon phase). But why Vermeer? he asked. I shrugged. He's not what he seems, I said. I told Gottlieb how at the Bilderberg Garden Hotel in Amsterdam, Vermeer had complained about the smell of mussels. He was walking around the restaurant sniffing at the buffet. I can't stand the smell of mussels in the morning, Vermeer said, fanning his nose; he seemed to have had a heavy cold. And all this fuss about the *Nightwatch*, the painter said to me, leaning over my table. How can anyone stay at a hotel called the fucking *Nightwatch*? He proclaimed he had fine powder. The management made threatening noises. They didn't know who he was. He had another name of course. It's all right, Vermeer said to them, though the waiters stood their ground, waiting for him to leave. I walk away, he said. That's what I do. I just walk away. Vermeer and I travelled much together. He taught me the secrets of his paintings: how he used himself as a model for portraits of women. It took three months before I came out of character as Vermeer's doppelgänger. I couldn't afford psychoanalysis. I still go in and out like that, in flight from the drudgery of being a gallery guard. Customers love it … I take them on tours with this patter. They come out completely disoriented.

Gottlieb was writing everything down on a napkin with a silver ball-point. If I seemed particularly dissociated that day, he didn't appear to notice. I'm sure he thought I was on drugs. I could have been mad of course, but there's no point in explaining madness.

My doctor, Judith Sarraute, says I am not mad. Listen to what the OED has to say about the fugue state, she instructs, lifting a heavy volume onto her silken knees. She licks a finger and flips over a page. Here we are: *a flight from one's own identity, often involving travel to some unconsciously desired locality … a dissociative reaction to shock or emotional stress in a neurotic, during which all awareness of personal identity is lost though the person's outward behaviour may appear rational. On recovery, memory of events during the state is totally repressed but may become conscious under hypnosis or psychoanalysis. A fugue may also be part of an epileptic or hysterical seizure.*

Judith encourages self-measurement. A fugueur needs points of reference, she says; compasses; hourglasses. Sometimes I see stars, I tell her. You may not know what innocence is, or guilt; or even murder, she continues, ignoring me. You will have these blindspots. You won't have a memory of your episodes.

But if you can't remember, then are you guilty? Or is it that you are guilty of invention?

13

In the West Wing in his mansion in Sydney, Gottlieb could never sleep when Marie was away in London or New York, at her art auctions. She could not obtain an export licence in France, despite the efforts of her father. Important works stayed in the country. The idea of France is starting to smell rancid, she warned, shouting at Gottlieb over the phone line which discordantly delayed every word and then echoed it, nothing new, she yelled, could come from it, since *all that had been gone through is being repeated*. Gottlieb used to ring me in the East Wing all hours of the night. He couldn't sleep. He didn't say he was struggling with originality. I told him it was on account of the contortionist who made his bed, the guillotine-nosed maid from Ashton's Circus. He agreed. I could hear him sighing at some sound from Blixen's bedroom. That maid, I said, walks in everywhere unannounced. She's waiting for the tumbril to take you to your execution. She's outside your door right now. Gottlieb hung up.

He pleaded with me to drink regularly with him. I believe he was already an alcoholic, though out of some unwritten protocol he tried never to drink in solitude. Even alone in a bar, he said, you can have a mirror-self. But privately, at home, there is only the dark end of all despair. Read Berryman, he said. I told him I did not have Berryman, that my confessive poets ran out at Lowell. Well, buy a volume then, or borrow mine. The whole enchilada. I'm gonna sample a double-maltski. What about you? Speaking like this, Czar Gottlieb was a sedated murderer come to life in his prison cell. Padding slowly from room to room, the only thing he menaced was the cat.

I was a slave to his insomnia, but it was saving me on rent. When Marie was away, Gottlieb ticked her secret rental book and told her I had paid. It was a modest fee for such grand premises, but we all understood the rules of friendship, hospitality and the unspoken principle of suicide-prevention.

The maid passed me in the hallway wide-eyed, a grimace on her face. She was carrying a pillow. Imprinted on her irises, dead flowers. Gottlieb was sitting in his Morris chair, a rare one with large castors. He called it his *fauteuil roulante*. He wheeled to the sideboard. You'll have to tell me another story, he said. He liked pathos. His head lolled to one side. He reached into his dressing gown and sucked some pills from a phial.

In all the years I'd known him, I'd often experienced this moment. The drooping head, the pathetic demeanour. What immediately followed was usually proprietorial overkill. I think all the years at the seminary taught him self-preservation through bullying. He was, how else could I put it, *lacking in refinement*. It was the way he brushed his hand away from his chest in irritation and impatience. It was the way he flicked his thumb with his index finger to indicate the stupidity of a remark made in his presence. This came from somewhere deeper, further back in the genetic helix, from the wilds of his Latvian ancestry. I see a young Gottlieb lugging firewood in a snowstorm, schlepping faggots towards a smoky post-war tavern. The mountains loom depressingly. It is already dark in the middle of the day. He's flicking splinters he's pulled from his thumb after depositing the fascicles. The swaying head does not obey his wishes. People think it's compliance, that nodding service of his, arriving with wryness. He understood his own foreignness, just as I understood mine. It's just that I had less trouble with my past since I invented myself at every moment. My ghosts, I said to Gottlieb, were benignly middle class, but I took risks. Forgery was not a game, except perhaps for academics. Gottlieb's phantoms were roughly of the *arbeitende Klassen*. Not like my father, who *fell from grace*, son of a major poet from Macau, I said to Gottlieb. Gottlieb senior would have got by on hard work in Australia, would have changed his name to Goodleap if it hadn't been for the registry forms which he couldn't hurdle – *Vot means dead pole?* Imagine all that guilt at having left for a new world; at having *survived*; worse, at having *covered their tracks*. Don't sign anything. *Pliss. Erase.* They were all vegetarian, having seen all that baby flesh bartered on bombed-out sidewalks. But here is the intellectual son ordering a story from me as I pour his drinks like the good waiter I am. He thinks I'm anarchic and childish, but he knows there is no mileage in the reflective life. You had to act; write; hear those typewriters clacking. He likes to eat, his pudgy fingers breaking bread upon the tablecloth; his jaw doesn't cease chewing and there is pity and fear in his eyes, just as cattle display when the truck nears the abbatoirs.

I began:
I have always caused the deaths of those I've tried to help.
Take Florian Gautier-Epstein. He was slumming it as a waiter in Paris because he couldn't get along with his father. He was simply waiting for his inheritance, a vast fortune. But he would have to reach the age of twenty-one, something he was unlikely to do since he believed that life was to be lived at break-neck pace. Indeed, he belonged to a secret society of bicyclists ... Thomas Hardy, Mircea Eliade, Bohumil Hrabal, Eugène Ionesco, Eddy Merckx, Slobodan Milosevic, Gavrilo Princip, Jozef Skvorecki, Tzvetan Todorov, Samuel Beckett, Marcel Duchamp, George Dwyer and the philosopher De Selby. One night, in the hotel kitchen, Florian told me a little of his life, of his association with famous people. Many of the latter were dead, he said. He said that in high school he had seduced his French teacher with an impressive command of the preterite tense, which conveyed a musty sense of bygone times, lazy Sunday afternoons on a Rover Cob (an English bike), riding from manse to manse, a written narrative he actually spoke and spun into instant seduction. He said he liked this tombstone conjugation, leaning and fallen, in need of a period. He dazzled her by singing it as one would recite Homeric epics with original scansion, turning them upon exact and erotic rhythms; disarticulated; clean. She was nearing forty and he seventeen, and she would squint while he declaimed, sitting backwards in his chair like Jimmy Dean. He confessed to her after Rhetoric Class that he was having a breakdown. His lightness

under stress attracted her and their butterfly courtship took hold mid-flight: he desired, she fled; she reached out, he left. She did not know why such passion was always predicated upon wealth, nor why her heart so compromised her. She drank. Love turned obsidian. She was romantic and a Communist. She had an ageing charm and ageing parents who couldn't make him out and when recalled to meeting him would exclaim: *Ah! The kike who rode a racing bike*. She was much more suited to old professors and archivists who had lost their daily lives in worlds beyond the present.

Florian was aged far beyond his years. By sitting at women's feet he got to know a thing or two. With domestic patience born of ancient craft, he was an expert at writing letters. It may never have gone beyond the epistolary if not for her active encouragement, for she hallucinated clouds of mentors and virile acolytes, believing her fertile period was not yet over. He took her out to lunch at Maxim's and they walked from the rue Medici where he'd obtained a first edition of her beloved *Bérénice* by Racine (in the bookshop the staff had caught another thief so he was totally unseen), and over Châteaubriand (the writer not the dish), he feigned romance, mocked the efficacy of inherited charm and she was wise enough to avoid the baited hook until the cognac and then the priceless book, when her defences suddenly all collapsed. She fell for poetry and deliquency. He took her home to his own apartment on the rue St Honoré and put on Santana's *Caravanserai*, his hi-fi scratching while she shyly slipped her slip between his covers.

A week later he disappeared from school without taking his *Bac* and her lessons fell apart. She rang him frantically. They met a couple of times in a gallery and a museum – he was aloof and dark – and she with bloodshot eyes, her face aglow then pale, would sigh at him while he would come and go, talking of Fra Angelico. She was too deeply in love to care how she looked, tossing lank hair, frowning too much, blind to his deliberations: *there are five different kinds of love which don't exactly fit our description: delictio, caritas, amica, amor and concupiscentia, not necessarily in that order.* I wonder if we shall ever meet again? He banked on being *in absentia*. She waited in rented, bare apartments in northern slums where she anticipated being taken from behind while speaking softly to the neighbours down below ... when in reality he didn't even show. One fine day she received a line: *Je voyage en Orient, ton Florian.*

He said he was going through a Cubist phase. (The disturbing thing is how angry people get with angles). His indifference was beginning to cut. He wrote that he could not love. In March she took some pills and had her stomach pumped at Sainte-Marie. By December she was spending five thousand francs a month on psychoanalysis. Florian stopped writing the following April. He had taken his fill of love with others and was last seen on his bicycle heading for Lille. She walked the windy streets, her heart threadbare, her position at the Lycée under threat. She did not care. There were flashes of him on every corner.

The Galeries Lafayette department store still made her delirious; the Samaritaine made her ecstatic. (The rain outside was cold. It helped to shop in order to forget.) She tried on fancy stockings just for him. It made her bold. One stormy Saturday, after a rush of blood in the lift to the top floor with two bags of shop-lifted goods: a roll of silk from the haberdashery department, a line of underwear from Shiaperelli of which she was so fond ... his careful tutelage had not been wasted ... she was spotted clambering over the iron balustrade to leap from the slippery roof.

It was all reported in *Le Monde* but Florian Gautier-Epstein's name escaped the final proof.

14

What do you mean? Did you try to help her? Did you cause her death?

Fabiana was concerned. What if it were the other way round ... that he couldn't handle the power of her love?

The wind was howling. It was always howling. Fabiana was sitting on the old couch in the silo. Around the walls were cubist paintings and on the floors her frames and palettes and tubes of oils. She has not moved any of the clutter. I have one small shelf of Montaigne's *Essays* above my stretcher bed. I have paid my rent, three months in advance. It gives me custody of these books. In the past, in France, I have used them as collateral. In Australia they weighed them by the kilo and tried to pay me in inverse proportion. Each time I redeemed them. No one was interested. Fabiana said it was good to have a man around the property. I said I was no good for farm work. No, she smiled and nodded. I think she envisaged me in a painting, wearing nothing but a vest, muscles bulging, massaging a clod with a mattock upon the stroke of noon. I think she wanted to oil me. But then I've never actually seen her painting. She uses the other silo as a storage shed. There are ceramic pots in there; bowls, clay statuettes. She keeps that one padlocked.

No, not *her* death, I said. I had no part in that, I said to Fabiana. Florian showed me some of the letters. The ones she wrote to him. They were novels. Everyone wants to write, Fabiana sighed. That's what's wrong with the world. There is no longer a reality, only celebrity.

I agreed. Though I would be the last to see that as a fault of the world.

Well, I was a gallery guard forging famous paintings, I said to Fabiana. I was now working at the Musée d'Orsay. After closing time I took colour photographs, using flashbulbs. Gottlieb was still in Paris and we used to meet at a brasserie at the Bastille. I told him Florian Gautier-Epstein needed help. I told him everything. Maybe he could empathise; that in this case, love did not counterfeit itself for money. The wealthy knew the wealthy. He could take Florian under his wing, make him a disciple of the preterite art of ancient feeling.

Instead, Gottlieb broke the story in *Le Figaro*. Marie helped translate the scandal. It made page three, but that was enough. I looked Florian up; knew he wouldn't handle the loss of friends and the family business. I found him in a dingy one-room flat in the Barbès district. He looked like Baudelaire, a black cat upon his shoulder; newspapers all over the floor. He offered *comté* cheese and a mild Bordeaux. His hair was greasy and he looked ill. I said: I had no part in this. I told your story to a friend in the hope he would help by publicising your poems. I said it was nothing more than a story kitchen-hands and waiters told to pass the time and that was that. I understood Florian's gloom – it was a bad meeting. I walked back along the Seine pretending to justify my lie. A giant ferris wheel revolved to Santana's *Caravanserai*.

Two months later, when everyone had forgotten him, Florian Gautier-Epstein opened a vein in his wrist and bled to death in his mother's bath in a four-storey apartment on the fashionable avenue Montaigne. That made much bigger news.

15

Water. I drink nine glasses by 7 a.m. It runs from a spring near the silo, spurting from a clump of rocks which you have to climb over and then the water descends towards a small cave. I sit above a sub-terranean river singing through grass and I look back at the small green towers at the top of the hill and then in the other direction, and I see Fabiana's smoking chimney, the long yellow stretch of winter grass and the unkempt sheds leaning in one direction, ready to fall like playing cards.

In my silo I have a sink and a wood stove. The tin flue goes all the way up to the coolie-hat roof and it draws efficiently. Each day I stack up fire-rolls near the door, which I split at dusk. Kindling I find in several old water tanks which lie on their sides, wedged against trees. Polished pieces from old parquet floors. It seems Fabiana's dead husband was a parquetier at one time. I've seen photos on her piano of him standing proudly on a newly-laid dance floor. Now I feed the jigsaw pieces into my fire, fry eggs and bacon and raise my cholesterol level, floor by floor, storey by storey, stories in polished wood. I burn what they have witnessed, these oblongs of varnished grain, parallelograms etched with small circles, thin sickles, stiletto-heels, marks of crowded afternoons, scandals and martinis. Time-sealed, these wooden cells reflect dinner jackets and cummerbunds, silks and suspenders. I take my reading spectacles from their little case. If I bend the lenses back and forth, I sometimes see debauchery.

16

I do not visit Fabiana very often. I like to keep intimacies to myself. I ride to town for provisions on my newly repaired Swift. It now sports two panniers. I take the other road from the property, the one nearest the town of B., where I have made the acquaintance of the grocery store owner, McCredie, a suspicious ex-army man who has decorated his shop with old swords and rifles. In the glass-fronted cooling cabinet he's got a helmet with a bullet hole through it, lying like an upturned turtle next to the ice cream. It is meant as a kind of display, but it is not tasteful. I tell him that it is not tasteful. It isn't meant to be tasteful, he replied. War is shit and shit is not ice cream, though some think it is. So you be the new chap? He is a small, lean man in jungle-greens. He has orange hair. So where might you be from? I don't know, I say. I hate his curiosity. My appearance: it may be a distortion. He scratches his head. Extortion? My prices are the lowest, he says defensively. Oh, that we agree upon. That settled something. It made him safe. Where did you live before? I do not answer immediately. McCredie was the sort of fellow who liked to catch you out. I begin a kind of meander, from here to Vietnam, and I have a vision of the nights he screamed in bed before and after his wife left him, though *during* her leaving things were exceptionally calm, the moment when the firing stopped and he wondered whether to collect the wounded and the dead, cockroaches on his wooden floor growing larger by the minute. The screaming. His wife. Anamorphosis. What? A deformity appearing in its true shape when viewed in some unconventional way. What? Holbein, I suddenly exclaim. Isn't there an army base there? McCredie asks. No, I say. Holbein was a painter.

At that moment I was thinking of Roger the parquetier and I was thinking how as I looked at his photo on your piano, Fabiana, I saw a man with a dark face and a turned-down mouth, not a face with a dark complexion but a face with a hardness and a hatred, as if he hated you at the moment you were taking his photo, and it occurred to me that men like Roger remained on the ground all their lives, having, as Nietzsche called it, only a *frog's perspective*, from the floor, and that they spend all their lives there unless they meet a woman like you who would encourage and arrange for their proprietorial talents, and in Roger's case, support him while he bought more land and then began to *philosophise* about land and nature. He had a frog-mouth, and it was apparent to me that he was *bitter* about not having discovered this philosophising talent earlier in life, but that he was pleased about having met McCredie, a friend with whom he could philosophise, telling McCredie about a French philosopher who strangled his wife, and so his life was bittersweet for not having his wife as a companion, choosing instead an army mate with whom he shared unspoken things, and it was apparent that you needed to give Roger everything, your full care and attention so that he could develop his full potential *as a veteran and an intellectual*, and that land-owning would at least supply him with the power to thrust his authoritative opinion upon others. Indeed he looked like one of the subjects in Hans Holbein's *The Ambassadors*, which features two well-fed Renaissance men with turned-down mouths leaning on a sideboard, while at their feet a rogue floorboard seems to have sprung up between their heavy calves (they were horsemen, though with thicker thighs they could have been cyclists, had Holbein exercised different muscles) and the Persian rug. At first glance it looks like a flawed painting. Viewing it with the naked eye, it seems as though the painter had made a bad mistake and had painted his palette in mid-flight, falling onto the Persian rug. It would cause a mess. Fortunately it seems to be landing the right way up. There is much here that is unperceived. The heavy curtain actually hides a bathroom, into which Holbein had disappeared for a moment to take a pee. If you use a cylindrical or conical mirror, you can see a human skull in the oblong flaw upon the floor.

Uprooted parquetry is only good for burning. I do not know why I saw your story, Fabiana, in a rectangle of wood … your fabulation … why I was thinking of Gottlieb when he told me he was seeing someone 'of immense talent', an artist, no, a writer, he said, correcting himself; though I knew at once that he was lying. I was not jealous. Perhaps he simply forgot what he saw there in the mist of love which came over his eyes. *Anamorphosis*: a change in perspective owing to an initial forgetting; a moment of inadvertance by the creator, accidentally knocking his palette from the easel.

I do not see Fabiana very often. Indeed, she drives to the city on the weekends, so I presume she has a lover there. I feed the dogs and keep the generator running on windy nights when blackouts are frequent and thunder sets the dogs to howling. Fabiana remains pale. The first flush of our accidental meeting is over. She leaves me alone at this end of her property. She has offered me the use of her car, though I have never driven, and have never learned to drive. The Swift is enough for me. I am conscious of Fabiana almost every minute of the day. I do not know the exact attraction. (I veer towards sadness with some women). I'm sure it is not a phys-ical one. My heart has stopped beating over such things. Blindness perhaps. Reversing the old saw. She asked me if I had any vices. I mean, in the nicest possible way, as a joke, with a smile. I thought it wise for any landlady to ask that of a lodger who heard voices and who conversed with the dead in the night. There was this one kiss. I retaliated with several. When you have suffered a lot of pain you tend to get through love; do it faster. Something about being *inured*. Conscious of the inevitable betrayal. Time's wingèd Iscariot. She cantered away. I could have followed up her question with a long thread which would have led to her bed. But she has left me alone and I don't complain. I gave enough rent to her. It would probably cover a year, but I didn't work it all out exactly.

One evening, over a bottle of Veuve Clicquot which she said had been given to her by an admirer, I asked about Roger. It was an ill wind, Fabiana sighed, which marked the beginning of the end. It was a year in which trees fell and the wind wouldn't let up, circling the bush and rushing down upon the house, and all the agonies came forth at once ... every turn, every move, became grief between Roger and myself. In the end it would have been better if his body had been found. It would have been better if he had died in a hospital. I can't help thinking he crawled off somewhere after the accident and animals picked him clean within a matter of days, his bones redistributed in various lairs. Fabiana clinked at my glass with the bottom of hers, as if all of this had been lucky. The way she clinked was vampy and suggestive and rough. That night I walked back to my silo, looking out for anything bleached, shards catching the moonlight.

My father was dying in a hospital bed vomiting some kind of foam. He looked as if he'd tried to shave. He was always leaving soap around his ears. The last time I visited him he was semi-conscious. I sat for a long time. I didn't see the point of just sitting there when he was almost in another world. What can you see? Nothing. Where are you? Nothing. I've seen the solicitor about the will. Nothing. I'm going to have to go. Nothing. Then as I was leaving he suddenly sat up. I think he asked for water. I was on the way out. I think I saw him do that out of the corner of my eye. But then I am blind on one side; peripherally occluded. I continued out of the ward. I jogged out through the corridors. Sprinted out into the carpark. It was mid-winter. The trees were bare. I thought it was the end for my tired heart. I think he was calling for me to take him to the water. He wanted a swim. Above his bed, a pub poster of Bondi

Beach: bronzed lifesavers; rolling surf. He died that night. In the water at Bondi.

Grey trees. Spatter of rain. I've never taken any notice of the naming of vegetation. Trees. Grass. A splash of colour. That's all that was needed. I could have said something about the scarlet sumac, blood brought up on alcoholic nights. Perhaps the colour was drained out of my eyes. I've never made much of nature. It wore you down. It was about attrition. Survival of the fittest. Almost every bird or animal I saw had something wrong with it ... a limp, a cough, torn ears, worms, lice. I got tired just thinking about it. The dying birds, the dying wombats. Preoccupied they are, with their condition; sex a long way in the past; sex even disgusting now. Just a smell, no heat. A whiff of burning tyres. Death a lingering tediousness. As we approach the thought of it, we are already dead. We moan and groan but are asleep. Montaigne would tell you so. Having fallen from his horse, he found his semi-coma sweet, his stomach heavy, slowly filling with clotted blood, his writhing involuntary, detached from himself. He had left his body behind. When he recovered, he experienced pain and pain was nothing but the *thought* of it, having to negotiate with it. He learned from this that we are often besotted with our knowledge.

In the slingshot rain I used to like to write by the ticking fire. I was indulged by art; selfish, self-serving. There was a rhythm. I was mostly unconscious. Fabiana awakened and attracted me because she said she never wanted to write. Everyone wants to be a writer. Even my dogs have started to look wise and cynical at anyone who even looked like they were writing, she said to me. I see the dogs nodding with half-closed eyes before the fire. They express nothing but their present contentment. No, if I should desire to be a writer, then one should shoot me, Fabiana said. It was a strange remark to make, while the hail was striking the window panes. I found great joy in her conversation. I write daily, I said to her. I wrote for her, though I didn't say that, knowing that I was *writing unto extinction*. I didn't realise it at the time, but now I see it clearly, that I was trying to reduce my readership to the bare minimum in order to express my ideal of possessing the perfect reader. But perhaps I was really expressing my desolation at never having possessed my own story, my grief taking on the unadorned nature of *one whose house had been robbed*. Surely Gottlieb had already written everything about my grandfather by now? Surely he would have observed my fugue-states, in which I *was* the poet Camilo Conceição? Had these just been *my* blindspots, or were they invisible to others as well? I certainly cannot remember whether I had been in this role, or how much I have revealed. I ride my bicycle and sometimes forget where I am. I am distanced, dissociated. Not for me the desire to be *in situ* or to be famous, to be the man on the spot. Not for me the common herd of newsboys leaning on their bicycles dreaming of fame or Olympic glory. I told Gottlieb stories and I became tired, and my anger grew more prevalent over all his thefts and misunderstandings. His interest in me was unashamedly professional. I was simply a conduit for his portraits, shifting in and out of the picture.

They are sitting by the fire in her house. The wood that Redvers had brought in for the hearth had been placed in a tin tub ... a kind of baby bath ... and there is an insect making a buzzing sound inside, trying to decamp from beneath the bark it has called home for so long. The dogs are roused and they soon begin to growl and are suddenly at the door; someone at the front gate. The postman, Fabiana says, on his late rounds. He rides a bicycle too.

We are sitting by the ticking fire in her house. The postman had just called. He left some parcels on the patio ... art books and music scores Fabiana ordered from abroad. Once a month Fabiana invites me to dinner, when she plays Bach for me. I tell her that Glenn

Gould, the famous Bach player, used to play like a cyclist, crouched egg-shaped at the keyboard in a kind of disagreement with any windy theme emanating from the notes, as though he, Glenn Gould, was trying to plumb the secrets of those rotary fugues which Bach had hidden from view because they existed outside time and like the motion of a bicycle, could only be brought into existence both corporeally and incorporeally, an exercise in transparent logic and absurdly stationary physical regularity. Bach, I said, was non-anxious, with his slight degrees of sadness wafting upon zephyrs emerging from lowly fields, when all the while these winds could have had the potential to breach the heavy doors of stone cathedrals and blow away the aroma of incense and the odorous corpses of seditious cardinals. Bach was not aggressive; he was discursive, like Montaigne. It was a well-tempered joy, not like that of my friend Gottlieb, I said, who had succumbed to the illness of romanticism. Every time I thought of Gottlieb I wanted to escape, ride my bicycle, engage in a back and forth motion, reciting my *Brief Lives* in order to revoke everything I have ever told him about myself. Or told him about others. A friend who was no friend. But you will have to read my book, my friend.

I revered Jacques Anquetil. For it is impossible to talk about cycling without speaking of Jacques Anquetil, whose Norse name meant *cauldron*, and who won the Tour de France five times, I was telling Gottlieb on one of those nights at the Bay Brasserie. Anquetil's name sounded like iron, an anvil, but his cycling style was as smooth as butter. What I liked about Anquetil, I said to Gottlieb, was that he never warmed to the public, and when I asked for his autograph after the brutal climb on the Puy-de-Dôme in 1964, he looked at me with dark humour and wrote *J.A.: contre toute façon* on my programme notes, playing on the phrase 'against the prevailing fashion' ... in other words he was inimitable, unique ... and the word 'counterfeit' (*contrefaçon*). It was this snakey scrawl of his which put me in mind of Baudelaire's story *Counterfeit*, wherein a man gives a counterfeit coin to a beggar, emphasising that everything is an act of faith, even our soul, and this faith is subject to cruelty and miscalculation. And also of Gottlieb's interpretation of Anquetil's autograph, which Gottlieb said (and I paraphrase), *was a serpent he was giving you*, and I took this to mean Anquetil was giving something venomous to me, as well as an intriguing tail of a tale, for Anquetil's life after his famous victories offers the enigma of a man who took too many amphetamines with his champagne, a minter of truth, a semi-recluse who married a woman who had been married to his doctor and who, as a semi-recluse, had an affair with this woman's daughter from her earlier marriage, giving the said daughter a daughter of his own, and when all that was over, had another child with his first wife's daughter-in-law from a previous marriage. To manage all this, there must have been a lot of counterfeiting, perhaps even of conception itself, as he went to great lengths to alter the names of his offspring.

But it was what Walter Gottlieb said to me afterwards that struck me more, even more than Anquetil's *esprit*, and that was his confession that one night, not long after Blimunde's death, he had attempted to take his own life and had chained and padlocked himself to the last pier supporting the jetty which stretched into the harbour from the bottom of his garden, and he had thrown the key far out into the water, waiting for the tide to come in above his head, while the lapping sea only reached his crotch – he had misread the moon's phases – and he had to scream for Marie, unfortunately rousing the neighbours, who then cautiously cut him loose. *I give you that story on credit*, Gottlieb told me, and I knew I would have to pay for it ... sooner or later. I find it hard to reciprocate such confidences.

And then there was the time while we were sitting in the same bar when Gottlieb turned to me (I was sure there were tears in the corners of his eyes), and said: It is only four in the afternoon, but it is always an eternity. I asked him what he meant. I wish I were elsewhere, he said, in another time, even if they were perilous times, but elsewhere in time must be under the same sky, must it not? To be in a moment which stays forever? Is that possible? I didn't understand him. The weather had always deceived humankind. He began declaiming in the mournful scale of an Aeolian monody: *I am writing to a woman: by means of this engraving, I am come alive; but O, how can one survive, when love is so enslaving?*

Gottlieb wanted advice on how to charm a woman through letter-writing. He said he had made a grand effort to forget her, but somehow there were reminders everywhere; her smile, like the sunrise on Copacabana beach. But you've never been to Rio, I said. You don't have to have been there to understand how a culture is genetically inserted into an expression, Gottlieb argued. For instance, the way you shake your head when you affirm something is purely Hindu. He flicked something from his thumbnail. I am not the best letter-writer, he told me spilling his coffee onto his lap. While he was mopping up, he wanted information, as briefly as possible. The technique. What is the technique? Patience, I said. There are no short cuts to seduction. You have to write with the right amount of balance, between concern and desire. It's best to proceed with curiosity about her situation, for Narcissus cannot love, I said. Write it down for me, Gottlieb ordered. I thought it a betrayal of a friendship to be used thus, an amanuensis to love, as if I were a Cyrano. The irony of it. As if I had really loved. Perhaps; and yet, perhaps not.

It appeared Gottlieb could only live by anticipation. He checked the mailbox a hundred times a day. He was in despair when nothing arrived. Indescribably lonely in a crowd, his heart ached in bed, lying there next to Marie, who was more aware of his agony than he thought, and who repressed it even further. He didn't want to acknowledge her presence. He clung to his despair as an accusation. It was *their* life that was killing him. But he would never relinquish his despair because it provided him with the possibility of another life. You know Redvers, Gottlieb said to me, love is harder than anything in the world. No one assesses its remarkable beauty or its excessive pain outside of yourself. I think Gottlieb believed Socrates' idiotic proclamation that love was absolute beauty. Who was the Greek kidding? Love was making a fool of yourself. Gottlieb later said these letters were a *return* to love, something he had scorned for decades, because by revisiting it, love had diminished his freedom to control its processes. Freud called this repetition-compulsion, I said to Gottlieb – the feeling of not wanting to return, but painfully going there again and again. I had heard all this before – the roundel of the unrequited. Love was never equal; always a lover and a beloved. It was tacky, this confession of Gottlieb's. He covered it up by making himself out to be a Casanova ... many fish in the sea and all that. He pulled out a photograph of a dark-haired girl with a silver streak in her raven mane, wearing a lace camisole and stay-up stockings. She was sitting on a cane chair with her thin legs crossed. He smirked and said nothing. The music had changed from a cello fugue to a drinking song.

Which reminds me, I said to Fabiana that evening, I cannot reciprocate these soirées of yours, as I do not play any instrument, and I scarcely cook inside my silo and I dine mainly on cold tuna fish McCredie sells me at a discount because the tins have been damaged. I have become a fish man. I have cat-breath. My body has shed its meatiness. By concentrating on my body I have been able to think about the present. To be *in situ*. We do not escape ourselves, the house we have built. You could have said I destroyed my house in order to build Gottlieb's with its stones, I said. Donated the tombstone of the past historic tense. But I live, I live ...

There were three minor lawsuits when *Brief Lives (I)* came out. A poet claimed he was never molested by a priest, a detainee never by a dog, a schizophrenic never by himself. Brezinski won them all. He was good, striding over the courtroom floor, hands behind his back; he had the profile of Abraham Lincoln. At six-four, he leant over the litigants. *The world is a bell with a crack in it*, he said. *Only a writer can strike a true note in order to flush out the pigeons.* I think that was his most famous moment. His next line was shit, but nobody can remember it. He had friends in the High Court. They were Masons. They wrote books on belfries. All the libel suits were dropped.

I suppose it was with the same ingenuousness that I answered Fabiana's queries about Gottlieb. When she asked questions of me, I actually learned more about her than she did me, because of the condition I have, which ensured I gave away almost everything I possessed and having been *lightened and enlightened* thus, emptied, a non-entity, I was filled with an hysterical pleasure which allowed me lines of flight without risk. This set others at ease. I took no heed of consequences: how I may have been interpreted; suspected. Indeed, she may have found me a bore, but she didn't indicate this feeling at all, and I took it that my self-obsession was perhaps interesting or entertaining for her. Through the gaps I learned that Fabiana spent weekends, sometimes whole weeks, in the city where she had a shop in Double Bay. My curiosity was aroused: in which street? Was it near the marina? No, she said, but it wasn't far from the chandlery. I sold craftwork; tasteful work, she said; fragrant herbal soaps and perfumes, dried flowers and wooden sculptures, candleholders and pipette barometers. She was in partnership with another woman, an artisan, for that was how Fabiana described her, and in the evenings she, Fabiana, played in a palm-court orchestra at the Intercontinental Hotel, to keep her fingers and her little knot of friends, she said.

She seemed at the opposite pole to me. I was trying to undo all knots. If you had to describe me you would say I was a *knot loosener*. Dispensing with friends of the ordinary variety, only maintaining acquaintances who were most likely to become enemies and who could then be shed without conscience, I acquired true solitude. The only time I felt lonely was when I lived on the banks of that French river with rats for company. The rats fought a lot amongst themselves. I didn't seem to have their attention. Back in my bourgeois life people always intruded. Even barged in when I was in the toilet, like when I was sharing the flat in Newtown with a couple who made noisy love all day. They had a big bed and liked manacles, whips and chains. It was a construction site with vinyl; I had to use a megaphone to enforce union hours. The hippy with angel hair cooked, appeared out of nowhere, offering lentil soup. Accosting me in the outside toilet one day, she suggested we practise constriction. She was twirling a little braid of rubber bands. Anyway, it's because I liked solitude so much that I have had these seizures, escapades, repetitions, I was saying to Fabiana, since I had been born to perfect my life according to my art and so much of both had already been dissipated by a failure to garner critical acclaim. Hell was other people. So her silos were a godsend, I said. (I had since moved all the paintings and easels and frames into the smaller bin, which only has one window). Fabiana said she didn't mind, so long as I didn't damage anything. Besides, it was cooler for the canvases in the smaller silo, which I called *Silo #2*. My round tower, which I heated with a wood oven until the walls started to peel and crack, was perfect for hatching, germinating, incubating flight plans. I bought a small tin bath, lugged it back on the Swift looking like a turtle; cars swerved, truck drivers blew air horns like Vikings. I heated water and soaked in peace – solitude at last!

I do not see Fabiana very often, yet I seem to know her well, perhaps because when she plays Bach's *Goldberg Variations* she always plays Variation No. 26 (or Variatio No. 25 if the Aria is bypassed), with sadness in her face. I read this in her ancestry. It was upon this Variation that Bach understood genius, I said to her, because if you listen to the key changes you will see *both destiny and chance* there. She looked puzzled. Yes, I said, it is a key change of pure genius, spiralling upwards, aleatoric because there is no willing, only chance, some rude questioning about the future, rising up like smoke towards God. No theme, no pure noun, no subject. Total risk. Like a Francis Bacon painting. (I was waxing lyrical now, eager to reveal my former friendship with the great painter). The love of the roulette wheel and the questioning of God, I said, are present in their genius, in both Bacon and Bach, and this genius howls in a minor key because it is ill, it is through with elevating the sacred, reaching upwards only because it is degraded, brilliant because abnormal, deep because it is denatured and cursed with catastrophe; sentenced to greatness, I said to Fabiana. It was the moment at which Bach understood.

Oh yes, Fabiana said. Oh yes, oh yes. The *Goldberg Variations*. How I love them!

She was having a love affair, I could tell straight away. Her benevolent narcissism, svelte good looks offered to all, willed malnutrition – the drawn hair, the tiredness, the secret pride which showed itself in the eyes as *experience* – all spoke of passionate living. A glow came off her. Nothing wrong with it, just the added attraction of being available to whoever was paying attention, to whoever would listen. A firmer clue came in the form of her falling asleep whenever I talked to her. *Tell me things*, she would ask, and all too willingly, I spoke freely, when after about five minutes she would be fast asleep and I would stare at her lips, which seemed to be always smiling, and imagine her riding my bicycle, her hips swaying from side to side, up and down, and I would understand the silences which engulfed her, which enclosed her in her world of friendships, and which wasted her great talents for the piano. Beauty demanded discipline, I would say to her sleeping form.

17

I had little time left. Judith told me as much, though she didn't elaborate on my illness. I went in to see her after fasting. The blood test drained me for the ride back. Judith asked how far I had come. I said I was going backwards. No, not your career, she bit her lower lip. Later she asked me to go next door, to the bakery, for some wholegrain bread which would sustain me for the hundred kilometers back. But here it is in the report. Pathology sent it in a plain brown envelope. I knew that meant the death sentence.

Time? I had no time. Fabiana drove up one morning. There was thunder. The black branches swayed, prelude to a storm. She wore jeans and high boots. Her swaying, lurching gait, hands in pockets, revealed the goldminer's daughter that she was, ashamed still of her large hands. Brazil '66; the year of her father's death. She brought me an oblong box, miniature coffin, hand-carved, and proceeded to unwrap the tissue. It was from her shop: a huge hourglass, big as a professional peppergrinder, bearing fine, white sand. Annoyed, I asked if this was really necessary. I had a telescope, I was about to lie to her, which cut through time, forwards and backwards. I did not need these shards of measurement, microscopic harbingers of my death, siliceous lineality. I fell into deep gloom. Fabiana was hurt, but she hid it well. That story, she said, the one you told about your friend Florian ... I was very moved by it. This gift is to ease your guilt. It was not your fault that someone else published your story. She smiled such a radiant smile her eyes ignited. There was something in her; sand ... as Mark Twain would have written ... misplaced. In my father's parlance, a coin of a girl. But not for me. She said she was going swimming in the waterhole. She sat on the front seat of her Rover, reached under her skirt, unrolled her stockings and handed them to me.

She drove away. Perhaps wanted to push me out of the preterite, into the present. But I had become unpredictable and the only way of attaining balance was to ride my bike, furiously at first, then upon reaching the first hill, more at one with frailty, and finally descending with supreme joy, ploughing over deep mounds of sand on the track, a volcanic pressure upon the heart, such pumping, its bellows firing silica into glass and the glass narrowing to allow sand through a fine artery, hour upon hour until chest pains. The sign of infinity: a bicycle.

My dear Fabiana,

Only I could have been so crude. To have accepted a gift with such an accusation. Etc.

I rode down to her house and left the letter on the front doorstep. I don't think she was in. I remember telling Gottlieb that when I lived in Paris I was a bicycle courier for a short time, constructing phantom books in my head as I rode, inflamed by the example of

Proust sending letters to countesses through couriers. I would linger in the courtyard with the concierge's daughters, girls in flower, tilt my cap and loiter in the shadows, waiting. But in reality I risked my life in heavy traffic for legal scrolls, stock-market statements, pathology reports. I turned the hourglass on its side. Infinity. Took out her stockings. Fine black silk.

18

My pathology tests came back. Dr Judith gave me these pills which I had to extract from a plastic strip, labelled with dates and days. For the stones. I took jellybeans instead. After all, they were kidney shaped. When I awoke each morning I began to wander. Night dreams were docile, in place, black and white. But in the mornings, magpies glided without a wingbeat to surprise competitors and mark out territory and I would prepare to leave again. Each morning, the tentacles of my fugue-work: branching lines toward the horizon.

My Chinese self sustains me. Franz Kafka had a Chinese self. So did Walter Benjamin. I buy provisions when in Sydney, ride back with panniers loaded: ginger, rice, preserved plums. When I eat for my Chinese self, I withdraw into the private gut. Saved by peanuts and ginger. Strength returns. It is a lucid occasion, uncluttered with thinking. No longer a guest. Home. How I pine for the pines, the terraced mountain-sides, the loneliness of the oak that was mine! I have lived away from my self enough to survive my last remaining days, but ... one false move and I still reach for the noose; to preserve it all. I mean, this shape which has not yet shown.

I found an old telescope McCredie was trying to sell for a hundred dollars. It was lying atop some books beside a can of beans. A brass instrument that needed cleaning. I blew on it. How would I play this? I offered twenty. He shook his head. Started to tell me about his ten years in the army ... Vietnam ... White Mice, the starched militia who shot people for jaywalking ... *Tet* made them tetchy.

I rode away. Rode back. Bought tuna fish. McCredie charged me more than usual. He said the *global price* of tuna fish had risen. He spoke less like an economist and more like a priest singing a High Mass. The twenty-five watt lightbulb above his head projected its mean orb. He said a barrel of tuna fish came in at ten cents more a kilo these days. I rode to the next town. After three weeks of absence, McCredie accosted me on the highway. He was parked on the side of the road in his ute and he wore a large hat with a badge on the side ... some sort of fan or sunrise you see on packets of soap. He brought out the telescope and asked me for twenty dollars. I gave him ten and said I would pay the rest if the price of tuna fish came down. He accepted this as a deal but not a bargain.

Now I had the means for a distended view, after much cleaning and blowing out grey worms in my head, *vers de gris*, grizzled verses, never mind, I got a long view of the long paddock and then focussed to see lorikeets scratching their ears ... birds have ears do they not? Or just a hole in the head? They hear remarkably well, at least, they frighten well. But let me set this up, this look back into time, for isn't that what we're seeing when we look at the stars, this old light reaching us, documenting events before bacteria crawled out from under a crystal? Let's see, swivelling, tromboning. I'm only going to attain half my fugues with this, but there we are, we progress by halves. What can we see? Fabiana's green tin roof from the top of this tower ... no higher point save the water-tank and then the windmill which could unjam at any moment and decapitate me with sharp blades ... try anyway, Fabiana's wind-vane swivelling just for me, a sign of my direction, the tail gamely pointing to signal game. I smell foul play.

19

The art of the fugue. Point and counterpoint. Crazy walking; street stalking; fast talking. Montaigne, having had too many pots of wine, encountered a group of women on the corner of a Roman street; danced a charconne with them, a slow waltz in three-quarter time. For one moment he lost himself in movement, in the swaying torches, the measured music, the elegant steps. He was escaping from his essays. The *Essays* were attempts to gain control over his daydreaming. The *Essays* demanded firm action from him, forcing him to discover himself through travelling. But suddenly, in this fugue, he wanted to be rid of essaying, the try-line receding before him. No logic, just chit-chat. Chatting up. A charm offensive. He strained to excise his non-committal smile, showing his teeth. Only in motion could he reinvent himself, pull off the tightening knot of false friends, the voices which gathered in his head. He wanted to be in a new place between each piece; match reality with reality in order to prevent himself from opinionating. Yet he wanted to be as deluded as poets and painters, to fly free, to *experience*. Perspective had to be fluid. But when he looked up at his oak beams in his hotel room, he saw dry reason. All those knots in the tree. He looked more closely: little fat men perched on their toes giving off bad odours, women with bad teeth, a child reaching out from its dirty blankets, left there on a corner of the street by a prostitute who at that moment was riding a couple of youths upon their naked thighs, someone vomiting into a trough, night pigeons making for the regurgitated mash, a lost dog circling aimlessly between the legs of shitting horses; and there it was, life in all its guises, the living intoxicated by the same music and gallant dancing before illusion faded and the pox or death arrived. The woman picked up the screaming child. He could have sworn she was at the spa yesterday. There he was, Michel de Montaigne, swigging a jug of red wine at the moment his equerries brought him a letter saying he had been made Mayor of Bordeaux. How did that make him feel? It made him feel dirtier than the others. A hypocrite with kidney stones pretending he was participating in society, not quite able to let himself go. Continence. Noble toady. In the uniform ugliness of the early morning light he smelt the putrid wind. There it was; old sex at cold dawn. Riding had made him hard; riding now on his stallion as the Mayor of Bordeaux; no more dancing with loose women. That's it. A putrid wind always came upon success. It made him feel both fugitive and lord, wary of the next turn.

Back in his mill-tower in Bordeaux, Montaigne wrote that we should reserve a storehouse for ourselves where we can hoard true liberty. He was in flight from convention; from his wife; fugitive, *fugueur*. Liberty had to be stolen, pilfered. He wanted a friend with whom he could discuss all, but he only had his writing. He was furtuoso, given to thieving from his own thoughts. A *furtuoso*. He could not bring himself to be passionate, chaotic and dangerous ... like poets ... but he took long journeys, *périples*, odysseys, to escape domesticity.

Back in my silo in Colo I write a letter to Gottlieb in his grave, telling him stories of Montaigne, reprimanding him with the fact that husbandry was a servile office. Gottlieb had been afraid of being abandoned by Marie. She had money. He had some kind of Catholic guilt and a terror of poverty. The priesthood made him fear destitution. He felt sick when he thought of going back to teach at the university. All those awful meetings; busy-work; stabbings in the corridor; septic language and management microbes. When Marie suspected he was having affairs with his former students she put a gas meter in his bathroom. He would need coins for hot water, bills for his wines, credit for his self.

I think now of how he made his life into a showpiece; Gottlieb as community stalwart, opening art shows, umpiring cricket matches, his hair growing wilder in the wind, standing at the wrong end of square leg insisting on wearing rolled up jeans which Father O'Hanlon called 'cowboy britches'. Then Gottlieb would walk home with his daughter, Blixen, who had now grown a little taller, thinner, bearing within her face a fine bone structure, her smile angular and subtle as she pushed back her hair, her walk athletic; everything that squat Walter and plump Marie did not possess, and the girl, in her twelfth year of life, knew the sadness that was inside her came not from the golden plane trees unleaved by the wind coursing through the park, nor from being unloved – for she was loved, with Gottlieb's hairy forearm on her shoulder – but from suspecting that unlike the foliage, she may not have scythed down from this particular family tree.

20

I have fitted to my Swift a peculiar thing. It is not a pump, though it looks like one, tied there to the top tube with a bit of elastic. It is not a stick, though I use it as a frightener for dogs who try to follow me. I ride to and fro, far and wide, over fields and along goat tracks, and bump over bracken, sail over fern. After months of eating very little, I have become quite light. In the afternoons I discover ruined abbeys, burned offerings bushfires have left, and I scour the naves for signs of spirits, while outside in the abandoned yards with their blackened tombstones ... the essence of this country, I was saying to myself, convinced it was a duty to the forgotten past to read lists of family tragedies aloud ... I conjure an Australia made up of massacres and the moral slaughter of the day-to-day, relieved by a breeze down by the waterhole, the ritual of a paternal rape perhaps, and upon the strengthening wind, a flight or two of dark imagination, spumante trails of landing blackduck. We have all but lost it now: this sadness of the land. In summer, pain lights up in white heat and there is a hatred that stems from the heat, a black sun which has no depth, no sweetness with the burn it brings, no mourning, only nostalgia for colonial vigour, and the nights carry no relief, simply a stink, which has built up inexorably like the benediction of carcasses. Nothing rings out, no crispness of bells in the valleys, just the hiss of swollen bellies, pregnancies of the earth which burst into bushfires, red tongues of grass spurting under fleeing reptiles and then dry scales of measure: a crusty revival, slow time with nightmares and no future imagination of this as the best it ever will be. For to imagine the country's history is to be ruthless with the truth, which used to spend itself uprooting families, dislocating bark humpies, destroying life on mad sprees; to imagine is to confront disgust, the insecurity of ennui, the phalanx of children and the loss of solitude from slab hut or stone bungalow to paste-board suburb; to imagine is imperious autism, the never-ending journey into despair ... inevitably, to murder. Oh, tense joy of the kill! This is layered in the land and we have all but lost it, paralysed from denial ... given up our hindsight for the faint haunt of unachievable contentment in the future, which is already smelling like curdled milk.

So down to the crossroads and then across safely, other side now, of the highway heading towards the river through a gap in the wire fence I cut yesterday, gliding down to the waterhole, a deep wide pool where you could have sailed a small boat back and forth, a quick swim in the icy depths sluiced with duck shit and comely weed around my privates, midges in my mouth, freezing now in the tramontano which whips over these hills, fetching, if not a sliver of snow, some icy blasts, memories of the Piedmonte, and I'm restored to fighting illness as I push the Swift up the track to the summit of the black hill from where I can survey all ... there she blows ... following the long road to the same waterhole with her Brazilian boyfriend half her age and she spreads out a rug on the sandy bank and the sun had come out for them at that moment, shining only on the waterhole where all around it was dismally grey with mist, and he undresses, his member attentive, a staghorn erupting quickly when she touches him, none of it very inventive or prolonged (she, being more modest, leaves her underclothes on, her thighs glistening despite that), then they swim – and I realise all my hours in the silo had not produced a fraction of this jealousy and eros, not even a hint of this exquisite and painful scenario, this exclusionary moment, this dispassion of having watched Diana at her bath being seduced by her Actaeon. She is dissatisfied when she emerges, but he is spent, and there she goes tearing branches from the trees to use as switches for bothersome flies. She stands, majestic still, unarmed and naked now, then lies on her back staring straight at me, one leg arched in defiance and she knows I am watching, annointing me with her permission for me to tell ... and as I lay down the spyglass, I knew I would always feel the itch in my right eye as a lasting memento, through with searching for what was pleasant and easy, scenes which tickled me. In the other hand I grip the leash of my brace of hounds, the beasts straining to tear the boy to pieces.

Of course I wasn't sure who they were, down at the waterhole; the water shimmering, a Watteau painting; and I wasn't going to mention it to Fabiana that night when she came up to the silo with a peace offering, her hair wet, a bottle of Glenfiddich under her arm, saying she would take back the hourglass if I wanted, though I said no, for it did mark out my day somewhat, since I'd started reading again, and I saw them leave the waterhole together; though of course I didn't say this to anyone. I didn't say I followed as closely as I could without being seen, standing behind trees holding up the Swift on its back wheel like a rearing stag, until the dogs began to bark ... hark, another measure of the day ... the sand holding me back, the wind, and after a brief twister they were gone.

But it was Fabiana who mentioned it first: saying quite casually that the woman who was driving that cow along the road with a stick on the day I fell into the creek ... that was how she put it ... that I simply fell in ... that woman Miranda, had found herself a boyfriend. A Brazilian; *tout court; un sauvage – totalement nu*, she led me to think. I did not believe her for one moment. Her black stockings hung on a branch, trailing in the breeze. Those wind-socks binding me to her forever. The little object of my lift-off. Whenever I see a woman in black stockings I have always wanted to order a bottle of wine.

21

With the aid of the hourglass I can see what Montaigne was trying to tell me. This timeless hourglass measures eternity. It is an Eternity Machine in a vacuum, which magnifies my daily life of pain; torments my obsession with measurement; exaggerates my folly as I stand hypnotised. To have one's measure. If we want to know anything beyond ourselves, if we want to transcend our limited capabilities, we have to edge just a little towards chaos. Fall off our horse. Go beyond measure. Indulge in frippery piperie.

I was trying to train my smell. How to train one's smell? I mean one's sense of smell. I follow the example of dogs. What delights them, what intrigues them, what is of no consequence or is no matter to them. Nothing actually disgusts them. They are devoid of the morality of smell. Montaigne said that the use of perfume only covers defects. *To smell sweet, is to stink.* I have seen dogs take great delight in rolling on dead and rotting carcasses. What one delights in, is a matter of experience. I stressed this to Gottlieb, when I told him a little of my childhood dream.

In my father's time they played a version of the game called 'The Love Pipe' in cabarets when the rains came to China – a circle of half-clad boys and girls inhaled a debilitating drug – they passed the smoke through tight erotic kisses from right to left until desire reached its peak and when the pungency declined, or the weather leavened, or the wind died down, began again from left to right.

It was 1947.

There was a slender spy within their midst who passed on secrets with an active tongue and who, though masked, was neither high nor dizzy but leant toward a lassitude not entirely beyond seduction. They said she was an expert in other things as well: a choreographer, torturer, writer of plays-within-plays, she could also dance and sing. Her name was Kitty. She was hung in '49 after the Communists took Shanghai, where such perverse production was henceforth forbidden. It was on her death certificate they wrote that she was he.

That same Kitty had taken me aside one day and teased my ear with whispered sighs. I was a child and understood nothing, but the words still stake out haunts on lonely nights, some echo that her courtesy could never overstep the mark: Excuse me, my lord – she addressed me thus – the liberty I take in undressing you tonight ... and she proceeded to place a silken mask upon my face and take my boyhood in her mouth, and intermittently, through poetry, her voice trembling in the evening breeze (while blinded thus I cannot now remember what the weather was, or even if the wind came from north or south), she began a slow inversion. I was overcome by vertigo while my bird was being swallowed whole in a nest of words high up in branches. Did you feel, she said in extrication of her tongue from some untidy verse, the power of ventriloquism? In fine, how came you to womankind?

From that moment on I've wanted to recapture this strangest scene to see if this play within the game of Loving Cup was real or dreamt. I had written it down long before, in fragmented fashion, and did not want to lose the thread of it, since the addition of perspective over years may have revealed a flaw in grounded memory. The drug in the Loving Cup was never described, but the odour of my aunt's breath remains memorable, like bruised lavendar. I have not smelt it again till now. Fabiana's stockings. Tinged with *Morpheus*, the god of sleep, it possessed a subtle odour between fruit and flower, accompanied by a scent of poppyseed. Part of it was in the wind after the harvest of pomegranates on de Nerval's estate. Some of it was amongst the tramps gleaning uncollected grapes. Yet none of these arrived together. There was a perspective of smell through the hourglass. If you gazed long at the twinned tulips, you would see a reflection of two faces. That is how one would describe it. There is no other simile; a smell without morality, reflecting a two-faced smile. Janus-like. Good and evil, painkiller and addiction. Vial or vile container. Preserver or liquidator. It was in Dr Judith's surgery. It was here. At first I sniffed Fabiana's hourglass and thought I was deceived. It was in the wood which formed the base; the columns on the sides; the sand perhaps, though that was improbable, since all was sealed. Maybe it was Fabiana's perfume, *L'Occitane; Thé Vert*. But no. This was much subtler than any scent. It occurred to me that I had not caught Fabiana's perfume since the day I fell into the creek. Since then, Fabiana herself *had no smell*. I circled the walls of the silo. It could be that the silo still contained some odour of fermented wheat. I sniffed around the shell. Nothing seemed to match. I thought of Fabiana's workshop, the locked Silo #2. That's where she said she constructed knick-knacks for her shop in Double Bay. That's where all these smells were focussed. Memory now crystallised them; gave them one description.

The smell of opium was a smell of *relativity*. The description of a smell was relative to a past ... or to the experiences of many past smells. You galloped past them. It led me to think that smell was a form of motion, I was telling Doctor Judith one day, having ridden all the way to Double Bay for a consultation. Kinetic smells led you through a spectrum of a life. Judith was having a particularly busy day and could only give me a few minutes. Hmmm, she said. Smell as a motion. A pathologist would agree.

That rather cruel remark aside, I had now become obsessed with this indeterminate odour of what I believed was opium, or perhaps morphine, and I was determined to have a look at the locked silo, Fabiana's workshop, and I began discussing how one would make a skeleton key or lock-picker with McCredie. Oh it's easy, McCredie said, in the army we learned that early; part of basic training to open the lockers of others, release padlocks from gates, unlock doors for discharge papers, gain access to the armoury. He said he once stole a Chieftain tank. He sold me a tool consisting of a series of hooks and files. We practised on several locked display cases.

Montaigne in motion. He could never see himself in the mirror. He writes about scents being left on his moustache and beard after love, but he is unable to speak about himself in love. He is changeable and he is centreless. He fails at love not only because he is as tender as a child, but because he doesn't work hard enough at it. He makes it a lifelong quest to be a good lover, but he fails. He feels he is nobody trying to be a somebody, but only because he sees other perspectives and is true to his nature. For many years I liked Montaigne because I thought he was a loser. In the end, I thought, he reverted to convention because he didn't want to dilute himself with deception, narcissism, drink or drugs, *never having reached the point of love*. I believed that's where he failed. Too cautious. If I hadn't read Montaigne, I thought, I would not have been so moderate, *discoursing on balance*. I would have lived more fully, pursued my desire to be a real painter. Immoderately, I would have passed away earlier. I would not have given up going to the Ganges merely to observe human duplication and liquidation and would have plunged into that oily water, gone caving in those submarine depths, pursued the horror of bloated faces and half-burnt skulls exploding from black and bony shelves, the multifarious and the nefarious still roped in jewels, and I would have stopped giving everything away to Gottlieb, harnessing silence, having squeezed out all, ending my days declaiming like Dylan Thomas when he writes that *Modesty hides my thighs in her wings,/ And all the deadly virtues plague my death* ... doing quite the opposite to weaving a wreath around my words.

Instead I am conservatively unlocking Montaigne through a smell. It is the smell of old cologne sealed in a folded hanky. If he hadn't been a mayor, he would have been a bank manager. When dancing a charconne, men and women sometimes gripped a kerchief between them, and one held on slightly longer if there was a scent of love. For Montaigne, writing prevented such fugues, their fragrance sealed by reason. He always let go of a fetish too soon.

Oils. I could detect the presence of palettes and canvases. The silo door rubbed against the stoop and creaked open. I shone my torch at all the works of art. Stars blinked above through the skylight. In Venice, Montaigne reported that the coaches had glass roofs, so travellers could spy on women at their windows. He greatly desired to be a coachman and a painter. Here, in this my *observatory-silo*, he would have found all those selves in these muscular landscapes; female swimmers; dizzyingly sexual. On the tables and shelves there were jugs, plates, pots, whole dinner settings, all in indigo and white, some heavy, some brittle. I shone the torch through them, so fine was the porcelain, that I could read the skeletal Chinese characters beneath. I was thinking how, by appearing conventional, Montaigne dissected himself and scattered his light through the perspective of others. He placed himself beneath the work of others in the same way that Vermeer drew himself first and painted women on top. I'm scattering light everywhere but I'm not finding the pieces that fit my shadow. Reverse for Redvers. A shattering. I wish I hadn't dropped that plate. I was just turning around and my elbow brushed it off the table and it smashed onto the concrete floor. I swept it up as best I could and put the pieces into my pocket. I hope it wasn't valuable. And that was when I caught the smell. Poppy-seeds at harvest-time. And there, in a large teapot decorated with indigo motifs of maidens in gardens with their scarves and robes trailing in the wind, was a packet of Benares Pure, the mandolin carnation, bittersweet chandu.

I have stolen the smell at midnight. In the presence of convention, not everything can be perceived. Many of the paintings are labelled. Drafts for commercial posters. Chinese advertisements for Red Lion cigarettes and Russian Veloski bicycles. I presume these were for exhibitions or auctions. They had 'C.C.' written on them. My grandfather's initials. Behind the canvas of one of them was stencilled: *Lesbians massaging each other with medicinal oil from the Leopard Eng Aun Tong Pharmacy Company.*

I am unsure what happened next. I came across stacks of bills and papers. A traffic infringement notice for $750 which was overdue. Of course I made a cylinder with it, lit something and inhaled. Always the prelude to mixing oils and then painting over an existing canvas, exactly, more brightly. Learning the brush-strokes, the secrets, as the Chinese had perfected it in the transmission of their cultural heritage. This painting-over, this restoring or *forging* a new road, experiencing the past and experimenting with the future, was what my grandfather did to unearth his poetic inspiration. My grandfather – the famous and infamous Camilo Conceição. I live under his shadow. What was he doing here? (Tomorrow, all this significance will look fanciful and ridiculous.)

22

Each morning I rise at cockcrow, go down to the shed where the milkers are waiting in their stalls straining with full udders and I scatter the chickens, sterilise the pails with boiling water, milk each by hand, in a daze, the cows in a daze, munching softly, a sound of silk brushing by and then unstitched, I dream of Fabiana. But then the cows are gently looking at me in the dim light, each kicking over their pails and I realise how quickly I had become another.

She invited me for afternoon tea one day I think it was a Saturday, though I only monitor the hours and not the days, and the wind gauge was spinning on the roof of the house, and she had made scones and even before I entered the door I smelt something, the rankness of goats, hairy armpits, rutting boars, and out walked a dark young man, half naked, wearing only his jeans, smiling at me. She introduced him as Sergio. Sergio, she said was helping her poison the blackberry which had taken over near the waterhole. Sergio, she said proudly, owned a nightclub in Newtown. She called him *her* Brazilian. Like a horse. He smiled all the time, showing off his white teeth.

I do not ask questions. Sergio's presence on the property has precluded any curiosity on my part. It suits me since I had broken a dish, not to ask questions which would raise any suspicion about that event. It suits me that Fabiana has hardly come up to her silo or looked in. It suits me that I have escaped the imprisonment of her hourglass since Sergio has proven to be a hard worker, a muscular worker, a handy, efficient, knowledgeable farm-boy. He smiles at me and sings his sad songs and then brings me berries he's picked. I do not ask anything about the art works in the studio-silo. I do not ask anything at all, keeping my eyes in a book, walking around with my hanky to my nose trying to be inconspicuous, sniffing at the *time of cologne*. I do not ask because I'm spying on myself from up close – it is a movement of pride – and I only ask myself how I could have heard Fabiana and Sergio discuss a field of poppies they were about to plant when the blackberry had all been cleared.

My bladder is full of heavy sand and I piss time like the hourglass. Kidney stones shoot pain with reckless skill. Spasms in my back arrive on the hour, when the world turns red. Astride the saddle of the Swift, I am numb in the nether regions and an occlusion rises behind my eyes, so I am forced to walk the hills, then coast down while balancing on one pedal, standing upright as on a scooter, a boy still in pyjamas, tranquillised with early dementia. The Swift has its own mind when not in harmony with a human body. It veers. In practising this walking and coasting method, I conclude that like an ass (I was leading and coaxing the Swift ... I mean that the Swift was like a stubborn, disdainful donkey), there is nothing more demanding and intransigent than a bicycle.

New South Wales is in the grip of drought. The trees are dusty with the deposits of deserts. Eagles stir puffballs over lethargic rabbits; fires cast dirty furrows of smoke through the bleached hills. I ride in search of water, keeping away from habitation where everything is sullied, where life is stuffed into a sausage ... I can see them driving their cars as fast as they can in mindless stupidity, not out of risk but from routine impatience and aggression ... snaking into a white electric fog. I cannot drink the water on the property any longer. It comes from a spring which has turned sour, full of minerals, salt, flavours of drowned mice, and I see Sergio holding each one up by the tail when he checks the water tank. I have become a connoisseur of water, of boiling, cold, tepid, dead, toxic, sulphurous, salty, heavy water. I ride out on the Swift, embark on a balance and a weighing up of dryness. I practise exagitation, stirring things up, muddying the waters in the district. I allow McCredie to spread the word that I am a diviner. When the melancholy humour, I say to McCredie (who is leaning over his cabinet of horrors – this time I see him remove a small red cylinder from beneath the holed helmet), is mixed with the sanguine (I watch his incomprehension turn to pain and I have to explain that mixing the melancholy and the sanguine is like eating a bloody steak with pity in your heart), then something divine comes forth. He finally hands over the waxed tube. That's gelignite, he says. If and ever you need it for what you do.

I cannot pass the stones. My urine is bloody at sunset. Not a death sentence, but I do not want to live. I cannot bring down fruit by shaking a tree; I cannot lift a sack of wheat. Endless unhappiness; endless failure. I find a thin stream of water and lay the Swift down to urge myself with the gurgling, but all I succeed in doing is to soak my books which are in the panniers. Novenas. I try to drink nine glasses of water every morning in my solitarium but I cannot filter out deception. What looks and tastes like sweet water causes me unendurable pain an hour later, like reading my grandfather's poetry which I had been clumsily translating from the Portuguese for Gottlieb before the latter's death; each line shaping like barbed wire instead of a teardrop. The sentiments in them were out of time, out of place. This was why I bade farewell to literature, which was pain through joy, lyricism garlanded with razors. As for the water I tested, it was life, but only if you wanted life. Sweet water seeped into graves and levelled out into the watertable and always pumped up salty.

On January the twenty-eighth 1581, Monsieur de Montaigne passed a rather biggish stone and other smaller ones. Before Montaigne went on his health trip through France, Germany, Switzerland and Italy, he had already suffered much, I informed Gottlieb on one of his particularly difficult nights. It was just after Gottlieb's stroke and he had taken to wearing a fedora, partly to disguise his rictus. I met him at the Brasserie in Double Bay and he ordered a bottle of whiskey and couldn't undo the cork even though the waiter had loosened it. He asked me to help him and I thought at that moment of the knot of friendship between us. I uncorked the bottle, but the knot was suddenly tighter. After the first glass, Gottlieb stared at me and spoke in his deepest voice. Have you ever wondered why I left the seminary? I shook my head. The sight of Marie, I was thinking, was not conducive to a *coup de foudre*. Some homoerotic scandal? Paedophilia? None of these seemed convincing in the light of his Vatican dispensation. I saw his eyes glinting; an alcoholic's teariness. Then he looked at me strangely from beneath the brim of his hat and said: *I have always wanted to be a criminal who incriminated others. A gangster with a name like Levine.* Gottlieb said he'd never experienced a fugue state.

The pains in Montaigne's kidneys had been present for some time during the writing of the first two books of the *Essays*, I said to Gottlieb, who wasn't interested at all in Montaigne and was gulping down his whiskey twirling his index finger around in it and rubbing his temples with the sweating glass, indicating, I think, that I should hurry up with the history and listen to his story, which he was eager to expound, but only for the moment, and then he held back. He wanted me to speak about my grandfather again, but I was not in the mood for my grandfather. Montaigne, I continued, had just published the second book of his essays, and took it north to present a copy to Henry the Third with great fanfare, though in private conversation with his coachman, he had remarked that Henry the Third was a *dissolute transvestite*. The king received the copy with feigned interest and spoke into the mirror whilst rouging his cheeks: *Would Montaigne like to join His Majesty at the siege of La Fère in Normandy?*

Montaigne had no choice. Throughout the blockade he regretted bringing a copy of the *Essays* to be read by the king. 'An ageing mannequeen,' he confided to his valet. Montaigne's kidneys hurt so badly that he had to stand in the stirrups, even swinging himself over to one side, hoping that this acrobatic jolting would dislodge something. The siege was a long one.

Gottlieb was snoring. At least I thought he was. (In hindsight, how mistaken was I?) His head had flopped to one side and his eyes were closed. I believed there was a tear secreting from the corner of one eye. Lately he'd been wearing a large silver crucifix around his neck, which he clutched in moments of spiritual doubt. He still had one hand on it. It was the same gesture Marie used to employ. His large head and lion's mane of hair was at odds with the contortion of his tiny trunk. It was as though he was tormented by a torso he could not forgive and was summoning the image of a tortured Christ as a hedge against mediocrity.

I continued with the story of Montaigne. His travel cure took him to Rome, I said, where he witnessed the circumcision of a child. After cutting off the foreskin, the rabbi took a gulp of wine and then sucked the glans and spat out the blood. Then he rinsed his mouth with more wine, dipped his finger in it for the child to suck and applied resin to the wound. A rabbi who had circumcised more than twenty infants had the privilege of never having his mouth eaten by worms after he was buried. He could speak from beyond the grave.

Montaigne, in his essays, does not repeat La Boétie's sonnets. He simply says Booty's twenty-nine verses are elsewhere. These missing fugues represent the circumcision of Montaigne's desires. He will never be a poet like Booty. He will never be a painter like Holbein. He only has this amputated prose as a *memorial* of what has been lost. Booty's missing voice is the voice of youth; Montaigne's the sound of worms busily eating at the night.

My dear Gottlieb, I said, leaning over the table (the brasserie was filling, the Saturday night crowd crushed together after rugby games and rowing regattas; youth was exploding with ignorant testosterone), I have not had a single physical desire for the last five years... how is it between you and Marie? As I spoke, I noticed his little black book in which he noted down observations. What I may have said that night inspired him. The notebook was closely guarded and it hardly ventured the short distance between his jacket pocket and his lap. I removed it from beneath his elbow. Opened it. It was empty, except for the last page, where he had scrawled the words: *Husbandry is a servile office between enslavement and blackmail. There is no third position.*

Montaigne conceived everything in threes. His best ideas came on horseback. Then he retired to his tower and he wrote. Three things he did almost every day. The ternary destroyed the dependency of the couplet upon its loving dialogue ... dissolved its poetry with thinking. The tower was his library and his memory. It was on

the third floor of a three-storey rotunda. There, he presented himself for dissection, where he was no man and Everyman. A reader
of himself. Open to all the deadly virtues. He had three windows. It
was a panopticon. He could view his courtyard, his fields, the public
road. He carved aphorisms and epithets into the wooden beams
and inscribed his aim inside a wardrobe; *i.e. to retire to the bosom of
the learned Virgins*, where he would find *freedom, tranquility and leisure.*
He spent some time inside the closet. Inside and outside. Three
windows. A triptych. He looked out and examined the limits of
himself. The wooden joists formed the spines of his books, the bars
of his memory. He liked the idea of prison. Each word a cell. The
cell as the basic unit of writing, he said to himself. He would use
his mind like a prism. Examine the flaws in each confinement. Find
the perspective in which there would be revelation or escape, all
the while knowing that his retirement, his voluntary coming to the
dark tower, was a willingness to end the trade in deception. But his
furtiveness and openness could never coincide. The third element
for this to occur was missing: a lover to whom he could confess.

I was not aware of Gottlieb's secret, of the practical nature of his
affair with Fabiana, the *prágmata*, the good *things* of friendship, that
had been perverted into the counterfeit of love ... and money. I was
isolated out here on this property and I had to watch my step. Not
ask too many questions. There was a net closing in on me; just a
jailbird's intuition.

A police car came up the track, jouncing. Its blue flasher lights
were on, the radio chattering and the dogs barking. I went out,
ordered the dogs to stand and stay, buttoning my donkey jacket in
the wind. Two of the braver mongrels went up and sniffed at a trouser
cuff. A dog should always have a bone to gnaw on. I thought one
of the cops was going to shoot. She was unfastening her revolver.
The driver was out of the car first, his cap pushed back. Where
are you from? What are you doing here? Who are you? he asked.
I answered backwards. Redvers. Writing on Montaigne. Paris. The
female flic wrote *Paris* laboriously onto her palm. She had heavy
metal around her waist. In Paris, I said, the gendarmes were not as

pretty. Her face hardened but her partner smirked and asked to see the silo. I displayed my books and paintings. No these are not mine, I said, indicating the ones in Silo #2. Hers up at the big house. Yeah, we knocked; the female uniform monosyllabic throughout. We're looking for a stolen car; so what do you drive? I said I don't. I had a Swift. What's that? A bicycle. You don't drive? No, I'm prone to blackouts. They both moved a half-step back. I squeezed oil onto a palette. My morning routine. Anyone else live on this property besides this Martins woman? Not that I know of, I said. Her husband died about a year or so ago. I added that for authenticity. We know, the burly woman said. She stuck her biro back into her pocket. It was a fire, I explained. My supplement was not an invitation for them to elaborate. They knew already. They looked around. I continued to squeeze out paint. I went into Fabiana's studio. They followed, made some secret notes. The dogs, the same two, sniffed their tracks when they turned their backs. I waved back the rest of the pack. The cops smelled of prison-issue. The police radio piped up. The woman went to receive. The man, stocky, needing dentures, told me he knew all about me. McCredie told him. McCredie had cleared me, he said. Then as he turned to go, he volunteered some information. There was a fire, he said, but no body was found. Roger, the woman was saying into the microphone. Yeah, Roger, that was his name. Well if you see any strange activity, car-wrecks, let us know. I nodded. I don't look out that much, I said. What? I decided not to repeat my remark. I waved. They drove over the daffodils I had planted along the sides of the track. The dogs watched them go.

Having opened up Fabiana's studio I smelled it once more. Opium and prison-issue uniforms. I went inside the studio, Silo #2. Opened all the windows. Turned the canvases around. Mixed the paint on the palette. I still paint Francis Bacon faces, full on, side-ways, distorted, grimacing, open-mouthed. I had been a scholar of suicides, had haunted the morgues in Paris. In Silo #2, I paint over Fabiana's cubist canvases, transforming their faces. These 'accidents', with the imploded features of people I still remember, can always be read backwards in recomposition, through a prism, where the living once again sit on their toilet-bowls to have their portraits painted.

23

Torpors, soma; I drowse at midday, living reluctantly. I would rather not live if not for this vigorous resistance of the flesh. The beginning of the long silence to the grave. Only the Swift squeaks. To be matter is my desire; it is at the core and pith of misanthropy. To be a bicycle. To be ridden by Fabiana. The midday sunlight. It was to that which Gottlieb was referring when he lectured on the fallacy of being taken in by emotion. From the panoramic triptych of the cinema screen with the closing curtains, the side walls, the back exit, we were ejected into the prism of sunlight through which everything decomposed. At the moment of disillusion even the Swift exploded into parts, its wheels splintering into tyre, tube and rim. Only at dusk could I see more clearly, composing with the aid of the telescope, and could pick up the movement first in the trees, an uncoordinated dancing of hot and pendant leaves. Now I am able to focus more precisely on Fabiana's house, her green roof with the furiously revolving weathervane, characterless, like me, at the mercy of every breeze, a prismatic compass of words and counters and now I can see her window, lit in the gloaming ... oh, erotic wind! ... oh, unveiling wind! ... parting curtains, blouses, skirts ... I adjust my square, and there she is, wearing a cap, which she's taken to doing when Sergio is around and she sports a pony-tail which she's drawn out behind through the adjuster-strap and she's reading, though I cannot see her book (I adjudge this through the periodic lowering of her right hand from her face), sitting, I presume on her modernist furniture ... she liked that period which is now no longer modern but which signified a departure from classical lines, full of steel and glass ... and I am reminded that Francis Bacon was a furniture designer first, before he was a painter and the figures who sat on his furniture, on his toilets, *secreting* their bodies into pools of paint made sense now, bringing into perspective both viscid death and the pungent reality of decomposing flesh. And there you sat, Fabiana, and I was mesmerised by the way you lowered your right arm and then raised it again and it was the thought of you and Sergio, who you said was helping you clear the blackberry ... though you had neglected to tell me anything else, why for instance, the poppies had grown so high in its place, *Nepenthes* they called it in ancient Greece ... opiate or alcohol, the fugue of forgetfulness which chased away sorrow ... it was the thought of Sergio and you Fabiana, as you sat reading in the silk dressing gown which I gave you and which you left opened, your book that is, the thought that he comforted you with his guitar, this *well-tempered escravo*, soothing you with his chocolate tongue ... not for nothing did Valéry write that love consisted in the privilege of *being silly beasts together* ... and all I could see was the way you moved your hand to the back of your chair and touched at your own hair and how your grip tightened as your breasts heaved, and it was this thought that brought back to me a fearful potency, Fabiana, which I believed had left me ages ago when I wandered the hills near Benares and they were harvesting poppies, lopping off the heads of the white flowers and I saw Salomé, not the biblical character but you Fabiana, deflowering all the monsters of isolation, and you looked out your window then, pausing, as you did when you turned a page, recounting to the kneeling Sergio, who does not read, your desires, and you were staring straight at me grimly through your window, as if you were ready, with one stroke, to lop off my head with the glass from its frame.

24

And there I was, slowly riding back from Fabiana's cottage to the broken stones around the twin silos – the sun was aslant this day –

when I saw her coming out of Silo #2, and she looked displeased, angry, her eyes full of stony disappointment. I was quick to speak, to ward off a painful pause, the moment when she would employ a platitude out of mockery, and I declared my breaking into her silo as an accident, related the incident of the police visit, all of which I said, was caused by a slip of the hand, a splotch of paint, a dribble of ink, because it was out of my unwillingness to help the police that I thrust myself into some activity, distorting your paintings, I was saying to Fabiana, because that is what I know best, I said, masking, covering up, cloaking myself in silence, which was different from lying. There was no need to tell the police about what was in the indigo porcelain pots. I think I was frightened of slipping into the skin of another me – a good citizen – when my being consisted entirely of being a Chinese mask, I said, which had its own morality by *not living for others*. That had been my life, I told Fabiana, a full-scale negation of authenticity. It was good never to have been observed, because others will find me out when I am long gone, peeling off layer upon layer of paint. But for now, I had ceased trading in enigma and I was falling in love with Fabiana, much against my will. Was I attracted because of her danger? Francis Bacon, I said, explaining to her the canvas she was holding, depicting a cubist woman now modified by my Bacon look-alike – the figure seated on an office chair beside a bathroom sink – one of those sinks I remember from the age of four when my father forced my head into it for not remembering to brush my teeth: *Shank*, the name printed on the porcelain had been imprinted on my retina – the figure now shanked on a meat-hook with the melting face of Walter Gottlieb ... Francis Bacon, I continued, employed prisms and circles and cages to hold his figures within a strict perspective; an intellectual limitation of the imagination so that the melancholy of space remains true: held them from exploding into dream and restrained them to themselves, all the while executing their swollen decomposition. His flat was an abattoir. Bacon sometimes feared his own art – not because of its withheld horror – but because he thought it so mediocre he suspected some unconscious fakery. To forge a Bacon therefore, was to take on a redoubled pain, t*o love with another's passion*, but at the same time to do Francis a favour by being his proxy, putting him out of reach, out of his misery, loosening the noose around his neck, releasing what had tied us together. *All responsibility for our friendship was abdicated*, I said to Fabiana.

Fabiana, understanding nothing except my distress, held my elbow and led me to the stoop whereupon I sat despondently, holding my head in my hands for some time. She went inside to get me a drink of cold water and I noticed she had set the hourglass upright on the table and had turned on the light before examining what I had done. She had been frightened by my logorrhea, and was now horrified by my images.

It was through that sandy prism that I recalled Walter Gottlieb's face, I said to Fabiana. When you gave me the hourglass, all I could do was to think of Gottlieb's face, how his insomnia had driven him into psychosis and his stroke had wrenched him into wordlessness and madness and he took to sending me notes, even though I was only in the other wing of the house … he sent little bits of paper in envelopes via Madame Defarge, the maid with the guillotine-blade nose, little yellow envelopes containing what he called 'conversations', though they were really 'interrogations', asking me to clarify what I had said the previous night at the brasserie, epecially about Florian Gautier-Epstein, the kitchen-hand who was about to inherit his father's millions. What happened after he committed suicide? Gottlieb wanted to know, and Gottlieb's prurience, his curiosity, even his *rat cunning*, irritated me no end, because I hated this curiosity sugared with false naïvety, for while Gottlieb pretended he wanted the story again to write it down in a different form, probably in a novel, for he had already published the facts in the Paris paper *Le Figaro*, I was sure he knew full well it was that publication which brought about Florian's suicide and he, Gottlieb, was simply trying to have me confirm he had abjured any involvement in the Florian Gautier-Epstein affair. I can still see the headline: CAPRICES DES GAUTIER-EPSTEIN – TISSU DE MENSONGES – FAMILLE EN CRISE. Stolen narratives have terrible consequences. Gottlieb,

I realised, was dangerous, even in his stroke state, and I began entering these 'conversations' with him by mutilating the subject of our friendship, employing a fugal device, a *stretto*, a narrow strait, a constriction, using the subject as its own accompaniment in another key, or as is known in painting, 'layering', or to use the painterly term: a palimpsest, where the painter has *re-used* an original – and so I used the device of the *stretto*, a final, narrow passage recounting Marie de Nerval's attempt on her own life soon after meeting Florian … whether she had slept with him I do not know … he used to show her his paintings, I told Gottlieb; and it was then, in Paris, that Gottlieb wrote that fatal article … the noose tightening around the friendship between Gottlieb and me, the subject screeching in another key, its arteries constricted.

Fabiana was looking at me intently. I knew that speaking about my mutilation of her paintings in musical rather than in pictorial terms would draw her out a little. You didn't touch my grandmother's work? No. of course not. She was looking wistful. She was dressed in a severe black jumper and black jeans and both were tight, which brought a Sartrean response to my mind's eye: peripherally, I was making love with her but she would have to wear stockings. Those paintings of mine weren't that good anyway, she admitted, and you knew that. All this time I thought you were writing a book, so you said, about a sixteenth century philosopher, when in fact you were practising deception, reconfiguring my work. And all this time I was attempting to paint like my grandmother Julia Grace, she of Cubist fame, who left these shores for France, achieving nothing because she was an attractive woman, and attractive women would never be able to attract interest in the genius of her art rather than in the beauty of her face. Oh yes. Fabiana shrugged one shoulder in that slightly foreign manner which had leached down from her ancestors.

I was at this moment touched by Fabiana's observation, not only because it was the first time she seemed to be forthcoming about her work, but because she had forgiven me, so I thought, and the tightness of her black garments seemed now to be a counterpoint to her discipline, loosening her secretiveness and untying her tongue. Julia Grace, I said, is a beautiful name. There are two paintings by her, are there not, in the studio? Fabiana appeared startled. Yes. Of course you would not have touched them? I had them turned to the wall. But you would not have touched them because you recognised their value. No, not their value, I said, but their delight, their masquerade. Why did Julia sign her paintings 'C.C.'? I asked. It was a fatal question. The look on her face said I had intruded much too far this time.

It was only after she'd turned away, long after she packed the paintings into a crate so as to *emphasise* my crime, long after she whistled up the dogs to accompany her back to her cottage, after the cold wind had risen, that I came to myself, so entranced was I by her. I laid the hourglass back down on its side and thought of Gottlieb. In order to see myself better, I had come up here, viewed my relationship with him through a different prism. Now this prism was showing me astonishing things. I was being untied from him. Solitude undoing the knot. I realised how pale I was in comparison to someone like Gottlieb, who had devoted his life to art and I had irreverently painted him seated on a toilet bowl, leaning rather heavily on a sink where the word 'Shank' was printed in the porcelain above the overflow slot. And it was only after I had painted over Fabiana's canvases that I realised the word *shank* had a meaning beyond being a brand name, a surname, perhaps of its maker, but that it meant to walk away, to leg it, to wander off, and that at the age of four I was already being instructed by words to *remove myself from things*, never to have settled upon anything, never to have persevered in painting or in writing, always to have wandered off, and it was only when Fabiana asked me one day (she was eating plums she had plucked from the tree by the river when I came upon her, and she was offering me one and the juice had squirted slightly and settled on the sleeve of her black pullover), it was only when she had asked me whether I had any children that I replied that the idea of bringing a life into the world horrified me. To think that I could pass on to a child the shame of existence! I said, thinking to myself that I was useless even in the most natural act of creation. And it was while Fabiana sat down on the bank, her toes wriggling in the soft sand, that she told me about her daughter, that same daughter whom I had not met, but who comes up to visit her, she said. It was a daughter she had given away, Fabiana said, a year after the child's birth, and now the girl had recently turned eighteen and had traced her mother through a diligent search of state records. It must have been strange, I said, but then I said no more, because I was really thinking how nauseating it would have been, not to have seen your daughter since she was a one-year-old, and to have her turn up as a young woman, your own flesh and blood, a separate individual, for whom you had renounced responsibility, and I was thinking, though I did not say it, that this to me, was like a seedling that had taken, expanding to become a tree, shooting outwards and downwards, never to retract, and it would not behoove you to cut it down. I do not know why, but I thought of how I did not go to my mother's cremation because I had an important university exam, and I thought how this would have been the mirror-image for Fabiana of that event, of having a child turn up after so many years, knowing you had abandoned her because families needed to preserve respectability, social importance, hiding the pregnancy from public scrutiny, leaving a cremated memory floating in the Ganges. But it must have been more than any of this. Fabiana must have been desperate. She must have been on the edge of an abyss; ready to jump off the deep end. I do not know why, but I thought then of holding Blimunde in my arms trying to keep everything together.

25

I saw Sergio driving along the Putty Road in a pink Chevrolet. I was sure it was him. Driving naked to the waist as he liked to do, speeding in a convertible, the top down, a joint between his lips. Sergio does not speak much English and he has no French, German or Italian, so it remains for him to stare at me, I who speak all four and he, smiling with contempt, simply to convey his proprietory attitude over Fabiana and her property as if he had sensed the presence of a fellow criminal, because I was sure Sergio was a car stealer and I was starting to regret the fact that I pursued intellectual matters, locking myself away in a silo, a sillographer, albeit one in the pits, one who had sunk so far as to be unable to understand human complexity, one who could no longer read books without passing quickly from one to another, strolling along the walls to pick at the shelves, achieving less and less with greater persistence. Without lightness, there was nothing, I was thinking, just at the point when the wind picked up behind me and I sailed on the Swift, weightless as a feather, just when Sergio sped past me in a powder-pink American convertible with fins.

Dark thoughts descend while upon the Swift; sooty, fork-tailed, they swoop. The Swift flies with them; tyres buzzing beneath me on the road to Sydney; red wheels and silver spokes carrying me with speed and grace; men stand up to look from their work in fields, children wave, and I, disembodied, flow upon double triangles, descending into the brown murk of the city to squeeze into the wealthy glare of Double Bay, its houses hidden from view, their walls rejecting intruders on this still afternoon of my unruly madness.

The little maid opened the door. She wore a cardigan, badly knitted. She scowled at me. For the first time I saw in her a divine blemish. She was someone who had devoted herself to doing one thing superbly in the circus, and when she fell from the trapeze and tumbled over the side of the netting onto the sawdust-laden ground she was forever deformed, not physically, though I was unable to tell that just by observation, but mentally. She carried this mental deformity unconsciously, with her guillotine nose and her permanent scowl. Her swift flights had ended. I asked for Marie. The maid said she would go and check, as if checking would determine my worth. Brevity would have been joyous, but the length of time I waited at the door determined this in inverse proportion. Presently Marie appeared, looking tired, wearing a sack dress which concealed her bulging body and which made her seem more of a nun than ever before. She was pushing her mouth to one side, screwing up her lips so I immediately recognised one of those unstable phases of hers when she would make endless novenas to the Virgin Mary, not out of a desire for redemption, which proved unattainable for someone as wealthy as she, but from superstition, a storing-up, an insurance against disaster. And disaster was what she suspected I had always brought. Though my peripheral vision was all but useless, I noticed that in a corner of the dining room the maid was extracting tea from teabags with her fingers. Marie and I discussed my situation. She came straight to the point: was I asking for money? Everyone was touching her for that lately. No, I assured her I needed nothing from her. The reason I said I was visiting the *Château de Nerval*, as I called it, was not to ask her to slip a few more Francis Bacon forgeries onto the market ... which she would not have done in any case, though she made a good profit from them in the past by later *exposing* them as fakes, for there was a profitable market in good fakes; in fact, one could have said that it was a status symbol to possess fakes and to hang them in one's Parisian apartment rather than displaying originals, and there was nothing quite like the Seine barges shining their searchlights up into spacious apartments during Patrimony Week, illuminating all the forgeries on the apartment walls ... anyway, the reason I had for visiting her at the *Château de Nerval*, I told Marie, was to try and discover whether there had ever been any issue between us. Issue? There were a million issues, Marie said, not least your little entanglement (*embrouillement* was how she put it), with Lisette ... and *while I was in the house*, she said raising her voice a little. No, I explained. There was hardly a month between my leaving Marie and her proposal of marriage to Gottlieb, who had

115

accepted eagerly. It was, as they both informed me, a *meeting of minds*. Therefore I was wondering ... and here I began thinking again of Lisette, Marie's sister, who had suffered from a spirochetes, which sent her into periodic states of euphoria, her hair falling out in handfuls into my shirt, into my books, sticking to the paint on my canvases, and it was in compensation for this alopecia that she always dressed magnificently, even while we made passionate love, obsessed with arranging her wardrobe *in order to please me*, and it was not only this sweetness, but her immense intellect, this beauty of balance, that convention was dropping away, which made me fall even more deeply in love with her, leading me back to the question of issue ... *Absolument non*, Marie screamed. The maid had entered from the back, she may have been clutching a carving knife. To think that you think such things! Marie asked the maid for another tisane. Then she confided to me in a whisper: the women in the Nerval family have never been able to produce children ... or if they conceived, there were always malfunctions, she said, miscarriages, stillbirths, premature deaths. It's a family ailment that goes back centuries, documented in the national archives in the *Palais Soubise* as *Le renvoi en marge de Nerval*, a marginal alteration to the family, meaning, of course, that there were countless mad bastards. Then Blixen and Blimunde? ... Marie closed her eyes at this point and began a silent prayer, shaking her head from side to side. We adopted them, she gasped. Walter was so pleased. He spent every hour with them and there were so very few. Tears were rolling down Marie's red cheeks. Her face was asymmetrical, completely calm on one side and distressed on the other, and somewhere in the distant past I recalled, I had also loved her with this asymmetry in mind. Dear Blixen is in her first year at the university, dear Blimunde, please watch over her, after all, they were twins and they still are. You know how twins never let each other go don't you? They were always together, like a mirror image, a shadow of each, a Rorschach ink blot ... Marie was now speaking quite rapidly and incoherently, they only ever saw the backs of each other's heads, because they did not need fictions of one another ... Marie was now invoking the heavens, rolling up her eyes, and then she began intoning prayers and I left her at the altar of her huge dining table, which appeared funereal, the silver placed perfectly, candle holders tarnished from disuse, and I walked to the door, let myself out while the maid watched me from the bay window as I retrieved the Swift propped against the mossy stone of the wall and rode to Newtown.

My former housemates had moved. In their place, another couple looking like the previous, time-encased, *outré*, flowers sewn on their flared jeans and pirate bandannas on their heads and silvery hooks piercing scaly flesh. I asked them if they knew Sergio, owner of the *Salada Salsa* nightclub on King Street.

26

Montaigne said when reason fails us we employ experience. How to tell a bad egg from the good. The bad one floats. I have never been able to see evil, though I have been quick to suspect it. Whenever I look closely at a so-called thoroughly *evil* person I find there unexpected charm and humour and I come away quite refreshed by the world. Floating. This judgment is from experience. Yet there are so many people one would presume *good* whose evil lies concealed in the presumed act of doing good, as in people who profess that their true aim in life is never to be dishonest or contradictory, and who constantly tell the 'truth' without a hint of contradiction, ending in a flow of constant gossip which causes irreparable harm, warning us of concealed dangers like a lighthouse which no longer projects light, but which rears up as an added danger at the last moment.

For many years I had felt an unease, or suspected a disease in storytelling, so much so that whenever I captured a story, I released it almost immediately, vowing never to tell stories, even though in my mind I had already formulated its beginning, development and ending, and I had in a flash, seen that this is what a presumedly so-called *good* person does, by simply saying it is a story, rounding it out, manufacturing its completeness, and by saying that it is of no consequence, that there is no use for it except to titillate us for a moment, perhaps make us wonder about it, but not for too long, and if it is a really captivating story, to stir us enough to desire it or to steal it for employment, for that is the kind of evil that resides in a dishonest mind. But that is rare, because only an idiot lives by stories; only a complete fool carries around a story trying to imitate its precepts and attempting to put them into practice in the hope of gain. Sometimes of course we admire tellers for their charm, but mostly we realise all is calculated by charm in order to charm, and in the end, those of us who have learned through experience realise there is a *religious* charism at work here and that in the end stories are fanatical lighthouses without light and appear only during the day, possibly in fair weather, but they are nothing to cling to in the deepest of nights, for we only have ourselves, the controls are in our hands alone, as we glide towards danger, suicide or resurrection. Snake-charmers do not have the well-being of cobras in mind. I have never tried to tell stories. I've lived them of course.

I was thinking these things as I rode back to Martins Boarding Kennels, dog-tired and dogged with cynicism. I thought about the dying Count Von Keyserling of Dresden. It was 1742. The year had gone badly for the former Russian ambassador to Saxony. It began with kidney stones, for which pain the Count took copious amounts of laudanum. The pain had spread to his bowels. He could not pass a motion. He sat on his commode for hours on end. He could not sleep at night. Others were going to the Russian Embassy Ball. Keyserling, of course, would be unable to attend, as he could hardly stand up without doubling over in pain and when he took his opium drops he flew into strange hallucinations, sailing through English gardens pursuing pageboys with cherubic smiles. The Count's court musician was an angelic fifteen-year-old called Johann Gottlieb Goldberg, a protégé of Johann Sebastian Bach. Count Keyserling asked young Goldberg to play the harpsichord in order that he, the Count, might try to sleep. Young Goldberg replied with caution, for the last time Count Von Keyserling asked him to play him to sleep, it was not the harpsichord that Goldberg attended. The boy said cunningly that he would have to ask his master and mentor, Herr Bach, for advice on what to play. Anything to stall for time. Anything that would not end in the eruptions of a fleshy flute. Anything with endless variations and striations and returns and endless ways of mutilating the subject. *Something smooth and lively*, the Count yelled from his bedroom commode. *If it doesn't send me to sleep it may at least initiate a movement.* Little Gottlieb Goldberg ran from the court and hailed a carriage. He asked the driver to find Bach's house, but on approach they discovered the narrow street blocked by a crowd. In the flare of oil lamps they saw stilt walkers and magicians and women dressed in translucent silks. There was a fire-eater and a knife-thrower expertly cleaving apples from a boy's head. Young Gottlieb heard music. Someone was playing a viola da gamba, another a lute. Several couples were dancing a pretty chaconne. And suddenly there was the Maestro, his right hand beneath his chin, memorising the tunes in passing, nodding at attractive women, writing the notes of the sarabande in his head … does any of it need an aria? … already sensing his protégé beside him without so much as a glance, saying to him that these tunes were not variations on a theme, because … and he cocked his head to one side … hear that? There was no theme; just each one varying the bass line in a different way. He looked down at the cherubic face. The boy was not going to have an easy time of it. Everyone wants stories. They will keep him from the court before too long; it was his name; a circumscription. Never reveal a theme or an ambition, the old man silently cautioned his young charge. The music grew louder and then it stopped. Bach pushed the boy along, his hand on Gottlieb's shoulder, guiding the boy to the house, bidding him to sit at the instrument and to play something that he had just heard. The boy sat at the harpsichord and played flawlessly: pieces of the chaconne; variations of the passacaglia. Slower, Bach said; faster here. There. You memorise well. Now the bass, progressively higher! Yes! Bach shouted. The maid knocked and came in to close the windows. There is a dusty wind coming from the direction of the

Leipzig Palace, she said cryptically. The old man understood these rumblings of the people. Even though he had a court appointment he had never forgotten that his great great-grandfather was a humble miller and still remembered the story of his ancestor turning up at the grinding mill, the round tower on the edge of town, where he played his cithern while waiting for the wheat to be ground. It was this musical relentlessness, the great composer Johann Sebastian Bach was thinking, which had been passed down the generations. Imagine the unceasing grinding. Yes, he said to young Gottlieb, that is what will put Keyserling to sleep. I will write this down for you. Even though there is no theme, I will call these the *Goldberg Variations*. As you play them, think of the millstone tied around your name and the rumblings in the distance, but above all, think of the delicate sounds of the cithern, with the dusty wind howling outside. Sleep is disagreement with life. With these words he sent Gottlieb Goldberg away, promising he would have a soporific solution within a week. *Every idea*, Bach said to himself while standing at his window, *is built from what is already known; created out of chance, counterpoint and somersaults. O, God, are you really there, or are you just a miller?*

27

A police car passed me on the way up to Kurrajong. Admittedly I was finding the hill difficult because gravity demanded energy and my energy was being siphoned off since I was thinking of Fabiana, of the time when she was living at Potts Point, in a terrace house shrouded by liquid ambers, long before the County Council trimmed the trees to prevent addicts climbing them to break into and enter premises from balconies. I was thinking how she told me she had met the notorious Levine, who came to her concerts and then sent her flowers and notes and obsessively invited her to dinner at expensive restaurants, brushing aside all her excuses, breaking down her defences and then finally charming her by finding her weakness for men with a shady side.

The two same cops were passing me in their police car and I waved, lifted a weary arm while wrestling with the hill, gripping my handlebars, and they did not wave back, but looked grimly at me and then sped off, as if to demonstrate that *power*, as distinct from mechanical efficiency in concert with human potential, led to *progress*, which is nothing so much as a concept at the mercy of history and history is always narrated *for the sake of progress*. As I climbed the hill in my saddle I thought how time always had a theme specially suited to narration since it was always interpreted in linear form, but time is never really linear, because of its superfluity, abundance, excess of chance which produces events in an entirely random way. I thought how Bach, in contrast, *confined* chance to a probability, so that his fugues were not random events but a highly disciplined re-configuration of time, *using it against itself*, so that time, which is mostly represented in its appearance and disappearance, is finally *felt*. That was how Bach understood the Jewish tragedy and its corresponding triumph, its flights and fugues. Little Gottlieb Goldberg was open to an uncertain future, facing an eternal return that was not of his choosing; and yet he will be resurrected, if only by chance. As I crested the hill in triumph I saw Fabiana's dark secret through the prism of my sweat, beads of perspiration clouding my vision:

'I don't know,' Levine said, 'isn't it best in the late afternoon?' 'What?' 'When one is drowsy and dreamy?' 'Wha-at?' Fabiana asked him again, the melody in her voice filling him with desire. 'Well, when one is drunk and lascivious,' he said, drawing out the needle from his bound arm. He used a phylactery. The shadows were lengthening in Potts Point. He had had such a terrible day, such a day of fighting off all of his despair that he realised everything had been formed by an emotion, inarticulate, inarticulable. There were men and there were women. Everything was liquid. 'I do not need to say what I want to say,' he said. 'All you will say is that we could never be lovers. And that has set me back thirty years.' It was a rejection like a used bus ticket. Fed through a system. Mechanically, without spleen. That was how he would have described Fabiana if he could have found the words. She teased. But then, so did he. He was thinking of her body. 'Anyone,' she said, 'who was not interested in seduction would not have slipped into your limousine …' and she could have added that she opened the liquor cabinet and watched him watching her as she poured, watching the sheen of her silk skirt reflecting the lights as the chauffeur pulled away towards his apartments in a North Sydney tower, crossing the bridge crossing her stockinged legs silvering beneath the thin black skirt while she plucked ice cubes from her glass and as she leant over to him already seeing the hardness in his trousers and while holding clinking glasses in one hand unzipped him with the other, working him out through his underpants, sipped at the droplets curling from her glass before running an ice cube over him …

In his apartment she lost herself; screamed and trembled in a zone which frightened even him. There were men and then there were women. Their dance and their warfare took place upon one understanding: addiction made them neither.

28

All of these visions are against nature; against Bach; against the bicycle, both of which have principles and laws; the way I am interested in nouns beginning with B; both proper and improper. I sailed down the other side of the mountain towards the Colo River feeling the bass-line of time, heavily thumping in my chest. Bach must have been a bicyclist. He noted at the bottom of the score for Variation No. 26 that 'young Goldberg sometimes sat at the harpsichord as though he sat a hobbyhorse, a trumpet-blowing cherub on a wheeled bench'. He may have seen the drawings by Da Vinci. I ride over the wooden bridge. I breathe in the river, measure the approaching hill, absorbed by the idea that all motion in the world is rotary, sitting yet moving, stationary while in motion, no gap and no pause as the world flies by the still point of my circular reference, one foot down, the other up and vice versa, repetition and difference, point and counterpoint, everything reciprocated through perfect control, filtered through detachment. Indeed, the Swift was incorporeal, yet still capable of divining the earth. Another fugue arrives.

The rain is filtering down through plane trees three weeks after they meet and they decide on a late supper, after which they go to his apartment, which consists of five bedrooms, three bathrooms, a kitchen and a warehouse-size living room with glassed-in bookshelves, Giacometti on the table, a magnum of champagne, cushions on the floor and a concert grand ... in the bedroom they draw the curtains and he feels the need for speed, but refrains, everything significant, in capital letters, fractured. The dark glass reflecting their single florid lampshade. Every move the beginning of something. A sentence about to form. Moving towards something they don't yet believe can end. Levine addresses her politely, undresses her a little, his hands like butterflies. Would you like me to walk for you then? she asks. Wait. He runs back the curtains with the remote control. The full-length windows bathed in nightlight and rain. She is translucent. Arms akimbo. In an adjacent building in the watched and watching city, a telephoto lens extends. He smiles, visualizing a frame of her spreadeagled on the pane, on the glossy page, while on the roof a green neon blinks and hums: *the architecture of a beautiful body*, and then the floor, shingled with stiletto imprints, he watches himself watching her, the rain streaking the window behind so she is filmy and wet, passed back and forth between negative and positive, her suppleness after babies, dark nipples, her shadows, her clicking heels. He is scarcely aroused, shakes loose his hair from a pony tail, always appearing louche, the pallor of his skin so different from hers. She walks, she kneels, he pushes her away. Her sentences do not hold. She is tired of playing Bach, realising all too late that in her attempt to will originality, she had become predictable. She broke it off with him a month later, sitting in tears in her apartment on Macleay Street ... the flaking *Pomeroy* apartments, once a mansion with croquet and tennis lawns, in which Julia Grace, Fabiana's grandmother, had lived and painted her Cubist panels.

I think this was the story Walter Gottlieb wanted to tell me, on one of those nights he couldn't sleep. I saw him come to life, blood rushing to his cheeks, animating him from semi-paralysis. He had dreamt Levine ... surely it could not have been a memoir ... and was asking my advice to push this story further. At least it was better than his poetry.

What happened? Fabiana asked me. What happened with the child that drowned, your friend's little daughter? I don't know, I said. I was asleep beside the pool, fleeing to the Ganges, always in flight. I couldn't do anything after the fact. I had let Gottlieb down. There was no more reciprocation, I mean, in a friendly way, and from that moment on I think I had to memorise every apparent act of friendship in order to imagine its opposite, waiting for the moment at which my negligence would encounter recrimination. But he must've given you stories too; he must've made you a confidante, Fabiana said.

I was not a real writer and couldn't use any of it. In secret, I was planning my *Brief Lives (II)*, in which there would be a chapter dedicated to Blimunde entitled: *Pavane pour une Infante Défunte*. Even though I did not say this to Fabiana, because I caught a whiff of her increasing curiosity, concern, or need I say, *alarm*, I was thinking that at the moment Blixen roused me from my slumber to indicate that Blimunde was not moving at the bottom of the pool, the instant that I woke, I felt the ineffable weight of time, a landslide of sand shifting inside me. It was like smelling or tasting the cold, when getting out of a warm bus into a grimy winter, flakes of grey snow brushing against dark buildings; or when entering an air-conditioned cinema on a hot summer's day ... each space a kind of *vault*, affecting the heart; both a leap and a withdrawal; systolic and diastolic; panic and paralysis.

It was then that I got wind of a forthcoming publication, a post-humous work by Walter Benjamin Gottlieb. The ad in the review pages literally blew across the stoop outside McCredie's store as I propped up my bicycle. It was one of those ill winds that occurred regularly, and I didn't feel good on my ride home with the folded newspaper tucked inside my shirt.

29

Sergio has disappeared. I have not seen him for several weeks. I can only assume he is renovating his dance club in Newtown, the Salada Salsa, a share of which Fabiana owns. My book on Michel de Montaigne is progressing slowly. In 1573, Montaigne was made a gentleman of the chamber to King Henry III. During this time he was witness to a number of royal debaucheries. The king was a staunch anti-Protestant, and Montaigne a luke-warm Catholic. The latter had to watch his step. Any intrigue not well handled, any information passing into the wrong hands, could entail a summary execution.

Yesterday I had another visitation from the constabulary. This time the two of them were accompanied by Fabiana. She said they were investigating the laying of poison baits in the area. Someone was doing it illegally and two of the dogs had lain dying, froth bubbling from their muzzles, writhing down by the waterhole. Which two? I wanted to know. They all looked at me. The two that followed you around, Fabiana said. She seemed unconcerned. She was explaining the layout of the property, the logging, the clearing of the paddocks, her plan to grow flowers for her store in Double Bay. All three stood huddled in a conspiracy, looking at me side-ways, and when I mentioned Sergio, how I had not seen Sergio for weeks, though McCredie said he had sold him some meat, Fabiana turned to them and with her back to me, made the sign of lunacy with her index finger twisting a stray lock of blonde hair by her temple. Sergio, I said, Sergio the Brazilian. The constables looked at me with a smirk on their faces. McCredie says you're a writer. The fellow showed his bad teeth. Have you ever published anything? Yes, I answered. *Brief Lives*. The policeman nodded. A whodunnit was it? Was there a Sergio in it?

I have never been forthcoming with authority. Authority requires simple-minded clarity and it produces an ugliness of language, a language which cannot encompass all the nuances of the body. It is at this point that I am closest to matter. I am simply active and reactive, and could be compared more favourably to the Swift, my skeleton taking on all the characteristics of the bicycle, which, with all its circularities, only defies gravity when in motion.

When the police left, Fabiana lingered, went into her studio-silo and I assumed, tried to paint. At a little after four o'clock, she knocked on my door and she asked me to come to dinner that evening, inquiring as to what I would like her to wear. The strangeness of some people cannot be underestimated. Montaigne said that we should not impose our value system upon others with vastly differing customs. He also noted that whenever there was a conjunction of body and mind, when the body made up its mind, so to speak, a form of dissociation occurred. My illness, for example, sometimes brought me a delirious joy. Likewise, love brought a terrible agony. I was surprised at Fabiana's invitation at first, but then again, I did not really know her, and at that moment began seeing her in a different light: the unkempt hair, the threadbare jeans, the darkness beneath her eyes. Having failed in eliciting memory from me, she was going to essay seduction. I saw how completely deceived I had been, over what I thought was her *charming* mystery, which had in fact become a malignant and deceptive plotting, my suspicion not taking root until I saw her interacting with the malevolent cretinism of the police. Women do not know perversity, but they know plotting. I've noticed how materialistic she was … the logging, the boarding kennels, the dried flowers she sold, the kitsch art she manufactured in her spare time. Now there was her association with Sergio, a sniff of drugs, the nightclub and poison. My disillusionment was justified when I read what Montaigne had written: that nothing was your own, not even your desire, and that only your control gives you a measure of the world, a control which is forever being corrupted by the need for love. Clarity was dissociation. He received this insight not through idle speculation, in repose, in comfort, but from being ill. Lucid in his fever, he saw criminality in obsession. The last thing he wanted to do was to become the mayor of Bordeaux.

I think the last thing I wanted to do was to have dinner with Fabiana. I think she was interested in poisoning me. I can see it now: my retching and vomiting; a slow death in the solitude of my silo. Like Gottlieb, she was blaming me for my negligence. I was not paying her enough attention. I was not reading the patterns in the parquet. Everything had to be re-thought in order for me to trace the flaw in her character. I would have to go back to the source, find the clear water which gushed from the spring and use it as a prism. Steal the water back for the hours I've missed while living in a state of love.

30

In the middle of the night, in this silo of mine, I prop the Swift up on its centre-stand and I ride, flicking on the flickering lamp, the wheels whirring in their revolutionary rhythms, and I traverse ancient cities. Repetition-compulsion. Pedalling up, pedalling down. Turning and returning. Round and round. This circularity wears down reason. The mind becomes disconnected. The body breaks down identity. Through mechanical reproduction, the original is worn away. *Chaos*: the tearing of a piece of cloth. In this gaping chasm, the world was born, copying itself, an erotic violation of God's original. But the act of repeating has made shameful what was not there to be seen; it has caused a rent through which we peer at our emptiness and at our loss.

I needed to tell someone of this trap of reproduction, just as I had warned Gottlieb of fame. But my friend was dead. There was no friend. Gottlieb's posthumous novel entitled *In My Briefcase* (sly old Gottlieb would have insisted on a space between *brief* and *case*, but such are the vicissitudes of sending a child into the world after the death of its father), is now a *succès boeuf*. It caused a scandal in Portugal.* Tarnished the image of one of their greatest poets, my grandfather Camilo Conceição. Portrayed him as degenerate. The book was dedicated to me, the author of *Brief Lives (I): Mon frère, pour renouveler notre amitié, avec les sentiments de la plus profonde humilité*. Gottlieb had finally triumphed ... without my friendship. Yes, I had sat by smoking while he suffered on the gibbet of his marriage and had made a careful triage of my loyalties to him, always with an eye to my lodgings. There would have been a trade-off. Montaigne was right about friends. Then there was that final twist of the knife in Gottlieb's will: he had bequeathed his library to me. Six thousand books; a lifetime's collection. He knew I was almost blind. Anyway, I had nowhere to store them.

The blue sky and the shimmering gumleaves bear down on this round mill. The landscape remains a paradox: wide-open, available, withholding painful secrets. So with only two hours of daylight left, I strap McCredie's stick of gelignite on to the top tube of the Swift and I bring my torch and cycle to the back portion of the huge property, the track becoming rougher, rutted with stones and corrugations, sloping down to the waterhole which is now dry, where the willows no longer indicate the presence of wind, their drooping boughs crisp with clumps of dying, drooping leaves, and I walk the Swift to the rocks on the dark side of the waterhole, lean it against a boulder. I climb the rockpile and make my way towards the little opening which allows me to squeeze into the small grotto where Fabiana once showed me Aboriginal hand drawings, and I light a match and wait to hear the sound of dripping water, listen

* The Portuguese edition, loosely translated as Walter's Briefs, had to be recalled because of printing errors. (Ed.)

for the resonating echo, contre-basses, cavernous counter-voices of the dead, searching for the god of Error, pondering my situation as the Emperor's troops have surrounded me now; rhythmic footfalls, soldiers of time. I scramble down in the dark. Feel the water running up to my calves. This is the channel which feeds the waterhole. It flows underground and then rises up at a different level. Water always finds its own level. I trace the ebbing wells with my toes. I walk the walk that I have memorised during my expeditions here. I now have to go further. There it is, I feel the aperture first with my foot, then with my hands, the damp and the moss. There is a little ledge just above my head. If I stand on tiptoe and can find a grip, I will be able to pull myself up over the slippery rocks. I have the stick of waterproof gelignite which I will place in the small hole where the spring has been stoppered by mud, rocks and tree roots damming up all the subterrenean arteries, and when the bung bursts open, there will be an almighty gush of water and time, uncontrollable, a diabolical pumping and shuddering circulation, for water is true imagination, memory dammed up over time, seeping from dense sources, and the earth is impressionable, receptive of such leakage, and both earth and water have heavy dispositions for they constitute the substance of Saturn. I was suddenly back in Benares, by the banks of the Ganges. It signalled the end of my illness ... of always seeing the corruption in things. That muddy water in India gave up its secrets and filled the mind and then erupted above me as I submerged myself, freeing me of my paralysis, my immobility. Unlike Narcissus, I was relieved of all my tortured daydreaming. Here was construction. Here, measure and squeeze through reality, the water already flowing faster; it forces me back, the mouth of death always cold. Outside, after the explosion, my bicycle will slowly submerge, but when the flood subsides, something will rise up on a parquetry of stone behind the bridal veil of water, propped against a vault inscribed by ancient peoples, a bleached cranium bathed in prismatic colours, grinning dementedly at the way we always represent ourselves as ambassadors of blindness.

The wind, the wind. All around, swifts are darting, criss-crossing the evening sky.

II

WALTER'S BRIEF

Baudelaire wrote no detective story because, given the structure of his instincts, it was impossible for him to identify with the detective. In him, the calculating, constructive element was on the side of the asocial and had become an integral part of cruelty.

– Walter Benjamin

Sunday

Coímbra, Portugal.
The slow drip of a Sunday complaint on the fourteenth day of January 1894 fell drop by drop with faint determination from the roof to my numbered door. Rosaries of rain running into braids of guttered music; downpipes of depression, smells of fungus. More:

Tomorrow I will leave my father's house lugging two small suitcases into the tumid tram smelling of horse, eyes cast down to run the obstacle course of half-digested oats, while up above, dark faces at the greasy glass will grin my discomfort. The air is thick with garlic and ripe overcoats. I garner no empathy. I'm from a line with an ancient deformity. Just five feet high and hydrocephalic. Family lore has it that we will always be granted one concession to beauty, unfortunately always illegitimate ... that's the fee.

The Conceição Concession hasn't fallen upon me.

Leaving home finally. I did not want my mother there. Her position was not one that was justified by marriage, instead she would have been out of place in her condition, amongst my father's friends and colleagues who were milling about the carriage. They sent me off in style, gave me money to continue my studies; even as a junior magistrate I did my father proud and he held me saying 'Sonny come back soon'. Then there was Hannah, my good friend's sister, letting herself be kissed for the first time on the mouth, my heart all a-flutter, her hard lips when she whispered I would be missed. Suddenly my mother appeared in her shabby dress crying aloud, her face a mess of tears and mud from the potatoes she had been peeling. My father had already turned away and disappeared into the crowd which pretended not to see what I had always feared – her imploring hands, her trembling prayer reeling between novenas. I placed some money in her hands, their backs still covered in farina, and saw her frown, and I ran for the horsedrawn tram, away from town, still hearing her exclamation: *I bore him from my loins, and now he gives me coins.* I am not proud of being amongst bad seeds which have sprung unplanned in life's dark row, but I shall not go down on hypocritical knees when my father has been my foe.

I sit in the carriage like a mouse with cheese and watch schoolgirls on my corner wave goodbye to me, giggling at the lawyer's son they knew was a bastard without beauty. The next century will be lit beneath a darkling sky and young brides who fasted for their wedding day will play their games reciting my verses (those which lasted), rung by rung, performed with a mocking bow: Camilo Conceição – a poet by any other name would sound as bad when sung with rhymes conceived in shame. Didn't you know his father had laid a coloured parlourmaid?

1

He was making for Paris, his face covered in soot – he kept sticking his head out of the train window on the way to marvel at the countryside. He had not seen such vast and open fields, endless rivers and hunched artists examining their easels in seas of lavender. His father's house in Coímbra looked out on rainy hills of habitation so the eye fell short, upon suits, umbrellas, a tight-laced bourgeoisie all smelling of wet newspaper. Nor did he like their town house in Lisbon, for there he could hear worms creeping in the night in his father's books. The laws of torts and taxation succumbed to their appetite.

In Paris the population glided on fumes: of alcohol, dead flowers and opium which he had smelt only once, when the dentist took out a tooth of his and later he had negotiated the streets in a swoon. He could never really sleep. It was just a lingering. Close to corruption.

He wanted to dislocate himself in a way that brought a deeper past, completely to transform himself into another, and was convinced this other lay buried in China. Just the mere mention of a place name and he was compelled to travel there: Marseilles, Morocco, Manchuria. He would work at all kinds of jobs. He would become frenzied, unstoppable. China. It was whence all flowers came. He could smell its poetry.

The fragment of the Portuguese self he carried within him was embalmed in dead law-books. It did not rise to the living world *because it had no great tradition*, only small-minded precedence. He was convinced his sleeplessness was a sign of something else awakening, something from a bottomless sea, an ancient vessel surfacing, upon which he would wander the world to find all the grand connections. Camilo Conceição: poet. The soughing of waves; the sloughing of sails. Stow it. Others would say such windy passions could only have been conceived by a defective mother suffering from hysteria. The tides, the moon. Conceição soon bore his father's symptoms: popping eyeballs, a restricted field of vision. He felt no pain in parts of his body ... he could stick needles into his tongue ... but his nether regions were hypersensitive and disruptive, calmed only by warm baths, one brush upon that fleecy place and Vesuvius erupted. He was untouched so far by women or philosophers on their daily path. He felt; he touched; if only.

Church

From an early age – I think I was six or seven – I cursed the Infinite for allowing me into the world. Not God, for he was a white-beard resting in heaven, in a storm-tossed cloud steadied by archangels, old man, cape furled, not at peace, ranting at the wingèd youth who sheathed bright swords upon the words of maidens. I cursed Time for bringing me *this* moment, in which I was cast out from heaven's beauty. Look, I am a centaur. My short hairy legs will carry me far.

The Renaissance ceilings in the cathedral of my childhood in Coímbra. I mistook them for legitimacy, authority, the inheritance of deep feelings; believed such art demonstrated my crime of being born outside the law. The world was full of exquisite cherubs. My countless faintings at High Mass was proof not of low blood sugar but of a flaw, something interlinear – an impure strain which anarchists bore, their thirst to scatter incense and explosives; I fainted before fanaticism, which opened its thighs to receive me – intensely, purely, obscenely. At Mass I cursed.

Unsurprising therefore I read Virgil, he who lived between two ages and doubted poetry's false scheme to line up beauty and reality. I was on a different search, not for rhyme but for the reason why the Renaissance thought a discovery of perspective gave it a superior view. I preferred Chinese art. I saw their porcelain vases in a local museum. They were fragile picture palaces and distance was neither here nor there, a discovery given only to the few.

2

His mother's name was Pereira. It meant *pear tree*. Stable enough. Humble roots. She became his governess as they moved from town to town and as his father grew in importance, little Camilo began wearing boots. He did not find out she was his mother until he was ready to leave home. She told him she always wanted to be married under a pear tree. Not realising she was his mother, he did not see anything strange in this wish. Her moment to be free.

Here he is: an indifferent pupil. A C-grade student. A short teenager walking with a stoop, the world too heavy for his four feet and ten inches. In Coímbra, a rainy old city, he attends university, writes sad poems about dawns and twilights and shows the first signs of clinical depression. Life, he writes to his friend Alberto Osório de Castro, was simply a matter of *getting through time*. He alternates between the past and the future and develops a fear of the present tense, which he associates with a miasma suppurating above the water pump in the square at night: a fog; now-time: time to go; those moments that have already embalmed their nostalgia. The sickness of his sadness.

Conservative and rebellious, seething between self-importance and low self-esteem, he betrays no other talent than that of following his father, a judge. He enters law school in Coímbra but is not gifted enough in that direction. He will not attain that indifferent dream of his to argue in the high court, to expound matters of state waving a large white handkerchief sprinkled with *eau d'Issy* to an audience of visiting jurors. His ideas of republicanism are cloudy with naïve romance. As a probationary notary in Óbidos, he is suspended between births, marriages and deaths. No entry of a birth, marriage or death is without a raft of stories; that is, without deception. By *deception* he also means disappointment: love is not a real emotion; issue is quite without the balance of the law. Something going seriously wrong inside his head. Once a week he takes a walk to the baths at Buçaco, where there are green hills and gardens and there he pays for a rub-down by a hoary attendant. Payment is his requital.

When he moves to the district court, he does not wish to call himself an advocate, *avocado*, that strange green Inca fruit known also as alligator pear, reminding him of his governess which he would never call Mother, even when she lay dying after the doctors extracted a weighty stone from her gall-bladder. He is not interested in advocacy, but in provocation. Something growing inside him, a poisonous seed.

In the newspaper room of the Club de Recreio he reads about the Italian anarchist Enrico Malatesta, whose manifesto declared that *the insurrectionary deed is the most efficacious means of propaganda*. He is secretly thrilled that this mindless advocacy of violence has made its way into the club room. He points out the headlines to his colleagues. Horrors have an enchanting effect on him. It is not yet cocktail hour, but most of the clubmen are already drunk. They snort at the news. The eponymous Malatesta is not sick in the head.

He is a product of rag-pickers and that is why he has the capacity to act, Conceição says. The others are bewildered. Such rapacity. They will consider banning Camilo from the club. Before the new century gets into stride, anarchists will have assassinated President Sadi Carnot of France, Prime Minister Antonio Cánovas del Castillo of Spain, Empress Elizabeth of Austria, King Umberto I of Italy and President McKinley of the USA, Conceição prophesies.

He brought suspicion upon himself. An ironic grin appeared beneath his black beard; little white teeth; canary eggs. He probably belonged to the Carbonária. He was a republican; secretive. His hand gestures, when he illustrated his views, were coded signals. Perhaps the clubmen should have had this Conceição investigated. In any case, he was reading a poem by a Charles Baudelaire. Now *that* was someone worth prosecuting, they concurred; a *communard*, no doubt. Conceição swallowed his cognac and lit his cigar. In times of terror everybody is a detective, he said. He neglected to finish saying what he was thinking: that a poet, in times of terror, was first and foremost a whore, writing anything that provoked requital.

Pancreatic Paris

Desperation. Finding lodgings.

I will pay, I can tell, for having treated my boring but comfortable life with such contempt.

I drink too much in compensation.

I did not want to hold up a deep mirror to the world, reflecting common perversities.

I did not want to say: On a cold afternoon in the *Hotel Californie*, Miss Edith Wharton encountered Mr Henry James on the carpeted landing.

Or that something was terribly wrong. That there was a dog turd on the rug. Left there by the fireside spaniel. Nothing alarming; not as if there were no fish left in the sea.

I had a deep hatred of novels, those embellishments of the bourgeoisie. Little commodities they took home in order to fry a *frisson* from an insecure world.

I had borrowed some of my father's money ... about half of what he held in a strongbox behind his books. He was back from work, wet with rain, and he reached in and notes were falling like washed lettuce leaves from his hand and he gave me his blessing. My friend Alberto Osório de Castro loaned me the rest. At the Freemason's meeting we secretly said goodbye. Touching.

There was a frozen dog turd on the carpeted landing.

I was in Paris and the first call I made, after a couple of glasses of wine, was to one of Baudelaire's dirty haunts – he changed addresses 27 times in one year – then I rented a room on the Île Saint-Louis near the Hôtel Pimodan to study what Baudelaire would have done behind the frosted glass in a chamber of that club with hardly any furniture, just couches upon which he participated in 'fantasias'.

Baudelaire wrote with a red goose quill. Hardly anything else on the table if there was a table. When the bailiffs took his bed he wrote on his lap, sitting on a chair made by his stepfather, with most of the stuffing gone, the material threadbare. His stomach groaned. Outside, all Paris was a *digestif*. It flowed with absinthe. In combat with his circumstances, he was tormented most by his clock. One o'clock: there will be no lunch. Six o'clock: no dinner. He lay comatose most of the time on the floor in order to conserve his energy for writing. He unscrewed the glass from the clock, ripped off the hands. Then he wrote on its face: *It is later than you think*. He wanted to travel to China. Hashish: his invitation to voyage.

My neighbour's cat slinks into my room. I remember something I wrote a year before when I haunted the museum in Coímbra ... how the Chinese can tell the time from a cat's eyes. I pick up the cat, stare into its pupils. Light reveals horror and night yields secrets. It is still before midday. In the present. Claws. What would the Chinese have done now? With this perpetual midday which never arrives? Sharp as a scar? A memory: I may have been Chinese; a grey Taoist day, on a beach somewhere near Figuiera da Foz; staring at a woman baring her breasts; her accusation; my smallness.

3

At the age of twenty-one, Camilo Conceição had not had any love affairs. Of course there were those little flutters of the heart, the flirtations which flattered him when all the girls were just taking on a dare, testing their resistance to revulsion against his ugliness. Always second-guessing. He had these big soft dark eyes with the lashes of an angel. There were further cruelties, but he took them as normal in the course of becoming a man, so he thought. One wistful, freckly nymphet allowed him to touch her nipples, little cherries which were no different from a boy's. At school, boys did the 'nipple-squeeze' to each other as a form of ambush. He wasn't sure if he should. Then there was Fernanda, who allowed him to court her when he came home from the university. It was like having a plump companion for whom you had to make allowances. He believed he lost his self-pity during this period, not his virginity.

And finally there was the prostitute Delicia, who hated kissing, and after the first embrace during which he was premature, still fully dressed, he could not wait to save up enough for her and thought he would marry her and rescue her from such a life, teach her how to osculate, and it was only when he walked in on her with another man, a bald and tattooed worker undoing his undershorts while she lathered his muscled thighs with salivary smackers, that he decided he would not entertain romanticism ever again.

In the streets they were staring at him. In the church they saw the black patch of sin pinned above his heart. Sooner or later punishment would come. A failure at his law exams. No reply to an acrostic poem he sent Matilda, the beautiful secretary belonging to his father's colleague; deceitful Matilda who teased him by telling him that if only he would wait, he may have a chance ... not today, not tomorrow, but soon ... only to hear his father whispering to her one evening that his son was probably an invert.

His ears continued to grow; not the appendages of a bourgeois, more like a peasant's. He did not know how he got such lugs. Maybe they were pencil-rests. He should have grown his hair long; collected paintings.

Sunday, Again

Emptiest day of the Lord.

Latecomer. Following the trail of Charles Baudelaire. Tail him like a ratcatcher in my grey greatcoat. He had to kill too; precursors like Lamartine, Musset, Hugo. Kill nature as they represented it. Portray Paris awash with grief and joy. He was intent on murder. Demolitions of buildings. Boulevards widened with dynamite. An underground rail network. A dull booming on the hour. They even blew up the cemeteries to make openings into the Underworld right next to department stores that opened their doors to a heaven awash with light. You hurry past at night. By day the white ray of progress plays tricks. You smoke a sticky jelly in your pipe. Achieve *trompe l'oeil* effects. Buildings veering from side to side. Clocks melting. On Haussmann's new avenues they drape tarpaulins so all will be revealed on the opening day; shrouded graves for resurrection. In the sky, clouds are simmering. Soulful recollections of a grander past. He hated such above-ground landscapes, preferring the smells of coffee, fish and urine. Then the sulphurous rain.

When I first read Baudelaire I said to myself I was finished with poetry. Now I was reading him again, standing at one end of the Pont Neuf waiting for my eyeglasses from an optician on the Quai Mégisserie wondering about the book I had intended to write in Coímbra on town-planning in the second half of the nineteenth-century, when, looking up from reading *Les Fleurs du Mal*, I saw his double. Yes, unmistakably Baudelaire, with that tic in his walk as though he was fencing with an unseen foe, the dark scowl, the coal-black eyes which burned into me. He raised a forefinger and then looked away, saying: *You are buggered by your leisure-time, just like the rest of them!*

I took that as a warning. The world was in production – arcades and emporia filled with pinstriped suits and spats, and I was searching for a cat which could be my timepiece, cornering Baudelaire for me finally and for all time. That cat had seen the devil.

4

The world was crude. You could say that from the moment Camilo Conceição was born, the world was already too abrasive. Being tossed out on to a towel like that. His skin too sensitive. A shade too dark for the ruling class, yet he sunburned easily when his father took him to the beach at Porto. His governess, Miranda Pereira, rubbed oil into his back and he howled with pain. Oil rubs out the darkness, she said. When he grew older he was forever running from crowds. Something about their darkness. Men on street corners reading newspapers; who stuck out their legs when he passed. It was the way you treated a dog, a charmless runt who could do no better than stack boxes at the fish markets. His father said crowds were like that: the crowd mentality was the mentality of the country. But how to whiten his skin?

His father said his skin was sensitive. What was sensitivity?

He was about nine when he discovered it. An emperor in a long indigo gown. There were cultures which prided themselves on sensitivity, achieved, it seemed, with barbaric cruelty.

Sensitivity was awareness, yet it was not consciousness. He discovered this when he was eighteen. Awareness was a predisposition to open up worlds backwards and forwards, worlds out of joint with the present one. Achieved without thinking.

Total frustration. But worlds backwards and forwards – they

stored energy as well as trauma and left marks on him, little anxieties that he believed came via antiquity, an awareness, in other words, that had been filtered through generations; a nobility earned through war. These sensations came upon him slowly, like the cool mist of the evenings. Whenever he thought consciously of his state of consciousness he became a tough guy. Courtesy of those boots up the backside on street corners. He tried to be an irate tough guy, but all that surfaced was a tame gruffness which others thought a good bit of discipline would shake out.

To move through crowds was to be conscious of them, of their venality, the way they jostled, each worried about the day. How to get their hands on coin. It was madness, this pragmatic pushing. The bitter smell of brass.

He was at odds with anything called friendship. He willingly gave up friendship for solitude. Solitude allowed him to experience worlds fore and aft, fantastically and historically.

He made these notes and then made up his mind that he would take ship at Marseilles. He had to plot his course quickly. Time and tide were running, consuming life too thirstily; Paris overcome by vertigo, poised between a vague recollection of history and the next industrial revolution. He would have to slide down into a more ancient world, one which remained within the rhythms of the natural. Slowing down. Slipping under. A water plan.

Ocean

What if it turned out I've lost the small erotic thing which cost so much to buy on long afternoons drilling ash into spittoons lingering by the doors of department stores waiting for the scent of a particular woman?

What if it turned out I've come to the end of the rope of life, home to a frayed mortality, my empty room, the practicality of two pairs of shoes, six shirts in queues, waiting for love, success, any omen?

What if it turned out I've cast off a country which had given me a ballast of small minds, the comfort of class and weightless opinions passed by a king who wore a ring on his masculinity so there would be no question of his divinity – that I too, had spoken of his assassination?

What if it turned out I could never return to a summery girl, to her reckless churn of fluttering eyes and blonde deceit, that I had voted with my feet for a poorer world of weaker violence reaching China in my mind, through engulfing silence and sweet sickness, that with the swipe of an unexpected knife, sex subsided into the ocean? Do I want to go?

I wasn't cut for revolution.

5

There was no summary girl, like an execution of his virginity. Instead, he met with some Portuguese republicans in Paris. The secret police had made some notes: that on the 4th of February 1894, Conceição met with Nado de Brito and Venceslau Almeida in the Café Poulidor in St-Germain. There were strange signs exchanged between them, though the agent, a *Tenente* Machado, could not quite describe them ... a way of fingering a coat button, the rubbing of an eyebrow, a nod with a hand on the heart. As far as Machado could see, no written notes exhanged hands. There was a woman at the next table. She was dark, she could have been a gypsy wearing a mink hat, and she was writing furiously on a postcard. He edged his chair closer behind her, scraping it so loudly that the three conspirators grew alarmed and disappeared, one by one to the toilet. He looked over her shoulder; inhaled the fumes of her dark cigarette. Mused about her undergarments. Agent Machado could not read much English. He had hardly finished secondary school.

But like a good secret policeman he took note of the address on the postcard by requisitioning it at the post office, and then made a few discreet enquiries with the receptionist at the hotel opposite, on the off-chance they knew something about the woman. Before long he was intercepting letters from a Julia Grace sent from Australia to a Miss Anna Ångström, *poste restante*, Hôtel Jeanne d'Arc.

Marseilles

Contestatory, in opposition, I strode down the rue Paradis. *Massilia*, founded by the ancient Greeks, it smelt of leeks. I came here to find a safe haven. Lunched on sardines and beans, found a girl and paid a fee. My first real experience. 'Lavinia' rose and fell, her pink blouse undone, smelling faintly of rosewater and sweat; they all wore pink; it was the colour of prostitution. I saw pink hills in collision with the sea. I saw pink-painted cottages against whose walls men preferred to urinate, beside the oyster stalls. *Huîtres! Aqua-vita! Con!* They seemed to be calling me. Last night I fought the Carthiginians in mellow smoke, and sided with Pompey until Caesar imposed harsh fines on fine wines. I wonder what my father would have thought of that. What was the real origin of taxes? The city was broke, then there were chimes: Marseilles proclaimed itself the first French republic in the 13th Century and turned to manufacturing laundry soap. Cantankerously Catholic, it had a cottage industry and some hope. It opposed Henry IV until his conversion – he was such a dope he praised his own desertion. The city rebelled against Louis XIV. Its inhabitants heard the sun didn't rise from his arse – his head fared worse – they joined the Revolution with their bottoms bared. *Vive La Marseillaise*. Bristling under the Terror, the city was subdued and razed. Blockaded because of Bonaparte, it supported the Bourbon Restoration. When Napoleon III regained the throne, Marseilles again became a republican zone, clandestine and contrary. Understanding its history, I was never happy on the rue Paradis. At dusk it was all blood. A russet sky. But see, there was always hashish and fish. I am Marseilles and Marseilles is me.

6

Conceição was on his way to take ship for the Far East. He was wandering around on the docks and they thought he wanted a boy for the night, but he was trying to see what it took to sign on as a sailor and on one ship where he requested to be considered as a squab, the whole crew laughed at him when he couldn't even make it up a ratline to the first spar. Hopeless at everything, his father had told him. But he was rehearsing at life; that's what he was good for; trying out everything to get the *tone* right; the half-tones; snipped lines of experience; collisions and ellisions. Caesurae smelt of unplied hemp, liaisons had tarry odours. He read Chinese and dreamt of courtesans and the smooth, taut cables of love, which stayed grammatical until the moment of orgasm, when tongues were untied, so he thought, in the gurgling of brooks, replications of centuries of sexual arts, vanishing points of perspective, man and woman undefined. He had no experience at all. That after love, a man sailed and schemed and grew hungry. He had to wait weeks before a suitable ship weighed anchor. One night he found himself sheltering under a stone bridge when a huge thunderstorm erupted. There was an old woman taking cover there, frightened out of her wits. He held her hands, spoke to her as he had never spoken to his mother. He said you could count the seconds between flash and thunder. Work out how fast danger was approaching. The old woman thought he was a priest. No, he said, a Freemason. So he would know about stone. Would the bridge be a safe place? Under it was fine, he said. He shared a piece of bread with her. She was so relieved she tried to give him love; embrace him. She had no teeth. He ran. He had no idea what was on her mind.

China

Sunday, December 1894. We set sail on a rusty vapour boat from Marseilles, a trading vessel smeared in oil, fumes forcing me up on deck in a soiled pea-coat.

From time to time, with no appetite to spoil, out of sheer fatigue at sea-grey monotony, I repair below, edge to my cabin at the far end near the boiler room past the 'temporary bar' set up for six professors of botany, fellow travellers to the East. Specimens themselves behind salted glass, they feast on boiled eggs and beer, a plate of sardines for those lucky enough to have the money. I pass. I have no means and they have no pity. They guffaw at jellyfish specimens they've hung on the gunwale, dissecting them with razors, prodding at a tentacle, which like nettle, produces a sting. Men laugh when stung.

In the denser darkness of night-time swells, strange glitters erupt ahead; from deep arcades and infinite wells, black water heaves up jewellery from the dead ... a glowing trail, *ardenthya maritima*, drowned souls making their frail way up to heaven. My crate of unread books wedged with tins of lima beans slides about beneath the bunk. I could drag this liferaft out before Cape Horn if the ship were sunk; or, hull holed by a pirate in the China Sea, I'll defend the decks with Dostoevsky.

There is no self in my notes from the Underworld – an infinity of texts without a shelf; I have no essence, my mind still furled, becalmed mid-ocean, stricken by the notion of equality before the law. That was when I saw Macau, shimmering before the dripping bow and I, vowing to abolish the unsavoury practice of slavery, saw a mirage of dripping coolies and read the word 'reform' writ large upon my scroll. But they would perish with my first decree, before any legal punishment of owners could prevail. Chinese troops would mass on the fragile border and there would be no food for freedom-lovers. Only death brought reconciliation. All else a veil of compromise. It was the Chinese way, I'm told. And I, a puny Portuguese. The sea had turned metallic then, and slabs of swell formed into colours, a marbled collation of seaweed and debris as the steamer backed up and from the deep rose a phallic gush, a rush of foam, a flush of catacombs, blind dream of ancient bone, a resurrection! I, standing on principle while reading the *Tao*, both prince and disciple of the *way*, take on this heathensong, the excitement of indictment, rush to judgment, ravishing maidens, tight nights of gentle jig-a-jig beneath a crescendo moan, a ring of tiny offspring ... born again, I, Judge Conceição, am here at the bow, to rule. Who could have been a better fool?

7

What Camilo Conceição called his 'profane illuminations' allows us to investigate how far he can deviate from the norm, playing God, before arriving at any reality principle warning of what could befall him in a strange land. The *Procurador* came to meet him at the wharf. It was raining steadily and had been raining for some days. The Procurador was a Creole, a Macanese, a half-caste. The Procurador was supposed to be clever, doing things by halves, because the Chinese could overrun Macau at any moment, and as the Viceroy of Canton Li Hung-Chang said, if each of his soldiers threw their left shoe into the harbour there would be no harbour at all. Doing things by halves was enough to shift Nature itself. But because the Procurador did things by halves under this hypothesis, hardly anything got done at all, since he was supposed to mediate between the Portuguese authorities and the Chinese, and fearing the Chinese, but seeking gain from the Portuguese, he trod a fine line, and in the meantime, as an in-between man, a tightrope-walker, he made a lot of money just by balancing and doing nothing. But the reason why they said Procuradors were clever was because they spoke many languages. Camilo Conceição did not like the Procurador upon first meeting him, a smiling man with gold teeth holding a waxed paper umbrella, speaking Portuguese in a kind of patois, as if to say: you are in my country now and you would do well to learn my lingo. The Procurador spoke many languages at once; some obtuse, some threatening, some ingratiatingly flattering.

Upon disembarcation, Camilo Conceição wanted to climb back aboard the steamer. There were massive crowds of people the like of which he had not seen before, with their smooth skins, their hard-worn faces, all with something cheap to sell: a comb here, a toy there, fish-hooks, rattan stools, fans, ivory earwax removers, joss sticks, salted fish. He thought it a terrible mistake to come to a place where his wealth could not buy anything of value. In a few days these contradictions worked their way into a justified feeling that he could not have gone further away to escape worth. Here he was, representing Catholicism and a King, when he was a Mason and a Republican. Here he was in a culture where there was no such thing as illegitimacy. Everyone acknowledged their children, if not by giving them their name, then at least by giving them some means of living. It was why the Procurador seemed to him so much more suitable to be a judge in Macau, but now the Procurador was calling him 'Judge Conceição' and the latter didn't know if such an address warranted offence. They hadn't had a Portuguese judge here for some years and the crime rate had dropped, the Procurador said. He added that he didn't like it one bit, this oily compromise with the law. The Procurador fished inside the pockets of his linen suit – there were yellow rings beneath his armpits – and brought out a mouldy cigar which he offered, a first gift to a first judge, so he said, extending the object from his palm to his fingertips in the way of a magician. No, thank you, Camilo waved it away. The Procurador lit it for himself and the smoke smelt bad in the wet air. Then the second gift: I have a case for you, Judge. They referred it to the Portuguese court, since they presume we would be more aggressive, I mean, in pursuing the case. They? Well, a woman and her daughter. Let me tell you, it is not a simple case of slavery. The daughter was considered a *mooi jai*, you know, a child servant you could buy. The custom here is that if you have no children of your own you can adopt boys so their filial duty is to take your name and then continue your family fortune; but girls are different. They are not so highly considered. This woman's daughter crept out to watch a Chinese opera. These shows occur at night on street corners. The Procurador took his arm and led him away from the Praia Grande into a narrow side street. Fruit-sellers beckoned to them half-heartedly. Dirty water slid down from the tarpaulins. Just here, the Procurador was saying ... (walls of a house covered with soggy posters, an umbrella shop opposite, empty crates stacked over the mud so Conceição felt he was on stage, everyone watching from their windows and shopfronts, dark suspicious faces) ... just here they built a bamboo frame and draped it with material, the Procurador said, stepping between puddles, breathing heavily so a whistling came from his nostrils. Musicians on that side, actors here, each having their moment above the lantern-light. It was here she was kidnapped, the Procurador smilingly reported.

Camilo was not very worldly. You can see from these yellowed pages of notes from his diary that he felt besieged by others. When they spoke to him he was assessing their grammar, monitoring their syntax. When they spoke Cantonese he was learning all the tones, listening to their expression for a way of responding to them in the same fashion. He was acting on their behalf. He had no suspicion of them whatsoever, but was afraid they may suspect his disingenuousness, since he was dissimulating in order not to get the better of them, but to *become* them in order *to breathe their breath*, to live their lives, to understand intimately a social fabric of which he would never be a part. It was as though every pore in his body was listening and sensing the world to the point where a deafening buzz drove him to repeat phrases used by others, to shout them out, to torture himself with the feeling he was nothing but another forgery of the world, an extra layer upon an already painted canvas. Perhaps this was why he learned Cantonese so quickly. He also applied himself to studying Chinese calligraphy, thereby becoming familiar not only with written Chinese, but with the art of writing; the art of art. He began to write poetry.

8

Camilo Conceição suffered from an anxiety of influence. He repressed any explicit mention of his precursor, Charles Baudelaire. From the beginning of his schooling, Conceição was obsessed with the Parisian poet who was forty-six years his senior. He secretly linked Baudelaire's name with his own. The *baudelaire* was a kind of cutlass. *Conceição* was a corruption of the spelling of *concepção*, or *conception*. The irony of his conception and the legal fiction of his mother as housemaid while his father remained his father the Judge, brought a particularly masculine edge to his ideas of family. He was cut out of the womb, a caesarean birth. He was not the product of a marriage, but a concept, a *conceito*, an arrangement which left a stigmata on his flesh, carved from the blade of virtue. Parricide was never too far from his thoughts. Conceição thought much about his hero's name. It was an anagram of *air de l'aube*: dawn air; a poisonous miasma from the polluted Seine; dew from which evil flowers sprouted. Bodies were found there, no cause of death established. When he read Baudelaire's *Les Fleurs du Mal*, he knew something monstrous had taken place inside himself. He would have to kill or be condemned to the flaw of reproduction.

9

Port Bou, Catalonia
4th April 1902

Darling Grace,

I have just left the studio at Cerbère. Port Bou is just on the other side of the border and it's a strange little town on the sea, with a neat harbour and one little railway station. What's strange about it is that the town is almost surrounded by scrubby hills very similar to those near Lithgow in

New South Wales, but it's much drier here, and there are practically no trees, just wind-blown bushes of fennel and stunted oaks and old women in black shawls combing the sides of the slopes for thyme or St John's Wort – like a funeral ceremony, their bowing and bending over the perpendicular earth. These hills also give off an eerie atmosphere, a smell of chalk and salt, of sea-breeze caught in an amphitheatre, and indeed the train had to pass through a tunnel from the French side, debouching into a glare of light. I am writing this letter in a bar and the locals are looking at me in a suspicious manner. I suppose they are always suspicious of an unaccompanied woman, but I've cut my hair short, I wear trousers and swing a watch-chain, so they really don't know what to make of me. Can't wait to get back to see you, but am already missing the crowd at Cerbère. Oh, darling, we must come here together in a few years' time! All is light and perfume. What can I say but that I love you too dearly for you to be destroying yourself teaching in a girls' school. I will be home soon, my darling and then we will plan our trip to China.

Fondest love. Anna.

Forever Sunday

Forever Sunday,
    Christianity has given us Sunday nothingness.

    We wait for work in the dreadful melancholy of tomorrow.

    We find there is some virtue in the idea of work, though we hate the idea of it, not work, but the cliché of virtue.

    On Sundays we Portuguese sit empty in our rooms reading the newspaper, wanting to be saved by writing.

    In this gentlemen's guest house in Macau, at 40 patacas a month, we have a bed, laundry sevice and passable meals.

    We have wine, although it costs a little more than in Portugal.

    On Sundays we play waltzes on the old harpsichord in the hall, trying to drive away our hearts, which keep turning towards Lusitania, in a westerly direction, across the sea.

We are men, are we not, with feelings?

On Sunday evenings we play with the two little baby tigers the owner, Hing Kee, has received as payment from an adventurous tenant. They scratch and bite and their pupils dilate and contract, like my blood pressure in the season of typhoons.

Sometimes we walk up the hill to the grand hotel, the Boa Vista, with views of Bishop's Bay, always conscious of Sunday, always aware of the emptiness of the streets, longing for a bath in a clay and enamel Chinese tub into which an attendant has poured fresh hot water, wherein we linger, keeping Sunday to ourselves, keeping our leisure running and our neurosis close.

For we are civil servants.

Some of us, the conscientious ones, prepare Monday's work in the drawing room, where there is a large billiard table they use for desk, where they spread out their plans and graphs and ostentatiously place a pencil behind their ears, making the rest of us uncomfortable, for already we have forgotten the time of progress, that infernal train we feel is driving us into slavery, and we can only read the time as Sunday, in the eyes of the tiger who yawns with a red mouth, a furnace, its stomach ignorant of schedules.

10

A young girl was kidnapped on the corner of the rua de Roma. The Procurador's secret police captured the culprit. There he is in a bamboo cage. His arms and hands are bound with rattan. Around his neck, a leather strap. This can be wetted down, not to cool him, but to strangle him when it dries. Then it can be soaked again. He is lucky, the Procurador says to the assembled crowd. Under Chinese juridiction, outside the enclave, he would already have had his side pierced with a knife, so the organs are revealed one by one. A lesson in anatomy. Then his arms and legs would be cut off with a chopper.

This would be done amongst the crowd, so people would have a close-up view, to participate in the carnage out of a fascination with the spectacle, with what is normally forbidden; the awe of the law.

The presiding judge was Camilo Conceição.

Portuguese law condemns slavery and execution, he begins. But he knows this is not about slavery, execution or Portuguese law, but about the customs of the Chinese. This was the ironic twist of Christianity: you could not apply Portuguese family law to heathens. It was liberalism by default. But Judge Conceição is of the old school. He believes one should be equal before the law. In opposition to the views of the Procurador, Judge Conceição declares that defendants cannot have it both ways. One law for all.

The judge looks at the plaintiff. She is attractive, in a hard-faced way. There is never a smile. But then again, this is not a smiling matter. She has plaited her hair up on her head, in an attempt to look more mature, perhaps. She cannot be more than twenty-four years of age. That means she would have had her own child at the age of twelve.

The prosecutor begins his speech. Kidnapping and slavery are serious matters. But Judge Conceição is not listening. The defendant has already stated he *bought* the girl. Yes, slavers are sending people abroad from Macau, but in Macau itself, there is no slavery *per se*. The Chinese buy and sell everything, including children. To prosecute every case, they would have to prosecute virtually every family in Macau. Minors are sold for adoption and domestic service. *But it is not about a price. It is about a gratuity*. Like a marriage dowry. No price is set, but it is about compensating the parents for the loss of their child.

All this is rattling through Judge Conceição's mind. He sees very clearly that the kidnapper had not paid enough. It was purely a money matter. His mind drifts to Paris. He sees Baudelaire and the black prostitute Jeanne Duval. Baudelaire understood prostitution: the wage-labour of his mistress; the prostitution of his art. Judge Conceição looked at the young girl, the mother's child. The child was extremely pretty. The child was smiling at him. She leant her head against her mother's breast. Madonna and child. Sphinx and angel, both almond-eyed and brazen. Conceição ponders over the fact that children are the oldest form of commodity in the oldest civilisation. Nothing was more of a mass article than *progeny*. Devoid of sex, desire was essentially the voluptuousness of buying and selling, of coinage. Just as Judge Conceição took pleasure in having to rewrite the law.

The Judge takes a drink from his water flask. It stands next to a clay pot, which is ochre in colour and decorated by a red and white motif: an old white-bearded man sits on a mountaintop meditating, his head in the clouds. A goddess on a distant mountain acts as a counterpoint, a siren depicted on the same scale, distracting him from philosophy. Chinese painters were never interested in physical scale. Like a Bach fugue, the mountains are piled, one on top of another, as if this multiplicity made them immeasurable and contradictory. It was conceptual art. Conceição had bought this clay pot at the markets behind his guest-house. They could have given it to him because it leaked. There seemed to be a small hole at the bottom. Maybe it was meant to be filled with soil, for a plant. But no, the barrow-man wanted a quarter of a pataca for it. He called it a *clepsydra*. The judge called it a bargain. The pleasure of the squeeze.

The prosecutor was droning on. Judge Conceição sweated just listening to his tumid style. The prosecutor waxed lyrical, drew out a white handkerchief, mopped his brow, his puffy white sleeves fluttering over his face. Conceição could never have prosecuted. He never believed enough in pure evil. He could never see the devil rising from hell in counterpoint to God's descent. No, good and evil were equidistant, like the northern Sung design on his clay pot, and all was adjudged by compass and square, not by the trickery of perspective. Each a function of the other. The prosecutor was using a well-known currency: aware that Chinese families purchased members in return for certain rights over them ... filial duties, concubinage etc., it would be better to pursue the lesser charge of kidnapping in order to secure a conviction, rather than take the hypocritical European stance on child slavery. The latter was an emotional issue, and the Chinese did not deal with emotions as something to be exalted. Emotions had no social relevance. One's behaviour, one's self-reliance, were far more important than self-expression of this kind. But the prosecutor was taking a long time about it. People in the courtroom were fanning themselves, falling asleep. They were already bored with this celebrated case.

In order to bring his mind back to the current situation, Judge Conceição made an unprecedented announcement. He cut short the prosecutor's closing speech by pointing to the clay pot on his desk. *The water has all leaked away. Your time has gone.*

Counterfeit

You could call me the counterfeit judge, but cutting time short brought value to judgment, worth to coin.

I had no real calling for it, to pronounce verdicts as though one had made a discovery of guilt when there was no such thing.

The law, any law when translated, is counterfeit. It is about the two sides of our nature; the two sides of our word which we give and then take back.

It is not about writing poetry on a Sunday afternoon, inspired by Baudelaire's clock.

I suffer, therefore, from something that is non-existent; the sliced conscience of the *advocado*.

But I am irritated by Chinese indifference to their own suffering. I am a double-man and the abyss is widening.

I pronounced that the kidnapper was guilty of forced imprisonment, and to emphasise the power of the European court, *in conjunction* with the wishes of the Chinese people, I referred the defendant to stand trial in a Chinese court for not proving he had paid for the girl. I assume he will pay quickly and be done with the matter. But there is always the possibility he will have his arms and legs chopped off.

This is what I call the counterfeit coin of Colonial Law. One can pass it off quickly, like water in a leaky pot; or one can pass it on slowly, where I'm sure the drip of water from a clay pot will be used as a vessel of torture and eventually, execution.

The courtroom is stuffy and the crowd is only half-satisfied. They flutter their straw fans at their breasts and talk loudly. No blood today. When then?

11

Camilo Conceição was a collector. He was an obsessive shopper. He went on sprees in the markets of old Macau. Old junk; *brocantes*; pots and pipes. It was raining of course. It always rained when he went to the markets. He bought a clepsydra and listened to it clinking and sloshing with ancient sounds: *kleptein*, to steal; *hydōr*, water. It had gear wheels and a floating dart carried by a cherub, pointing out the hour on a drum marked with lines. Water was syphoned off from a small aperture by a waterwheel. He set it up in his bathroom. He was so consumed by this purchase – he paid too much for it – that he fell into a kind of swoon. The object had taken on a value beyond itself, and within its aura he had become very small, shrunk to nothing, wishing to pass though a vanishing point. The eye of a needle sees much.

A few days later, Conceição was trying to adjust the time when his pocket watch slipped from his hands and fell to the floor, shattering the glass over its dial. He looked for a repairer and found one on the second floor of a dilapidated house and there behind a counter sat a girl with very nimble fingers, whose sole job was to fix watches. As he looked on, she removed the shards from the dial and screwed on a new glass. Her enslavement to this task in this dark room, her devotion to this object which normally sat intimately in his trouser pocket, her presence as an industrial slave whom he had purchased for a few minutes, produced a dilation of his desire.

Watching her fingers, he grew intimate with her in the small space of her infinity.

He's not sure what to make of these feelings of contraction and expansion. He can only relate them to his heart, which is not in good shape and which pumps erratically, shrinking and dilating so violently it feels constricted by coils of water serpents. His body tries to escape from itself through a small hole in time. The girl charges too much, but he pays. He is happy enough to be used; if only he could do something to rescue an unknown talent from her abjection.

Chromatic Insanity

Several months now, I have been sinking into this place; the oily glare grounds my canvas; sheen of white light over the muddy pane of the delta; lazy rattan blinds sway over old balconies where my haemic respiration keeps sex at bay, so far from sleep, so close to death the latter has become familiar; bones crack in the cemetery, where ancient explorers, used to the thunderclaps of storm and cannon, moulder beneath stones unkempt and forgotten; temple dogs stray over them, rabid, cowering and dangerous; in the shops across the street foetuses doze in glass jars; I stand before them, deciding between snake-wine and powdered tiger-testicles, strolling from chamber to chamber in the cool darkness which smells of worn wood and dried herbs and I am absorbing a humid illness, which will turn me into dusty matter, drive me into my own portrait, a small disappearance into indifferent monochrome, that of a man without consequence, whose heart, meatless, has stopped hungering for Europe.

My bowels are bad; I hire a vehicle; a tricycle, a contraption ridden by a man pedalling in front, his ribs rippling beneath a yellow skin tanned by sun and anaemic from opium, his chest rattling wet bellows; I buy a small tin bathtub to place in my rooms, away from the noisy operatics of the other civil servants; I wash often to keep clean; my intestines ache and maybe there is something missing there, perhaps I am semi-colonic; threading our way now through the narrow streets I know by heart; Macau a small place; I do not need to travel any distance, but am reaching further and faster in this vehicle powered by a human narrowly harnessed to life; I negotiate a price with him; it is his livelihood; he doesn't want to sell; I meet his boss, a Mr Lok Yu, who can arrange for me to own one of these trishaws, but I would have to buy the licence as well; we come to an arrangement; I could pay it off on instalment, but I would not be allowed to carry any passengers; I agree; the trishaw keeps me above the crowd, allowing me to fly past without brushing against them while remaining very much in their midst, smelling them, hearing them; I am in graceful motion, I tip slightly, but am still in place; a rider of a black iron tricycle with an iron bar in front and a cushioned bench and a fold-down canopy. Every morning a new desperation; I have the luxury of melancholy, accursed for having been a judge; and because of my laughable body which only wants to sneak through a tiny aperture in the world to escape the small fate of a fat-arsed judge, because I lament the useless speed and the deadly mass and the deafening hysteria that western industrial time will become, where I will not be able to dream for the acceleration of colours, where I will not hear the echo of my awareness of the world for the hubbub of the maddened crowd, where I will not breathe the air of freedom because of its small-mindedness, I shall give it up; judging, that is; and attend to the eye of the needle and all that; consider it accomplished, this exile. I bought several long indigo gowns, the kind Chinese men wear.

Each morning I ride the small triangular route of five miles between the Leal Senado, the Border Gate and the Boa Vista Hotel. In this daily round I am able to gauge the vital rhythms of the heart which work against the brain.

The kidnapping case has been a watershed. It has divided me. I will no longer represent the King, Catholicism or Portugal. I have taken a job as a schoolmaster. It is a step downwards. Sometimes in the rain I see myself and my children absorbed into China, plying this route on their trishaws in sodden blue pyjamas. Everything goes downward. Blue anyway.

I have come to an arrangement with the mother and child. I have paid money to release them from their employer, along with the understanding that they will live with me, the woman as my concubine, her daughter as my *mooi jai*, or bond-servant. Silver Eagle and Nickel Hawk. Birds of prey. There is no problem here with the counterfeit of marriage. I paid 1,000 patacas to the mother's pimp, freeing her from prostitution and rescuing her daughter from the same trade. I enclosed 500 patacas in a red and gold lucky envelope and gave it to the mother as a good-will gesture that I will look after her daughter. Oh, and I have moved to a two-storey house on the Praia Grande, right on the embankment, so that the glare of the rippling water is projected on my embossed metal ceiling when I doze on Sunday afternoons, my heart pounding with exhaustion from all that vigorous coupling.

After that I play the piano. A passacaglia. I am dancing with pretty women in the street. One is not carried away completely, as in a fugue. Dreaming of Coímbra. My deep melody is not what sentimentalists call romantic love, though that is something for which I have never stopped yearning. Unfortunately, Nickel Hawk's growing beauty only shows up the ugliness of my playing. I stop.

12

The letters to and from Australia keep cropping up in the Conceição archive in the vaults of the National Museum on the Rua São Paulo in Macau. Now that we know he was a collector, it isn't so much of a mystery. He obviously bought the letters from those junk shops you find in the East, down an alley, the doorway covered by a curtain, where it was always dark inside, so you can't inspect very carefully all the copies and forgeries, calligraphy by Genghis Khan, for God's sake. On the counters you can find boxes of photographs, letters, stamps, incense, pens and brushes. But these letters he has kept don't seem so valuable. One can conclude from them that the two women correspondents were artists, one a potter and sculptor and the other an oil painter. Conceição was of course very interested in collecting art. The Chinese collection that was sent to the Galerie Kahnweiler in Paris contained some gems.

Conceição's poems seem to be minor things, little impressions, tiny watercolours he recorded about Macau, no doubt inspired now by his new domestic circumstances, preparing his lessons for the boys' school, his Portuguese classes filled with desultory students, sons of diplomats and civil servants, privileged offspring of wealthy Chinese merchants eager for a European connection. And Conceição? What about him? He doesn't like his job. He moons at the classroom window, unfolding his dreams over Bishop's Bay. Each morning a new desperation. His pupils have no revolutionary spirit. Don't they see that the King's days are numbered? That Portugal will no longer be the colonial power that it once was? That it is management of the colonies that is sending it broke? Young poets were committing suicide: Mário de Sá Carneiro; his good friend Antero de Quental; all impotent romantics and rhetorical republicans. It was good that he had left Portugal. At least his was a slow suicide.

As a dozy Chinaman smokes his long pipe,
as a cured fish gazes blindly
into the fumy night,
flanks skewered with chopsticks,
Portugal lies in its fix
sleeping unclothed,
sunk in dreams, feverish.
A cold wind rushes through
the colonial arcades
and another red-haired Autumn flees.

13

Darling Grace,

... the excitement of such love generates the same heat as most other passions, but the difference is danger. Conventional love confronts you with another being, a man, entirely different from you, with his smells and his harsh and hairy body and his belligerent mind. It is his job to hunt, not to linger over passion. In our kind of love however, you too often discover yourself as a lack – because a mirror of your own weaknesses is constantly displayed; a doubling of sameness (not a tautology!), and a multiplication of self-hatred. Companionship teeters precariously on the edge of this narcissism. This is the danger: an obsessive dependency turned into a thick cobweb of feeling too intricate to unpick on a daily basis. Sometimes it is a numbness. Sometimes you wish to be swallowed up by the other.

My deep, deep love is for you, my dearest.

Your Anna.

Sapphic love is either infernal or divine; perhaps both. That's what Baudelaire said. But his was a man's mythology, raiding antiquity for justification. He wanted to call his volume of poetry *Les Lesbiennes*, rather than *Les Fleurs du Mal*. Baudelaire was a dandy. He was obsessed with his mother's long silk skirts. How he hid his face in the folds. Fetishists had revolutionary instincts: the effete and the abject were powerful political tools. It was shock value for the bourgeoisie which was always threatened by the lack of boundaries. The smell of silk and perfume and the lure of fashion. Baudelaire couldn't afford to wash. Prostitutes no longer took off their clothes for him. He pushed on, through the folds of the crowds, over the barricades. Abasement fascinated him; his lover a prostitute; both commodity and stimulus. As much a silk cravat as the green jelly of hashish. This may be the last beautiful moment of the century, wrote Camilo Conceição on a paper napkin.

These items were all there in his archive, together with his manuscripts, between the pages of which was a pressed and dried lily flower.

Living Money

She smiles like a cat, unmistakeably sly, but teasing still, revealing silver teeth. She sits on the edge of my bed, but it is understood she has her own quarters. Behind her, the wide window frames bat-winged junks gliding between misty hills. At the back of this house, with stairs leading down to the cool courtyard, she is mistress. She looks after her daughter well. She keeps a good house and goes to the wet markets for the best deals. Then she prepares the meals while I teach at the Boa Vista, a former hotel which is now a secondary school, up on the incline overlooking the Praia Grande. Each day she notes down what she has spent in one column, what each item of food has cost in another. Her figures are neat, impeccably calculated. Outgoing; incoming. I pay her a little more for public holidays, when she goes to worship her ancestors or sweep the graves.

She has laid out my suit for the day. I have more than two pairs of shoes now, more than six shirts. She presses my handkerchiefs with a flatiron heated on a coal stove. I jingle the coins in my pocket before I leave for work. This makes her smile. In the common room at the school I examine my coins and find amongst them an American silver dollar. There is an eagle on the back. In God We Trust. I don't think I will change my mind about God upon my death. I wish for no afterlife; get me out of this one. Of course I would like to die like a book; but it will be certain no one will come to my rescue, no friend to edit friendship for itself, cut the pages to air my soul.

Illiteracy is my attendant. But really, all this talk about finality is a little short-sighted. There is no final day; the quotidian is death, each day a day of the dead.

She smiles, even if she doesn't feel like smiling. She may not understand feeling at all, because she said it was very inconvenient; a burden, she said, which she had disposed of many years ago. She overcomes pain by soaring above her prey. I call her Silver Eagle. Dressed in her rough black silk, walking flat-footedly with her plaits flapping, she is an Indian squaw we see on magic lantern nights at the school. The other teachers, weighed down by families they had brought with them from Portugal, look at me with some envy. It makes my heart lighter for having entered passion on a different floor.

Each day her daughter becomes more beautiful. The girl-woman flowers like an orchid. I teach her Portuguese and watch her mind opening to the day with the sound of birds. I call her Nickel Hawk. Malleable and ductile, occurring in combination with arsenic or sulphur. I educate her aesthetic instincts, almost as rapidly as I develop my own, in the categories of greatness in Chinese painting. I tell her about the four levels of human formation: skill, cultivation, wisdom and spiritual insight. I said cleverness was not enough. On the lowest rung, that is, on the level of skill, formal beauty is all that can be attained. A surplus value. I did not mention that a woman could go no higher. I think she understood this was where she was heading, though I probably confused aesthetics with biology when I explained that *a girl in flower* was a beautiful image in French, but haematose in English. She should always try and do better.

It began to rain then, while we were sitting on our stools in the courtyard feeding the chickens. I gave Nickel Hawk the book I had purchased, on early sixteenth century Chinese painting. She liked the illustrations of grasshoppers and shrimps. She astounded me by saying how beautiful the images were, compared to the language, *which was vulgar and vile*. She also said that flowers were not as important as fruit. I was completely taken aback. Then by giving you this book, my language is less vile? I asked. Oh yes, she said smiling. And then she hugged me. And for the first time in many months, I returned to writing poetry; from the fruit of my viscera.

14

... we arrived at Victoria Street Potts Point, before a row of terrace houses. We were let in through an iron gate by an old woman who, from the way she smelled and swayed, was drunk and she led us up to the first floor where a rehearsal by a chamber group was in full swing. They were all women, in various stages of intoxication. There was a Courbet reproduction on the yellow wall. They played lewd music on their instruments. It was hard to imagine such a coven in staid Sydney. The din and chatter deafening. Somebody had closed the shutters and the heat was stifling and a few people in the audience started to undress, first exposing corsets and modest pantaloons and then showing off their backs and their legs. It was all laughter and fun, but not for a country girl like me; it seemed punishable, saved by the fact that it was athletic. In Australia, mannish women seeking female companionship was not uncommon, Anna said. I've not seen anything like that, not anywhere. Anna said Parisiennes threw up their skirts without provocation, though there, it was accepted, but only if subsumed by an aesthetic. Anna was always the bold one. Much more intelligent than me. She was eyeing off one of the girls, a boyish blonde, thin in the hips, who was wearing nothing but a bow tie around her neck. Another was sliding out of her dress. I felt relief, not jealousy. Anna began to kiss and fondle the bodies, and soon the whole room was roiling and seething with buttocks and shadows and breasts, humid with female odours, the walls swelling with all that heat, the air heavy with groans and sighs. Somebody approached me and rubbed her hand over me. She had a very deep voice and a German accent and her hair rasped against my thighs and her tongue began to drive me wild ...

Asthenia

I suffer from a debility. At times I am so exhausted I cannot even raise my pen to write. I put it down to the air pressure; another trial for me to undergo. I do not have strong emotions, and my words are pallid and insipid. Even the ink looks anaemic. They say this part of the coast is particularly prone to the infestation of typhus. It sweeps up from Canton. My physician, Dr Gonzales, bleeds me and makes me even weaker.

Nickel Hawk is now thirteen and a half years old and at thirteen and a half the Chinese consider her a woman, of marriageable age, ready to be sold, ready to have more than her dowry returned by her husband, ready to have children, ready to have a son whose filial duties would be to create or continue the family's prosperity. Looks do not come into it. Feelings do not come into it. But I am different. I am a Westerner. I am Portuguese. She teases me with her guile and her innocence. I do not sleep at night. I buy her embroidered silk pyjamas. Her little breasts bulge. Within a budding grove down by the Governor's gardens I observe her at play, dancing over stones placed on the cinder path. My brief career as a judge has trained me to be controlling, to manage the rowdy courtroom. This self wants to come to the fore. But as one who has poetic ambitions, such a self should be the last thing to emerge. Few poets really understand this: to be passive, receptive, free. Baudelaire understood too much. He collapsed outside a church and died soon after. He shattered the windows of the reader's stuffy consciousness and let in fresh air, so one could tell the difference between that and the human excrement which was being regurgitated all across Europe. It is Baudelaire who keeps me from judgment; also from acting. A tightrope. That is how my sex feels. Wound achingly like a road into the hills where a mist comes down in the evening to blind acuity. But there is nothing wrong with intellectual adventuring is there? I have to keep my failings better veiled. Even if Nickel Hawk, in a fit of pique, embarrassed at my observation, has left her silk pyjamas rolled up at the bottom of my bed. I went to the old cathedral and mooned about before the black façade.

15

While a typhoon sweeps around the South China coast, Camilo Conceição is wrestling with young Nickel Hawk. He makes fun of her, while she clambers above him, half angry and half triumphant when he pretends to submit. This is a close bond. His permanent depression seems to have lifted. He is rejuvenated. The shutters flap. One window is flung open and his papers fly. His precious collection.

If you look at his photos you will see he has been play-acting all along. In every single one he does not face the camera fully. His eyes are crossed, his big beard makes a mockery of his small body, that of a dwarf's, staring darkly straight ahead, at an invisible Snow White in the wings. It is true, he said his optical nerve entered his right eyeball at an odd angle. Once, disguised as a medical student at the university in Coímbra, he observed the instructor removing the eyeballs from a human head. He wanted to gag behind his mask. He then realised there was always a mask. He grew his beard longer. When you posed for photos you had to stand there for a long time for the exposure to take hold. To be exposed to death. He understood this exposition. He understood how we would be looking at him in the future. A portrait of Conceição captured in dead time, reproduced in biographies, on the covers of his collections of poems. The same photograph, mirrored everywhere in the glass of bookshops, reaching all the way back to that day in the photographer's studio, when he saw his eyes removed from his head and understood decomposition. What he does not tell us is how secretively he had preserved his original face with that beard. It will never fall apart and we will never know it.

He worked hard. He overworked, studying Chinese, reading

ancient texts in the original, preparing his lessons, learning about painting, writing his poetry. The last was the most difficult. The ghost of Baudelaire hovered heavily in the humid air. He had yet to find his path, but from his study of Oriental painting, he learned that first he had to copy the master and then slowly to steal his secrets. He learned by first placing himself at the opposite pole, in exile from industrious Europe, by immersing himself in this moral slag-heap which was even more commercial, full of graft, material gain and perverse sensuality. It would be impossible for him to have the same feelings as Baudelaire but he could assimilate this language, make it his, so that his own heart would be transformed along with it. He would do this by translating Baudelaire's *Spleen et Idéal* into Chinese. He would recover his strength if he improvised hellishly, breaking the rules of style. What would Baudelaire mean to the Chinese? They would like his indifference.

Cat

Nickel Hawk appeared stark naked at the door to my room while I was writing. I admonished her severely. I said she lacked decorum. I said only cats were so brazen, and what if we had visitors? Her mother heard the commotion and ran upstairs to drag her daughter away. Then Silver Eagle began to scold me for teaching her child *European ways*. There is nothing left for you to take away, she shouted, except her innocence. It is of no value to you.

There is a perfume left in my room; a mixture of muslin, velvet, silk and fur; it makes the rules of language seem porous and transient; perhaps I could soar on the wings of my beating heart. While I work, Silver Eagle spends nights away from the house. I know from what Nickel Hawk tells me that her mother is earning extra money. I do not ask what she does. We lead separate lives and providing she looks after my needs I do not question her. Yet this gossip has stirred me. Of course I am jealous. Of course Baudelaire was jealous, imagining his mistress in the arms of rough men. We are men first, not poets. We compose with the exultation of revenge. But we live with the idea of possession and the threat of abandonment. One should act first. I should turn it to my advantage, by teaching everyone a lesson. I have bought a ticket to Lisbon for a rest cure, as advised by Dr Gonzales. Silver Eagle and Nickel Hawk will weep and moan in case I do not return. Their golden goose has contracted asthenia.

I disembarked in Marseilles for an old calling. Increasingly unbound, I did not feel like returning home.

16

At this point the documents reveal nothing. A faded train ticket. A strand of horse(?)hair in a small red envelope with golden Chinese characters wishing everyone a happy new year. Strangely, what Conceição didn't dare experiment with in Macau, he tried in Marseilles once again. Observe the honey-coloured stains on the inside of the envelope: the indelible marks of the amber balls he kept rolled and bagged like jasmine tea which caused a little flaring above the candleflame; the three puffs he took, coughing slightly, for he had chronic bronchitis form the sea voyage; the way the day opened up inside him when he woke. There was no occlusion, which he experienced after heavy drinking. There was no semen over his eyes, which is what he said blinded him when Silver Eagle refused him sex.

He sat on the terraces of restaurants observing the faces in the morning. He wrote, without embellishment, of his newly acquired interest in physiognomy, of not having seen so many European faces for a year or so. He found them ugly, fleshy, too large. Chinese heads were nothing but waxed skulls. Here, these people were feasting constantly, their mouths open all day, chatting, yawning, eating. Red mouths, bulbous lips, yellow teeth. Hydrocephalic heads about to explode. The constant convulsions of their bodies.

He made his way to bustling Paris. Such hysterical crowds, driven into a stupor by the idea of Christmas. *Fin de siècle* insouciance; delirium; exhaustion. Easy optimism flung from lush salons like confetti. It would be a new century of horror, the world cheated by science. He took a train to Lisbon.

Restaurante em Lisboa

I am not one for discussing money.

My friends know that. Fernando, they say, you don't even spend words; you inhabit those of others. My name is Fernando Pessoa. I'm a poet. But I also have many other names. They are poets too.

You'll see me in second-storey eateries; dark, wooded, heavy places above the taverns. On Sundays they fill up a little. Noisy families with drooping faces straight from shopping in the arcades off the Chiado. Here in the 'Brasileira', António Botto and I sit at two small round tables, drumming out poor rhythms, chatting without wit about the riots at the university. Since our parents moved to Lisbon we have hardly ever left this city.

A small man enters, sailing to a nearby booth, tacking like a lorcha, bat-winged in his cape, jerking here and there to get it right, his beard before him, his dark eyes crossed above like large billiard balls nudging the heavy felt of his eyelashes. My friend António coughed and pointed with his chin and said that was Camilo Conceição. He had two poems, visions from Macau, in this quarter's *Orpheu* magazine. Botto introduced himself to the dwarf and beckoned me over to them, speaking with his hands as he always did when wildly excited, whether by poetry or by lipstick. The bearded poet looked alarmed. At first I thought his lips had fused behind the forest of facial hair. Then there was a tiny laugh and glittering teeth blackened by what we knew: oracles didn't come cheaply. Steering away from opinion, we chatted slowly about the relative merits of hashish and opium. Sooner or later, we experienced the feeling of oneness; sameness. We were doubled and tripled by the amorous joy of what we had previously inhaled in solitude, which now crackled into daylight from hidden pores. Immensely polite, we had no wish to offend. We spoke of painting and perspective, viewed under the influence. Conceição said he saw every painting as destitution or fortune; you could talk it up or talk it down. Like hypnotising roosters.

Botto, with moth-like transformations, powdered his nose and waved a horsehair violin bow about, conferring a ridiculous dignity upon our meeting, which had now seemed destined, and one fine grey strand from the poor animal's tail floated into the poet's beard. The latter did not seem to notice, but said, after a moment's hesitation: 'There's still life in old hobbyhorses'.

Botto later said Camilo was the pope of tropes. Of course he was referring to the bicycle, Botto exclaimed. He's writing a poem. Lisbon is crowded with bicycles, poets and hobbyhorses. Conceição had written down my name before he left. *Peso*. No, Pessoa, I repeated. A person; it's no one. That was the one and only time I ever met the celebrated symbolist. We paid for his meal. When he had gone, Botto shrugged, loosing off one of those remarks of his I'd always found fatuous. Nature spends us, he said. Look at my stomach.

We were aloft for a moment, believing we were poets, that there was significance in human memory made out of human words … before a slow lobotomy adjusted the balance. We watched the other patrons eating slow-cooked African chicken, and listened to the rain outside. At our age we were all interchangeable.

17

It was a chance meeting between two poets. But through greater fortuity, Conceição, intoxicated by Lisbon, deliberating whether or not to return to his family in the East, tossed a coin to decide the matter. He could not act like the judge he used to be, yet he still rationalised, even after the coin lay still on its 'Oriental' side. For him, Europe would be all repetition. He had to strike out on his own. He called on his friend's sister, Hannah Osório de Castro, with whom he was 'involved' in an unrequited love, and melodramatically begged her to write letters to him so he could inhale her perfume when he unsealed them. It was an overture and a farewell. It decided the matter. Having said this, he could never go back on his word, for it would be grave cowardice. He said he would never return. She was disturbed by this, but could do nothing. She did not love him. He was like a little dog, charming and helpless. Her feeling was quite different from passion or love. Camilo knew this was all play-acting; he couldn't help it. He imagined a permanent camera lens pointing at him. His little provocations. Steadfast love was not for the ugly. In Macau, a wife could at least be bought and this freed him. Exchange value untangled all kinds of emotion. With this secret safe in his heart, he would be able to relinquish that organ for poetry. Hannah spent one sleepless night and then dismissed the idea that he was serious. She wanted to help him without being compromised. She had a small annuity. While the oblique rain swept past her window, she fantasised: she would invest in a small printing press; she would make him famous.

It is almost unimaginable how difficult it is to get a glimpse of Conceição; how he keeps fading when you look too closely. There is no diary, no serious biography, only scraps of poems, some of which had been published by Hannah Osório de Castro, some of which remain undiscovered until now. Camilo Conceição reveals and conceals himself in rain and mists, pumping out poetry in a periodic diastolic and systolic motion, contracting and dilating like the arteries of his heart. Sometimes the world rocked with his body. Dictated to him.

18

Hannah was his childhood sweetheart. It was only when he went away to the Far East and then returned briefly to Portugal on account of ill health that he saw her again with new eyes. She had blossomed. Her flaxen hair waved in the wind. Her *celéste* silk dress fluttered about her shapely legs. She had put on weight. When she undertook the journey to Lisbon in order to meet him, he thought she had developed a love for him. Not knowing how love works, that it is, in its passionate variety, a weakening at first sight, he thought the other could *grow* into love. In his isolation in Macau he dreamt of how he would love her and by dreaming in this way, imagined himself into love *as it would be expressed* by Hannah, who was burgeoning like a blue hydrangea.

So when she met him on the corner of the Rua Augusta and walked with him at his suggestion, to the Almada Negreiros exhibition, he felt it to be a major coup. She had declined lunch as she was meeting a friend earlier and luncheon in a pavilion by the river would have run like a ladder in her stocking into the late afternoon and there would be pauses and soon a change of heart. But here she is, holding on to his arm as they step off the sidewalk, her long dress almost too stylish with its lace and swinging tassels at the hem, brushing against his unironed trousers, his shabby coat, the holes in his armpits. He was saying to her how important it was to write from experience. Under his other arm, a folded newspaper. The headlines had proclaimed a huge disaster. An earthquake had hit San Francisco. A huge fire had followed, and most of the city had been destroyed. If it were not for his anaemia, Camilo Conceição said, he would go there, to see for himself. Don't be so silly, Hannah said. You are such a one for first hand impressions. Doesn't a photograph capture it for you? No, he said. He was thinking how he could never just visualise. He had to feel it in his heart. When he looked away from her ... indeed, he was incapable of looking straight at her to study her because there was an earthquake in his heart and he was crossed-eyed to boot ... when he looked away, he thought how beautiful she had become. It was the glow of sexual experience, which would darken for him at a later stage.

Hannah however, was hardly ever silent about feeling, so had she never expressed an interest in him, no matter how slight? Here she was rattling on about earthquakes. On All Saints' Day, she said, on the morning of November 1, 1755, two shocks, forty minutes apart, raised the waters of the Targus. A huge tide swelled up from the riverbed and thundered through the city. Churches collapsed; fires erupted. Thirty thousand lives were lost. What can be learned from disasters, both man-made and natural? she asked.

I think apart from platitudes, that all of this is both cyclic and immanent, he replied. It is only newspapers and photographs which have brought us the catastrophe as though it were new; made it ours as a novelty; but these are perpetually without reality. It is the way we have decided to speak... at arm's length from the disaster which 'will never happen to us'... which disengages us from life, but it is also this necessity which unites us. So what we can learn is to speak less of catastrophe and more of human experience. In other words, to see and feel proximity for ourselves, rather than simply to fantasise. In this way we quickly learn that living is a daily tragedy.

He meant his failing attempts to engage her love. He somehow meant that if there were an instant catastrophe she would immediately fall into both his arms. In his clumsiness he let the folded newspaper slide into the gutter. She laughed a tinkling laughter. Hannah never let a good argument go past. On her own admission, it was because she was Jewish. But she delighted in arguing with her friend from childhood. She liked to tease Conceição, who was small and bristly, like a little bear. Of course it is the case with everything that there should be more reflection, she said, more sympathetic imagining – which, I think, is quite different from inserting oneself into the event in order to understand it. If one can understand something only by washing it through oneself, then what a tiny little world that would be!

The water in the gutter was black, like the gutters in Macau. He thought about picking up the newspaper, but was paralysed by what she would think. Then again, it conveyed an important tragedy and could not be left in the dirty water. He decided against it. He had bought the paper after all. He could buy another. Let the gutter water wash through the catastrophic event. For a moment he saw that one of the rapidly soaking pages bore a headline that read *Silver Eagle*. No, it was the price of silver. It had gone up. He had sworn to keep that part of his life a secret.

I would agree to disagree over the tiny world washed through one's experience, he replied. I would say that is the only thing worth reading ... the tiny world. It is the truth in its experience. I take Degas' cautionary remark about 'painting falsely' to heart. The price of tin was up as well, he noticed. Brazilian mines were closing down. Of course, he continued, the imagination can enlarge and can profoundly open one's way of viewing; but there is a danger of gilding the lily. A tinny sound emanates from false flowers. Though when the cracked bell of the world is struck by a real artist, Hannah interjected, it begins to ring true.

That was the problem. All this talk. What was he feeling? Indifference or empathy? He was no good at it, but was simply happy to have her there. He noticed she was in good spirits, her forearms up, fingers outstretched, raising each shoulder alternately. She had rouged her lips. Then he had a thought like a blowfly he encountered in the country which stuck to his forehead persistently, winging off whenever he raised his hand. She had been lunching with someone else. There was a scent of alcohol with her perfume. A touch of garlic on her breath. How idiotic of him to have assumed she had come to Lisbon simply to meet him!

Hannah adjusted her hair. She pinned it back and reset the angle of her black hat. She let a silence ensue, which no doubt he was misinterpreting as a reflection on his words. No, she did not think he was a true artist. At least not yet. But what she had to tell him was not that. She was going to tell him that she was getting married; that she was already secretly engaged to an important man, Diogo de Melo Sampaio, a minister in the government who owned a publishing company. It would be Sampaio's second marriage and he did not want this to be announced prematurely.

I am intending to publish a selection of your poetry ... she said to Conceição ... in a limited edition.

She saw the joy in his face beneath his beard. Perhaps it was a sign of the transition in him: from not being worthy of her to being noteworthy in the world. Just as well. He heard the gurgle in the still pool, the small earthquake in his heart, the tidal wave of his ambition. Something at least had been rescued from his disappointment. But still, the residue. Her blue figure in the distance as he left her. The crack of the wind of experience. Don't you run away, he said to himself. But he did.

Praia

To arrive at a seawall. The point beyond which you can no longer go. See how the waves crash over the stone and froth up on the footpath. In years to come the passages between these islands will silt up with sand, causing time to collapse ... I will be able to ride my trishaw across all of them in hardly any time. Time, which has always been a law, will be defeated not by sand, but by writing. How can this be so? Because the discovery of my poems will open up new worlds. I write this on the back of a cheap painting I've bought, to a woman I've loved, but can love no longer. It was an association brought about by my sickness. She loved me because she could pity me. I loved her perhaps because she didn't care enough. That has always been the case with love from time immemorial. But what has this to do with time? Well then, we shall see.

Every morning I ride my tricycle to this point on Coloane island in Macau, innured to the irritant of its wheels squeaking against the worn brakes. I stop and watch dealers selling paintings here by the sea-wall. They are here when the sea is calm. It would seem like a better idea to sell paintings in galleries or shops, so there must be a reason why they are risking the unpredictability of the sea. Perhaps because they, the sellers, do not know worth or quality, obsessed by the easy money that passes through their hands. I look at the faces. These are not coarse. Not the worn, sunken cheeks of coolies. Their clothing is drab, but remarkably clean. They stand here by the sea-wall and prop up their paintings on the stone and watch for the sea drilling a small aperture at their feet. See how the water drains back through the tiny gap. They did not paint these scrolls and wall hangings. All part of their family heirloom. They are selling them off because the revolution has begun. The last emperor has abdicated and the Manchu dynasty has collapsed. Last night a man presented himself at my house and asked for my support. I thought at first he was a fugitive, a political refugee. I received him in my bath. It took me a while to recognise him. He was in no need, I could see that. His high collar was immaculate. He wanted the support of the new Republican Portuguese government, which had taken power from the monarchists a year before. I told him ... he had a sensitive round face, a salt-and-pepper moustache and a winning smile ... that I had no official standing in the enclave. Nevertheless, he said. He shook my hand for some time before hastily departing. My bathtub is a throne. He had refused the tea Silver Eagle brought upstairs, where he had insisted we meet in the strictest privacy. I believe he thought I had had something to do with the assassination of the last Portuguese king.

19

They are selling off their silk-screens, their pots, their silver and their gold. Members of the old imperial regime. They have no shops in which to display their wares. They have no time. The time entombed within this art is irrelevant. Collectors like to argue down the price. It helps when a knowledgeable foreigner acts as a comprador, a dragoman, a translating dictionary, who can supply catalogues of these works for visiting connoisseurs. It goes without saying that catalogues too, can be inspired, tipping the scales this way or that, guaranteeing that the chinoiserie which ends up in Paris or Rome is authenticated by weighty time, by the time of Han and Sung, not by the stamped and rotten wooden frames out of which bespectacled collectors, those wily borers, have emerged, feeding off pale-faced Mandarins.

He trails along the seawall in the mornings, studying art. This has now become his specialty. The dour and down-at-heel Mandarins kowtow. They know him as a former judge with high connections. Gossip did its rounds about his trips back to Lisbon, how he took six paintings with him and returned with overflowing pockets. Untrue of course. They present their collections to him. He is their saviour, Macau the exit-door for them from the terror that is still to come. Dr Sun-Yat-Sen writes to him from Nanking, asking: *How's your bath?* When he met up with Dr Sun-Yat-Sen in Hong Kong, the future leader was on the run from someone or something. He kept looking over his shoulder, even in the China Club, where it was so dark and so heavy with teakwood beams he had every right to do so. Maybe he was thinking of carving inscriptions on the ceiling. But after their one cup of tea at the table near the bar, the great man leant over and made his excuses. His last words to Conceição were: *China will be democratic, just like the bicycle.* He is well established now, he informs Conceição, and was in thrall of a beautiful girl who brought him a case of Californian fruit. *Chingling,* her name like wind-chimes, he wrote. 'I am not sure,' he added, 'if it is a box of truly Californian fruit, since it arrived in Shanghai on board a Filipino mango clipper. But I was very touched and as Director of Railways, have given her a free pass – as well as several for her friends – to travel wherever they wish in the new republic. However, I would like to entice her back, and would appreciate your send-ing me a painting by Liu Sung-nien, whom she admires greatly. Anything by him will do, as I am well aware from your catalogues that thirteenth-century painters from the Southern Sung are being picked up for a song in Macau.'

Each morning he checks the condition of the light. Then he takes his stroll, zigzagging along the Praia, to peruse paintings. If the light is good and there is not too much haze, he should be able to see lorchas and tankas spreading bat-wing sails to make for the channel. When he looks at the paintings he sees a repetition everywhere. Ancient Chinese painting is a re-creative art. It works by appropriation, through copying and expanding. When he sees a painting that takes his fancy, he tries to buy it for a bargain price, claiming it to be a copy. Sometimes he succeeds, but when the seller doesn't smile, when he looks seriously depressed, as though an expert has discovered something, a flaw he himself didn't know about, then Conceição is assured that the painting is worth a lot more than he thought. He takes it home, places it on the floor in his bathroom. The floor is made of ceramic, clay and gilt-wood tiles. A Chinese parquet. He lies down in his empty bath and warms up a honey-ball and takes a pipe. Two puffs. He can only get it down to two. Sometimes he takes three. Experts only take one draw. He has his darkness and then his ecstasy. In the afternoons, when it begins to rain, he has no classes. Language is best transmitted in the morning. In the afternoons, he heats water and takes a real bath. Here he can consider the art that he has bought. Water and weather corruscate feelings, sand down romance. He takes up his brush and works over the silk, without any ink or paint, dabs and swirls over the scroll in a dry run. If it is a landscape by a good artist, he will be able to determine the moment by the movement of the master's strokes. Rapidity. There is always a 'moment' in the best paintings when all is revealed. Hear the rhythm. When the weather changes, the sky turning to rain, or there is a moment of fog, perhaps it is the evening mist, then there is less contemplation in a painting. One can feel a pressing need for expression; a desire for motion, to get in out of the elements. Yet there is this resistance to action. He refuses to colour in. That would only lead to grief at the point of the original. He can feel the pulse of the master.

Chiasma

These fogbound solitudes are rare, the room's my own for an hour before the women return with the smell of food, wet fish, all the stuff of life which makes me tremble before its generosity. I have no appetite, no stomach for the long fight with complex prose, with its inversions and crossings. Recalcitrant, I have my purchased indolence, tracing disappearing moments in the ordinariness of things: an evanescent conversation with a guest in a river pavilion; its paper walls reflect the candlelight and something primal strikes at understanding – place and fire – the placid river running beneath. A humpback bridge. See these clumps of branches forking over the cool summerhouse. I could have learned how to represent that once; heard the trout jump at dusk and fall back like a sexual sting, the slap of water, and then felt how nature undermined desire, it was so much vaster and surprising, with dark terror held in reserve. But let me attribute these paintings: to Liu Sung-nien, to Ma Yüan, to Hsia Kuei. You may not know them, but they have hidden secret signs in their paintings. As a Freemason I know something about signs and symbols ... how they work in stone. An emotion does not come upon you, but the other way round. You chance upon it because you have made it available. Because art is time mastered. Hidden there, it surprises you. Only because it has been long forgotten. A river-bend. A cracked teapot. Yet you have expected them all along. I paint *The Conversation with a Guest in a River Pavilion* all over again, and this time I have already invited Hannah into our scenario. I do not want to know Hannah's other game; her other lover, her artist friend who is not her husband-to-be, scurrying into the mountain hut with her, making the best of the moment before her marriage. For the teapot at the river-bend is a sign, a warning for all of us who relinquish friends and guides and mentors ... tramping through the solitary pass to our ruin ... this is what is hidden within us when the weather changes: the lonely river-bend, the broken teapot.

I paint *The Conversation with a Guest in a River Pavilion*. The side of the wall closest to the viewer is open. It is an open conversation, the sort we carry on in a restaurant that is not crowded, so that the table over the other side can hear everything we say very clearly. The moment is a moment of secret confidence, given in friendship, to be overheard. It is a testimony to others of our sexual conviction. Currency for this moment only. They have brought the first course of minced pork patties, made from pork cheese and olives kneaded together, dipped in beaten egg and bread crumbs and fried in butter. The musicians are setting up. They have brought in a famous *erhu* player, a refugee from Manchuria, whom I have specially requested. Hannah picks up her chopsticks delicately. With a cup of rice wine we begin our *almôndegas*. Hannah's eyes are blue and they are sad. I catch myself in one of the Chinese mirrors on a pillar and find myself ugly. It is how things always begin. My feelings intensify because of this disparity between us. If I were handsome, love would only occur briefly. There would be no suffering. I would move on. Maidens stand at the door to the kitchen, their arms in their sleeves, singing softly. The rice wine warms my stomach. The only way I can keep Hannah in this painting is to be disinterested. I ask her about her new husband-to-be. She smiles and lies. Her eyes are wet. I pretend to look at the menu. My hands are moist, my heart is pounding. The weather outside suddenly changes. It has become achingly cold, without a wind, without a storm. Subtly, quietly, the ice maidens crack when they move. I am done with dusk. Liu Sung-nien's painting darkens on my clay, ceramic and gilt-wood tiles. Why am I not roused? We are served the second course, *caril de camarão*, shrimp curry, cooked in tamarind, chillies, saffron and paprika. But as I trace Ma Yüan's *Banquet by Lantern-Light*, I am no longer with Hannah but eating alone in a mountain restaurant with the mist layering above. I have forgotten my guest, and now I paint with the idea of a gift in mind. The dark peaks loom behind and their fearsome size makes me shiver and I feel that my enhance-ment of these historic paintings ... my desecration of them through my lazy doodling, my restoration of this restaurant ... they all open aspects, scenes, perspectives which I did not know were there. Dark,

dark, the almond-smelling night, pine-needles beneath my feet. Third course *bebinca de leite*, milk, sugar and lemon rind, cornflour in coconut milk, stir in egg yolks. Grilled slightly brown and cooled. I am painting over *Tall Pines by a Mountain Lodge in Snow*. This is not the same as copying. While copying might be a transmission of culture, painting-over is not an imitation, but a divining of the ancient master. A restoration of feelings by walking the road oneself, aware of the immense danger of destruction on one side ... one false move and the original trace is gone forever ... and on the other, the possession of a secret, which once acquired, can be re-used, where the true heart is a trained heart *confided*. My second pipe after dessert. Flurries of snow drifting under the door. I am working fast, but not up to standard. I am giving away much competence and relying on improvisation. The icy formalism of this hanging scroll has forced me to place it over my bamboo screen which partitions my room from the landing. Thus I can hear sounds of entries and exits, the social condition of my house which binds me to the world. But when there is a small movement behind the screen, a soundless step, the glimpse of a familiar earlobe which slender fingers have revealed by pushing back a strand of raven hair, I grow deaf to all save the avalanche in my chest, the subsiding snow on the opposite slope. But when she moves away from the threshold and glides down the staircase I see all the flaws in my screen, the knotted joints of bamboo, the clumsy strokes, the inability to turn the weather from rain to mist. Then a pain. Jealousy. What was she doing at that moment? What was her intention? Her time given now to others. My *jalousie* screens me. The discipline of work is not to hope. Hush! She returns. Her innocence before her, she waits by the opening. Normally in her nightshirt, she comes in to tell me about her day at school. She learns the things I have already taught her – how to tell the tone of a painting or a poem – between what is crisp and natural, without labour, and what is affectation. Only what you can lament, I said, was without affectation. She did not understand, but saw the tear in my eye. Mr Crocodile, she calls me. I admonish her. It is not right, I said, to sit at the foot of my bed each night in your nightshirt, especially when your mother is out. It seemed she understood that as an affectation. And so for several nights I was able to work without interruption, stretched upon equal tensions, my moral wrack, upon this dunghill of a city. I paint without eyes. I don't intend these works to be rediscovered; no bleaching to reveal a palimpsest beneath. She passes behind my screen again. The shine of red silk pyjamas, the little hairclip I had given her moving along the top of the lacquered partition. Without eyes, I try to absorb the moment when the painting changes. Suddenly, a drizzle, then a storm. Hsia Kuei's *Rainy Landscape*: hillocks, wet foliage, misty lowlands.

Could I not have travelled to Europe instead?

Beethoven, deaf, unable to converse without signs, received his guests, two fellow musicians, I was saying to Nickel Hawk. (Yes, lightly she has come to the end of my bathtub). He had written something. Macbeth, Beethoven had said to the others. The landscape of Macbeth. It is not Scotland; it is not China; it is a place in his head. A ghost, it refuses to disappear. They rehearse the 'Ghost' trio. Key of D. Flurry, then melody. The impatience of an old man. His fingers fly over the keys. On a slope, lined with trees at the top of the hill, a figure walks across a bridge. I can hear her wooden clogs. Two buckets and a bamboo pole slung across small shoulders. Warm water. She has brought warm water, pushing aside very gently the *jalousie*, standing now behind me, pouring the water upon my back. Second movement. I remember: I was suffering an influenza. I could not stay quiet for more than two minutes; sneezing, coughing. I timed myself with a watch. I was in London. Living in a very cold, mouse-ridden flat. I did not have the stamina of Baudelaire. I walked to rid myself of the ague. For miles and miles I walked. Then I walked back to Russell Square, where there was a small concert in progress in a small church off Kensington Road. Beethoven's 'Ghost Trio'. I show Nickel Hawk the importance of the painting, the change in the weather. It was hard to keep my cough under control during the recital. I had fallen into a feverish love for the violinist. I gave the last of my gold sovereigns to her after the performance.

Are you not afraid of soaking, Nickel Hawk asks, with all this steam and water and coughing? She means the paintings. I have placed them on the edge of the bath. The bamboo blinds filter steam through their ribs. Beethoven was too deaf to realise his piano was out of tune, I said, ignoring her warning. Some of the keys produced no sound at all, only a kind of muffled hammering. He heard the music only in his head and he raced, slowed, without listening for his cellist and violinist. It was horrendous. All this steam and horror. Close your eyes when you approach me in the bath, I ordered. She turned away. She turned her back. Stood at the door. 'How can I learn about the change in painting then; the moment at which the weather in the spirit turns?' she complains.

20

Cold. Conceição shivers. He has sent Nickel Hawk out to the shops because he needs things to inspire him. More opium from the pharmacist, from the old man with snakes in bottles, foetuses in jars. But also more of the cheap scrolls from the dime shops, for which she will have to bargain. He is teaching her. Well, how to recognise what is artless from what is art, for one thing. Is a foetus art? No, but it is a creation of the body. But *Camilo* (Nickel Hawk uses his name because he said it was a present for her ... not even her mother, Silver Eagle herself, could do this, use his first name, for he was always Sire, or Don, or *Mestre* ... though Nickel Hawk could only address him in private with this valued currency) ... Camilo has collected the moods of his painters, capturing all those atmospheres, saving them up like slow money for use in his poetry, dark depressions which he can study and then release. Camilo said this was *capital*, something which Nickel Hawk thinks is very powerful, seductive, like her little budding breasts, which the old pharmacist is gleaning with his eyes, sweeping this way and that, not lingering, remarkably swift and agile, tiny black swallows, very mobile for an old, supposedly weak-sighted man, sharp wings of glances which take in pleasure from beauty; almost the real thing. Soon. Capital for her.

Conceição has not only collected paintings of dubious value since the rest of the world knows little about this period of Chinese art, but he has collected a family as well. He purchased them. Given that Nickel Hawk is turning out to be a beauty is pure luck or grief for him. *Eurasian*; looked down upon as a curio. A relic of historical traces to be treated with semi-respect because it is impure, though not in-bred, thought to be clever, immune to diseases and above all, since it draws from disparate cultures, sexually potent, nymphomanic, highly strung, emotionally dependent. Jealous-cheating-possessive. And on the other side, seductive-sultry-passive. Conceição's shock at the discovery that Nickel Hawk was the daughter of Silver Eagle and the Procurador has changed his feelings. He no longer has this ideal 'secure' little family he has purchased. She told him as much, his bartered wife. No way back when money has changed hands. But now he cannot touch Silver Eagle; I mean, he cannot bear to be near her because he imagines her thin body beneath the Procurador's, which is oily and fat and even though he knew of her past, her lovers were faceless and he had rescued her from them; but now ... now he cannot remove the Procurador's pock-marked face from his mind and he cannot touch her, for fear of contracting a hatred for her. Jealous-cheated-alien. Silver Eagle was part of his collection. She was bought, possessed, and restored. When he collected her, he purified her, saved her from being a commodity, returned to her the dignity and aura of a wife and woman. But now ... what about Nickel Hawk? She didn't even have the status of being classed among the *cabritos*, children of white men and half-caste women. Thinking about lineage gave him a sexual tingle; that it was possible to procreate ... redeem Nickel Hawk's pale visage, her light-coloured eyes which burned in the street ... possible to save her from predatory men and rapacious history.

Desejos/Desires

I teach Portuguese with a headache, waiting for the world's destruction, a tidal wave ringing the South China Sea to vomit up yellow silt in the corridors. The maids had to clean the floors this morning; choleric, the boys before me sick from breathing in this city of rotting cats. A cholera epidemic. Why not watch out of my window instead, the schoolgirls in their starched blouses hopscotching through the miasma with the pride of innocence?

Above the flat sea a hawk hovers, kingfishing for shrimp in translucent water made fresh by the morning tide, running with the ebb to pick stragglers off the sand, silvery crustaceans coiling, droplets of water spilling from its beak.

Yesterday, Sunday, we lay head to foot in the long bed, lazy from sunlight. In no mood to wrestle, we read instead, Robert Louis Stevenson, though I recall nothing of the story, save the way Nickel Hawk tickled my foot with her hair as she turned the pages. None of this could you call uniquely paternal love; besides, it is a long journey from ethics. And why not? The moment was given to examining the way Western culture has always presumed that the moral high ground belonged to innocence. There are millions of examples of the world not operating this way. There is no innocence in Macau.

Not going there now though. My class of boys are reciting Camões with correct pronunciation. Their voices are soft and tentative, but one day they will yell and curse, burn these poems to symbolise their independence, leave school behind, riot in the streets and then find jobs in order to dress like me and work in an office only to learn again, the correct grammar of their bosses. They will take girls who are not their wives to their beds and one by one they will return to Portugal and dream, on magnetic nights when the moon is full, sailing in their baths, nostalgic for their little beautiful *cabritos* and the possibility of finding pork dumplings in Lisbon.

I discard my high collar and my tie for good.

I take over the cooking, wear a long white linen gown which is soon bespattered with sauce.

For the filling: 1 onion, finely chopped; 1 clove of garlic, finely chopped; olive oil for frying; 1 teaspoon of finely sliced fresh ginger; 2 fresh chillies, finely chopped; 1 carrot, finely diced; 2 potatoes, cut into small cubes; 100 g (3 ½ oz, ½ cup) green peas; 1 tablespoon ground coriander; 2 teaspoons curry powder; 1/2 teaspoon saffron; 1 teaspoon salt; 1 tablespoon lemon juice; 2 tablespoons breadcrumbs. *For the wrapping*: spring roll wrappers; egg white; oil for deep-frying; cut wrapper into strips, brush with egg white; fold.

There you have it: *chamuças*. Samosas. A triangular pastry. He sits between the women at the dinner table, a concept between two raptors. They eat in total silence. Something has changed forever. He has crossed over … there is no perspective and they are confused, fearing a loss of their livelihood.

Svelte, She Appears

She wades ashore, wet.

I have a panic attack, disorientation, vertigo. Not because of her white silk pyjama suit. Not because it is filmy, translucent as a jellyfish cruising off the island of Coloane; Portuguese man o'war, hydra headed, trailing stings of rebuke to my liquid meditations. Out there are swimmers of the unconscious and I need to be a judge; rescue some, drown others in shameful strings of evidence. I feel protective. A life preservative. Tightly it clings. Wet, she wades.

Today I failed to go to work for good. Night sweats, a strange fever which left my extremities freezing. Let's go to the beach! Nickel Hawk dragged me to the dinghy I kept moored near the temple. Somebody has evacuated himself in the boat, using the gunwale to hang his legs over while musing upon the sea. Never mind, turn the boat over in the shallows, retrieve it with my weak arms, lungs like gasping bellows – I try to present a strong face. Suction as we drag it out. Bail water. Clean. Catch the oar in the deep green, standing one foot on the transom, waggle out Chinese fashion.

Wet she wades, treading the ginger bottom of an old sea. Willowy, still innocent, swaying, squeezing dry her dark brown hair. She's grown taller. I've failed to work today; failed to teach her, failed to write. What matter when she surprises me from behind, landing on my back with force, her breasts, her quivering heart conjoined! In the clear shallows we mime seahorses, the glittering water clouding briefly, mirroring the sky. How can I reach, she splutters, cleansing her face of all false dignity, the second level of experience? You mean in art? Of course, she sighed, knowing more than I, in this time of failure. The first level, I said, was simply the level of competence and cleverness. Hard work patching together design, scraps of beauty. The second level is to banish thought – to swim in the sea and not to know why things flow the way they do in accordance with any truth until the moment of enlightenment – it is said only men can achieve this kind of detachment after many years of meditation. She scoffed at that. Pure selfishness, she said. She was wrestling with me in the sea. I have to kill the hydra-head now, for it will grow in time. A brief braggadocio upon my moral victory. I am not Heracles. In my bathroom, much later, the clepsydra drips out its tortured time-scale and my desire is stilled. The water-serpent, preserved in a vessel, this friend of orators, whispers a filibustering wish-wash. Today I did not go to work; I stole my life back from routine; I stole her in sleep, the never-purchased sylph who swims among jellyfish, wet and sea-salted. Oh, how I melt!

You see how his dish was presented. His confession, which is folded in a dream, served in a moment of private conversation with a blonde female guest in a river pavilion.

After that particular fugue of Conceição's (his *Dinner by Lantern-light in a River Pavilion*), on the 21st September 1916, when he imagined he was confessing to a woman of the future about his moral failure ... obviously with an eye to the posterity of his poems ... he would write nothing more for several weeks. He was trying to attract catastrophe. Because he saw every experience as a *rehearsal*, he purchased what was possible in order to make what he had rehearsed, real. He doesn't tell you how to cook the samosas; that the filling had to be sautéed, placed in an oven at low heat etc. He wrapped what was raw. It was never meant to be the final product. He thought he had time for that; for marinading morality. He thought if he *rehearsed* life, his imagination would converge with reality and everything would be fulfilled and accommodated. But by not enforcing reality, by not facing it, he invited catastrophe.

He had collected more than two dozen poems at this stage and was on the verge of sending them to Hannah in Lisbon when Nickel Hawk confided to him that she was pregnant. There are no personal notes or poems which register his reactions. Nickel Hawk was confined to the house and Silver Eagle was going to pass the child off as her own. It surprised him how easily he accepted the news. He had already rehearsed all that. There was even some joy. He walked back and forth along the waterfront, among the stalls in the marketplace, talking to anyone who would listen. Yes, he was about to be a father, can you believe that! The Chinese were complimentary, some even overjoyed to hear from this foreigner who spoke such good Cantonese, that his Chinese wife was pregnant. They envied Silver Eagle; producing a son with a Portuguese man guaranteed her a golden future. They didn't talk when they heard it was Nickel Hawk. At the blacksmith's, the Procurador watched a cutlass being hammered out over an anvil. He was being promoted. Now, he said to the engraver, the judge is one of ours.

22

The Conceição archives yield some juvenile sketches. No, not by him.

August, 1916, sailing to China in a wooden cabin on a creaking ship, sails collapsing periodically when the wind dies, the moist, cold air eroding your face. The two women had left Sydney a week before. They are standing by the port rail, at the back of the ship, on the third deck, talking passionately, sometimes one touching the other, because this is how it works ... there is the lover and the beloved, and it is the lover who instigates everything, because the beloved doesn't need to ... and perhaps is flattered rather than anything else. She touches the other on the back, kisses her cheek. One blonde, the other dark. One taller than the other. Edge closer to hear the conversation. They are talking animatedly now, their phrases catching in the wind. Nothing anyone can make out. Speaking English with a slight twang and flattened vowels. Yeh, yeh. Off to China. Intepid women. Delphine and Hippolyte; heroines of modern travel. It is their industry that impresses. Even on board ship, one of them, the fair one, is constantly sketching. The beloved. The beloved always has time. There she is again, leaning her pad on the iron rail which smells of paint, but she is used to paint and loves the different varieties of smells so they have a colour, these odours. But on board ship she cannot drag out all her own paints. Besides, the lover doesn't approve. Why do you have to be preoccupied all the time? Surely we can have moments of dreaming together, of laziness, of pure indolence? But the beloved cannot help herself. Her industry is pure, for no reason, perhaps simply because emptiness is a gulf for predators. They swoop. Men, women. Upon her lips. She has thin lips, which makes her fragile-looking, nervous, flighty.

The lover takes this in, watching a wisp of hair drag itself across her beloved's mouth. Despair befalls those who stoop to drink there! The lover is dark, her hair cut short, shorter than current fashion allowed. In Australia she sometimes wore a wig because construction workers on the building opposite her King's Cross studio called her a Nancy Boy. A harsh place for women, Australia. A hostile place for artists, even though she called herself an artisan, because she didn't believe in art for art's sake. An impossible place for the warrior in her. Not because of her fear, but out of fear of her temper. What she might do. Her Swedish father had eaten raw seal meat off the coast of Tasmania in order to survive his geographical expeditions. He placed himself beyond them all. His wife, her mother, complained day and night, then on her deathbed, blaming her daughter for not having taken care of her. That was enough. That was the end. Her father returned to an empty house. He had a mistress but he didn't want to lose his daughter. He gave her money. An annuity. He said: Anna, you will not extend the Ångström line, so I have had to find other means.

Motherhood. She could not bear hearing the name. All sticky blood. In France, at the potters' studio in Cerbère, she starved herself. She thought that if she grew thin, she would be finished with all that blood. She fell ill and the others were worried. Meister Gleize, the cubist painter, sent for the doctor from the next village. The maestro said her work did not demand such sacrifice. Perhaps if she went home to fetch her beloved and returned next year? But then she would not return. She was starting to discover something new in France. She urged Julia Grace to investigate it fully, though she said this new thing, Cubism, it was called, was 'a domain proscribed, out of reach of photography, but still servile to architecture.' It was becoming a favourite of Freemasons, and signaled the end of emotions. Anna wrote long letters to her uncomprehending beloved.

If only Julia could prolong this moment. Time aboard ship is always time forgotten, because it is only an interstice for the sake of the journey; a time for the goal of arriving. That is why she is making every moment count. Look at the way Anna stares at her, kisses her, looks out across the water in a dark sea change. Julia tries to avoid the plenitude of time, which is always a gulf. Only the moment counts. She turns her back upon the sea and rests her folio on the canvas cover stretched tight over a lifeboat. She thinks of her sheep farm, her mother, the maids, an isolated, genteel life. She believes in Anna's politics, especially when the latter says women needed to be freed from the price of their bodies. Only then could a woman be truly creative. Julia really does believe, but knows the price of the body is still there, whether paid for by men or by women.

Julia Grace leans over the lifeboat and sketches. She appears very beautiful at that moment and shivers slightly in the moistened air of a sea-stroked dusk. Anna places her cape around her beloved's shoulders and leans over her to see what she has drawn. She has sketched a portly man wearing braces and a red bow tie, sporting an enormous mane of greying hair, looking anxious and worried at the opposite rail, his right thumb stroking his moustache, a cigarette between his pudgy fingers, looking equally ostracised and equally vulnerable, as though he'd just been surprised on the toilet.

Violin Arcades

Every morning I check the condition of the light over the Pearl River Estuary. I am mostly disappointed at the verses I disgorge – shrimp scurrying towards the fake glimmer of love. I buy paintings, bargain for the right price. The quality is dwindling now, the lesser known, lesser works of jaded masters. I understand the way they offered themselves, took on prostitution for a basketful of fish. They had to eke it out, salted fillets of their talent, dessicated in the noon-day heat. And so I elaborate, varnish their stroke with mine, and being word-obsessed, write catalogues for their enhancement.

I collect dogs as well. Three or four small ones. Pekinese varieties. Jars and vases, porcelain and bronzes. Nickel Hawk frets at home … she's started vomiting … but now Silver Eagle takes an interest in the fact my father has passed on, leaving me seven thousand miles away, much richer than when I first arrived. My birds enlarge the house preparing for more prosperity, though they are forbidden to remove my rolls of Chinese paintings rotting against the humid masonry in my secret rooms, my soul. I have become a reprobate.

The Procurador's son came one day, a simulacrum of his father, oiled with baby fat. He offered to buy the best preserved paintings, but I exaggerated the prices, turning mediocre works into master-pieces, and in the end I bought his concubine instead, having once glimpsed her swaying in the old arcades in the central shopping district, her silk *quipao* split to reveal perfectly formed, perfectly normal feet, her toenails painted. She went cheaply because of them. Even small deformities fetched greater prices. She will be Nickel Hawk's companion and nurse. She walked behind me. She was tall and willowy. The crowds pushed us together and the human heat formed a foetid bath. Macau was a material and moral rubbish heap. I felt her small pointed breasts cushioning my earlobes. At the markets she blinked uncomprehendingly and fondled the dogs and smiled. I name her Number Three. Later on she will take on the name of 'Peregrine' rather than concubine. This higher status as mistress (involving emotional attachment) entitles her to a share of my possessions. She only told me later that she had ben married before and had come upon difficult times. She bore the rather aristocratic name of *De Rivière*. A first husband, you see, who was French. Who abandoned her of course, when he went back to Europe, gloriously eligible, already thin with cancer. My son by Nickel Hawk, whom I will call the Monkey, will adopt her name instead of mine. You see what vipers we bring into the world. A whole zoo. I allowed the Peregrine to bring her mother to the house and then I found that she had a sister, who shared her room. Her mother had a cousin, who shared the former's little quarters near the back of the court-yard. I built more rooms, hired coolies for the job, selected the stone myself from the pile of rubble left by the foreshore where dissidents had blown up a statue of a former governor. The Conceição For-tress. Silver Eagle is not happy at all.

I yearn to be transformed by something more than sex. In a house now surrounded by trees and women, I lie like Marat in tepid water waiting for rising jealousy to disgorge violence, a woman who would plunge a knife into my convulsing chest with professional detachment. My sheets are holed with burning cigarettes, I keep my opium near. The canopied bed rocks on high seas, its mast bearing a crown and two brass fish. In the spring my son will be born. We will name him Macau Conceição. A rhyme at least; Macau being a gambling game. Such eponymy; such economy. Little Macau, my dusky baby-chance, will be known by the unfortunate diminutive of *Macaco* or monkey, and will officially be registered as the son of Silver Eagle and Camilo Juanzinho Pereira Conceição.

23

15 February 1917

Dear Family,

Anna and I have finally arrived in Hong Kong. To think that it has taken almost three weeks at sea to get here! We stopped at Timor, Makassar, Manila, and it got more and more crowded as we steamed north. I am fine, but poor Anna took ill with fever and was laid up for days. It was rumoured she ate a bad pork sausage. She's a lot better now. Hong Kong is a haven for English speakers. An English doctor saw to her and she recovered almost overnight ... left me with the freedom to wander alone ... ate noodles at a stall and watched a Chinese opera ... they were trying to sell me vases and wooden boxes in the back lanes, claiming them to be antiques ... but the whole idea of antiquity is not well known, indeed it is invented, and there is a strange collapsing of time and treasures to be had ...

The prose is unnoteworthy, but you can see Julia Grace starting to

think on her own ... you can see from this letter that there are apha-
sic moments, *points de suspension*, into which she vertiginously falls.
She is curious. She wanders alone in a foreign place which is not
known to be safe for young blonde women. A smiling Chinese man
approaches. The alleyway is dark, full of squatting hawkers eating
rice, smiling, the grains falling from their lips which they retrieve
from the ground, trying to interest her in their teapots and jewellery, pathetic mounds of beaten tin, coloured glass shards strung
into necklaces sitting beside the catshit. The young man has very
smooth skin, as smooth and unaccented as his English. His breath
is warm with herbal cigarettes and mounds of vapour erupt from
his mouth to caress her hair. He says he will take her to Macau,
where there is very fine art to be collected. Not this rubbish. His
smile seems honest. She says she will think about it; she will consult
with her friend. You see, there were two of them and two would not
be easy to deceive or to rob. The young man will appear at the door
of their hotel in the morning. And the two women, yes, the Australians, would have already taken the early ferry to Macau.

As the steamer slows, entering the middle harbour in Macau waters, a
sampan appears, trolling a rope in its wake. Two women, one with
a small baby, are calling to passengers leaning over the rail to buy
some of their bric à brac. Humid scrolls depicting river gorges.
Copies, no doubt. Reproduced daily. Bronze pots, brass fish. Anna
waves them away. Anna uses her deep-throated laugh to indicate
scorn for their wares. But Julia begins to bargain over a painting.
A rainy landscape. She uses her fingers to indicate the price. Anna
tells her not to be fooled. Julia persists in the game, but Anna is
the heroine of communism, disavowing trade, erecting her moral
and infernal dominance over her friend and lover, she waves back
Julia's arm which extends over the side holding out a coin. They're
not beggars, Anna scolds. But Julia is already making a testament.
The divine ordinance to shed one's possessions is medieval, but it
is also the opposing half of the collector. God's voice: dispersal and
reclaiming. The coin clatters onto the deck of the steamer and as
she retrieves it, the package of letters she had been gripping under

her arm is released. Julia was hoping to give them back to Anna. Letters amongst letters. Anna's letters to her from Paris, from Cerbère, from Port Bou. Her own letters which she had kept from sending. She thought of destroying them. She had bundled them together but now they were all scattered and they floated down upon the two women in the tiny boat. Anna's entreaties. Julia's rebuffs. Freud would have said Julia's unconscious acted of its own accord. She was not comfortable with this evidence, even though she was a collector. The beloved acts; a teasing, spoilt child. Anna shouted. Ahoy! Can you give them back? The fisherwomen had already examined them and had put them into a basket in their sampan, thinking of throwing a rope up to them, but suddenly their tiny boat was dislodged from the wake of the ferry and the foreign women held up their hands in a gesture of futility as the sampan turned and sliced towards outlying islands.

All those formalities at the customs house. Green uniforms, red braid. Julia attracted gallants with moustachios, leering, smelling of cigarillos; *obrigado*; she smiled; she had no Portuguese; they could be saying anything to her and for a brief moment, the thought of a rough man above her – surprisingly, for the thought crept up out of pure fancy to dare and challenge Anna's propriety, her Edith Sitwell eccentricity, mad staring down of rough men, her superior look which men often received with disgust the moment they sensed that kind of business ... *if you like that sort of thing* was the remark they made – the thought of coarseness excited her; but for the moment there were smiles all round. They brought her a single rose. No, letters. Lost letters. They understood. The post, they said was very efficient. The women were catching a pedicab because they thought sedan chairs a demeaning practice. The rider looked half their size, pulling them through the soup of human bodies, *laila, laila, laila*, he shouted, threading his tricycle through the laneways up the hill with their boxes, to the Pousada San Francisco; a quick bath, separately, this was understood, bathing together not yet on the agenda, and some champagne out on the balcony listening to the cries from the hawkers and the Chinese water clock dripping below in the lobby, the humidity still cruel.

24

In his room a street away, Camilo Conceição lit up a third pipe, his poetry a bluish flame on the page. How could expression look so fake when examined? Words caught like insects in sticky ectoplasm. He hated his words. Baudelaire's ghost stuck to it so he couldn't think originally. Glued to the past which was also the future. He would be humiliated. He could see it all: Hannah's support for him; her defence of what others will call *forgery*, because it was always the words of others which he purchased, like the women he purchased, like the child, which was his, certainly, suckling now at Nickel Hawk's sore breasts, darkened by his own gummy lips; the child: which he had already seen greedily sucking everything from him, because *it had a claim on him*. He had no wish for any social approval. Caught in this sticky amber. There was no going back to a social world. No return to Lisbon where others will hoot at his insect aspirations while licking their fingers and turning the pages to explore his lascivious maidens from the East. Paris-Macau. Baudelaire-Conceição. It almost rhymed. He drew on his tattered shirt and walked outside and he was as one who was sleepwalking, shuffling blindly up the street along the Praia a tremulous hand against the low stone wall. Then the revulsion. The crowd hemming him in, elbowing him, slowing his flight; the future will dispense with him; the future was this crowd, spitting him out. The walk from his room where Baudelaire's handless clock sits on his night-table, to the clepsydra in the lobby of the hotel across the street where he will take his morning coffee, is a journey that takes more than one lifetime.

On the way, he gave alms to beggars. He wore no shoes. He could not act other than to give alms while dressed as a beggar himself. It purified him; gave him the sensation of levitation. His alms-giving had caused much pain in the household. Silver Eagle scolded and nagged him. The Chinese don't give alms, she said, unless it is to help their family. The clan. He hated the idea of the clan. Selfishness began at home. One day Silver Eagle, dressed as a beggar, wearing a torn, black veil over her head, stood in rags before the soot-smeared façade of the Saõ Paulo cathedral. When Camilo gave her a coin, she drew off her veil. He was outraged. He was about to slap her. She stepped back and he caught her by the arm, shaking her. So typically Chinese of her, he shouted at the top of his voice so that real beggars scattered along with the pigeons. He understood at that moment that the poet in him had turned into a monster.

He dragged himself to the little courtyard at the front of the hotel where they served coffee in the mornings on bamboo tables over which the flies hovered hot and lazy, making a soft blue sound. He sat down, looked behind to eclipse his shadow, rubbed out the monstrous double weighing him with meaninglessness: *um cómico defunto*: a dead comedian, playing at poverty. Baudelaire's dark humour welled up from real destitution. His own, from the stage. Water was falling over a stone wall ... up above, someone hidden in the shrubbery with a watering can. He sat there until the waiter came and took his order, a boy in a white jacket with gold buttons like those worn by sailors. Conceição smoked. Little cigarettes he rolled himself, anxious to fill time with the fragrance of pleasant memories. Remember love? he asked himself. No, he could not, except as a monstrous laugh at the non-existent reason for his having once loved. Fatuous now. Hannah's hips melting into middle age. Then what he thought was love ... momentarily, when he caressed Silver Eagle's breasts, tiny bulbs he tweaked as she presented her back to him like a boy. Then Nickel Hawk's ministrations. Now Peregrine's expert mouth. The Falcon. All of these did not constitute love. He was a non-lover. He could not fall because he could not feel. Not even the swipe of a cutlass from behind. But he could experience the sound of the drops of water from the clepsydra, the slowly revolving barrel atop the paddlewheel, its pointer running along the marked hoops, a device which could not find the time, but simply marked out rough duration, a set period in which he had to establish himself. Someone will see. Someone will protect his future. He had no fear of dying.

He was nursing his cognac. There they were coming down the stairs into the courtyard, the dark woman and the fair one. Conceição looked and turned away so as not to appear curious and then looked again. By God! It was Hannah. He rose, he ran, stumbled, knocked over the chair he was sitting on, Hannah!, So you've finally come! She winced, frowned. His was a kind of delusion which often occurred in the East. It came with gin and tonic. It was particularly common in fair weather, when there was no other drama. But it was the dark one who spoke first. One does not know you, sir. He recovered his composure just in time. *Desculpe.* Mistook you for somebody else. But the blonde was smiling at him. She spoke in English. A strange lilting tone. No, it is we who have disappointed you Sir. Were you expecting to meet a friend? A friend? He chewed over the word. No. My dear Senhora, I am so sorry. A friend. I have lost all my friends.

And so began a conversation, broken by so many translations, mis-translations, smiles, apologies. He invited them to have coffee but they declined. He asked if he could smoke, and they said to go ahead. This gave him confidence. You see, he said, a smoke is a friend. They smiled at this. She was an interesting one, the blonde. She was daring, and was quick to take up any hint of intimacy. When he said he was a teacher, she grew attentive and invited him with her eyes to linger over the story of his life. He said he was washed up, here in Macau, a bit of flotsam. She did not say she collected flotsam whenever she was on Sydney's foreshores, trawling the wet sand when the tide had just gone out, picking up bits of crockery, splinters from sunken ships. They agreed to meet for dinner.

25

Conceição in his Forbidden City with his concubines. He escaped it, took his daily walks swimming in an opium high, a *rausch* rushing through his veins. How could he possibly have written poetry? But there they are. Published in 1926 by Hannah Osório de Castro. When did he write them? They must have come in a rush, their beauty insurmountable, the time bomb of their symbolism, his devastating attack on industrialisation, his indentification with his mother, his ambiguity. *The Water Clock Poems*. He wanted to slow down time. And yet it all occurred in a rush, in a lather of sweat, with a cold wind coming off the sea. He had to get through the portal of redemption, opening up for him like a passage through the water, waves held back for him, the Garden appearing green in the distance. How had he managed this, having forsaken Lusitania, a deserter by no other name, a decadent, an ugly duckling, a purchaser of concubines, he who called his little son a monkey, he who was a failure as a judge, he who taught languages with the dryness of a grammarian, lazy to the bone, slanderer of his father, imperial coloniser, pederast ... how did he manage this poetry?

They met that evening for dinner at the Pearl River Pavilion. He, pale, in a cream suit which was too small and tight for him, but which showed off his posture, straight and stiff, a gentleman of the old Lusitanian establishment, or so he tried to appear. His mouth had been somewhat blackened by opium, so he rouged his lips. Grotesque. Anna was not in favour of this dinner. She would insist on paying for her share, of course. It was the Australian way. Pay as you go, but only for yourself. Grand gestures were not her specialty. Impressions were not part of her interest. Julia, however, convinced her that if they wanted to look over some paintings, those reputed to have some value, then they were to be polite to Conceição at all times. They let him pay. Julia was rather impressed by his attempts to scrub up during his several visits to the bathroom. She was wearing her blue dress, her transparent muslin, her little box hat. He smoked between courses, after advising them against the cod, which he said had been caught too close to the effluent shore. His little cigarillos. Anna turned away from his smoke. Julia inhaled it. During dessert Julia suddenly exclaimed: A writer! As though she had just discovered the only true one in the world. Anna rolled her eyes. Yes, Conceição admitted for the first time that he wrote poetry. Not to anyone, but only to one woman; to her perhaps. Ha! Anna scoffed. But I am listening. He ignored her. No, his discourse was directed to Julia, whom he was finding to be marvellously in tune, laughing at his compressed irony, quick to pick up his suggestions of double entendres and she was thrilled to be talking with someone who did not perform the literal act day after day, throwing pots from earth, submerged in earth, dedicated to clay, playing at being an earth-mother. But she wasn't interested in making Anna jealous. No, that was already too catastrophic, since Anna once exhibited such fury she claimed Julia was nothing but a puppy, or worse still, a *pussy*, which (yes, the impersonal became her), was nothing better than a feline with loose lips and a tight sphincter. Fired up, Anna had a way with words. Pots flew. Shards littered the studio in King's Cross. Julia however, could not help herself. This ugly man opposite her was playing a terrible sadness upon flowery jokes. On her father's station once upon a time there was an Aboriginal man who possessed the same physiognomy: wide nostrils, dark beard, and he sat on the stoop at the back porch relating sorrow in broken English. A well-worn tale. Not his, but hers for the telling. Now this Conceição, refined, educated, with the same pathos. He spoke as though he had no choice in the loss of his profession as a judge in Coímbra. In Portugal, he said, it was impossible to possess a sense of literary nobility. A poet *feels*, he went on to say, at his own expense. Yes, she agreed, but an artist works. Anna tried to add something here, but they were not listening. I feel, he said, always under the light of others. As if the lantern of brilliance they concealed under a bushel was what I tried to imitate with my little candle. Only I set fire to my bed. Speech, you see, disfigures everything. She was laughing – a generous laugh which revealed dimples and charms and an even row of white teeth.

He had not had such a conversation since Hannah's muted rejection of his work. The latter would probably continue to turn it aside. He was not depressed for it was not his best work. He admitted all this to Julia. Anna looked as if she were going to throw a tantrum or a pot. She was bored. There was no conversation with this man. He did not see her. He was not impressed by her mind. So she let it be known she didn't like poetry. She didn't like poets. She then said she would walk back to the hotel slowly. Julia did not like the adverb at the end of her sentence. Take all the time you want, she said and she saw Anna's face flush with anger. They all rose. Then, in a moment of independence she hadn't exercised before, Julia said Camilo would walk her back later, wouldn't he? Conceição bowed. He would be delighted. They would take a detour via a tea-house by the river.

None of this would have come about without reflection and meditation on Julia's part. For months she had been imprisoned by Anna's will. For years she had suffered the older woman's experience and jealous scorn. Julia was always frightened of the conversations Anna had when others were present. There was always a moment when Anna would turn to her and say: *But, my dear, the large canvas does not suit you. Your cigar-box lids are perfect. You are what you appear to be, small and perfectly formed.* Or something to that effect. It was however, Julia's personal fortune that supported both of them. Travelling the world on the sheep's back.

Reminder: the word baudelaire is a kind of cutlass. And it was probably during that night, while taking coffee with Julia, pausing between each mouthful to reveal a black cavern, the rouge of his lips imprinted on the rim of the cup ... it was probably then that he cut himself off from Baudelaire. For Julia did not find him repulsive. She saw in him a beauty which was not illegitimate; an honesty. She urged him to move from second-hand poetry to lived composition. *You must act*, she told him, *you must use your despair. That is when you will regain your happiness.*

The moment he got home, having escorted the blonde painter back to her lover's room, the moment he heard the women of his household shifting uneasily in their apartments ... rumours were already abroad: *A white concubine!* ... at that moment, he began a poem without Baudelaire. He cast his opium pipes aside. The poppies had been lopped, but now he heard a single flower opening in the night. His fight had not been useless.

Day of Useless Agonies

The day of agonies is over; its egress marked by the title on this cover: *The Water Clock Poems*: thin wings of words, hymens easily broken, pains of love. I abandoned Baudelaire, and immediately the day of useless agonies passed from my burnt-out mouth. He had always feared women, most of all intelligent ones. He said he 'slept with a hideous negress', because he could not perform, counterfeiting his limpness with feigned boredom. What a face. I was his negress. I am leaving him now. I live my hell without recourse to doubling, double-dealing with him. I left *Les Fleurs du Mal* with Julia, my only copy of it, worn from the pressure of my hand in countless failed attempts to learn from him. It must have been Julia's resemblance to Hannah which made me want to give her something. I thought the book my inspiration, but now I know it was my failure. Something which I had always carried around. A personal millstone; portable gallows.

I left her lucid and pale beside people dying in doorways and threw her one of those kisses into which I would have thrown my life, as water in the grand harbour swirled and lights from rickshaws glimmered upon her teeth and a young man coughing up blood in my path. Down from the blackened façade of the São Paulo cathedral, burnt down in 1601, a nightbird swooped. One by one, Chinese lanterns up in the hills were slowly extinguished. The night settled in close. On our walk, Julia, slightly drunk, told me she practised body-building on the family farm, out of sheer boredom. Hoisted hay bales and steel rails like a navvy and in a lather, in solitary self-confinement, released herself. And yes, beneath her coat she placed my hand and I examined like a doctor the shapes of muscles hardening and softening.

Lucid and pale, I stood on the threshold of a sickened city while he passed his hand across the sky, brow burdened with verses penned before and better penned. I'm just a girl in a bustle sewn with stars, simple in design, fine for the nightwalk and did not see the dirt beneath my feet. As we lingered upon a seat by the arcades in Sintra he came alive and was not shy, his finger stalling, just once, between Venus and then Mars.

26

In his room, alone, in the small hours of the morning, he unwraps the little parcel of her letters, purchased from the fisherfolk he knew, for a bargain. This was what inspired *The Water Clock Poems*.

He had not been able to act because he had no desire save the desire to die. Reality disappointed ... he had seen everything already, the end coming out of a new century, the muscles of an avenging angel, her name given to an act he had already rehearsed but never fulfilled, and it was by this grace that he was still alive that night, given back to life. Useless except in reverie, only seeing between wakefulness and sleep, the way she took his hand a revelation to him, a lead, a guide, he was no longer a man. He was given a parcel of letters by a comprador; they had been scattered on the sea and were now collected and dried like fish. Out of these he plotted his path, a poetry which had become a duty. His act of contrition for his guilty secret.

There was a murderous dew that night. He wrote poem after poem to the drip of water while sitting in his Mosely folding bath. Roughs, which he will later rework for weeks and months. But for the moment they poured out without a subject, or at least it was a subject invisible to him. He had invited Julia to visit him in the late morning and he wanted to have something to show her. She had assented, but hinted that it would be a difficult permission to obtain. *Permission!* He took that to heart, too pained to ask if it were only a figure of speech. But he had imagined the stranglehold the older woman had over her. The woman of the world. He had imagined, when he wrote that night, the words: *Obscene hydra, under the weight of my virginity!* What did he mean by that? Guilt crushed under the heel of blindness? The water-serpent of fantasy reaching into territory he did not know? He was hardly innocent. *Mea culpa*, strike your chest, pectorals, *peccata mundi*. Behind him, through his window, the lonely harbour lights. He sat there bleating, that was what he called this, his writing, a call to be succoured, something which had never left him. He was compelled to reassess the present: Silver Eagle downstairs entertaining another man before going out; Nickel Hawk waking and rocking her baby, his little monkey, whose hands he already imagined would rip his life from him, a child he would not educate, her child, and though Nickel Hawk showed the promise of a felt life, there was no hope; not in this city; nor was there anything he could call upon in Portugal, for it simply could not be done, to return with such baggage ... it was for their sakes ... and so it was all hopeless, plaintive as the Peregrine's snoring in the third room, a woman of some means who wore all her wealth in her teeth. He sat and wrote bravely, fragments of fantasy which had neither adornment nor false feeling. That, he was satisfied, was his truth: kaleidoscopic shards which tumbled together, forming new perspectives: Julia's breasts a template upon which the Romans had modelled their armour, and she, neither passive nor aggressive, softly disturbing his erotic field with whispers, bending flowers in the tumid night and then his drooping disinterest (opiate induced) activated by the process of a switch on her hardened buttocks, suddenly Anna there, the cold punishing light of a distant star and he could only watch, his eye behaving telescopically; leave it to them beneath the dim lightbulb: *Grace under Ångström*; his bathwater freezing; everything measured, tempered, alone again.

27

There he is, coughing up blood, sitting now by his window which looks out onto the Praia. He has contracted a germ from the crowd, two months after Julia Grace and Anna Ångström left Macau on board the *Finca*, bound for Lisbon. Lonely, these two months, filled with work, filled with blood, his lungs, trying to relieve the congestion with iced red wine, consumption he thought he could cure, red for red, but was only concealing it with colour. Must have been the sewer-gases, miasmas, horse manure, human faeces which passed it on. But his angel had left him, bound for Europe on the Finca. He could only recall the way she smiled when they took their last walk together, saying that spontaneity and improvisation in art were ways to mask intention. He was not quite convinced. He could see it in her, that muscular strength forcing her material to bend to her will. *To be mastered by her!* That was the intention of his poetry. But there was something else. Taste. You could not write unless you had taste. His mouth grew blacker. He was triangulating the positioning of his house. He had bought a painting, a rather mediocre early one of the Macau waterfront. He wanted the perspective; how to accommodate a view from an illogical standpoint; the Eastern mind sees what it wants to present, not as accuracy, but as the truth of the artist's intention. He brought out his Freemason's compass. His telescope, *the thousand-li-mirror* is what the Chinese call it. Its range is probably about thirty *li*. Art is measuring. His reckoning was that Macau's art markets were located in a double triangle. Side by side, like the frame of a bicycle. At the apex, the crumbling gambling houses on the Rua Nova de São Lazaro, where rich crime bosses dealt out dirty money and cheap, plywood coffins. At the bottom, there was the waterfront in the inner harbour, where items were sold, brought in on sampans: paintings by ancient masters, lyrical elegies from the Ming dynasty, scrolls of calligraphy in blazing red which Camilo had bought for two patacas. In his big house near the Boa Vista, there were fifteenth-century screens and panels, priceless porcelains, seascapes in sandalwood. Triad gang-members lolled about outside his door. They knew nothing about art, but were learning the market. He wrote catalogues for them.

When she visited him that memorable evening, Julia had brought lilies. There was nowhere to put them. The rooms were chaotic, spread with paintings, dogs lying on couches, cats stretching. What he thought was an intimate environment must have seemed like a ramshackle clutter of junk and chaotic collection. It was not the house of a lawyer, judge, teacher. It was an extravagant pile of guano belonging to an eccentric gatherer of waste. There you have it. What Julia would have seen and heard: a cacophony of Chinese voices and barking dogs, flapping chickens. Indeed, when she visited, she wrote that there were probably fifteen souls living there. Mainly female, with their squalling babies, their itinerant, extended families, helpers, loan sharks, hangers-on, prostitutes. Scratchy Chinese opera music came from a back alleyway. A smell of cat urine. For a poet, it was not reflective of calm or meditation. Reflexion, he told her, was a nightmare he chased down in order to extort from it a pleasant dream in daylight hours. He was hurriedly writing something down. Hollow sounds of dripping water from somewhere in his room; saliva sizzling in his bamboo pipe. Julia showed her disgust. She didn't know about his refuge. She didn't wish to know. By the look of his morning attire, he could not have possessed a bathroom. She didn't conceal her views, just said his house was a kind of rotting birthday cake ... a bat cave ... those were her words. She apologised for her plain speaking. Australians had a democratic tendency to criticise what they did not understand. For his part, he collected women and progeny. He was kind to them. He called them unfinished fragments. They always had hope and they weren't out for closure. He was against what Julia stood for; not her sexuality, which excited him, but her persistent need to acknowledge her bourgeois tendencies. She asked him straight out what he was going to do with his collection. He said he had already bequeathed it to the National Museum in Portugal, but that he also favoured the idea that a part of it should go to the Paris gallery whose curator had befriended him and who had helped him find Baudelaire's rooms. He patronised Julia. Did not allude to their intimacy. The fact that she presented herself as a conscious artist from an English colony, devoted to work at all costs, unremitting in discipline – she hardly perspired, it seemed – her ambition to be *seen* as an artist – this fact demanded scepticism. This seemed to him false, betraying the artist with the *idea* of an artist. She was coming to the stage from the wrong side of the curtain, and while her upbringing brought her much confidence, her beauty gave him pause. Beauty could not bring about art. He did not say all this to her. A single look was enough.

28

The anti-royalist was dying, surrounded by his mistresses and their extended families. He no longer received visitors in his ante-chamber. He asked them to visit him in his room, while he sat in his bath which Nickel Hawk or Silver Eagle periodically filled with warm water, and Number Three, the Peregrine, who was now promoted to preparing and lighting his pipes because she had strong and steady hands, glided in and out, making sure his visitors did not tire him, all those bureaucrats and aspiring writers who had got wind of this house of death in which, still lived, so they had heard, *Baudelaire's equal*.

He would not have coped with that. Grimaced beneath the beard, probably. There was always, even amongst those he called *friends*, the great dead writers on his shelves, a usage. T*he human being was manufactured*. He wrote that in one of his letters to Hannah. You could hear and see his doubles emerging from the telephone, the gramophone, the camera. He was very concerned about his young son, he wrote, *because there is a stigma attached to being a Creole*. He knew how Nickel Hawk felt the moment she began to understand painting; her fear and panic at the notion of enlightenment. Now he began to tell her of her origins. She was creolised, a product of her mother and the Procurador, lacking both direction and a racial passport. It alarmed her. She was suddenly dispersed and reconstituted. Her next steps would be ingratiation, *passing*, then dissolution. She would become a prostitute. It happened to the best of them. What about her son? Conceição saw everything in advance. He had nightmares about the little monkey growing wise, robbing him of everything in the house, selling the collections. *Macaco* the monkey would set up a little business with what was left from squandering all the money on gaming tables, starting a dark and dingy bicycle business in the red-light district on the Rua da Felicidade. This was his copy. He might even grow a black beard. Make himself all the more recognisable amongst the Chinese as a foreign devil. Then he will try to 'pass' by claiming European identity, enabling him to borrow money more easily. He will not like people asking about his race. A face like teakwood. Every morning he would swim the channel between Taipa Island and Coloane. He was proud of his gloomy bicycle-repair shop erected under an awning beside the Senate buildings; proud of the colorful posters advertising bicycle brands stuck on the back wall ... Omnium, Onyx, Orient ... he had come from nowhere ... he was not an artist like his father. Women found him interesting nevertheless, balancing themselves on his bikes, giggling, chatting. He would tell them how he was born in a pedicab, his thin-hipped mother rushing to the midwife in the middle of the night, a lantern at her feet next to his protruding head, foreigners whistling, hailing them to stop, believing she was touting. Yes, he said, he was half a bicycle. They were welcome to ride him.

Conceição had fallen in love with Julia Grace. She had been horrified at his circumstances, intrigued by his 'savage riches' as she described them in one of her letters to him ... an interestingly intimate letter, apologising for her initial reaction, her forthrightness at such squalor and grandeur before she was able to assess his priceless paintings, his antique furniture, his ancient ornaments and scrolls. Her collector's eye had been clouded by his women, her covetousness confused, blushing helplessly when Silver Eagle stared her down. She had been ushered in by Nickel Hawk, through two museum salons which were impressive despite the dogs and cats and chickens, and she turned right, following the girl, whom she mistook for his daughter, and she brushed aside the drapes which Nickel Hawk had let fall onto her face and saw him in his bath with the yellow screens behind and the untidy bookshelves and the cupboards full of jade vases, jars, porcelains and bronzes, and there were paintings stacked against the wall, damp from the steam of his bath. His tub folded back into a wardrobe with a mirror, revealing a sodden Persian rug, the whole affair arranged along one wall of the large room. They had a long discussion while she sat beside his bath and Silver Eagle poured in water and the Peregrine, swaying and willowy, lit his pipes. They spoke about drugs and then about fugues. He said he was peripatetic, prowling around the back streets, lost in the vortex of the city, but now he was tired more and more, his urban revolutions smaller, his map marginal. He was coughing up flecks of blood onto his handkerchief. She was caught between disgust and her fascination with his silken women, intrigued by their indifferent silence. She suggested buying some of his collection ... the paintings, of course. Outside, beyond the shuttered windows the city exuded an unhealthy mist, fermented the air with decay, tang of wet markets, fish stalls closing for the night, cobbles gleaming with blood and silver scales. She had walked here and the hem of her dress was still damp against her boots and she had had to elbow her way through a thick soup of people, thinking of her farm at a place called Putty, in New South Wales, Australia, where there was always the health of the grain, wet wool of sheep, the sweetness of silos bursting with store, flavours of roasting lamb and the sharp crackling of red gum burning in the grate, and no people, and she thought of that peace which was not here, the stillness of the night and the proximity of the stars.

When they were alone he began to speak more eagerly about his dry-brush copying, the hand revealing the will, the experience, he said, of traversing the same road as those Chinese masters, a true imbibing of the weather, and that was what it was like with his poetry. Julia then saw sadness, a wind-blown shade come upon his face when he spoke about his son, of the fate of those born out of wedlock, the *perfilhados* – perfidious, he claimed, sons without faith – so they always turned out – for the very reason that in Macau they had the same rights as their fathers. The monkey was on his back, pushing him one rung further down into the grave. The son was his copy and would extinguish him; and then his son, and then his son. Brush him out. He wanted to put himself out of reach. She wanted to show him that he was wrong, bring him to another place where there was the sweetness of timber and the crispness of air, the inhalation of life and taking the washcloth from the side of the tub she began slowly to wash him, first his feet which he had propped on the rim, and then his shoulders and his thinning hair and as the water became more tepid, knew refilling was a disturbance, a displacement of pleasure taken from the already-dead, and so she submerged her hand beneath where there had been no more feeling and brought him to the present. It was the one thing for which there was no correction. The rest is history. The clepsydra dripped.

29

There is a very small entry in Anna Ångström's diary, which was left behind in the studio at Cerbère ... fortunately rescued by the patriarch of the artistic community ... the small entry made on the 5th January 1928, almost two years after Anna had visited Macau, which does have the ring of truth about it, indicating a mystery which had not yet been digested, since all jealousies and betrayals entail consequences and speculations which become more lucid with time ... the entry of the 5th January 1928 notes that:

... something had happened to Julia ... it was most certainly the result of an encounter with that awful Rasputin. They had met three times in our short stay and even though Julia made it quite clear that she was on a mission that was purely business, I could not quite trust her. I'm not

sure if I was jealous, for time has passed quickly and I cannot remember if she had been disloyal, though I knew that deep in her heart she was not that way inclined. I therefore began to suspect her motives. Why she was spending time, for example, with a man who was at the end of his minor career as a poet? A man at the limits of his talent, who admitted to her that he was always having to make such a mental effort with modernity he could never return to Europe. A man who hated everything about modern art, since we were sailing towards the future: Modernism; Cubism; Surrealism. That Camilo creature knew nothing of what was going on in France. He had gone backwards into Chinese painting and exclaimed during our one brief meeting at dinner ... an event I was fortunate not to have to repeat ... that he was 'always looking for midday at two o'clock'. Passé. He was absolutely passé in his thinking. A man of the past who destroyed the past. A passéiste who painted cheap advertisements over once-worthy canvasses. A man who believed in symbols of commodity, who fathered children indiscriminately and who bought women for his pleasure.

My suspicion of Julia began that day we set sail, when she suddenly expressed the desire to go home. Indeed she only spent a month at Cerbère and it was a desperate month for both of us, for we argued constantly and Meister Gleize had to counsel me for what was rapidly turning into nervous exhaustion. A break-up, as it now turns out. But Julia was running back home. I know how she would have waited breathlessly at the post office at Putty, waiting for news of him in that Australian heat.

If only Julia knew that Conceição was raving mad by this time. He sent the Peregrine to bring him his pipes. He liked the honey colour of the Macau Opium Farm brand. Long after Julia had departed he asked Nickel Hawk to put lilies in a vase. He said they were grown in a honey-coloured valley. He directed her to it, somewhere in in the heart of China. Nickel Hawk said there were no lilies. The woman with the lilies had left a month ago. No, Miss Grace will do it herself, Conceição said, and filled the vase with bath-water. He saw the flowers being nourished. *Autumn is gone now, the cold returns* ... he wrote of her as Ophelia, her hands translucent and cold beneath the water.

In the mornings he walked as far as he could but suffered from a chronic pain in his joints, a pressure behind his nose, a head that would not tell the time. The walking was all there was – a forward movement toward a narrowing gap. He walked barefoot in his long indigo nightshirt like a beggar, zigzagging between people, crossing and re-crossing the streets out of some superstition that buildings may collapse, tiles may come tumbling down, for catastrophe may occur at any time. The world was discontinuous. He walked barefoot to feel the state of the ground, to detect the fine tremors of future earthquakes, to configure his position with regards to the earth because he felt he had come to the end of his time and this ending was fortuitous, and his bare feet felt the cold stones and the coldness gave him back something that was not entirely wasted. The thought of the gift of his death lightened him; released him from another rehearsal of a life in which he would be overcome by ambition all over again. It would only be at the last moment – when he became discontinuous, when he had already fostered discontinuity, having fathered useless words and children – it would only be at the last moment that he would find that this imitation of life had no meaning; except for his taking revenge on the rhythm and circulation of time itself. He would need to teach Nickel Hawk how to escape through this aperture, how to recognise originality. He would teach her that by submitting herself to the command of the work, she could collect other people's memories and free her own vision. She had already created. She should teach her son about painting.

Look at him lifting his feet as though he were cycling, careful of the dogshit. Or maybe he was pedalling a foot-driven watermill from which the Chinese word for *bicycle* is derived. Going through the repetitious motions of life to sample all the scales of emotion. He rolled out his tricycle. It was garnished with rust, suffocated with cobwebs. He walked it through the streets, struggled with it up the hill to the school. He would ask for his old job back. He was a teacher. The measure of his life was as a pedagogue, a reproducer of failure. Cobwebs had been stuffed down his throat. He stood outside the gates. Heard the muffled recitals of verse. He wasn't dressed. Barefoot, dirty, he would have to dust off his jacket. Mournfully, he wheeled the tricycle around. Sat on it and sped down the hill. The contraption squealed. Words running like spiders in his brain. He flew. The brakes gave way, levers like sponge cake beneath his fingers. At the bottom of the hill he had a moment of rational calculation: the sea-wall; if he turned at the right moment, he could spin the vehicle in such a way the back wheels would take the brunt of the impact. But there was no balance. There was no weight. It rolled and he toppled; surprised, disoriented, uncharted; and then there were perfumes, flowers, sweet paradise.

His dogs were sleeping faithfully on his cold body when the women found him in his dry tub – you should have seen their look of horror, the realisation that their welfare had suddenly disappeared – and there he was, divested finally of the fugues he so favoured, having come to rest when he thought his work was finally and uselessly done. Passing on. There was a smile on his ravaged mouth, a glow on his cheeks where a savage beauty had settled.

30

And now I await something which may not make itself apparent. I, Walter Gottlieb, am waiting for a life sentence … the interminable future of one's reputation. Had I not interrogated Redvers, absorbed his memory, found out all I could in order to glimpse the palimpsest of Conceição? Had Redvers knowingly lied and I blindly followed, or had he lied blindly and I followed knowingly? Have I not mined Conceição's archive to discourage future fabulators? Am I not wearing a red bow tie? A clean white shirt? Please be assured I have staked my life on my credibility and my research. Conceição has been my life's obsession. His descendants, save for one, are dead or untraceable. How else but to lure the survivor into my confidence? We fell out of course, in one-way traffic. He fled to Paris, his safe haven.

I have this little phial of morphine I stole from my doctor's fridge. I do not know what it will do to the heart. Some kind of *étouffement*. Suffocation; constriction. Miraculous calm there is, in deceit: liminal, between two realms. What? Erect at a time like this? Alert, this organ? No, not my heart. A change of heart. That's what all these drugs do; they turn life into a drowsy variation of thirty short dances between depression and excitement. So brief. No rush now. Coming into a transit zone: counterpoint ... step and turn ... pulsing ... flesh ... inert matter ... step ... an anamorphosis ... pirouette ... my bleached face melting beside the toilet bowl, finally, those useless muscles in the process of articulation. Just a little bit more then. *Dr Walter will write you from the future.* I am at the jetty again, chained, waiting for the tide, only this time nobody will hear me. I am at the border. It is all too familiar, my *ennui*. No one writes to me.

I shall go to Lisbon, thence to Macau to meet Conceição, to sit and converse with his ghost, find out the truth. But before that I memorise my room on the upper storey, the rug, the desk; I mentally photograph these tesselated tiles, this cast-iron, claw-foot tub, the baroque mirror on the ceiling, so that I can accurately describe to others in another world how these crossings are accomplished by raiding the past. I turn on the taps. Here, in my absence, those who remain behind will feel they had forgotten something; a briefcase perhaps. Downstairs, they will be reminded by a small leak in the ceiling. Readers will experience a certain familiarity with things out of time, having encountered an invisible stranger from the future who, like themselves, is a perennial lover of life. To learn this new identity, to be open to a world brimful with hope and happiness, is like learning how to ride a bicycle, moving forward while sitting still, pedalling faster to avoid falling, conquering borderless territories by means of a sweet union with the earth.

III

SARRAUTE'S SURGERY

I am glad not to be sick; but if I am, I want to know I am; and if they cauterise or incise me, I want to feel it.

– Michel de Montaigne

Ingress

Something had gone terribly wrong. There were no fish in the sea.

On this very fine, very blue morning, in Rim Cove North Queensland, the jellyfish have taken over. That's what the mini-bus driver told us last night when we arrived at the airport and were shuttled to the resort in the warm and glutinous air. Plastic bags. From the South Pacific to the Andaman Sea. Plastic bags which turtles mistook for jellyfish. So the turtles were all dying, choked by plastic which they swallowed, thinking they were jellyfish, jellyfish which they loved, transparent blubber, never-ending 'hors d'oeuvres', nourishing protoplasm with a touch of spice, a whole underworld of eating and drinking. Now the turtles have gone and the jellyfish have taken over and the fish are dying, stung with poison, trapped by curtains of tentacles, deprived of fish food. That's what the mini-bus driver told us in the black night lit only by the lights of the resort, while a light tropical mist descended, bringing odours of frangipani. We need guns, the driver said. For the plastic bags? I asked. No, for the pigs. Feral pigs are like jellyfish. Breeding. Destroying the land. Like ... he looks around the back of the bus ... catches my eye and smiles a sly smile ... like them Asian property developers, hey.

But now this bluish morning. A hazy horizon. Something wrong when there was not a single person in sight. Warm already, full of sea-weed smells; the raw and the cooked. I hang my Italian sandals around my neck; I wear white flannels rolled. Fine, clean sand squeezes between my toes, cold, hard-packed; softer pockets further up on the small dunes, still cool beneath. Everything groomed by a small tractor which trawls up and down at dawn and sunset. No glass bottles, no trash. The oncoming heat bears with it an anxiety that the day is already lost. Prickles of shells, squeak of soles. Sea pineapples bowl up and back, frothing and rippling. Later in the forenoon I will frequent the marketplace, stroll about, loiter in the shade, lean on doorposts to glean local knowledge. The 'agora'. With the market-crowd, all that matters is my own silence. And then they will tell me everything. I need to buy a lantern. Find an honest man.

Last night I ate alone at the Biarritz Restaurant. Open to the beach front, windy, warm, with barbecued smells of shrimp and steaks, all you can eat, Queensland style. The restaurant was blurry with smoke, staff in the fug and panic of a small kitchen fire. Busloads of tourists arriving. Confusion is what I cherish. The woman next to me (our tables were small, French style, in a row, along a continuous banquette), appeared professional and busy. Real-estate perhaps, but definitely a local. The waiters were obsequious. I may have drunk a little too much. Not much recollection, but I'll try it in the present, so I can go in and out. The woman next to me has long black hair and intense dark eyes and she catches me glancing to my right, over at her, so I look away at the glistening sea sparkling with ... well, glowing sea-critters. I'm not one for too much nature study. I gave that away when I shaved off my beard. Someone else inhabits me now. She eats quickly, studies a pharmaceutical brochure, lifts a long finger for her bill. Pays, slips out the other side of the table. The staff are preoccupied with smoke. I take her money, put the bill on the empty table on my left, leave twenty of her dollars beside my plate and am just about to ease out of the confines of the banquette when I notice she has left a book behind. A leather-bound notebook, black, lying on the red leatherette. I take this to be fortuitous. Red and black are my favourite colours. If stopped by anyone, I could say I was simply chasing after her to return it. It's a ploy I've used before, an exit strategy, though this night I felt happy, adventurous, leaving everything to chance. I carry the book under my arm into the fresh breeze, thinking of the skinny blonde girl I met on the plane, who said she too, was heading for this same resort. I had told her (after several small bottles of airline bubbly) that she was beautiful, and she smiled in a way that was neither embarrassed nor dismissive. I was looking forward to meeting her again by the warm salt-water pool. In the meantime, I sample French champagne from the Honour Bar, which for me bars all honour, as I read the spiked slips which have been turned over for secrecy, and graft onto my honoration of the best wine all the best room numbers.

Clean-shaven, I look much younger than my years. Faces, at any rate, are melting moments. One never sees them entirely, since they change like the weather. In Rio, I thought I recognised many people, all from my past. Ex-lovers, ghosts, maybe. In their new lives they deserve not to be recognised, so I did not approach them. I certainly don't judge people by their faces. Judgment is acquired from a distance and the face changes as one approaches one's subject. Tropisms, for instance, occur in the noonday heat. Re-assessments take place after a good meal. Alcoholic vulnerabilities settle in during the late afternoon, when desires or disgust arise. Perspectives are sharpened. It may explain why sane and sober people are often paralysed by unconscious and unclear moods, dulled by emotions with the consistency of jelly.

The shutters in my room emit a smell of the east. Sandalwood, perhaps. I'm not an expert in the varieties of wood. Driftwood more my style; bleached and salted. I think of the skinny blonde. Imagine making love to her, but nothing fits. Roll a little rush of ideas. Light up. This loosening gives me a better grasp. Who was the raven-haired executive next to my table? Inhale. Fold back the covers of her black notebook.

1

From the Journal of Doctor Judith Sarraute

Something had gone terribly wrong. There were no fish in the sea; not even little reef sharks, which used to nose shorewards at dusk, black shadows darting between clouds of sand.

From my surgery window I can see Janet Cordillion hanging from a parachute, being towed by a powerful speedboat out near the reef. An oil tanker is heading north, spewing smoke. Gosh look at my reflection. My beautiful long black hair turning grey. The gap between Janet Cordillion and the tanker widens very slowly, and the smoke looks like it's engulfing her. It must be her. She's para-sailing every morning about eleven, when the wind comes up, with the speedboat driver and his assistant, skiing into the air and when aloft, kicking off her paddles then hovering in the updraft, a weathered eagle; I know the crows' feet behind her shades. No idea why she does it; she's fair, yet deeply tanned, and will get skin cancer. I copy this from my journal onto her patient card. I note that above the card I have also written *suicidal* – she expressed that to me when she asked for the sleeping pills which I was reluctant to prescribe, but she would have got them anyway from the doctors in Cairns, driving there in her dark green Porsche. I hope she wasn't storing them up. Janet *Coeur de Lion*, was how she pronounced her name. Her husband Carter Cordillion is the district's biggest property-developer. He's running for Parliament. God knows why. It's not for the money. Somebody will probably shoot him.

A sonic boom from a low-flying aircraft no one can see, shakes the windows. No fish in the sea. At this time of the year the box-jellyfish have taken over. Scientists do not know how to exterminate them, so tourists can swim safely all year round without having to don smelly wetsuits. *Exterminate.* I'm worried about their use of this word. Out here, in the calm, unruffled waters, nature cannot be controlled. Much of my surgery time is engaged with first aid, treating stings by *Chironex fleckeri*, which can be fatal. Box-jellyfish are cubozoans. Picasso would have loved them. Totally transparent, four-cornered, each corner sprouting up to fifteen tentacles. Three-eyed cubists trailing three metres of deadly poison, fired off through hollow shafts. It's simply a reaction, on the part of both jellyfish and victim, a kind of neutrality of the sting. No party intends it, for both are in the abyss of a chance encounter with nervous systems. In a more pleasurable and benign sense, it's like encountering music or painting ... initial incomprehension and then the horror of dawning reality, ambushed by surprise and anguish. The pain experienced by the victim usually becomes more intense as time passes and in a few minutes, the heart can stop beating. The common symptoms ... lower back pain, muscle cramps, nausea and vomiting ... occur within half an hour. A symphony of symptoms.

Vinegar, when applied immediately, can slow down the process and alleviate scarring, but it's not an antidote. There is no known antidote. Ambulancemen bring me marinaded patients, their privates shielded by towels, their faces distorted, arms outstretched like victims of crucifixion. I inject them with analgesics, principally with morphine. Then it's a balancing act between the dosage and toxic side-effects. My whole life has been a balancing act. Judith ... my father said to me ... you must balance your life and not be like your mother. That was probably during one of his more sober moments. When my father talked with me about my mother, I would run from him and lock myself in my room on the rue Marie Curie in Paris, opposite the laboratories where he did his research in tropical medicine. A Bach fugue playing in the background. Point counterpoint. His hi-fi with six stacked records guaranteeing eternal return. Through the misted windows of his office, I could see him sliding his palms up skirts as though he were palpating an orchid. He liked to kneel, embracing their thighs. In Paris in the nineteen-sixties, it was *de rigueur* to have two or three mistresses at the same time ... if you were a famous professor.

There's Janet Cordillion descending, rather ungracefully, over the reef. The tanker has disappeared. Her chute folds down on top of her. Let down by men who know the ropes.

2

Between November and May one should not be in the water. *Irukandji Syndrome*: a slow incapacitation named after a local Aboriginal tribe near Rim Cove. Cramps, difficult breathing, lower back pain, a feeling of impending doom. This last an interesting phenomenon. I've had patients who were not stung by the Carukia barnesi, but who experienced impending doom for most of their lives. Patients in Sydney. Walter Gottlieb, for example, who soaked his bread in vinegar and dabbed it onto his lips. It was a peculiar gesture. He rang me just as he'd finished writing the last lines of his manuscript – a moment of triumph which his wife Marie was not there to share ... she was in Paris curating a photographic exhibition at the Pitié-Salpêtrière – telling me he had just run a bath ... he was depressed, he was saying to me on the phone and he was alone. I alerted his neighbours just in case. They must have knocked for quite some time. It was just moments after his death, his leaden eyes staring up at the gilded mirror on the ceiling.

One should always deal with impending doom intravenously. Morphine, for instance. For years, they treated sting victims by rubbing on vinegar, which had no restorative power, for it was only a temporary salve. Or they bathed the patients in water and wintergreen, which sent them mad with pain, sometimes inducing pulmonary constriction. Besides, baths are enervating and bathing in a tub is not a particularly hygienic form of cleansing.

For years, my father took baths, even during the war. In Paris, we had a giant double-ended roll-top Bateau copper bath with a wood patina finish. Even with such a tub he had to go without soap. There were ersatz products, but he declined using them. His desire for soap was so great he developed an obsession-compulsion. Lack drove him to become a soap fetishist. He always carried a small, genuine cake in his pockets, so his handkerchiefs smelled divine and his hands emitted seductive fragrances when he positioned slides under his microscope. Look at that, he would say, swinging my chair towards the instrument. He breathed into my hair. He carried soap like others carried chocolate; warmed, for personal use. His soap fetishism did not pass onto me, but his concern with lack did, imposing an iron discipline, driving me in my studies so that my medical qualifications were second to none. I still do not bathe in a tub. I shower instead, and there is a plenitude of efficiency there. I could say like my love affairs, but that would be untrue. From my father I inherited the habit of never saying too much, thus cleansing words of their impurities. It's my soap. That is why I am a doctor and not a novelist. But that may be untruthful. I have a cast of characters, a plinth of notes, grammatical prosthetics made out of necessity: I tell some of my more hopeless cases, old men with fatal prostates, that the word Viagra did not possess magical powers, did not even have as much virtue as a good bath. Of course they keep asking for the former.

Sans vie, my father used to say ... without life. He was referring to what he was examining, dead microbes, but I rather think he used the term to disapprove of restricted moralities, teetotalism, lack of risk-taking, satisfaction with smallness. For him, death itself was a failure. His excesses were legendary. I guess that's why I've taken on an observer's role. I have not left the microscope. Smallness is about first things. The first discovery can never be a copy, even if it is a discovery of one thing among many which are still not named. It is the naming that justifies all kinds of primacy. Dr Jack Barnes, for instance, gave his name to the box jellyfish which causes the Barnesi Syndrome. I study his findings and read his work deep into the night, refusing a dinner invitation from Carter Cordillion in Port Douglas, even though Carter was hosting the president of Bayer Pharmeceuticals, who was staying at Cordillion's Temple Meridien resort. *Envie* ... which is not in life, but outside of life ... envy is the sad embalming of lack and of desire.

3

Things slide about. If you place a jellyfish under the hot light of the microscope it liquifies. It has the ability to be transformed into its own medium; the merest illumination and it becomes transparent. Few swimmers have ever seen what stings them. There are people like that. They sting invisibly while they are living their lives, just by living their lives. I try not to imagine the lives of my patients. I note what they have to say and that's all. Then I make general observations. My father taught me how to assess what is general. All people, he said, fall into categories. They become predictable even when they seem to have unexpected urges. If you imagine them, they become too unique; if you observe them, they do not differentiate too much. Like jellyfish, people too, melt into their own medium.

My surgery is in an old house right alongside the beach on the wilder side of the resort strip. It is reached by a dirt road and sits beneath some palm trees and there is a small lagoon which is washed clean by the high tide every month. The 'clinic' as the locals call it, is made of weatherboard and stands beside several double-storey holiday homes which all look out to sea. I have bought one of these modern houses which is linked by a walkway to the surgery. I keep the front room of the old house for my practice. Patients seem to feel calmer when they sit on the old captain's chair next to my desk and gaze out at the green water. The house creaks like an old boat. I deal mainly with geriatric cases, long-time residents who have seen the waterfront develop and their friends sell up. They come to me to complain about everything. Some amongst them have minor chronic illnesses. The terminal ones are mostly silent. Now and again, the odd tourist who has cut his feet from broken glass, allergies, skin eruptions, will ask advice on real estate. In the summer season, from November to May, I deal mainly with those suffering from the Irukandji Syndrome. You can't tell people not to go near the water. Water is a heavy magnet. There are netted areas for them to swim in, but there will always be a few who will display ignorance or bravado, then they are brought into my clinic whimpering and wheezing and tell me they are dying. My geriatrics in the waiting room cluck their tongues like castanets. They've seen it all before. I reach over to my small locked fridge and extract a vial of morphine. My heels click. I do not bend my knees. I used to learn ballet as a child and this habit has stayed with me. My patients are always distracted by what they call my *flamenco gestures*. I wear a white smock and I keep my toenails painted. Patients come from as far away as Cairns to see me and they don't mind waiting for hours. I must say, this practice is getting too much for me, but I don't want a partner. Here I rule. My tunic may look odd, not nearly as professional as a lab coat, but it doubles as a priest's vestment: a *sarrotus*. My name might be a challenge for them, but they queue to confess nevertheless. Patient records are stacking up and take up most of the room in my offices at the back of the house. I sometimes take out the files and re-arrange them in the order of their seriousness; then I shuffle them randomly. The ones which keep coming to the surface form a critical pathology, a baseline which is continuously varied upon by bad luck and tragedy. But if you remove chance you have an epidemiology. Discourse, you see, spreads. But not yet. Not so fast.

Carter Cordillion has high cholesterol and wants to buy my clinic and my house. In fact, he wants to buy up the whole strip, but no one is selling. We have monthly residents' meetings to protect ourselves from surprises. I have another practice in Port Douglas. On weekends I work in tandem with Dr Priscilla Kwan in the heart of the Swordfish Shopping Mall. I intend to cut back. I have floated the idea of change. I want to turn my house into an art gallery. Sick people would no longer be shuffling in and out. At least it would not be a hotel or a restaurant where intoxicated Japanese spill out over the dunes and vomit onto sand.

I have to go now to meet Blixen.

Blixen has flown up from Sydney. Whenever she comes to the resort she stays with me and I always look forward to that. We go shopping, we drive up to the Daintree rainforest in my open Porsche, we go out to the reef in Carter Cordillion's cruiser, which he has placed on permanent loan to me during the Irukandji season, for reasons I will not go into here.

4

My surgery is my observation post. What crosses my line of vision is the grifter who works this area. I've seen him several times, here and in Port Douglas and sometimes in Cairns. He looks different on each occasion, but there is the same gaze, the same camera-eye that he employs ... sometimes I wonder if he is tracking me. I see him lift the tip money from plates; I see him placing his order of Moët on the room numbers of others. I see him counterfeiting a signature from what is obviously a stolen credit card. He is moderately handsome; moderately non-descript. He is quiet and well-behaved, with very pleasant manners.

He crosses in front of my surgery, which is my repair shop. I re-adjust my perspective. Old Pivot is sitting in the captain's chair, spinning around and around. He is drunk, doesn't really want to live, but in my company he comes alive. There's that drifter again, he says. I try to keep Pivot functioning as long as possible. I inject him with vitamins and saline, insure he is irrigated. I caulk the seams in leaky boats.

You're a real corker, Carter Cordillion told me when he was drunk. He had on a dark blue shirt and polka-dot braces and he affected a five o'clock shadow looking like the gangster Sol Levine, whose photo appeared in every newspaper at the time ... for his drug wars and art thefts ... and Cordillion certainly looked like he may have been a dope dealer or an art critic ... pushy, anyway. I don't know what he meant by that remark ... a corker. I thought of Levine and heroin. He had his hand on my knee. It was at the Lions Club centenary dinner. A string quartet was playing Brahms. That was when Cordillion made the offer of lending me his cruiser, a powerful boat shaped like a shark with many thousands of horses, as he said. I don't care for cruisers, with their gurgling throats frothing up the surface of the water. I thought he should have bought a barque; an elegant sailing vessel. I thought of my father's *bateau-bain*, his bath shaped like a deep-keeled boat. I thought of Baudelaire and his *Invitation au Voyage*. Bad Baudelaire. I thought of the dripping tap. Gott-lieb; Gott-lieb; it went, into my father's bathwater, roseate with his blood. I put on my gloves and turned off the tap. I thought of Gottlieb again. Got leave, he used to say to me; out of this world; on leave with Bach; permeable with the element in which he was floating. I could have saved him with love. It was neither accidental nor intentional that I didn't. I should go back there. Survey what had happened years before. Do some caulking. *To sleep. To lie down on deck and sleep, with all one's clothes on.* I always slept with my clothes on. A habit in war-torn countries.

Jellyfish do not survive by learning or by memory. Their reproductive instinct is their perdurance. They multiply out of mimicry, producing polyps shaped like vases or ancient water clocks, from which dozens upon dozens of copies are spawned. They are a culture of copying; an *exemplum summum.* Composed of ninety-five per cent water, the jellyfish is carried away by its medium, although it does have the capacity to steer through it. A box jellyfish reacts, like most of its species, to light. It may be that it also reacts to colour; the colour red, for example. Perhaps that explains why Janet Cordillion is out there on the reef in her red wetsuit. A tanker is heading down the coast, sending out black smoke.

The fugueur, a person who loses himself or herself in a fugue-state, is very much like a jellyfish, carried away by its medium. We no longer use the term *fugueur* in its romantic and non-perjorative sense. In history, there were many famous fugueurs, Jesus Christ being a notable one. Einstein may have lost himself in flights of fancy when he discovered relativity, as may have Kafka in his parables. Whatever the case, they may lose track of the subject, venture onto sidetracks, only to return, synthesised into a different pattern; but only temporarily, like a kaleidoscope. The same and yet different.

Bach wrote fugues. The important thing about a fugue or 'flight' is that all the voices are equal and independent in counterpoint. They are all relative to each other, and in this organised complexity, they speak together, drop out, become fellow travellers, form pairs of dialogues, and in general, mutilate the subject by inverting, augmenting, truncating, or copying it.

As with most things difficult and complicated, we label rather than learn from them: *phylum: cnidaria; from the group that stings; class: scyphozoa; cup-like.* We could say the humble jellyfish has the same qualities as a prophet, divining from a cup and stinging with words. Janet Cordillion certainly thinks so. However with humans, this process of the elevation of the humble is being reversed: *prophetic; oracular; bi-polar; obsessive-compulsive; schizophrenic; mentally ill.* It is not stretching things too far by saying all Bach's fugues were gloriously ill; schizophrenic, obsessive-compulsive, bi-polar, oracular, well organised voices of prophetic intent. Things come round. Speculation is affirmed.

There's Cordillion's cruiser pulling away from the jetty with its searchlights blazing. It is not yet dark. The lactic evening disgorges poets. Jellied hallucinations.

5

I met Marie de Nerval in the hot springs in the Gellert Hotel in the Buda part of Budapest many years ago. She was there, she said, for a cure, though I must say I started smiling at that point. Hot springs cured nothing of course, except perhaps some very minor skin blemishes, or they provided relief for simple or tortured minds. I wouldn't have said Marie de Nerval was simple-minded, but she certainly was a tortured soul. She was an art dealer and worked at several auction houses and was in Budapest for some rest. In the baths at the Hotel Gellert, we waded round and round clockwise, and then anti-clockwise when the attendant blew a whistle ... all of us, large and small, mainly round women, all in bathing caps which was *de rigueur*, though none of us put our heads under the water, afraid of what we would see or ingest. And it was on one of the anti-clockwise rounds that Marie de Nerval confided to me, because she always confided in doctors, moreso with female doctors, who were rare in Hungary, at least those in whom you could confide, that she could never have children.

All stories began in hot springs or baths. I believed and vowed never to believe anything said in hot springs. It was only later that I started writing things down, stories told to me by Marie de Nerval, who had become a sort of patient-friend and who consulted me in exchange for advising me on art, which was becoming a growing interest of mine. But I only began to write things down in concealment, under a sort of cachet of client confidentiality, of doctor-patient secrecy. It was Marie de Nerval who first told me about Walter Gottlieb. Walter, having been driven mad from having lost a daughter, was wandering around Europe and China in a demented state, trying to assuage his grief, attempting a grand *walking tour*, as he called it, in order to *stop thinking*.

6

Slide #1: Carukia Gottlieb. Cubozoan

You see him moving out of the light. He comes forward then disappears into the dark. He doesn't swim on the surface. There are many perspectives you can take when observing him. I think the most interesting one was a written one; the one in the Common Book belonging to Fabiana Martins. She sold these blank notebooks in her shop in Double Bay, along with dried wildflowers, clocks, hourglasses, barometers, microscopes and telescopes. You know the kind of book I mean: skin-bound, with an elastic strap, with ruled, squared or plain versions, endorsed by the writer Bruce Chatwin when he was jotting things down in Patagonia or Australia. For some reason Fabiana preferred the squared ruling, so that her words were vertically as well as horizontally spaced. I suppose she picked up this fondness for squared pages in Paris where the notebooks originated, or perhaps in Shanghai, where the graph paper suited the formation of Chinese characters. She seemed to have had a fondness for cubic spaces, and Walter Gottlieb's little room in the university college was just such a space, neatly arranged so that three walls were completely lined with books and the fourth looked out from a casement window onto the courtyard and the playing fields beyond, from where he could observe all the comings and goings of his students. It was said that Walter Gottlieb preferred standing to sitting, and paced around his small room lecturing even when there was no one present ... the cleaners had discovered him thus several times ... speaking in a loud voice, which he said was a *pedagogical conceit*, that rhetoric was its own enactment, a form of dramaturgy which authenticated life. Of course Fabiana was just repeating his words, since she was in complete awe of the Master ... *Maestro*, she called him ... from the moment she heard one of his lectures on Socrates, which he, as always, at the beginning of each term, insisted on as a prelude to his literature courses. That Fabiana Martins had sought to meet with him in private not once, but several times in his room is well documented, since Gottlieb was Master of a male-only college, and an attractive woman walking into his room in high heels and mini-skirt in the fashion of the times gave cause for rumour, which in a male-only college, tainted Gottlieb with an ambiguous reputation: half heterosexual centaur and half betrayer of gay and aspiring youth. But it seems that Fabiana, having diligently researched Gottlieb's past as a failed priest and academic, felt a strong urge to confess to him and to seek his advice. She wrote everything down. Gottlieb, of course, never wrote anything down. At least, you never saw him doing it.

You can imagine him moving into and out of the light from his window. He was in the middle of lecturing to no one in particular, speaking in a low voice and then a louder one, as in a dialogue; something about Dante's circles of hell, and he had on an academic gown, you know the kind, lined with ermine, even though the day was fairly warm, and he turned to you mid-sentence, having invited you into his room without addressing you until now, and said that if all punishment matched the guilt ... and since he had no appetite for life until now, having been brought to the ultimate stage of man's weariness, *Weltschmerz* ... then what was he guilty of if not for a kind of original sin ... why had he been persecuted thus? Fabiana turned on her heels, believing from what he said that she had suddenly been scorned as a temptress, sent to torment him as some college prank, but he placed his fingers lightly on her arm and detained her. She had brought him a present: a notebook with squared paper.

You can imagine him moving back into the darkness of his shelves, where sat ancient volumes in their uniform of dull gold lettering. That was when she fell in love with him, something so deep, beyond obsession. Several meetings later, Fabiana sat on his bed and told him about her marriage: how she had been seduced by a man who owned property; how she needed security and money; that she was on the verge of having to sell her grandmother's art collection. Roger was a tradesman, a parquetier, and he paid off her debts, gave her a gold credit card linked to his account for her birthday, bought her a small apartment and a baby grand piano beside a bay window. Nothing could have been more ideal, when she entered the front drive on the weekends, the car loaded with dresses and ornaments, the air smelling of moist hay, to know that he was out in the paddocks on his tractor, all the home fires alight for her. A double life. There was companionship but no love. It's how we waste others. We do not know the moment when love turns to hatred under such benign circumstances. We do not know the moment because we have taken on the original sin of choosing life above fidelity, which inevitably involves suffering. He knew she was having an affair. He spent more time on his tractor. Until he couldn't anymore. He stormed in one day when she was on the phone. You're just an old cunt! he shouted. She ate blood oranges all night, simpering in the spare room while her skin glowed. In front of her mirror she asked what it was that must have disgusted him.

Some music, she said, saddened you immeasurably, and she was saddened for no good reason, and the yearning did not cease and she returned to her music, just to sample the sorrow. There was no music in Roger, Fabiana said, and she had never quite realised what a gap this would be, a lack which was, as she put it, *in the composition of blood*. And this was an indication that she was on the right track, that this incompatibility would become an attrition of their relationship and that she would have to leave him sooner or later. He drove his tractor; ploughed further afield. He could not express himself in any other way.

When he went out to fight the fire on the property at Putty, she left for Sydney, frightened of him, she said, whose generosity was matched by equally selfish and violent expectations of wifely duties. She was through, she exclaimed to Walter Gottlieb, with home duties. It was at this point that Gottlieb placed his hand upon her silken knee. You are very lonely and lovely my child, he said, and then with a Tennysonian flourish, added: 'more beautiful than day' and he began to stroke her hair, which was fine, like goose down. Her face was half in darkness when she told him they had never found Roger's body. The fire had exploded in the pine forest where he had towed the trailer with the large water-tank on board. They found the truck overturned and charred, but there was no evidence of any human remains. Then she told Walter Gottlieb something that he would carry to his grave.

It's the fourth corner that makes a cubozoan jellyfish. Gottlieb found himself stung with passion. It was tortuous when she left that evening, her perfume on his academic gown, the fragrance of her kisses on his brow. He had succumbed to what Thomas Mann called *the late adventure of the feelings*. He ploughed a furrow walking on the football field that night, lecturing through the fizzing voltage of cicadas. The next morning he wrote a letter to the Vatican, asking to be released from his vows. He was still wearing his cloak, which was pinned with dead fireflies.

7

My living quarters are behind my surgery. The side facing the sea is glassed in, so that light can flood the open-plan living area. Even the bathroom and bedroom appear to sail out to the horizon. I had the architects design this floor as a replica of the Mies Van der Rohe *Tugendhat* house, using what they called 'smart-glass', which is one-way and can be lightened and darkened manually or automatically with control filters ... like the lens of a microscope. When I look out from my shower, I can see waves in the distance, breaking on the reef. Boom! I suppose that's what it would sound like. Now and again there's a fast-moving speck, not a bird, but a military jet fighter. Boom! Mid-point, just this side of the reef, I often watch Janet Cordillion hanging from her dragon-winged para-sail. Swivel past her and you can see the coastal tanker at eleven o'clock. Directly to the left of the surgery, on an outcrop called The Peninsula, is the Cordillion estate, a white stucco mansion built like a Mexican hacienda, totally out of keeping with the Australian environment. This triangulation between Chinese kite, Acapulco estate and the Modernist repair shop of my surgery counters any hint of transcendence or of any assured culture. Here, on this stretch of coast, there is no nostalgia for history or for aesthetic absolutes. Perhaps this is a good thing ... that in this country, we copy without understanding. How terrifying therefore, even to know history!

The Romans understood how false time could be. They used words like *fama* and *fata*. *Fama* was storytelling and self-promotion, instant fame, man-made; no other evil was swifter because it acted upon the present but was nourished by rumour; a grand illusion. *Fata*, however, was one's fate, the future which 'explained' the past. *Fata* was enduring time. It had legitimacy. The afterword. The gods had decreed it all along. It was hindsight as foresight; a divine prolepsis. It all depended on the time of speaking; on perspective, on the calibration of the sundial, or the dripping of the clepsydra. In the end, these measures were still man-made. Divination was artisanal; and because it was humble craftmanship to build such instruments, stone-masons were always reflective and saturnine. Obituarists.

I meet Blixen Gottlieb in the lobby bar of the Temple Meridien resort. I sit next to the stone fountain, which features twin mermaids. The air is moist and cool. There she is, looking a little dishevelled but smiling fresh-faced, her blonde hair in a ponytail. She is twenty-four today and when I hug her I feel her fragility. We do not speak for a little while. Tonight we will dine at the Rastoni, where they have a seafood carbonara that eliminates everything else from the menu.

When Blixen stays with me she always remarks about the weather; not in any ordinary sense, not in the phatic way most people speak about the weather or the climate. Blixen sets free her ponytail and then refashions it expertly into a small chignon pinned with a tortoiseshell comb. She observes that it practically never drizzles or rains for a prolonged period here in the tropics. There is the afternoon storm which is irregular, and a night rain which lasts less than an hour. It suits me, Blixen said. These are my reasons to be happy. In the year that Father died it rained for three months. Blixen has not really gotten over her father's death. Not like me, who practically forgot my father's disappearance in the space of a year. My father, the great *Professeur, le docteur Émile Sarraute*, achieved his *fata*. He is there on all the plaques, crowned with laurels, in the science buildings in Paris. Intaglios and imbroglios. Blixen does not speak much about her father. Walter Gottlieb, it seemed, had achieved very little at the time of his sudden death, there in the bathroom of his wife's Double Bay mansion, a vial of morphine in his hand, which I had to pry loose as rigor mortis had already manifested itself (Marie was away in London and Blixen was in boarding school), before I could write my report. It was raining, I had noted ... though this seems strangely irrelevant and it was not usual for me to note such extraneous circumstances, I detest formless interventions, lyricism, irrelevant conjunctions conjured up simply to paint a scene ... though Blixen's comment about the rain, made as she stretched her shapely legs out over my balcony while replacing the sunglasses she had on over her forehead ... forged an uncanny connection with the autopsy report. Gottlieb's body was still dripping when I arrived. I smelled a woman's perfume in the bedroom. Something French. Blixen suggested, half-jokingly, that I turn the Rastoni restaurant (which wasn't doing much for me I admit), into an art gallery. I listened with interest. There are enough restaurants in the resort, she said.

The Irukandji jellyfish eats and excretes through the same aperture. I am not a great eater. I've always preferred small, meagre dishes to large Queensland-style meals. I do not like places which display signs that say: *All you can eat.* I'm more inclined towards emaciation. I had never really wanted a partnership in the Rastoni restaurant. It was Carter Cordillion who made me the offer; a rather generous one. Carter would like to get me into his bed, but not while Janet was alive. The thing though, about the Irukandji jellyfish, is that it has three eyes. It sees things differently; so much so I thought the art gallery a good idea.

Grifting

The dark one and the blonde one. It was the dark one who left her diary on the banquette. I'm not returning it now ... that would mean I had probably read it ... besides, identifying myself is not something I do, and the blonde one will recognise me. I wear nondescript clothes ... blue jeans, loafers, pastel shirts. I always wear different glasses, sunglasses, reading glasses, mirror shades. Sometimes I shave, sometimes I sport a light beard. I practise walking with a stoop, limping a little, walking straight-backed like an army colonel, briskly, effortlessly sliding over seats, easing out of doors. Absent-minded eccentricity is my greatest cover. I never feel that I will be caught, in order to preserve, as naturally as possible, a demeanour of affronted self-respect when the moment occurs. If challenged, I always distractedly produce authentic credit cards or sometimes I even pay in cash.

Grifter/grafter: a sneak thief. Not a polite etymology, since some believe the word 'graft' comes from the word 'job', meaning excrescence. I agree. I blame my truncated education. Not a great one: waiter/barman; barman/waiter. At least I know the workings of hotels. I know jobs. When the chambermaid, for example, is in the bedroom, she always turns on the TV. Making beds can be monotonous. No one can hear anything when Oprah Winfrey is on. When the maid does the bathroom, I scan for briefcases and watches. In corridors, during mini-bar replenishments, I pick off whiskey and cognac from the drinks trolley. I make sure I go up and down the lifts a few times so the staff recognise me. I fiddle with plastic room cards if confronted, complain about demagnetised strips. I never go onto a floor if I hear a walkie-talkie. Fire escapes are the best exits. Sometimes you can be lucky. The early-bird checkout will drop his card into a slot in the concierge's desk. You ring the concierge from an in-house phone – you need him now, you're maintenance and the lift-door is stuck. Collect the card from behind the slot. Sometimes they forget to wipe the code for the next guest. Sometimes you can only break into the gym or the poolside deck ... where you can have brunch on the same room tab. Now and again I ring for a late checkout, queue for lunch, study the room carefully, go to the toilet when the buffet is crowded and slip out, walking briskly, heading for free drinks at the next gallery opening; canapés at a book launch; unbadged convention dinners.

I was attracted to the blonde one on the plane. Now I'm rather interested in the dark one; the older woman. They are so happy to see one another they don't notice I'm listening in. Sometimes you can find out where they're staying. But I'm not getting much from this conversation. I pull out her diary which I've re-covered in brown paper, try to match the voice to the writing.

8

Blixen is in her last year in medical school and I'm trying to talk her out of going onto an internship where she'll work double time for no money, learning on the job to do what I did for twenty years, a jack of all trades, prescribing drugs, delivering babies, cleaning out pus, suturing wounds, picking out glass, giving myself regular hepatitis shots, tetanus shots, flu shots, looking down throats and up anuses. You've got to be dedicated to people, I said. It would be better to specialise. Why didn't you, Jude? Blixen asked. Because ... well ... you know the answer. Blixen nodded. Your father the specialist. No, the researcher. He wasn't interested in people. A doctor? he used to ask, who wants to be a doctor? You think I want a dingy practice in Pigalle peering at penises or breathing the foetid exhalations of old crones? Have patients steal my ether for personal sniffing, hear them snivelling behind doors, pushing their children forward onto my knees, kids whose bums are seething with worms, their noses oozing, while I listen to their hacking coughs and catch their spew in a basin? You think that is heroic?

You see how I was not interested in his rhetoric. Words should cleanse, not sully. It was those ready-made phrases which came out of him so easily which pushed me in the opposite direction. *Words are physicians of the mind* ... Aeschylus. Don't quote Aeschylus to me please, Blixen said, and I saw that she was disturbed by what I was saying. Her father had quoted Aeschylus to her: how words should dissect, fumigate, sterilise the physical loathsomeness of sin. He made everybody heroic, Blixen said, speaking of Walter Gottlieb her father, so much so that his book was a tribute ... the whole thing a tribute to failure, Blixen said, and all you speak of is success, the success of art, the success of business ...

I thought Blixen was going to cry. I thought I had touched a raw nerve, but I am always doing this to people I think are worthy of being touched. Rastoni's was filling up. I ordered the seafood carbonara, the Stella Maris water, the Lacrima Christi del Vesuvio 2001. Gastronomy mimicked religion and anticipated medical methods. Surgery, after all, is not only a cutting up of sacrificial victims ... you learn from observing pork butchers how to put it all back again, festively, in the window. Your father wrote his book whilst suffering a fugue, I said, just to change the subject. Blixen sighed and looked away. Her eyes were glassy. I tried to fill the awkward silence which followed. It now seems to me he intended it to be read only after his death. He spoke as a dead man, Blixen murmured ... out of time, about things which the living couldn't recognise. My father tore up his manuscript you know, and then pasted fragments of it together. Reading him was like ... I don't know ... reading a history of wounds. His publisher did well editing and marketing it. Yes, I said. Then came Jason Redvers' hatchet job.

There I go opening up wounds. I didn't mean it. I didn't mean to stir up Blixen's painful memories of how Redvers' book came out just before Gottlieb's novel ... the former consisting of allegories of the master stealing from the student, the professor filching stories from the acolyte. It tarnished a good novel, I said, trying to compensate for my mistake, and that publisher of his ... Blonsky? ... Kapuszinsky? Brezinsky, Blixen added helpfully, yes, Brezinsky the libel lawyer, I said, would have known how to turn an allegory into a claim ... the plague of plagiarism, or some such thing.

I stopped there. I didn't want to hurt Blixen any more by getting into such a conversation. There's that pale drifter again. I've seen him lifting the tips from tables. He thinks he's not being observed, but I watch the back of his head reflected in the mirror on the Rastoni wall, beside the photograph of Ernest Hemingway and a huge swordfish.

9

Blixen gets distracted, in the same way her father used to be sidetracked by mirrors. She peers through a kaleidoscope, not a microscope. Then again a kaleidoscope is not that distant from a microscope. While she allows fragments to fall into place differently each time, serendipitously, my micrological procedure isn't any more objective than hers. I frame a particle of jellyfish to search for its thickness and it melts away from the light to reform differently. New worlds come to life under illumination. Reconstituting and repairing. But first I have to slice through the jelly. Surgery as sculpture. What looks disfigured in its everyday impenetrability, appears properly ordered from another point of view. I am far more aggressive than Blixen, and I sometimes wonder if I have lost my life for having no romance. Take the *Chironex fleckeri* box jellyfish, which was thought to be the most common jellyfish around here, locally known as the sea wasp or sea stinger. This venomous creature was known as *Chiropsalmus quadrigatus*, from which the common name 'quadie' was derived. But this is not the same as *Carukia barnesi*, which is far more lethal. True, the latter is a cubozoan, like the 'quadie', but such single-minded, single-eyed obsession over having four sides may be limiting. I squint but I don't see where the two animals have diverged. I only see my patient record cards, my ordered laboratory and shelves of drugs, my victims in their vinegar bath. Jellyfish deserve more poetry, more than my quadratic field.

Blixen is far less restricted. She has her colourful kaleidoscope: her gorgeous body; her childhood memories; her innocent personality; her heroes and heroines. The first principle of wooing is to make oneself sevenfold, wrote Walter Benjamin.

10

I'm busy treating Mickey Jones for burns. He's old and his hand is blistered from trying to douse his flaming barbeque with brandy. He's of the old school, a Francophile, wears a beret, but has never travelled overseas. He relives the First World War although he wasn't even born then. He comes to see me because he says French women speak beautifully and they give him a hard-on, although he no longer remembers how that felt. I change the bandage on his hand with care. I do this tenderly, more tenderly than usual. Perhaps it's because Blixen is working as my nurse, observing everything I do.

When we have a free moment between patients, I speak to her of my art gallery idea. I'm feeling flippant and I tell her I'm going to call it *The Museum of Forgery*. After all, no one knows what I'm going to put in it. World-famous reproductions, perhaps. Oh yes, I do, Blixen says, and kisses me on the neck while I look out to sea and observe Janet Cordillion, finally aloft after several failed attempts. I'm going to call it the Galerie Kahnweiler, after the gallery which used to be at the end of my street in Paris, I tell her.

It was mid-afternoon when the first sting patient of the season was brought in. A boy of about fourteen, of Middle-Eastern background, his mother beside herself with worry, pulling at her chalabi, not having been warned that Australia was full of venomous creatures which you could hardly see, full of danger signs in a language few who come from distant cultures could read, full of words just as deadly when unseen. Her jewellery flashed beneath. The boy was sweating, his arms and legs in severe cramp, moaning with every intake of breath, his voice trembling. I asked Blixen and his mother to restrain him from touching the stings. He's shouting in Arabic now, and his mother embarrassed, apologises. We smile, shake our heads, it's okay, we do not know the words. I draw a hypodermic and he is silenced. Normally, I would inject a dose of Fentanyl – with no known neurotoxicity; but there is a new drug on the market. I ask his mother if he is allergic to sheep, to sheep products. No? Then 2 ml. of Parenteral injected slowly into a vein perhaps; no, I think 6 ml. injected slowly into a muscle; his suffering finally punctured. The results are good. Before day's end they've brought in three more cases. Jellyfish are being washed up on the beach, nematocysts discharging into those who swept upon them unwarily.

Blixen and I open a champagne. Let's hope there are no night swimmers. They've set up arc lights on the beach, hammered in warning signs. They do not know that light attracts jellyfish, which are most numerous eight to ten days after a full moon, their canopies extending so they rise further up to the surface of the water. But you can't tell functionaries to turn off their lights. It's a matter of public safety, they will say. Times are such that everything is a drama, an emergency ... it's an obsession with flashing lights and sirens. No one reflects on the idea of plagues, of epidemics as having biblical precedence, cyclical occurrences, wheels within wheels. No one reads the implications of why terror comes from not knowing life's reproductions. Why do we name a species of jellyfish, the scyphozoa, the *Medusa*, for instance? Formerly a beautiful virgin whose gaze could turn men to stone, Medusa slept with Poseidon, the god of the sea, in Athena's temple. Athena was livid with rage and transformed Medusa's hair into live snakes. She was hydra-headed. If one serpent was killed, another sprang up in its place. It was a ghastly reproduction of beauty. Medusa was the victim in the end ... because she was once seductive. One sample is intriguing. A million is an invasion. For that, people have been exterminated.

Look at Blixen. Her mind inseparable from her body. She watches television in order to spot our little beach on the news. Your great-grandmother, I began, speaking over the voice-over on the screen, came up here for holidays. Mmm, she said, drawing up her legs under her in the way little girls did, then stretching out a hand began to stroke my hair, that white lick which has persisted in my coiffure since early adolescence, something I put down to my father's experimentation, a vial of peroxide or something more evil. I breathe with difficulty upon another's touch. I never knew my great-grandmother, Blixen yawned. Her chest filled like an hour-glass and suddenly Blixen appeared like her great-grandmother Julia Grace.

I'm tired of patients, Blixen said. Others are too much in me. I recognised this last statement. It was a complaint heard often in my surgery. Patients who had suffered some mental breakdown. Too many voices in the head. Too much for the system. After all, Blixen was a twin of a dead twin. She lost Blimunde, half of herself, at the age of five. Drowned in her father's pool. But I don't need to go into all that. All the business of Fabiana's psychosis. The history of her breakdowns, the way she lived several lives; city lives, country lives; how she always returned from the city looking for respite from all those people inside her. Before they were settled with their father, the twins alternated between the flat in Potts Point, the shop in Double Bay and the farm at Putty. Roger, her husband, enjoyed having the twins on his lap, showing them the burrs he had picked out of his lumber jacket, making sheep noises. But I think he grew tired of Fabiana's absences. She would just get up and leave him there; she would go missing days at a time. He suspected it was a sort of concubinage in reverse. She sojourned in several houses. He didn't know, when he married her under that big almond tree behind the big house at Putty, that she had this fracture in her. He didn't know she was quite incapable of raising children normally, having dragged them in a pram from flat to flat in King's Cross, neglecting to pay her bills, her electricity supply cut off. When she bought a car, she drifted off while driving and rammed several vehicles outside the Conservatorium of Music and a wheel came loose and bounced into the Botanical Gardens, knocking over a fertility monument shaped like a breast. The police found two babies in a large cardboard box on the floor of the back seat. Roger didn't know about that because her friends hushed it up. Nor did he know that her neighbours had tried to help her and that she had accused them of interference, screaming obscenities while she threw bottles at them as they rang the child-welfare authority. After they had been married a month, she and Roger began quarrelling virtually every day. It was the result of a mixture of alcohol and provocation; seduction and jealousy. Minor squabbles turned into suicidal odysseys, and once he had to rescue her from a cheap motel in Darwin, where she had been held captive by a complete stranger. The police were not called on that occasion. He hadn't researched her past carefully enough. Otherwise, he would have found that it was stubbornness, it was pride, it was the injustice of it all ... that she had not been gifted with the maniacal discipline of a great artist.

It was equally unfair for Walter Gottlieb. He had just left the priesthood. He had little money. He had to marry Marie de Nerval to convince the authorities of legal custody. He just had to make it work. And then on a cloudy day, with his friend Redvers sunk in a fugue by the side of the pool, Blimunde had floated out of her inflated angel wings and had found bottom.

11

From the notebooks of Walter Gottlieb

The sixteenth-century mind was not the same as ours. There was a lot more doubt. A lot more superstition and speculation. In comparison, we are quite uninventive. We fear failure. We adopt received opinions, sitting in our cages constructed by others. We live for them. We speak their inanities, just to make noises. We no longer ruminate like Montaigne, who described his breath as 'excremental', pushing out only digested thoughts. As Redvers used to say, even shit could be philosophy. On his death-bed, Montaigne's remaining moments contained a dialogue with imaginary servants as he clung to the social meaning of dying together (commourans was the word he used), under the seductions of sleep. *Meet me at the next tavern*, he said, *I have never succeeded in keeping some part of me from always wandering.* He didn't mean a smoky chamber at the inn. He wanted to be in a *convenient* part of the house. Nowhere moreso than in the bathroom, being bathed in brine for his ulcerations. In the sixteenth century, hot baths were said to have caused madness by overheating the liver and putrefying the humours. It was observed how flowers wilted when placed in a hot tub. These observations were noted down in flowery figures of speech, excessive in their encouragement of tepidness and moderation. The bath, apparently, was morbid. It provoked thoughts about death. For Montaigne, it had a familiar feel. He was a melancholic.

He always referred to his friend Booty, or Étienne de *La Boétie*, as La Boitie, unconsciously associating a limp (*boiterie*) with a lure (*boête*). Booty suffered from terminal melancholy, which Montaigne was trying to avoid without success. Booty lived under the sign of saturn. In a Zürich library I once came across this illustration. It's a portrait of Jason Redvers ... I've seen him naked, asleep on my lawn. He may be holding a crutch, or the handle-bars of his bicycle. He's just lopped off desire with that sickle.

A dialogue and a phone call

I found Blixen in the bath. It was a bright blue morning and no tourists were walking on the sand outside, no one stepping between the mounds of jelly. The beach was deserted and the jetty was devoid of cormorants. No one was fishing. I heard voices, and at first they seemed to be coming from an open window, but it was Blixen in the bath. I knocked and went in. She said she was exorcising ghosts. Exercising? She smiled and then I saw that she was in tears. She tried to hide her face in a wash cloth. I took it from her gently and scrubbed her back. She was better then. I said the bath was not a good place to be on one's own. This was the wrong thing to have uttered. I'm going to leave soon, Blixen said.

I try not to speculate. When I observe, I am silent. When I speculate, I always say the wrong thing. I do not know how to fill the silence while waiting for fragments in the kaleidoscope to fall into place. For Blixen, this silence is a condemnation. In the sixteenth century it would have been accepted as a form of *skepsis*. A dignified doubt which served coherence and unity. I am not one for soothing words when there is no intellectual solution which justifies them.

Your father always walked with a slight limp, I said to Blixen. I asked him about it several times when he came into my Double Bay surgery for his blood-pressure tablets, his Prozac, his Viagra.

You lie back in the bath while I place a hot towel behind your head.

It was not a real limp, you finally said. He zigzagged all over Portugal with that lurching gait. Doing research. I've shown you his notebooks.

Montaigne also walked with a limp, I said. Perhaps it was from falling off his horse, but I rather doubt whether it was a real physical disability. Baudelaire, I believe, walked erratically, bobbing and weaving.

Yes, I know, you said. Redvers had written about it too. I don't know if any of it was true. He was a piss-taker. I used to see him shaking himself on the lawn at midnight. He was probably making fun of Daddy. Redvers always scorned hospitality, and to urinate on Daddy's million-dollar lawn was employing his own freedom of expression.

I don't think so, I said. Redvers had a prostate problem which was going to kill him. The boot was on the other foot. Come to think of it, they were both aware of their mortality. Montaigne wrote of his love for cripples because they resisted being dragged along by the current. Erasmus declared that since Amazons crippled their future studs, it was crippled men, not crippled women, who were more sexually desirable. If that's an affectation, it's a positive one for me nevertheless. Friends, after all, were crutches for all kinds of repression.

This argument of mine was unconvincing. I noticed you frowned. You hold your breath and slide for a moment under the water. I know this moment of yours. See nothing, hear nothing. You rise, blowing like a seal. Why do you hate baths? you ask. They are so purifying.

It's good to attend to yourself, I said to Blixen. Then I left the bathroom. I did not mean to upset her. I did not mean to imply her father had been unethical, faking an intellectual limp to cover his tracks. Those who do not attend to their being are ready for a fall. I know Blixen is half Blimunde and she is not always in control. She has bath fugues. You cannot drown in a bath unless drunk or drugged; given over completely. After our talk, Blixen now bathes in private and she has locked the door.

I'm in two minds about locks on bathroom doors. Builders install them as a matter of course, though the number of deaths in bathrooms should be a warning to us all: Jim Morrison – heart attack in his suds; Keith Relf – electrocuted while flaying his Fender in the tub; Catherine the Great never emerged from her visit – she was pushing at the door the wrong way when she had a stroke; Claude François – the teen idol with the sequined suits who sang *My Way* – Clo-Clo, as he was known – electrocuted himself in the bath while standing up to change a light bulb. I am totally against cheap hotels. Then again, if Marat had had a lock on his bathroom door, Charlotte Corday would not have been able to stab him to death. And despite W.H. Auden's public praise of Man's private bath – his *Encomium Balneae*, as a site of Edenic and carnal pleasure with a lock on the inside – it was the unlocked door which saved Carter Cordillion.

Carter Cordillion was frantic when I received his phone call last April. He sounded really desperate, and was in great panic. Please come right away, he pleaded. My place. Break down the bathroom door if you have to; the neighbours aren't home. I wasn't going to do this without further information. It occurred to me from the sound of his voice that this was not a joke or ploy to get me into his bathroom. Can you tell me what the problem is? I asked. No. He could not. Something intimate had gone terribly wrong. Could I please come now? It would be your duty of care, he said. A failure of care, he insisted. Why don't you call the ambulance? I asked. As I said, he shouted. It's intimate! Johnny Smee … he's my mechanic … his brother's the town paramedic. I can't call them. Can you hurry?

I drove over to the hacienda. His palm trees had dislodged some of their green coconuts. The red gravel on the drive was bright. The red tiles on the roof were too bright. The red brick path blinded me. I put on my sunglasses. Knocked on the front door. No one. I opened the door. Carter? I called. I heard a grunt. Judith! he yelled. Upstairs. Quickly. I walked up the sweeping stairs slowly. It was not a moment in which to be surprised. I did not want him appearing naked or in a towel, his gold chain around his neck, complaining about his gout or water in his ear. In the bathroom! He was struggling. In some pain. And there he was in the huge spa bath lying on his side with his head lolling above the oily water. I've got a lemon up my arse. What? I've pushed a lemon up my bum, he gasped. It's stuck ... all the way in. Hurting like mad. I helped him up. Hauled him over the edge of the tub. He was a big man and he used all the strength he had in his arms, but his legs were like jelly. I placed a few towels under him. His splayed legs were hairy. For an instant I thought of Montaigne, who contrasted the size of his imagination with his scanty penis. *Mentula minuta*. Carter had never shown much imagination, but now I was rethinking that. Pain shrivels. I searched in my bag and gave him a shot of muscle relaxant. Put on my gloves and fished out the lemon. I did not ask what he was doing with it up there. He looked immensely relieved. He smiled inanely and begged me not to tell anyone. Then he recovered himself and added that of course I would not tell; I was bound by professional ethics. I let myself out of his house. When I arrived back at the surgery I took a long time cleaning my arms with Hibiclens, removing all the bath oil, continuing my dialogue with Blixen, only the bathroom was empty and she was gone. The house was as bleak as the weekend ahead. There were no fish in the sea. I made myself a gin and tonic. No; no lemon.

12

It's official, now listed as an 'epidemic', though the word really means a disease prevalent among a people, which has entered them from an outside locality. The word 'plague' is perhaps closer to the truth. Mounds of jellyfish have been washed up on the sand, now being cleared away by bobcats, pushed into pits and then covered over. Come look at this.

Slide #2: Carybdea Rastoni
This little creature is called the 'Jimble'. It's not deadly, though it can cause a wheal on the skin ... see how vinegar inhibits the discharge. Now watch as I apply methylated spirits ... all the nematocysts are firing. The sound of firing and the smell of methylated spirits. 1943. My father doggedly continued with his experiments throughout the war, his smell the odour of ether and methylated spirits. He married my mother smelling like that in the church at Montmartre, and all the time the firing, now close, now far away, and while they were going home in the Métro a Jewish woman threw herself in front of the train and workers had to drag out her body, my father placing a handkerchief soaked in ether over my mother's nose so she could be led drowsily back through the streets and later, much later, long after the war, he told me she would never have survived even though he had married her, because her memories would have caught up with her in the end, but while all the firing was going on, they enjoyed a rather bourgeois life, despite the rationing, going down to the little restaurant at the corner of the rue de Vaugirard and the Boulevard du Montparnasse, sipping minestrone, and all she could hear was the crackling which she thought was distant gunfire but which turned out to be the backfiring of trucks as they came speeding down towards the Seine, turning eastwards with 8,000 Jews being deported to work camps, where they would later be pushed into pits and then covered over, my mother gripping the edge of the white linen tablecloth as she listened for the trucks, my mother who had a morphine habit on account of her guilt, on account of surviving by imposture, a Jewish woman married to a Catholic man who was a well-known specialist in human skin diseases, who kept morphine liberally stored in a cool meat-safe, and there was my mother finally, stretched out on the table at the morgue when they had fished her out of the Seine ... it was ten years since the end of the war ... her

dress over her head, and my father was shouting to the attendant to shut the door through which I was peering, and the door was pushed so hard it slammed onto my nose, tears of pain welling up into my eyes though it was not the same pain as that which lay in my chest as I watched my father bathing with his mistresses in his apartment, pouring champagne taché into the water, the women giggling with fleshy stupidity and shameless ignorance, when I saw through the keyhole with one eye what it was like to be enslaved to desire.

13

The condition of awareness is sensitivity to form, I said to Blixen as we drove up into the Daintree rainforest to get away from the volume of patients. Blixen enjoyed herself that afternoon, hopping over the huge boulders in the river. Parrots swooped at great speed through trees, leaving just a dab of colour behind. Riverine birds, less colourful, dipped and swung up to misty peaks and the roaring and gushing of water drowned out conversation. On the other bank some Indigenous people ... you didn't see them at first until you glimpsed the red of their bandanas ... were drinking the day away since no one paid them as guides anymore, and they drank to the reality of their rock-spirits haunting the places from which the un-aware would fall, deep into the ravine, for having violated the laws of form.

Julia Grace violated the laws of form. Some of the letters between her and the poet Camilo Conceição have survived. You could have said she expressed too strong a desire for the cloudy lack of perspective in some of the Chinese paintings that he possessed, where distance was not accounted for, where mountains met the di-mensions of prophets, and women, suspended midair, sailed in their silks over deadly gorges. Instead, Julia Grace said she did not think such paintings had much value. They were talked up in catalogues, she said. They didn't subscribe to the principle of originality. What was certain was that a shipment of them had arrived at the Grace property a few months after she had returned home from France.

Blixen, fixing a stare upon the roaring waters, said that she would like to give them to me as a gift. But a gift was always tainted with debt. Best to give a gift away. Friendship rested on divestment, not investment. Further surgery on the idea was needed, I said to her. I could see she was disappointed with my response, but the murky world in which these artworks had come into her possession through the coincidence of Fabiana's disappearance overseas was not where I wanted to go. Besides, I didn't wish to take possession of anything that was tainted with ancestral tragedy. God knows, I've already seen part of the Barringila collection from Putty which had been brought to Walter Gottlieb's place at Double Bay and I had recognised some of Jason Redvers' works among the Chinese collection, paintings he was forging in Milan in the late 'sixties, mass producing Francis Bacons with sales going to the Red Brigades. When Bacon moved studios he abandoned quite a few canvasses, simply because they were too awkward to push through the narrow doors. He encouraged friends, poor artists, squatters, itinerants, to paint over them. One could come into possession of a genuine Francis Bacon beneath the top coat, just as one could come across a genuine Ma Yüan beneath one of the Conceição restorations. One could also buy an inane despoliation. I sat for him once, I said to Blixen. No, not for Bacon, but for Redvers. The result was not a fake and it wasn't badly done either. He even signed the back of it *Justine de Reviers*, no doubt making fun of the way I'd always got his name wrong. I wonder if he knew that the infirmary at Auschwitz was called the Revier. You expected to die upon entering it. My mother would have preferred to expire there, perhaps would have willed it to arrive sooner, exhausted from her hard labour, making the most of a bed and a blanket with less lice. That's where she would have given birth to me in May 1944. That's where they did some experiments, coating newborn babies in lard and leaving them in the snow, timing their survival and their liquidation. One or two out of a hundred survived. Those who did, saved their mothers as well. All were given lukewarm baths in the Revier, their mothers set to work carrying crates of bottles containing blood, and then the same bottles containing a colourless liquid. There were potted plants in the corridors; tiny saplings.

On the morning of the twenty-fifth of September 1940, at the border between Vichy France and Fascist Spain, the philosopher Walter Benjamin rested his head on his briefcase beneath an almond sapling. There was a warm westerly wind. Benjamin had less than twenty-four hours to live. Walter Gottlieb found that almond tree, fully grown, laden with nuts, at Port Bou. He told me that when he sat beneath it, he could recall someone else's memories. He said: *if you listen closely, you can actually hear the other's recollection, gathering like a swarm of grasshoppers on a mid-summer's evening.* This habit of sitting under trees may have been his refuge from his wife Marie de Nerval. But the sussuration of grasshoppers – for that was the sound Fabiana was making beside him that fateful night when Marie was in Paris, the sound of Fabiana removing her skirt and her stockings, the sound of her climbing on top of him in his marriage bed – signalled a plague. He was losing his mind; losing himself to desire's swarms. Gottlieb, I said, could not have been a Jewish name. God, after all, could never be named. Blixen ducked under the water. She was beneath the suds a long time. Then she rose and I handed her a towel. Not in Hebrew, she said. But it's possible in German. The real family name, she said, was Goldberg.

So Walter Goldberg made his way to his bathroom at one in the morning after Fabiana had left, every artery in his body constricted with guilt ... there would have been a tight knot around his heart and his penis, flashing lights erupting behind his eyelids; there would have been wheels of fire, blacksmiths with eye-patches, their red arms in molten metal, weaving a net so fine through which only time could escape ... and in the bathroom he would have glimpsed, in the tiny aperture of his remaining moment of consciousness, the whole machinery of the Underworld.

On the Cook Highway we pass Carter Cordillion's gold Mercedes speeding the other way. Do you know him very well? Blixen asks. Not very well, I say, but Blixen knows I'm lying. I wonder if I should tell her the truth about everything. Trade a secret for her secret. It may have been what Fabiana told Redvers just before he accidentally blew himself up with a stick of gelignite down by the waterhole on the Putty property – bits of his clothes were scattered all over the branches (the locals said it was a very windy day; gale force winds which may have provided static electricity in the air, causing a spark in the leg wires, which Redvers had not insulated) – it may have been what she said to him that made him go down there to try to blow a hole in the rock with his gel. After all, when the wind blows, the mad are distressed. 'If a dead tree falls,' Fabiana said to him, 'and is wedged in the fork of another, you might just alter your perspective and not notice it. On the other hand, if you are obsessed with it, you've got to figure out how to fell it – at some personal risk.'

Anyway, that's what the shop-owner McCredie said.

Wood for the fire; grist to the mill. All stories are caught in the forks of others.

14

It was at the Temple Meridien resort some years ago, when I first moved up to Queensland, that I met Carter Cordillion. I was looking for a place for my surgery and ideally, a double-storey building so I would have a view of the sea over the gorse. Carter was walking across the lobby with a hand outstretched, a palm which was remarkably soft, though he was quite rugged in appearance, and he was un-shaven, dressed in his immaculate Armani suit, saying: 'It sure is a pleasure meeting you ...' in what I believed to be an Irish accent, but which turned out to be trans-atlantic. It was a good meeting. Cor-dillion was true to his word and I picked up some promising real estate, since the Temple Meridien resort was at the far end of town on the paved concourse, my property only two houses along from it, on a small dirt road. Cordillion said mine would become the best street in the area, and as the second property facing the beach, the architecture of which he described as *Carribean tropical vernacular*, my pavilion home would make a good business investment. Especially since the present occupant had had remote-controlled windows installed and the Italian Saturnia marble floors laid by real artisans. Carter liked my idea of doing the clinical business down in the old cottage and enjoying an unfettered private existence up the slope. Only the best patients would come to you, he said. Then he asked me all about toxicology.

It was during my second meeting with him that he introduced his wife Janet to me. We met for dinner at the Poseidon Bar. Janet had taken too much sun and glowed like a radium dial, destined for a cancer ward. Her dyed ash-blonde hair and bottomless blue eyes interlaced with crows' feet gave her the appearance of an alien. She and Cordillion didn't seem as if they were 'together'. She hardly spoke except when we talked about reef sports. She invited me out on their cruiser and suggested para-gliding and underwater activities. I made a feeble excuse. Flying and diving were unnatural for humans. Carter guffawed, loosened his tie and before I knew what he was doing, had his hand on my knee under the long tablecloth. I had on my moiré skirt. It was a cold hand and I didn't shift my leg. He let it lie there like a dead fish and then pinched at my stocking with little minnow gestures. I just wanted to see how far he would go. He didn't. When Janet looked uncomfortable enough he brought his hand back up onto the table. There was a pulse which kept throbbing in the vein in his neck. This diastolic moment dilates the heart. The systolic contracts it. One extends and dissipates the body, sluicing it with blood. The other contracts the body in order for it to build force and escape from itself. Carter was trying to flee his own body. On his fifth visit to my surgery, he wanted some advice on sexually transmitted diseases. I sent him for a blood test, but not before he insisted on my examining his penis. I was not interested in such suggestions, unless there was some medical connection. But let me write this differently on his card. His *mentula*, as Montaigne would have put it, was swollen. I thought of my marine research: *Ascidia Mentula*: predominantly occurring on the upper faces of circalittoral bedrock with little tidal flow. It has a rather barren, pink appearance due to grazing pressure from sea urchins. Cordillion's member displayed signs of contusions caused by ligatures.

Time also has a diastole and a systole, like a water clock; the dilation of a drop when it gathers momentum is followed by its contraction and dissipation when it splatters. The pressure and pleasure of my moment with Blixen was bound to be shattered. While I was attending to Carter, I saw his bronzed, towheaded son outside in the waiting room, engaging in an animated conversation with her, and she was excited, fawning, smiling just a little too much, looking just a little too young and pretty.

Grafting

I am a drifter. I work by association; sleights of hand; petty theft. I have always lived this way, and have been caught out only a few times. You learn from being caught; it makes you cleverer on the next occasion. I've found out that she is a doctor, the dark one, with a successful practice in town. Dr Judith Sarraute. Her network of associations is a very interesting one: high flyers, resort owners, developers; the big end of a very small town. Of course they are hardly ever there. Seasonal people. Like me.

To graft: to insert a graft into a branch or stem of another tree; to propagate by insertion; to implant. I suppose Dr Judith Sarraute has done some surgical implanting in her time. On the hotel internet I discovered something about a bungled sex-change operation. Sarraute was not the chief surgeon. She returned to being a GP after that. Fled Sydney. My profession, however, may be an even older one than surgery. For centuries they have been taking twigs from ancient trees, grafting them onto younger ones. My associations go back to Adam. We branch out; we connect and proliferate ... sometimes to no end.

I sit in this restaurant drinking sweet wine and study the hybrid rose they have in a vase on the table. The sun shines with a metallic glare and the sea is sick, heaving, dirty green. I notice these things because my survival depends on noticing. The white tablecloth burns my eyes and the fried fish I have eaten layers the emptiness with bones. There is hardly anyone in the restaurant and that spells trouble for me. It means I will have to leave when the waiter goes to the kitchen; slip out the side between the heavy plastic which they've let down to break the salt wind ruffling the tablecloths, knocking over the roses. A gold Mercedes cruises the waterfront. I recognise the heavy build of the driver; the five o'clock shadow on his cheeks, the slouch to one side, the way he works the wheel with one hand. I've seen him park at Cairns airport. On a connecting flight between Sydney and Los Angeles (I was stopping in Sydney, mingling with transit passengers ... you never know what kind of duty-free you can collect from under seats on sleepy stopovers), I saw him embracing a woman. He was holding shopping bags in both hands. She looked like a porn star, dressed in a short golden chiffon skirt, leopard skin tights, black top with much cleavage. There was something about her that wasn't right. For a brief second, I looked again ... it's not good for me to stare, not in my line of business. But there was something strange that stood out. I couldn't be sure about the woman part of her. It was as if it had been grafted on. But then what do I know? I have to stay pallid, wallflowery, in order not to be noticed. It never pays to be too analytical. It's hard work, going with the flow.

The word 'work' is the original meaning of 'graft'. But the meaning has slipped, deteriorated. One root has been corrupted, one branch rotted. I still consider it a trade, a craft. But look what they've done with it: scammer, sharper, chiseller, swindler, gouger, clip artist, con artist, beguiler, cheater, deceiver, trickster, slicker, welsher. People who use these words forget one thing: we are all codes and copies, melting, merging. Look at this DNA map they've just produced. I found it in a catalogue. They tell me you can buy it at a huge price, the litmus paper dissolving beneath your microscope into key molecules from which you can distinguish double helices, twin spiral staircases of life, mortal coils. It's strange, but I've always felt cheated by science, by scientific people. None of their results benefitted me; they did not make me happy beyond the three seconds or so of happiness I enjoyed every six months. I'm like the fish bones on my plate ... left behind, fossilised ... dead fish eyes won't be seeing rainbows out there over the sea ... in school I learned human skin colour comes from rainbows ... it changes when seen through a prism ... was it Mendel or Mendelssohn who discovered the chromatic scales? My brief forays into amphetamines have ruined my memory. I think I'm alone; singular. But really, I'm born to look like someone else. In my brief forays into sex I've often had the bored concentration of a barramundi in a drying billabong ... beyond help ... foggy ... staring with fried cataracts at the harsh light of the tropics which turned a graft into an open sore, thinking how we loved one another because we were blind ... oops, there he is, Cordillion, looking like a TV weatherman, coming into the restaurant, checking the sky through his mirror sunglasses ... flesh, all too fleshy ... how are you? Good. How's Janet? I will ask him. He'll try to flip through his mental Roladex ... who the hell are you? ... I will make the observation that it wasn't Janet at the airport, the woman with whom he took the flight to LA, that he may want to pay for my meal ... and another bottle of the Sancerre. But I think better of it, say nothing, and slip out through the side, briefly parting the plastic, my cheeks stinging with salt.

15

Chinese art is non-representational, I was saying to Blixen as we lay on our banana lounges on the lawn in front of the beach. We have been working fifteen-hour days at the surgery and finally tourists have got the message about stingers. Now we are taking a day off, relaxing in front of the Pacific Palisades watching the water turn pink with coral spawn. Blixen was speaking about the Conceição paintings. Ancient Chinese art, I continued my lecture, was not about realism, nor about the copying of reality, which is really a kind of trickery, if you think deeply enough about it ... you know, the discovery of perspective destroyed narrative and emotion, I was saying to Blixen, who was not listening at all, her dreamy eyes wandering all over the beach, waiting to catch a glimpse of Travis, the Cordillion boy, who any moment now would saunter up rubbing his abdominal muscles with its protruding navel, smiling behind his shades and Blixen would melt into embarrassment ... for God's sake, she's twenty four, it's as though she's never had a date with a six-pack, spending all her life studying and sipping atrocious coffee with bespectacled nerds at the university. Perspective made you melancholic, I was saying, it put you at a distance, and you suffered from being at one remove, never arriving, but always being held by the vanishing point. Well, there's such a lot Blixen doesn't know about, and I guess I have to let her go find out herself.

It's not as though she didn't know about her mother Fabiana, who was always looking for adventure in men with whom she shouldn't have become intimate ... she was incapable of detaching her eyes, anxious she would not be admired ... sleeping with her neighbour's boyfriend, so that what's her name ... Miranda, yes, that was it, flew into a frenzy of rage and jealousy and fired guns up at the house in Putty, and it was not as though Blixen didn't know about Fabiana's increasing instability, her obsession with her analyst and with hourglasses and with Brazilian boys who ran dodgy nightclubs, guitar players who helped her grow marijuana on the patch of land cleared inside a pine forest, where she stored drugs in a silo protected by dogs ... where she watched time like a cat watched goldfish. It's not as though Blixen was entirely innocent about me, since she already knew of my career as a surgical specialist at the North Sydney clinic where I did sex-change operations and that I had given it up when I was convinced it destroyed too many lives, and it's not as though I hadn't written about how it was better to have left trannies in two minds rather than to be implanted and grafted, forever dissatisfied and forever to be pumped full of drugs until the body's hormones revolted and flesh fell into fat, shape into silicone, all melting like a Bacon painting into lonely grief, paranoid-schizophrenia; suicide ... it's not as though Blixen had been sheltered from all these things ... from her father's investments in coastal property, his dealings with shady financiers, so that when he died, much of it passed onto her. He was her hero. Of course Blixen hadn't gone through Redvers' writings since she found the latter's literary style impenetrable and therefore would not have read that chapter in *Brief Lives (II)*, where, without any need for allegory or subterfuge, he outlined the venal motives of his friend Walter Gottlieb, criticising the latter's need to 'divine' fame for himself, exploiting rumour, buying the public's belief that he had been let into a secret, when all the time he had been stealing his, Redvers' stories ... so Redvers said ... adding that he, Redvers, was a descendant of the Portuguese poet Camilo Conceição ... Redvers, who was always broke; Redvers, who envied his erstwhile friend, mentor and benefactor Walter Gottlieb, and Redvers, who wrote that beautiful elegy for Blimunde. No, Blixen didn't know about Redvers and me.

But I wasn't going to say this to her. Not while she was infatuated with Travis. Just as I wasn't going to remind her that at the age of fifteen, after a weekend in Putty, she had run back to her father Walter Gottlieb and had tried to encircle his thick waist with her thin arms. He didn't hug back. He never did.

Slide #3: Tripedalia Fabiana

The bell reaches 14mm across and has many warty mammilations containing nematocysts. There is little information on the Tripedalia species. Wait for the sting. (Buddhist monks ring a bell; hit one another to keep concentration.)

I wouldn't go so far as ever to insinuate to Blixen that her mother was a murderer. No, Fabiana was simply trying to get Gottlieb to leave Marie, trying to get him to live with her, the love of her life, the father of her children; she would have killed for him even though she would have betrayed him a hundred times. But Gottlieb wasn't going to leave the luxury of his existence, the preciousness of his harbourside poetics, the weekly reading-group to which he now belonged ... and most of all, the safety of Marie, because he was through with risk, through with self-doubt, with the insecurity of faith, hope and love.

That's the romantic version.

The gossip in the forest was that Roger the parquetier found out how much the 'Chinese' paintings were worth. He exploited Fabiana's naïveté and took possession of the works, in order, as he said, 'to put a value on them'. He met up with Marie de Nerval in Double Bay. The first thing he said was that his wife was cheating on him. He wanted those damned paintings catalogued. He intimated that divorce would be a messy business and that he was a simple man. He hired a private detective named Levine. Redvers told me all this. The third version, my dear Blixen, I cannot repeat to you. Redvers said your mother was a complete narcissist.

16

– Jude, who was Redvers?

– A drifter who lived on your mother's farm; a ghost, a phantom.

– Did he die there?

– Well, he disappeared, Blixen. Just like Roger. No one knows what happened to Redvers. He suffered from fugues. He said there were always thirty of them in one's lifetime. I think he was a melancholic; a sad fellow. He was always trying to live up to the myth that he was a great painter. He went everywhere on his bicycle; always appeared at moments when secrets were about to be revealed.

– What is a fugue exactly? Not that I'm going to specialise in psychiatry.

– Sufferers usually had two alternating personalities; a kind of double consciousness. Doctors first discovered these cases in 1885, in Bordeaux. Then in the 1880s gleaners, tramps and vagabonds discovered the 'safety' bicycle and an epidemic of fugueurs was reported. It was a kind of pathological tourism. Economy class. They terrified pedestrians, these manic travellers, poor workers for the most part, who did not appear out of nowhere. They had history on their side. They were stuck to their bikes in their 'other' state like former knights on their horses. They had eminence and precedence. Melancholic artisans without access to any nobility. Driven to movement, not humility. Three centuries earlier, Michel de Montaigne, the essayist and nobleman, was similarly obsessed about dying upon his horse whilst on his travels in the 1580s.

– Wasn't he the mayor of Bordeaux?

I play a CD of Bach's *Goldberg Variations*. I'm trying to understand Blixen's mother. How a talented woman like Fabiana followed such a devastating path in life. She did not have any self-esteem, Blixen said. Blixen in the bath, taking her time, wringing out her long blonde hair. Variation No. 26. I listen to Glenn Gould's historic 1955 debut recording. Taking his time. You can hear the pedals being pressed and released. The resonating aftertones. Bach's key changes indicate some form of destiny ... Bach speaking deeply to himself as though he had no real will, only questions about God's harmony in the disharmony of the world ... God's voice, Gould's touch. I listen to Glenn Gould's 1981 recording of the same Goldberg Variation he played in a concert in 1955. It is much longer. This time there is a haunted humming as well. He's an older man now, enjoying his mastery and his argument. His voice adds another conversation. He's not there for others. It's no longer a disagreement with God, but a kind of resigned *abnormality*, as though being a detective in these solitary fugues needed indifference and cruelty. I can hear Blixen humming along. Her cheating voice doubling Gould's. She's going to have a summer affair with Travis Cordillion. I said this aloud, irritated at myself for having been so unproductive in my research, for not being able to read the future. Ever since Blixen's arrival, ever since the epidemic, I have not discovered a single thing beneath the microscope. Squiggling molecules. I haven't given enough time to considerations of beauty, having spent much of it in cynical observation. What did you say? Blixen asks; she's come out of her bath, looking divine, wrapped in towels.

17

The relentless blue of the sky. The endless thudding of the small waves on the sand; the green water churning over masses of white jelly. The queues of patients and the smell of their vinegar baths prefigure a crucifixion. Someone must be sacrificed. On the horizon you can see the kite rising, hovering ... Janet Cordillion, suspended there beyond the reef where there were few stingers ... too cold, too dark in the water for them. She flies, towed behind her cruiser. The cruiser is a present from Carter. I think she has orgasms up there, Carter told me over a crab salad. He was drinking a whole bottle of late-picked riesling by himself. I don't disapprove of people drinking at lunch, especially when I make them sign what is necessary. How's Samantha? I ask. He looks at me and takes a minute to think. He told me about Samantha. He's crazy about her. She's fine, he says finally. I'm the one you ought to be thinking about. It's okay, I say. You'll get the results by next week. I can't ... he begins ... I won't be able to ... you know, with Sam. Not if you're responsible, I tell him. He looks over the papers for the Rastoni again. It's all in order. I wanted a six-month option, an installment plan. He signs. If you speak to Angus Cattle my solicitor, we can lay off staff tomorrow, I tell him. They'll have no trouble finding other jobs. The stingers haven't put off all the tourists. They come here to be social, to party. They prefer to swim in the pools anyway, I say to him. You know, Cordillion mumbles, preoccupied with something entirely different, Sam's not sure about the operation. Then she shouldn't have it, I say ... I'd seen pre-ops at suicidal pitch because they'd taken too many hormones.

I'm watching Janet out there on the reef and I'm depressed by her loneliness. All sky and sea, all alone except for the cargo ships swollen with fuel oil, fat to the Plimsoll Line, smoking up and down the coast, threading the Grafton Passage and the Trinity Opening between the reefs, ploughing up dark blue water. Why doesn't Janet want to know about Carter and Sam? Samantha, I think to myself, was beautiful ... I'd only met her once. She was cute, slim and dark, wearing black lace and stockings, sitting on a cane chair, winner of the Singapore Transgender beauty contest. The room sparked with camera flashes. She was electric, a mix of cultures, like the cocktails she liked to drink. The risk was not in the operation, I said. I wanted Carter to be aware of this. Men were the real danger. In the end men always killed abnormality. Carter was silent. At the moment he may have thought he was in love. There will be a time when such feelings will vanish; when he will become confused and not understand a single thing about dysphoria.

I said this to him again in his lounge room when he and Janet invited me to talk about some share options he was offering in his multiplex organisation. Janet was in the kitchen at the time, making titbits, caviar on biscuits which seemed to lack all imagination. Carter wasn't really sensitive to my warnings. He was lighting a cigarette. Do you mind? It's your house, I said. He stubbed it out, but the damage was done. My warnings increased his self-loathing. We argued about Sam without mentioning her name. I said her participation in these anti-pageants was a need for recognition, a risky procedure. I tried to point out the huge pain of being born with a body that was opposed to one's mind. It was wretchedness generated by an identity crisis, not, as Carter thought, a sexual come-on. His house was dark, billowing with curtains. Outside, a blind God was still blowing jellyfish ashore.

18

My father, the professor of tropical medicine, had the best collection of venom in the world. In his laboratories in Paris, he had two large cool rooms filled with compression shelves in which he stored venin and poisons from all over the globe: everything from funnel web toxins and snake venom to deadly nightshade. When I was twelve ... the age at which he said I had become a woman, he gave me the key to his rooms. I walked among the shelves. On one side, the dull transparency of death appearing harmless as saliva; on the other, colourful antivenins. He taught me all the properties of blood. I observed: coagulants; corpuscles; my father making love to an assistant. Sticky components. Contortions. I learned to extract venom from cobras, blood from human veins. A boomslang snake, I noticed, went into contortions after biting something, presumably out of excess aggression and the need to generate more venom. Then it would grow tired and you could pick it up by the tail. I always worked backwards, picking things up by the tail. My rear up in the air. My father with his large hands around my waist as I bent my eye to the microscope. Even though I hated my childhood, I respected the privilege of having the key to such things.

19

Blixen no longer rides with me to Mossman and back. She's always complaining of tiredness. I wanted her to send some blood samples to the pathology lab before the week was over. I went on long *randonnées* with the over-fifties club, though they were much too slow for me. On these group rides I heard all the gossip. Cordillion wanted to build a casino up the coast. Janet, they informed me, was riding up front, showing off. He's off to Africa next week. Who? Carter of course. He's always off somewhere. It's all very unhappy for her.

Blixen doesn't show up at the surgery that often now. She stays out, presumably with Travis. Passed into another's life. Comes home late, goes to her own room, sleeps until midday. I don't like my stepmother behaviour. I don't like staying up waiting. I don't like suspicion or fantasy. I don't speculate on scenarios. I have cold showers. I am punctual and methodical.

I have inherited my father's collection of poisons and antivenins, though these are more for the sake of historical data on aggression and stress in animals. Every now and again surgeons in the field of gender reassignment call on me to clarify the problems of hormonal reaction to surgical stress – any incision is an aggression upon the body. But my real interest is not in these areas of stress and anaesthesia, but in the psychosis patients develop after being bitten or stung. Over the years, I've built up my own collection of venom and anti-poisons, which I house in a Chinese teak cabinet, locked for obvious reasons. Downstairs in the surgery there is a steel safe for dangerous drugs. Collecting is contiguity: one item placed next to another without real meaning. All that matters is that there is a kind of 'system' ... an alarm clock which calls decadence to assembly. Look, these moments of my life: this phial in which I have preserved toxins discharged by Irukandji jellyfish, painstakingly extracted from the microscopic strings of pearls along hundreds of tentacles. Books too, can be necklaces saturated with poisons ... Zola's *Thérèse Raquin*, in which almost everybody dies, a damp copy of which is beside the bath Blixen has just used. Among her underwear, her father's rosary beads.

20

I catch myself acting like a stepmother with Blixen and stepmothers are not naturally good. I look at Blixen's slim body, her blonde ponytail, her lazy athleticism, the way she walks on the balls of her feet in her pink Converses, and she matches Travis Cordillion, in height and lightness. Though give him a few more years and he will turn to fat with his beer, as they all do, driving his car too fast on a winding road. Blixen left the door of the steel drug safe open. It was carelessness I could not overlook. That kind of thing could get me struck off, I said. She laughed, though she could see I was serious and gave me that look which said I was a little old and stuffy. As a stepmother I am too bleak. I take a bit more time with Travis. I am patient, entrusting him with courier work, transporting samples to the lab. Carter says enforced idleness is not good for his son. Because of the stingers, Travis hasn't been conducting his diving tours out on the reef. I've seen him staring at me, watching me in my pink Lycra, straddling my bike on the concourse as I ease out into my ride, past the grifter, who's stealing glances in my direction, and with all this staring I want to sprint ... an itch which will become furious, a fast-twitch muscle ticking in my mind, deluded about my erotic authority, angry with Blixen for having left dangerous drugs unlocked. There it was, wide open for any addict. Luckily, nothing was missing.

My cycling is a recycling of the body. Getting everything to work is in fact anti-aesthetic, since beauty doesn't produce discipline, and discipline doesn't produce beauty, but being in motion is vertiginous and seductive. There is nothing to be revealed about a body. To assume a body is simply to care for its needs ... to be a custodian of its duration while it memorises its pathways. After my exercise I shower and find myself hardened, my thighs more powerful, my breasts pouting in defiance. I have had many suitors in my time, but I have not had enough time to consider them, those men who cannot understand anything I say, as I cannot speak ordinarily, though I am intent on conveying ordinary things like the weather, and each time the suitor would end up feeling cheated, as if I were mocking what he had to say, mocking his defensiveness, his submission even, and it would be left to me to puzzle over what I said that was wrong; the slight tone of supercilious dismissal, the mildest indication of scorn. Now in my fifties, I have been pegged at thirty-five, but I don't spend time worrying over appearances. There is Travis observing me again and I can see him considering his Blixen (for surely I have given him Blixen? I have given her to him as a gift only to know her better, for her unfaithfulness to him will increase my propriety over her), measuring the girl against the older woman, thinking a thought with his body which puts his mind under stress, a clearly painful curiosity. And as I pedal along the coast road I feel the heat rising up from below, the same heat that Travis will now feel under him on the sand at the far end of the beach and next to him Blixen will be turning over in her black string bikini so that the sheen of the material over her backside, appearing under patches of wet sand which have slipped off as she turned, blinds him momentarily with desire, as though a landscape had subtly eroded and revealed not a woman next to him but the emptiness of the memory of his father's mistress ... a memory of Samantha, always immaculately dressed, slowly peeling open his astonishment as she rose up in the escalator, this encounter in a department store in Sydney, his father stammering behind, making small talk, introducing her as a business associate though it seemed obvious to Travis she knew nothing about his father's businesses, and now as Travis looks across at Blixen he will be encountering something different ... suddenly she is without mystery and he will not be patient, resulting in Blixen's abrupt departure, flinging her towel around herself, having sensed his distraction, believing it was I who had displayed myself too readily on my bike, mistaking the I who could not have distracted him ... I, who lifted my rear into the air, who could have had no interest in him except to remind him of worlds which may not have existed and which formed an idea beyond him.

21

Blixen returns before I am able to finish my ride. I guessed that she would, when Travis looked that way at me. The work of the female nude in paintings over the ages confirms the fact that posture and poise, point and pose, sublimate defects ... which then return as disturbances. Blixen returns, is unsettled, begins to drink early. I sense this already, out on my ride, and I turn around at twenty-five kilometers; make my way back. I find her lounging, disgruntled, moody, snapping like a turtle. I soothe her without words, massaging her back, rubbing her feet. I carry her to the bath, which I've filled with oils and calm her down. My surgery is also a repair shop, unguent, perfumed with care. Mindful of how much I can administer, aware that soap runs out as it did for my father, I leave Blixen to soak. Downstairs, in the surgery, I wipe my forearms with surgical pads soaked in alcohol. I look out the window and expect Janet Cordillion to fall out of the sky onto the line of the horizon, the oil tanker providing a smokescreen. It's a battle on the Coral Sea.

Stung patients have not stopped turning up at my door. Those that have already been treated, return with side effects: some patients have severe pain in their backs but anaphylaxis has not yet occurred. Pre-treatment with adrenaline may have prevented their mild bronchospasms. I am irritated at myself for having missed these contraindications. I notice that I have been forgetful lately, leaving lights on, my car keys stuck in the boot, bills that I have paid twice. I am overworked, but I have also exercised excessively. All this I have called The Blixen Effect. She reflects me in my worst light; perhaps it is my increasing intake of alcohol which she encourages, bringing back all sorts of exotic recipes for cocktails so that at the end of a long day it is almost impossible not to slide into a sort of coma, and then she will bring out the make-up that she has gathered, all the mascara, rouges, lipsticks and we will paint each other in drunken barbarism, faces dotted like island chieftains, this epidermal pointillism resembling nematocysts on the tentacles of jellyfish, each dot a copy, a plague of dots replicated to achieve the overall result of ferocious abnormality when viewed up close, but which appears at a distance as a benign and camouflaged uniformity.

22

Cordillion was optimistic in his report to his consortium. He was wrong. The Chamber of Commerce noted that tourist numbers had been declining; sales of luxury apartments and houses had almost come to a standstill, though their prices still hadn't dropped. Commercial fishermen are out of work, restaurants have reported fewer customers, boat owners have started to sell up. I renegotiated the price of the Rastoni with Carter. He backed off and then agreed to lower it. Renovators would start work on the gallery immediately. It was a small infusion of business confidence. Every little bit helped.

The stinger season has almost come to its end, but jellyfish are still thick in the water and people complain of feeling nauseous when they go out in boats, as though the masses of jelly increased the pitch and yaw of boats, made the water heavier, prolonged the swell and slowed the waves, and a viscous blubber was now forming beneath them, and even on shore they feel its pull dwelling at the bottom of their bellies and they cannot eat, any slight smell of cooking oil sending them out into the courtyards, beachfronts, parking lots, retching, heaving, vomiting. The pharmacy is inundated with customers. Travis brings me the pathology reports and hangs around in reception, but Blixen does not appear. I try to encourage Travis to go home. He's shaved his head. It's made him aggressive. I don't like him observing things through the open door of the surgery when there is break between patients, hoping to catch sight of Blixen. It's as though he's become too familiar. Yet I feel that if his presence was missing, Blixen would pack up and go back to Sydney. She has found his persistence flattering. She has booked a room for a week at a lodge in the Daintree, a room overlooking a waterfall. It would be a good break for her, as she hasn't really had one since coming up here, but it would mean I would have no help in the surgery. She didn't want me to mention anything to Travis.

Alone, in a dry bath. I sit there feeling the contours as if she had been there; for a week, the insulting blue outside, the offensive glare and sheen of bright sand and in my dry bath, fully clothed, I brighten and darken my windows to achieve the effects of cities, seasons and sounds, the lamplights frosted with green, heralding the coming of spring in the Place Vendôme near my childhood apartments, the brown waters of the Seine in flood during autumn, the glow from the stoves of the chestnut vendors at night, shouts from the illuminated haze above the Parc des Princes during the six-day bike races. But the light here is unrelenting, unmodulated. Almost antiseptic, it conceals a monotony which induces a pressing need to wander, to break out; an irresistible, purposeless need to travel as erratically as possible. It isn't something that is obvious or general until it is named. The bath fugue may still have its day in the Australian sun. Free to wander without imprisonment or punishment. Up there in the Daintree Forest, Blixen is sitting in her bath trying to hear the waterfall. Down below, there are no jellyfish; the water in the river is cold and fresh. She plunges into it from her balcony. I hope she understands form; measurement; the depth of the water before the rocky bottom rises up.

When Gottlieb told me about Fabiana during an unguarded moment in my surgery in Double Bay, I made it a point to visit her shop. Women have an instinct for allies. Fabiana invited me to her spring, her waterhole, to swim one windy summer's day. But down by the water there was no breeze since it was shielded by willows and the waterhole was in a depression, cut off from the wind, calm as an oasis. There, Fabiana, who was in a psychotic state as she often was, told me that we were being watched, by whom, she didn't wish to say. The story of the spring was true, she said. What story? I hadn't heard of it, I explained to her. Oh, everyone around here knows. The mystery of Roger's disappearance. It was true, she said, that her husband, who had begun life as a parquetier, a floorer, if you like, had bought the Putty property from the Grace family, the last of which was a surviving male, to whom the place had been passed. Roger had bought it back for her, his beloved Fabiana. It was true, Fabiana said, that Roger had gone out to fight that bushfire by himself and that the water tanker had dodgy brakes and somehow, while making the trip between the waterhole and the forest fire, the truck had disengaged and rolled into the flames. It was true that Roger's body was never found. But as you know, there are a whole lot of subterranean rivers and springs out here and in the past, cavers had come, asking permission to dive, which I've always refused, Fabiana said with a sigh, since it was too dangerous. It was I who told the police that Roger may have sought relief from the heat of the fire by plunging into the spring and had somehow been dragged down by reeds, into the strange and unmapped apertures beneath. It was true that the police sent down divers, but were incredulous that any human body could have slipped into those small crevices, let alone be sucked through them into subterranean caves. Fabiana then told me something that she had not told anyone before. She said that she thought Redvers was in love with her. He thought he could solve her mystery by widening an aperture with a stick of gelignite.

One death was an accident; two was carelessness; three would have been intention. Gottlieb pre-empted that. To be tortured by Fabiana would have been agonising. I know. I've met her. It was much worse than being tortured by guilt. My dry bath provides me with a memory. I had written on Redvers' card that he was a fugueur. He needed to travel for no particular reason. Always riding his bicycle. If someone had said to Redvers: *Don't try to be a detective, you can't possibly ever be one*; or if someone shouted at him: *Look, you're stirring up the dogs with that crazy behaviour, you have cyclic automatism*; or if they simply said: *Stop acting on hunches, you're just sleep-walking and dreaming in circles*; then Redvers might have survived, simply through knowing how he appeared, how he was named. Once classified, he might have watched himself, fictionalised a normal existence.

23

Slide #4: Chironex Cyclops
You have to read Redvers backwards. The reason why he claimed your confidence was that he only had one sighted eye, and that with an optical nerve at the wrong angle. The other was blinded by a stone thrown up from a car while he was riding his bicycle in India. It made him an extraordinary badminton player. He learned all the best strokes in Delhi; all the acutely angled, unreachable, unreturnable shuttlecocks geometrically calculated to perfection, flights of impossibility. He could glide from one side of the court to the other without being seen. But this made him obsessively one-

eyed and saturnine because he couldn't see himself. It didn't enlarge his understanding of others.

The huntress Diana spent much time by a river washing and hunting. She never ate the animals she killed. She donated her catch to the Cyclops, industrious slaves who served her. Her extraordinary skill was to convince the Cyclops that they were the masters, captors of an Amazon, carrying her from her bath dripping wet, laying her on silk sheets to be ravished at will. But in reality they were held captive by her; by her muscles, her power, her deadly aim. Her victims watched themselves being caught in the trap of a never-to-be-satisfied desire. They grew thin in her cage, fretting, fragmenting, thinking all the while of the impossible freedom to fuck her. It was because they were one-eyed. I without the You. Unable to think as someone else, they could only guess at perspective. Jason Redvers had chosen to die rather than to have surgery. His prostate had metastasised. He told me the fig had dried. It's like a rule in rugby, he said. Use it or lose it. He ran a high fever the last time he came to me so I put him in a bath of ice. He said his grandfather was a poet who wrote verses in a tub, reciting one from his *Water Clock* series entitled 'Perspectiva'.

24

It has grown dark outside. I must have fallen asleep, still in my clothes, but something has woken me; a sound from the bedroom? Nothing. I get up out of the bath, turn on all the lights. The air conditioning is humming soothingly, the sensor lights on the alarm pad indicate it is only my presence in the room. More body heat and mass than my own would have sent the system pulsing with loud beeps before a full alarm. I check all the doors, go down to the surgery and test the system. Ring the security service to report a trial, not a break-in. I go back up, undress, decide to take a real bath. I let it fill slowly and while undoing my silk organza gown, I pass my hands over my breasts, looking for any irregularity, performing my secret rites, squeezing my thighs together, feeling the ropes in my muscles, transformed, from Diana to Aphrodite. I do not touch myself down there. The steam is soft and golden as I negotiate my way to erasing any original sin.

I have fallen asleep a second time. It is deeper and more peaceful than before and when I wake it has been an hour or more by the little clepsydra I keep over the spa and I feel a little groggy watching the little cupid with his arrow rising up in time to mark the water that has passed. I recall a phrase from a strange dream in which I walked out the back door and saw Travis Cordillion clambering up a sand dune as though sand had been building up behind the house and now he was sprinting and I couldn't even make the first few steps without falling back and he was saying something muffled, telling me there was somebody left behind ... *passengers* ... it sounded like he was saying a passenger had been left behind on the reef and it must have been something I was reading in the papers the other day, when a diving party failed to account for all the passengers on a boat out near Wallaby Reef and returned to shore and it was five hours before they realised that two were missing. The fear of not being missed. I thought of Janet Cordillion and at that moment I woke again, and my previous waking was only a dream of waking, and I realise how tired I must have been. Taking a bath rather than showering has been a new experience, enervating and tinged with dissatisfaction, causing me difficult dreams. I am confused, not knowing whether I dreamt someone had been in the house, or whether there was a real presence and I am annoyed and irritated by the checks I still have to do. Had not I done it all before? It is late. The Chinese cabinet swings out its carved wooden doors as I pass. That teak cabinet in which I keep my collection of venoms and antivenins has been unlocked, the key which used to be on my keyring left inside. Its wooden doors flap uselessly against the sides. My heart leaps. I feel violated, raped through my own negligence. The rows of bottles are regular. I cannot tell if some phials are missing. I will have to take an inventory, fudge it if there has been a theft. All this carelessness has been my fault. Lack of vigilance. Inadvertence. I will not be able to report it, to state that I was in the bath, in the process of erasing original sin, not hearing anything.

I rush out onto the balcony. To the left, several cars are cruising slowly on the Esplanade, their lights dimmed. Passengers. Are there any passengers in them? In my dopey state, still clad in my organza gown, wearing my black booties with the white lace cuffs, I do not know whether I was dreaming when I caught sight of a car towing what looked like Cordillion's speedboat. I know the boat, the one Janet used on the reef before it dragged her further aloft – Cordillion's speedboat, which was shaped like a swordfish with the name *Passionjuice* painted in purple on its side. I don't know. All speedboats look alike to me.

Implant

They've grafted a little microchip under the skin near my heart. It keeps me going after the bypass. I'm like an old car stalled on a slip lane; the motor needs a few turns, a few coughs, before things get unblocked. At night I lie on my mattress in the caravan I've rented and listen to the sea, and my heart beats irregularly and all that arrhythmia makes me cough ... just a slight cough, though a persistent one, and that is bad for business. As a drifter, I risk being noticed. I shadow Doctor Sarraute. My 'I' hides in the shadow cast by hers.

There's that Cordillion boy dragging his jet ski up the coast where the stingers aren't that numerous. I've never understood how the rich play ... how they can never really relax without doing the next deal ... the deal is the play. I don't know why the Cordillion boy always takes the inland route up the coast. Why he always stops off at Butchers Hill at an old house on the Peninsula Road before going cross-country to the Cedar Bay National Park where he launches his jet ski at night.

A lot of the pines here have been transplanted. Just up the beach on the other side of the national park is a military area, off limits to all. I have been to the fence where there are signs warning of 'live firing', and 'unexploded shells'. A row of yellow buoys are strung out in a line across the water threatening straying craft with fines for trespass. During the day, sun-bathers speak with American accents. I step silently over the cones and needles and watch the calm sea. There is no moon, so I light the lantern I bought at the markets. Perhaps I will see jellyfish rising to the surface. Perhaps that's why Travis Cordillion goes surf-skiing on moonless nights past the nets and marker buoys, where he doesn't have to plough through jelly. The pine branches wobble as I part them, tensile, like aircraft wings in turbulence. They've planted more pines to keep the dunes in place. To transplant: to dibble, inoculate, vaccinate. A surgeon is also a gardener, grafting parts onto wholes. A Caligari.

Protection. That's the doctor's job. She doesn't know about me. My friend Ross, the cook at the Rastoni, has lost his job. Without him, I have very few good meals that are free of risk. Ross complains to me at the markets on Saturdays. They've gutted the Rastoni, and soon it will turn into an art gallery, with high walls and embedded lights. Graft, implant, embed, bury. Maybe that's what the good doctor is doing. That's what Travis is doing when he comes back on his burping jet ski. Burrowing. I blow out the flame in my lamp just in time. The pines have shielded me. Travis is burying something he retrieved from a small boat. He does all this in pitch darkness, squatting on the ground, hacking away with his army trench tool. Then suddenly, as if warned by a sound, he looks up, straight at me, though I'm sure he cannot see me behind the branches, and he picks up everything and comes in my direction, holding the trench tool in one hand, and I back away with a silence that comes naturally to me and when I regain the track, run in the opposite direction from the carpark. I'm good at such evaporation, but I've left my lantern behind. My chest aches; I know this pain. The microchip does not like visible and physical risk and it is letting me know.

I'm afraid there has been a break-in at the surgery, I was saying to Blixen when she returned from the Daintree. I had been waiting three days to say this to her. She looked alarmed. More panic than was necessary. Her first words were: Did you inform the police? Not: What was taken? This gave me the cue to lie. It was her scurrying which set me off. Yes, I said, and there is an on-going investigation. Her face turned pale and she bit her lower lip and this was a gesture of hers I knew was brought on by guilt and I sat her down on the lounge. Blixen, I said, when I was twelve my father gave me the key to his room of poisons, entrusting me with the responsibility which came with knowledge. It's the essence of all learning: to use what is known to reach the unknown *responsibly*. The fact that you left the key inside the cabinet demonstrates part of that responsibility. You wanted it known that it was an inside job. There are only two of us, Blixen. She undid the clasp on her ponytail and smoothed back her hair and then tied it up again. This too, was a gesture of guilt, stage two: the point at which she is found out. Blixen is a moral creature, and it is an admirable quality to have for a doctor. You knew it was me? she asked, nodding as she said it, reinforcing the affirmative. The alarm system records my body mass, I said. Unless Travis lost forty kilos, it could not have been him. I will trade you one piece of information for another. This is not a gift. Somebody with a serious heart condition came to see me at the surgery yesterday. This person observed some of Travis's activities. I presume you didn't see him up at the Daintree during your week there? She shook her head. Leant back in the lounge so her small breasts were defined through her silk top. She was exhaling heavily. Blixen never wore a bra. I don't know why I held this against her. I was more angry with this non-wearing of bras than with the fact that she broke into my cabinet. I felt like saying this was why Travis stared so much at me, imagining the satin and lace bra I wore, even under my cycling jersey. I withheld my full breasts from his gaze, I was going to say to Blixen. I imprisoned my breasts because of their unnatural size and their acorn nipples. I was like the Muslim woman who came to save her son from the effects of Irukandgi stingers. She was not concerned with politeness. There was a lot of strength in that. In her hijab; in her flowing abaya. Without seduction. One of my patients, I continued, implanted the thought in my mind. What thought? Blixen looked angry and horrified. Travis is a drug runner. He picks up sunken contraband. He does more than diving for a living.

It took some time before Blixen spoke. He was trying to make some money to help his father, she said. I'm sorry, I explained to her, I don't quite understand. The afternoon outside my windows had broken into a grey squall massing on the horizon. Soon patients will be queuing in reception. My evening regulars: the middle-aged women with sinus problems caused by low pressure and humidity; the jellyfish victims no longer boisterous with bravado. Sometimes the wind turns everyone anxious. It seems, Blixen said, Carter got into difficulties in Africa ...

I didn't urge her to say more, because this is the way I was brought up by my father. You neither urge nor encourage. They soon tell all. My father was not urged to make statements he later regretted, first about the Aryan status of his wife, then about the Vichy régime. It was he who forced the Kahnweiler to close in 1943, writing an article in the *Croix de Fer* news-letter about the gallery's 'decadent turn'. No, one's urges should be one's own and one should take full responsibility for them. I suggested Blixen take a hot bath. In it, she let me rub her back. I pointed out significant moles and asked her to take notice, have them checked. I did not mention her fair skin. How she looked just like a younger version of Fabiana. She should spike up her hair with gel; immerse herself in the balm of things past.

Difficulties in Africa ... the rich indulge in deliberate wastage, I was about to say, when Blixen informed me she was giving up medicine to join a Buddhist convent. I didn't tell her she was throwing everything away. I didn't say what a mad idea I thought that was, that the rich indulge in deliberate wastage, that they let themselves be carried away by a rip-tide, that the Nerval-Gottlieb fortune should be squandered on a child who could have been a Schweitzer, but who chose to push prayer wheels and chant mantras to child gods. I did not say anything when Blixen told me she was turning over all her paintings ... inherited from her great-grandmother Julia Grace ... turning over all of them to me, to kick off the launch of the Kahnweiler Gallery, in a stunning exhibition of old and new, in a *vernissage* unseen in this country, attended by dignitaries and art lovers from all over the world.

Blixen had an unstable lineage. Someone will have to pay; someone will be sacrificed. I retreated from the bathroom. Maybe she was missing Blimunde, 'connecting' with her. The twinning theory never worked for me. She was escaping from malevolent time ... giving away her legacy; her inheritance of guilt.

26

Slide #5: Carukia Fabiana
On the other side of her family, the tearaway Fabiana. You can imagine: fine hair ruffling in the Harbour breeze. The twins. Blixen came first and she averted her eyes from the baby; could not bear to look at what had been inside her, the demons of Gemini ... was there something from Siam as well, a message? The child was trying to attach, imprint, find its mother, its unfocussed eyes roving, folding back. Then the second. Blimunde. She looked. It was all right. They were not joined. The doctors were right. How clear to her that she cared about normalcy! How she cared. Then came a dark cloud and it settled on the mother's face. There was no hormonal rush, no spurting breast. She could not give any more. All had been taken away from her. And now, so were her babies.

Years later, Levine's be-ringed fingers. He had grown old with addiction, thin and dark. Levine, the North Sydney dealer and private investigator ... whom Gottlieb tried to imitate in a grotesque and ludicrous pantomime was rubbing his fingers over her unproductive nipples. Levine drove a big car. You couldn't imagine Gottlieb in a pink Chev. Or maybe you could, his hair flying in the wind while discoursing on Hegel. But Sol Levine, whose jealousy ran his reason, produced a razor in his hand and held it to Fabiana's jugular. Have there been any children? From me? You better come clean, girlie ... if I'm whacked I need to have them in the will. She knew Levine was broke. She hired Sergio for protection and let out her silos to itinerants and went nowhere without her pack of dogs. It was only a matter of time before Levine called on her again, following an ageing cyclist from a Newtown nightclub. Levine drove out to Putty in his pink Chevrolet. It was just a matter of luck for her that Redvers had his accident that day, and when Levine heard the explosion coming from the waterhole, he legged it to his car, only to find it gone. He hitched a ride on a semitrailer and disappeared in Sydney. Six months later, Fabiana left for Rio. From there, a third country with no extradition treaty. She bequeathed Barringila to Blixen, and it was there that Blixen wanted to retire to her Buddhism and meditation. She would build an ashram out of the ruins. You could imagine all the ghosts. Maybe incense would cure the air and chanting would drown out the voices, ream out all the skeletons from hollowed trees.

27

We came to this country with poisons, my father and I, after the suicide of my mother. Dr Sarraute (in Australia it rhymes with 'carrot'), crated his whole collection and had it shipped under refrigeration. When the right technology came along, he told me, this will be like gold dust. It was the 'sixties, when France ran with recriminations, revisions and revisitations of what one's father did during the Occupation. The Algerian war exploded lives for all to see in the newspapers. Was my father a collaborator? Did he save my Jewish mother by erasing her past? He knew about DNA. Undoubtedly, as the journalists pointed out, he didn't rescue her. He wrote letters to powerful friends. He was careful not to incriminate himself. This was cause to be reviled. Nor did he save himself; neither with his champagne baths nor his determination to forget, wandering off to other countries to find a tropical hideaway. He died in Fiji while I was in medical school in Sydney, of a rare blood disease. I kept a sample of his blood in my industrial fridge, building on the micro-array of codes documented in his deoxyribonucleic acid. I found toxins in the mitochondria. At the university they called me a vamp. *Vampire*, to make it clear. Not flattering. A blood-expert. Blood orange, they also called me: My black hair of which I was ashamed, which I had dyed red, still left a white streak.

Carter Cordillion's pathology report turned up today. My receptionist rang and left a message for him. He didn't call back. Blixen was making preparations to build an ashram at Putty. The Kahnweiler Gallery was starting to look like a real art gallery, with a spiral staircase in the centre of the ground-floor, circling up through permanent artworks to a space above for current exhibitions. Carter didn't press me for payment of my installments. Instead, he sent me a note, written shakily on what felt like papyrus. He would brook no discussion. He wanted me to have lunch aboard his cruiser on Tuesday. If I didn't turn up he would rescind the property deal.

That morning Janet was not skimming the horizon, hanging from her Chinese kite. The tanker was nowhere to be seen. It was an absolutely blank day, a glazed, layered painting of grey lines with a filigree of dark tentacles where a tropical storm was brewing. I walked down to the jetty. I was about half an hour late. Carter's cruiser, with its exhausts curdling the water, its transom bubbling like a cauldron, bobbed slowly beside the jetty. Mounds of jellyfish rode the swell astern. He saw me walking up and came out from the bridge to greet me. He had a shadow on his cheeks ... that wry, defeated smile which said we had once been intimate and that I had not played the game. He held my arm and helped me aboard and then let his hand linger for a brief moment. Although the day was not hot, his palm was sweating. The aft deck was set up with a table and chairs, wine glasses, ice buckets and a basket of prawns. He said butterfish was on the menu. He offered me pink champagne, which I refused. He asked me to unhitch the bow line and he eased the boat out into the glassy cove. I was slightly nauseous. In about ten minutes we were near the reef. Carter showed me where we could glide over the coral, where it was colourful and shallow, without jellyfish, and then he took the boat out into the blue, serious water. Before we dine, he said, what's the prognosis?

The water became rougher and when I told him he looked away from me to the stern and nodded as though he had expected this news all along and it seemed he had suddenly aged ten years, his shoulders slumping and his cheeks sagging, a look which I had seen on others when I pronounced a death sentence, and you just have to observe their reactions, make sure they don't turn suicidal or hysterical, but most of the time they are resigned, and Carter was even looking a little happy, relieved, knowing he had less than two months to live, because the toxins had caused the cells in his blood to revolt, caused them to die inside his veins, and he was already dead, and knowing this was like jettisoning the life-buoy, any hope which had been weighing him down ... it was the worst thing, hope. But now all the fight had gone out of him, and there was peace, and even a need to square one's conscience, reveal what one had spent one's lifetime concealing, the rapacity that had been driving him from the moment he was born, naturally enough staving off hunger and despair, but which had killed any empathy, anything other than material wealth, so now he didn't quite understand this sudden need to be human, why now, why this moment to look inward. The fear of not being missed. There was nothing much inside. I asked him where Janet was, why she was not para-sailing and he looked at me in an almost aggressive manner and then smiled and said she was at home, but he was distracted and gunned the motor so the boat slipped from the crest of a wave and began to bounce and slump, spreading more foam from its stern.

I wasn't in Africa, Carter said after a while. I think I knew that already. Everything bad Carter contracted came out of Africa, but I took that to mean a place he shouldn't have gone. I went to Los Angeles, he said, with Sam, and she took me out to an African snake farm where they had hundreds of varieties of poisonous serpents and she was learning how to milk them and make them harmless for a short time because she needed to dance with a boomslang coiled in her bosom ... it was for a floorshow in Vegas ... and the snake-keepers, they had a fancy name, *herpetologists*, warned her the common tree viper from sub-Saharan Africa was an extremely dangerous, greenish-brown snake, delivering a potent hemotoxic venom with its folded fangs. Sam always liked extreme risk, Carter said. She was going to read out all the snake information at the beauty pageant and then produce the reptile and allow it to nestle between her breasts. She had been bitten many times by other snakes and some of the poisons sent her into a sexual frenzy, she said, and I stupidly volunteered to be first to be bitten by a milked boomslang, what the heck, maybe some of this snake venom would drive out all my other viruses, I figured. Well, it all went horribly wrong. I thought I could hold the snake in a trance. They gave me an anti-venom serum but I was allergic to it and then I had to have blood transfusions and chased ambulances all over California, finding doctors willing to diagnose me, washing out bad blood, getting a high each time they stuck the needle in.

You're a fool Carter, I said. I couldn't help feeling sorry for saying it, but he smiled and said he was committed to death and he was sorry he asked Blixen to get him more poison and the dear girl brought him morphine. You trained her well, he said flicking a cigarette he didn't light into the sea. He was pushing on the throttle handle and the boat lifted its nose and he was making for a tanker which had appeared unnoticed by me, on our right, blowing black smoke, and I thought for a moment he was going to crash the boat beneath the ship's rusty bow, readying myself to leap out, but he was warning it to sail further away from the reef. Damn pilot's asleep, he said and blew the cruiser's klaxon and then stepped out on deck to wave the ship back into the inner shipping route and a seaman on the bridge waved back, mistaking it all for some drunken game rich white guys got up to in this part of the world. Then Carter was on his radio and he was calling REEFREP, to report dangerous shipping and the radio crackled and I wondered if I would survive all this heroism and finally I said to him I'd like to go ashore now, and I think I disappointed him by not wanting anything to eat and only accepting a glass of mineral water, a bottle of which he reluctantly dragged out of the fridge. Carter poured himself a whiskey and threw the prawns overboard and was back to his old self, making sure the cruiser was docking safely in the marina, fussing over hawsers and buffers. On the jetty he handed me a manilla envelope. The gallery is yours, he said.

Graffiti

It means inscription; claw; scratch. They found those in the ruins of Pompeii. Ash-embalmed victims in the act of scrawling their names on the walls. They wanted to be named, to be known in death. Make their mark. Kids have already painted graffiti on the ochre walls of the Kahn-weiler Gallery in Rim Cove. They've drawn huge penises. This is an old practice. In the sixteenth century Montaigne complained of this penis desire, three times as extravagant, he emphasised, chalked on the walls of the great houses. I've got a casual day job with the Council scrubbing off graffiti with a high-pressure steam hose. I didn't give my real name. Graves, Robert. 'Gravē' – to dig, inscribe. I once worked for the Council digging graves. Whenever I'm short of money, the Council is a good bet for some day labour. I've got a name on all the lists, copied from grave-stones. Graft. It's worth following up.

I guess I can always hold this journal over until I work out a way of getting a reward for it. One has to do this carefully. I don't know what Dr Sarraute would do to get this back. She shouldn't be using confidential patient information like this. I could maybe copy something from it to show that it is authentic and that my interest in helping return it is genuine. Graft – a pencil-shaped shoot. That's all I possess. Graft and no boodle.

There was no moon that night when I went out to the pine trees again, on the edge of the promontory in the national park at Cedar Bay. I thought I was dreaming that night when I saw Travis Cordillion burying something in the sand and now I was trying to find the spot, see if there was a trace of his digging, but there was nothing, just empty beer bottles left by amateur fishermen; burnt driftwood where they tried to start a fire and gave up, as driftwood is hard to burn unless you gather it further inland, and out on the reef there was a light which wasn't moving. A tanker? Dropping off another load of drugs, weighed and marked by crayfish buoys which Travis would pick up? But the light wasn't moving. I stepped back behind the pines. Sat down on the needles and watched for more than an hour. These narrow channels through the reefs are dangerous for shipping. The Messiah will enter through an aperture. Every day I dream of a catastrophe, which will install a new time. That is the grifter's salvation: that things will not be the same again. I heard the familiar burp of the jet ski. It was coughing and spluttering and it seemed that Travis was having some trouble. He waded ashore and dragged it onto the sand. Backed his trailer up. It wasn't Travis. In the dim light of the cabin console I caught a glimpse of a face. It was a black man. Perhaps someone wearing a balaclava. He took off without lights and bounced dangerously over the verge. I walked down to the water's edge, very slowly, just in case he decided to return. The water was black. The fact that there was no moon made it all the more sinister. I took off my sandshoes and tested my fear. Amorphous, elemental sea. It buoyed me up. The water was warm, heavy, with a coating on it. My feet came away black. The tanker I was watching had run aground on the reef and was leaking a massive amount of fuel oil.

28

When Dr Judith Sarraute looked out her surgery window that morning, she could not see anybody para-sailing on the horizon. There was a sharp glare coming off the water and she observed an oily sheen on it which still made her nauseous. The tanker was still aground on the reef and it would take several hours while the tugs waited for the tide before it could be towed out to sea. The incident had already made all the national news bulletins and it was reported that Rim Cove developments would take huge losses. There were no fish in the sea. And now an oil spill.

Towards the late afternoon they pulled the tanker off. The bay was ringed with lines of booms. Volunteers were spraying detergent on the beaches. It would take weeks, they said, for everything to return to normal. It was almost evening; martini hour in lounges and bars in normal times. The sky had turned a steely blue. The tourists had gone. Dr Sarraute stirred her drink on her balcony. She only had three patients today. One case of hemorrhoids; a woman with an in-grown toenail; Mickey Jones wanting Viagra, sitting there smiling slyly beneath his beret. It was just upon sunset when they found Carter Cordillion's body entangled in prawning nets. They called the only doctor on duty. They had a floater, the policeman said to Judith over the phone.

When she looked at Carter's body he had no face left. She saw bloated meat, a Francis Bacon study, a white object, grotesque and bland, in conformity with what appeared to be a human body, swathed in black fuel oil and wrapped in netting. She studied it with the disinterest she had applied during her years of surgery, matching appearance with reality when bodies crossed over. Yes, she confirmed it was Cordillion ... the telltale tattoo inside the left thigh which he and Sam decided to get on a night out in Bangkok. She said they would have to phone for a forensic pathologist. They would have to transport the body to Cairns. The tall policeman, the one with a head that looked too small for his body, wanted to know if they should Gladwrap the corpse. He's marinated, but not in extra-virgin, he said.

29

It had been a thirty-day epidemic and now the stingers were gone. The oil had blocked out their light, Judith Sarraute was saying to Blixen Gottlieb when she saw the latter off at the small Cairns airport where they were swabbed for explosives before they could get a drink. They talked about how foreign tourists were putting up shrines in the shower sheds to ward off future plagues. Carter Cordillion had committed suicide, Judith was saying. She was quite certain. There were other client details she could not speak about, but Blixen knew most of those anyway. As the call came for boarding they hugged, and then the older woman whispered in the other's ear that all dirt dissolved in soap. The coast would be cleaned and the fish would return. One simply had to be observant, single-eyed, ambitious. The moment of understanding would come. The younger woman nodded. I'm sorry about breaking into the morphine safe, she said. Judith Sarraute shook her head: I'm just glad you're finishing your studies. You'll see that little by little your flights will diminish. It's a bit like a thirty-day epidemic. Sooner or later fugues resolved themselves. They only had a limited range, a small number of octaves; they were made for portable harpsichords and clavichords. Sooner or later they returned to where they began. And then you will discover yourself outside yourself.

How much do you think a grifter could get for a doctor's notes? And who is asking this question?

Egress

To shoot: to depart, to get away; shoot through.

Landscapes, seascapes; they all overwhelm me. I don't know why, but they come upon me with great sadness, a tree-lined corner here, a track leading to a wind-swept lookout, a public garden. They all possess a bittersweetness, like an old suppurating wound. It was because I was not busy that I suffered. I experienced the suffering of others, became engulfed by their sadness, suffocated by the lives I thought they lived. It was my own projection. They were not in the least disturbed by their lives, not in the least affected by landscapes and seascapes, save for some banal marvelling at nature.

It had been a couple of years now since I'd come down to Rim Cove. The place had been dead a while and then revived. No more oil spills. The authorities didn't allow tankers anywhere near the reef and they'd forced them out into deep-sea lanes. Stingers come and go in their season, drifting like me, and at the Ocean Temple bar they even have a cocktail called a Stinger, and you see that couple over in the corner? Well ... just imagine ... he's passing his hand over hers and they gaze into each other's eyes and soon they will go upstairs, and in their room they will draw the curtains and he will feel the need for speed, but will refrain, everything tending towards significance as though in a dream, but the dream is fractured by their anxiety, the dark glass reflecting light from their single florid lampshade. Same old story. Each move is the end of something, yet moving towards something they don't yet believe can end. He addresses her breasts, undresses her a little, his hands like butterflies. Showtime. Wait. I remember it now. It was years ago. I had picked up a stray credit card. Followed them to their room. The same girl. The same strangeness about her. The way she seemed to have been grafted. He runs back the curtains with the remote control. The full-length windows bathed in nightlight and sea-salt. She is translucent. Arms akimbo. I had brushed the large cash tip he left for the waiter into my pocket. I paid for my drink and left the bar with his camera slung over my shoulder. I walked past the security chap in the black suit. As a rule, I do that early in the morning and often during the day. I make my way to the sand where wooden tables wait for lonely observers, night-owls framed by their own investigator's eye, and I click away up at the window with a telephoto lens ... you never know, the return of flow ... love's rhythms all but lost ... my digital instrument automatically sharp in the darkness and in the glimmer of brief light, old light, I could have sworn it was him; the property developer with the mirror sunglasses. There are no simple stories; the wind comes up; I pull my lumber jacket around myself and smell my odour; I've not bathed for days, though the sea is warm and clear of nasty cubozoans. I return to my caravan for the night and rap on the tinny side of my neighbour's rig for him to turn down his country-and-western music. I cannot abide sentimental ballads. I swear I've also seen that she-male before.

Morning. I have just bathed in the pristine sea. I am free from threat. Salted with vitality. The world, my oyster. A subtle change in wind signifies a change in season, which passes virtually unnoticed at this latitude. A sea-bath always turns me inside out. I am wide open; stretching to the horizon. Clean. There are no jellyfish; no fish at all. The mayor of Rim Cove is accusing the military of causing this calamity. Janet Cordillion was quoted in the local paper, claiming that toxins draining into the ground water and the sea from the base have mutated species and produced fish which cannot spawn. Inland, feral pigs are dying in their hundreds. The northerly wind is said to be deadly for children in the indigenous community next to the test area.

I stroll over to the Kahnweiler Gallery to have a look at the exhibition called 'The Culture of the Copy'. Chinese paintings which they cannot quite assess as 'originals'. Some are copies, done by apprentices. Others unknown; perhaps masterpieces. This is how a culture is passed on. The copied text becomes known through the soul of the copier, since he has to traverse the terrain it commands. A bequest from some woman artist who was famous in the nineteen-thirties has left the nation this collection. It bears the thumb-print of the Chinese copier. I read up on all this before I went to the Kahnweiler opening a year or so ago, in case someone engaged me in conversation. No one did. I hardly ever participated in conversation since I have lived alone for many years and am happy with my reclusive life. I did not know who Julia Grace was. There was no food at the 'vernissage'. Not even finger-food. Just plenty of bubbly which I drank to excess. Rolled out the door last and got to plant a small kiss on the cheek of the somewhat puzzled Dr Sarraute, who didn't know why there was this intimacy between us. This display of touching and affection and breaking cover is not what I normally do. Retreating, I palliated my appearance. I am bland, believe me; beige; instantly erased from memory; a correction of the work of being born. You are? ... My life has always been thus, getting by on the fiction of first names. I slide into the slender recesses of a system card. Three lines cover me. I take pride in never having worked for more than two consecutive days. Judith brushed back the white lick in her hair and asked if I could help carry out the crates of empty bottles. Outside, the misty night. She was distracted, still trying to recall my face, confused by crowds of copies, as if her numerous patients had turned impatient, all wanting to be recognised with the same face. The eternal return of the same. Some people kill to be different. She's frowning. Something in her unconscious. The unconscious always wants you to be found out. It lays out its traps: scattered on the wind, liquefied in rain, revealed by sunlight. She opened a door with a key. In the packing-room I realised how Judith had made her money ... by an epidemic of diagnoses. In the packing-room, boxes upon boxes of her patient records. She was disturbed. By the fog ... by me ... by names.

The Kahnweiler Gallery. It sits on the other side of the road which runs through the resort town, so that if you stand on the beach you can see it directly behind, on a green hill surrounded by date palms. On the left, facing the reef would be the peninsula upon which Cordillion built his mansion and his ritzy estate. To the right is Sarraute's surgery. The gallery is at the fourth point where you box the compass. A cubic stinger. They say Cordillion gave the doctor the site and the building. For her *services to epidemiology. 'Gratis'. That is my name for today. It's better than 'Graves'. Cordillion was a philanthropist. The rumour was he was bonking her on his cruiser.*

The Kahnweiler Gallery is sad, melancholic, built out of white stone with dark teak window frames, and it has large dark green doors and there is a courtyard in the middle of it, sprouting deep palms, so that it appears like a colonial mansion in Singapore or Macau. I can vouch for the architecture: a great copy of imperial construction; the edifice of edification. I ride up to it upon my bicycle. It is a grey aluminium racer I found abandoned at the local tip. On it, I am almost invisible. As I approach, the gallery looms large in my anxiety, although it remains hidden and squat behind the palms, a hum emanating from it, for it must sit on the matrix of a powerful electricity grid. The whole site is completely flood-lit at night. A northerly wind is blowing strongly.

Enter. It is very cool inside and the slate floors hold tight patches of sunlight which warm the soles of my feet. Today I am dressed between an ageing hippie and a food writer: loose cream shirt and three-quarter length beachcomber trousers. Beige canvas shoes. Almost colourless. Entry, I noted, was free. On this level, around the courtyard, there is pottery and sculpture, which I find to be mostly primitive, naïve art about which I know nothing, but at least I know what I like, though that is probably not the best way to approach art. A roomful of ceramics by Ångström. Wasn't he the founder of spectroscopy? I have Judith Sarraute's journal in my khaki canvas bag and I intend to leave the leather-bound volume on a bench, on one of the padded seats in the Julia Grace gallery, the one on the second floor featuring Australian modernist paintings, where someone else will find it and not knowing to whom it belonged, may just return it to the front desk. Bach fugues flow from the sound system. Perhaps I will leave the diary in the bookstore, where others will read it, try to purchase it, along with a volume on Giacometti, his sculptures photographed at the Victorian State Gallery ... here, a shot of them being admired by a short rotund fellow looking like Alfred Hitchcock; there, a beautiful, tall girl in black lace with her back to the camera. My life is premised upon such juxtapositions and coincidences. Suddenly, an aria piped through the speakers. One should bypass arias. Here on the first floor, the Chinese paintings. They seem to be curated according to the weather. A gentle breeze on a lake here and there, and at the other end of the wall, an overcast, windy landscape, trees bent in the direction of hills. Then a misty sequence, starting in a valley where gnarled tree-trunks stretch into foggy mountains; tracks which lead to a promontory lashed by rain. There is hardly any sunlight. No perspective. These are landscapes from prehistory, representing a region after a catastrophe, craggy peaks about to topple. Everything hangs in defiance of gravity; suspended because reiterated, repeated and contrapuntal. That is how the eye reads. It reminds me of something I was taught at school: too close to depiction and distance is pierced. My pacing from one picture to another, my walking … retreating and approaching … changes all perspective. Perspective is a sentence. 'I'; 'you'. The pleasure of observing a grifter comes from a glimpse of his escape. Through slight variations, he comes to be accepted as the return of the same, as in a fugue … he's an early-morning riser; an express check-out; a noon-day stroller; a late-diner … too close to depiction. At the moment of his disappearance, at the vanishing point, there is a distrust of the eye. Gravity-defying, he leaves … nothing. Off to somewhere off-limits and without limits.

I walk on. This section is on poster art. Look here. A whole series advertising Chinese bicycles. These must have been the original designs, done in oil on canvas. Two scantily clad women advertising 'Sa-Bei' brand cigarettes while riding their 'Forever' bicycles; here's one with a girl in red silk and mink stole, her left breast fully visible, 'The Wu-xi silk company: apparel for women cyclists'; and this one called 'The Sitting Monk'. He is squatting amongst seven semi-naked women leaning on their bicycles. It's for a calming medicine. Beneath the paint could be an original landscape from the Sung Dynasty, or vice versa, it all could be one gigantic sting … or chance … I was convinced there was a painting that would tell me all of this.

These little rooms inhibit strolling. A gallery should have rooms which follow one another in a straight line, so one does not have to turn corners suddenly. All of the art can be seen from a distance, in motion, forming and reforming according to one's arrival and departure, as in the Musée d'Orsay in Paris, where one could view a Soutine two

hundred feet away, and if you squinted, whole new worlds appeared,
parallel universes, the skeletal structure of each painting visible in its
embalmed death, smells of despair trapped in paint, a renaissance of putrid
meat, then if you head south towards the Van Goghs you experience a
similarly purulent frenzy, distempered dripping, a deep shimmering in
the noonday heat, hear the falling water of the wash-shed where there
were once hissing vipers and upon approach, the sunflowers would grow,
shine, wilt, and finally melt into microbes before the guard reprimands
you for nosing too closely.

And so to the contemporary ... the somewhat present. The air is cooler
here back on the bottom floor. This seems to be where the interest lies ... I
count four couples and some art students in front of the Francis Bacon;
pretty girls in sarongs sitting on the floor sketching. This room has an
informality about it ... an untidy aspect that comes with boldness, strong
colours, fleshy montages. Nothing very interesting except for a portrait of
a girl in a cane bath-chair in black lace, her beautiful legs crossed, with
long dark hair and wide smile, innocent, somewhat disabled in her thinness
... and I notice it formed the beginning of a series that had once been hung
for the Archibald prize, portraits of celebrities, though of course celebrity
is something I stay well away from and have never been curious about
people who have achieved it, so I do not know many of these names. I step
over the art students to get a closer look at the little cards on which is in-
formation about the artist and the subject and I spend more time looking
at these cards than at the paintings themselves, feeling that I can hide
up close, peering at the text rather than standing back in the spotlight of
colours spewing from the canvasses ... and at the end, at the very end of
exhibition, there is a small portrait, done on squared paper, a scientific
study ... all this time I have not missed the strange quiet, the polite silence
which no one has noticed, but now there is a murmur of what seems like
discontent, a desperate argument kept at very low decibels, the kind of
silent disagreement one often finds among spouses in art galleries when
one partner, out of the need to assert an opinion, cannot wait patiently
before breaking the silence like a familiar fart, uprooting an old argu-
ment that had been germinating beneath for all those marital years, and
the whole round begins again, a murmur ending at the wall at the end

of the corridor leaving behind half-expressed frustrations, nasty games, and I wonder what had provoked all this and I walk up to the scientific study on squared paper to get a closer look at the controversy and here I am, hunched over it, hearing the sound of a toilet flushing behind the wall, wanting to poke at this portrait, wanting to find out why it caused such disagreement amongst ordinary townspeople, this painting of a ... of a surgically-masked woman holding up in her gloved hand a jellyfish which, when stared at long enough, resembles a man's head, the translucent tentacles of the jellyfish hanging down like dreadlocks, and in her other hand, a scalpel ... as though receiving her applause like a violinist at the end of a difficult fugue, as if waiting for the bearded, severed head to answer, speak up, tell the truth. Her eyes alight, all-consuming ... they speak of her secrecy, the purdah of this jelly-like thing ... behind which was her strength, her oath, this anti-memory, this silent reproduction of deadly codes which had given her both life and fame.

To disappear behind a mask, beneath the surface of things. He slid over the waxed floor and the art students shifted uncomfortably and they looked at one another for they had only felt a slight breeze, as if nought but a ghost had passed between them and as he made his way towards the exit the bored guard noticed a shadow that had zigzagged ... everyone was disturbed, it seemed, by that portrait – it gave them vertigo – the way it was set at a slant, skewed, the fact that the woman's left eye was missing ... and the shade stopped by the gallery shop to purchase the reproduction, yes, the one entitled 'Judith and Holofernes', yes, that one, by Redvers, and yes, that'll be on credit ...

Acknowledgments

The quotations from Montaigne's *Essays* in the English are from the translation by John Florio, 1603.

The illustration *Saturn and His Zodiacal Signs* is from *Von den XII Zeichen des Gestirn*, 1470, Zürich, Zentralbibliothek, MS C.54 (719), Fol. 14, Vol. 2.

My sincere gratitude to Marion May Campbell and Isabel Morais for their generosity in making so many resources available to me.

Prior research was carried out during a Macgeorge Fellowship at the University of Melbourne. My thanks to the Potter Foundation and to the English Department at the University of Melbourne.

This project has been assisted by the Commonwealth Government through the Australia Council, its arts funding and advisory body.